Chronicles of Stephen

Kenyon T. Henry

Jumpmaster Press
Birmingham, AL

Copyright Notice

Choice of The Mighty, a novel by Kenyon T. Henry

Library Cataloging Data

Names: Henry, Kenyon T. (Kenyon T. Henry) 1977-

Title: Choice of The Mighty / Kenyon T. Henry

5.5 in. × 8.5 in. (13.97 cm × 21.59 cm)

Description: Jumpmaster Press™ digital eBook edition | Jumpmaster Press™ Trade paperback edition | Alabama: Jumpmaster Press™, 2018. P.O Box 1774 Alabaster, AL 35007 info@jumpmasterpress.com

Summary: Stephen returns home hoping to find a cure to his curse. He soon learns his curse is anything but and begins training to better understand his ability to read minds. In the end, Stephen is thrust into the middle of a war that has been fought since the beginning of time.

Identifiers: ISBN-13: 978-1-949184-30-3 (eBook) | 978-1-949184-29-7 (POD) |

1. Good Versus Evil 2. Speculative Fiction 3. Warrior Heroes 4. Magic Curses 5. Secret Societies 6. Myths and Legends 7. Christian Fantasy Fiction

Printed in the United States of America

For more information on Kenyon T. Henry
www.kenyonthenry.com

Chronicles of Stephen

Kenyon T. Henry

Dedication

I dedicate this book to my wife, Shaunna, and our children, Hope, KK, Erin, Zane, Jayden, and Ella. My family has been supportive, understanding, and encouraging throughout this entire process. At times, writing this story has consumed much of my spare time and used up enormous amounts of physical, emotional, and psychological energy leaving me to feel spiritually drained. They have listened to me brainstorm out loud and talk about the book for countless hours. I am certain that they wondered if the book would ever make it to print. Together we have persevered and now get to see this story have a life of its own. I wouldn't want to take this journey with anyone else. I love you guys! So, thank you Sunshine, Babygirl, Starshine, Princess, Tex, Little Man, and Little Girl.

Acknowledgments

First and foremost, I want to thank the Lord Almighty for all that I am. Without the mind that my creator has endowed me with, I never would have been able to come up with an idea for a story, let alone write a book. He also placed me in a country where I am free to chase my dreams and desires. Writing this book has been a dream.

Thank you to Mom and Dad for teaching me the value of hard work and perseverance. I needed a lot of that to finish this project. More than that, they love me and gave me a safe home to grow into the person that I have become.

Thank you to Jesse and Joy Thornton (my second parents) who taught me how to fight, not only in the ring, but in life. Without the drive to get back up after being knocked down, I wouldn't have finished this book.

Thank you to Mrs. Jane Duffy, my high school history teacher. She was the first teacher I ever had who called me out for just getting by. What usually passed for an "A," she gave a "C," warning me the next time would be a "D" or an "F." I needed to start saying something of value in my papers, instead of riddling them with "glittering generalities." This is when I started to appreciate the art of writing again.

Last, I want to thank a select group of people that have supported me in my project with either advice, prayers, or some other form of help during the writing process. Thank you to all the members of the North Georgia Writers Guild: Pamela Pettyjohn, Linda Peters, Caleb Kelchner, Rachel Cates, Judy Stephens, Barbara Papers, Elizabeth Jewell Headden, Anne Ford Melton, Ted Dickerson, and especially Bruce Gaughran, for nurturing and fostering an atmosphere of growth and support for all the members. A big thank you goes to Matt Hensley who read more than one version of the book and offered his honest criticisms, positive and negative. And a heartfelt thank you is due to Teresa Burse, who continually pushed, encouraged, and checked in on me during all the ups and downs of the writing process.

He walked alone down the sidewalk. With each step the man took, freshly scattered salt crunched between boot and the concrete. Although walking along familiar streets, it was still strange to him to look up and see the Gateway Arch of Saint Louis, a sight he last saw nearly five years ago.

He somewhat enjoyed the thick layer of snow, which blanketed the ground, reflecting multicolored lights that illuminated Gateway Park. Distant sirens, yelling, and loud music from a passing car, however, polluted the night air. Nearby office windows offered him some glimpse into the lives of people who appeared engrossed in laughter, carols, and of all the joys the season offered.

He continued down the street, clenching his coat collar around the neck with one hand, the other holding tight to his stomach to secure something hidden. Occasionally, he paused and looked down an alley or backstreet, searching for a sign indicating he'd found the right place. The streets grew darker as he moved further away from the park and other well-lit streets. Garland woven with strings of lights illuminated the windows he passed, helping him navigate through the darkness. Still, the festive Christmas decorations did little to provide any meaningful light to see by.

Where are you? He focused his thoughts on trying to find his mentor, his old friend. He continued to search, glancing down alleys, walking up and down streets, listening for the slightest sound that would reveal his friend's location.

A cat pounced from a nearby dumpster, causing a homeless man to jump. "Stupid cat," the homeless man yelled, pulling a blanket up tight around his neck. As he approached another alley, he stopped and peered into the darkness; no lights, no faint glow of Christmas decorations. It was pitch black. *There you are!*

He turned down the alley. The smell of the grease trap from a nearby restaurant caused him to withdraw for a moment. Sweat dampened the inside of his gloves. His eyes slowly adjusted to see faint shades of gray and rigid outlines in the dark. He continued.

As he neared the back of the alley, he felt nervous, and his head ached. He stretched his neck, leaning his head from side to side, but found no relief. He stooped down next to a crate draped in plastic. Peeling back an edge and peering through, he could barely make out the figure of a man, curled up tightly beneath a woolen blanket. He swallowed the lump in his throat.

"Waltz, wake up." He spoke softly, as though not wanting to disturb others. But there was no one else around. He waited a moment before nudging the man and speaking more loudly this time. "Waltz, get up!"

Waltz jumped slightly. He turned sharply and peered into the darkness where the plastic had been peeled back. “What? Who is it?” He struggled for a moment but managed to sit up.

“Waltz, it’s me. It’s Stephen.”

The old man crawled out of the crate until, on hands and knees, he was face-to-face with Stephen, eyes watering and lips quivering. “Stephen?” He reached toward Stephen’s face, stopping just shy of touching it, his hand trembling. “Stephen, is it really you?”

Stephen took the old man’s hand in his. Waltz threw his arms around him, squeezing him tighter than Stephen thought possible. “Please Lord! Dear God, don’t let this be a dream. Please Lord Jesus, not a dream.”

Stephen hesitated before reaching around the old man, one hand across the back, the other cradling the old man’s head. “It’s not a dream, Waltz. I’m home.” Stephen felt tears touching his cheek, but they weren’t his. Uncertainty kept him from being truly happy. Though glad he found Waltz, so much happened since he left—so much of it bad. He knew Waltz would not understand. Still, he needed him to. He needed Waltz to help him escape the darkness that had found him, followed him, and fought to conquer his very existence.

Stephen took a deep breath as Waltz released the near-death grip he had on his arm. He strained to see Waltz, but not much caught the light in the alley where the only illumination came from the stars above. Not even the moon was visible. Stephen heard Waltz’s thoughts. *Where have you been? Why did you leave?* The pain Stephen felt there was nearly unbearable and made him exit Waltz’s mind; giving the old man the privacy he deserved.

"Waltz, I have something for you." Stephen reached into his jacket and pulled out a gold-colored flask with intricate inlaid designs of a sword behind a shield, with stone in the middle. "I kept it. I didn't mean to take it when I left. I just had it on me and didn't realize it until I was gone."

Waltz reached out, taking the flask and loosening the lid. The liquid inside sloshed around as Waltz's hands trembled. He sniffed, then took a sip. "Hot chocolate? You remembered?" He took another longer sip. "Aaah! That's good. Thank you for this. But you can keep the flask. I'm just glad you're home."

Stephen looked around as Waltz sipped from the flask. He knew the place well but did not understand why Waltz slept there. "Why are you here, in the alley? I remember we used to come here to give things to the homeless. But, why aren't you at Uncle Bernie's place? I went by his shelter. A man outside told me you would be here. Is Bernie okay?"

Waltz looked at Stephen. "This is the last place I saw you. I've stayed here since. When the weather gets too bad, I go and find shelter, like everyone else—usually at Bernie's. But I've been waiting for you to come home. My whole world was gone, and now it's back."

Stephen rubbed the back of his head, running his fingers through the wavy hair that stuck out just below his toboggan. "What is it, boy?" Waltz placed his hand on Stephen's shoulder.

"What do you mean?"

"Ever since you were little, you've done that. You rub the back of your head when you're tense about something—whenever you lie, or get into trouble, or are just stressed out."

Stephen stopped rubbing his neck. "Really? I never noticed."

"It's your tell. You get it from your uncle Bernie. Obviously, it's not an inherited trait. I think it's from playing cards with him and the others. He's done it as long as I've known him. You started about a year after you came to live with us." Waltz paused a moment before continuing. "Stephen, why did you leave? Where have you been?"

Stephen knew these questions were coming. He already heard the thoughts inside Waltz's mind. He wished he could tell Waltz everything with ease, like he used to. Still, he had to tell him. "Whew," Stephen said, the word sounding like air escaping through his lips. He came for help and knew the only possible way to get it was for his old mentor to know everything.

"Waltz, let's gather your things and head to Bernie's. He's only, what, five or six miles from here? I'm back now, so there's no reason for you to be here on the street."

Waltz sat looking at Stephen, not moving.

"We can talk along the way," Stephen added. "I'll tell you everything. But let's get moving."

Waltz nodded and turned back toward the crate to gather his things.

It surprised Stephen to see how little Waltz kept with him. Besides blankets, a sleeping bag, and a half-eaten sandwich, he had nothing else. The two left the alley and headed down the road toward Gateway Mall, back to the lights of Saint Louis and the arch, which rose high overhead. Waltz seemed slower than he remembered. Stephen couldn't tell if it was his age or the cold that slowed him.

"I need your help, Waltz."

"My help? What could you possibly need my help with?"

"Well, it's complicated. And it'll sound crazy. But I really need you to keep an open mind."

"I will." Waltz's face softened, just as when Stephen was little and would go to him for help.

"When I left, it had nothing to do with you—not really. If you remember the last time you saw me, I didn't say anything to you. We were in the alley, and you must have asked a thousand times if I was okay because of how quiet I was."

"Yeah, I remember. You were awfully preoccupied. Your mind was somewhere else. You worried me. I guess, rightfully so." Waltz shivered. "Brrr. At least it was warm that day."

Stephen now saw Waltz a little better than before, thanks to the plethora of Christmas lights. He noticed how gray Waltz's hair turned in the years he had been away. His clothes, too, looked somewhat tattered. Other than that, he appeared to be the same Waltz, with the same piercing blue eyes.

The two turned the corner. About a hundred yards ahead, Stephen saw Kiener Plaza. The water flowed down the stone feature toward the pool. It wasn't frozen yet. "Up ahead is where it happened, where my life changed forever."

"At the park?"

"Yeah. Remember we stopped there earlier that day?"

Waltz's expression turned thoughtful. Then, a look of realization caused his jaw to drop. "Yeah, I remember. You wanted to hang out a bit. I suspected it had to do with some teenage girls playing in the water."

"Yup. That's the day. I was sitting there with my feet in the water, when I decided I'd been there long enough. I couldn't work up the courage to talk to the girls. As I got up and turned to walk away, this incredibly beautiful woman bumped into me. Rather, I bumped into her. She smarted off about my being a lazy youth, saying she was tired of supporting people like me, and I needed to go to school and get a job. Whatever. I just remember thinking how I'd wish she'd throw herself in the water. Then, she did."

They walked up to the water's edge and stopped. Stephen waited until a young couple holding hands walked by before he continued. "Waltz, I've never seen anyone so scared. I couldn't understand what had just happened. Neither could she. I was scared and confused. I later came to understand that not only had I implanted the thought in her head, but the emotions I felt afterward were her emotions on top of mine. And she had never spoken a single word. The more I thought about it as we walked toward the alley, the more I realized her lips had never moved. I had heard her thoughts."

"My boy." Waltz spoke tenderly. His voice sounded sorrowful and anguished. "I wish you had told me. I could have helped you. Why did you run?"

Stephen turned toward Waltz. "I was scared. I began feeling different inside. I didn't understand. It's darkness. Like there's a monster inside me—trying to get out." He looked around for people within earshot before returning his intense gaze to the old man. "I don't know what to do. I'm losing myself."

"Losing yourself? What do you mean?"

"This ability has changed some over the years, grown. Now I can pick up certain things effortlessly. It's like being in the same room with a crowd of people talking. I can tune them out if I want. But I couldn't always. Each time I get inside someone's head, their thoughts, feelings, even memories become my own. I can make them think and feel what I want. But their memories and feelings stay with me, as though they're mine now."

"You've been dealing with this since you left?" Waltz asked, eyes wide open, and a fearful expression on his face.

Stephen shrugged. "More or less."

"That sounds horrible, an incredible burden for one to bear." Waltz voice sounded feeble.

"Yes, or no. Heck..." Stephen was agitated. "I don't know. It can be useful, sure. I've seen a lot in the minds of people, some memories and thoughts that I wish I had never seen. People can be truly horrible in ways you never want to imagine, and I retain it all – good and bad. The problem is, I have trouble remembering what I've done, which memories are mine. I've seen a lot of horrible things in other minds. Now, I can't remember if I'm that horrible person or not. What did I do? What haven't I done? It's getting harder to tell."

Stephen's eyes welled up, nearly in tears as Waltz grabbed hold of him and pulled him tightly to his chest. Stephen laid his head on Waltz's shoulder. "Shhh. It's okay, boy. We'll get this figured out together. Let's get you to Uncle Bernie's. Okay?"

Stephen pulled back, wiping the tears from his eyes, and nodded. "Waltz, there's more."

"Well, okay. Tell me, it'll be fine." Waltz nodded at the street. The two began walking again, away from the arch that stood higher than any other building in the city.

"When I left, I was scared of the ability at first. I thought it made me some kind of monster. When I was a kid, like all kids, I dreamed of having abilities, being like Superman or Spiderman. I remember running around the house with a cape on. At least, I think I do." He looked at Waltz, waiting for a response.

"Yes, you did that often." Waltz smiled. Stephen felt some relief knowing this was his memory.

"Well, it wasn't fun having an ability, not at first. Eventually, I got used to it. I began understanding it, how it worked. I went to see the first Batman movie not long after it came out—"

Waltz interrupted. "I assure you, boy, it was not the first Batman movie." Then he chuckled.

Stephen grinned as he rolled his eyes. Waltz picked a strange moment to lighten the mood. But it worked and put Stephen a little more at ease. "Anyways," he continued, "The movie gave me the idea to do some good."

"And?" Waltz asked.

"Well, I did good. I was able to stop some bad people from doing bad things."

"Really? How did it feel?" There was an exuberance in Waltz's voice.

"It was great. Some things were harder, trickier than others. I can give you stories and details later, but man, what a rush!"

"A rush? Like what kind of rush?"

"I don't know, like adrenaline. At first it was just nice to do good. Eventually, it was thrilling. Finally, it's like I was the ability, like we, me and the ability, were one and the same. My life seemed tied to it and revolved around it."

Stephen stopped. "That is, until something went wrong." He turned and looked at Waltz. "A kid died. He was only sixteen. He was into some bad stuff and would likely have died anyway, but he was a good kid deep down. I can see that stuff, Waltz. I can see a person's deepest, darkest secrets, desires, you name it. Nothing is hidden from me. I can see the good and bad in a person. This kid wanted to be good. Instead, he died because of me. I watched him die from the inside. I was inside his head when he died and could feel it all."

Stephen grabbed Waltz by the shoulders and looked him square in the eyes. He felt guilt and concern inside Waltz. "I know what death feels like. It's the most horrible thing I've ever felt, and the most powerful. There is no hope, no compassion, no strength. Nothing." He let go of Waltz and continued walking as Waltz followed.

"There is always hope, my boy."

"Ah, you're talking about that Jesus stuff, right?"

"Jesus stuff?"

"I'm sorry, Waltz. I don't mean to be disrespectful. After all the stuff I've seen, I just don't know if I believe anymore. Heck! I may never have believed. I know I was eighteen when I left, but I was still a kid. If it wasn't for all I've seen, both through my eyes and others, I'd still be a kid. But there's a real darkness out there."

"Yes, there is." Waltz smacked his lips. "All that darkness just means the smallest light can shine that much brighter."

Stephen searched Waltz's thoughts. He had expected Waltz's reaction to be stronger and negative. The emotions continued to be on the surface for Stephen to soak up. The thoughts, however, seemed hazy and distant. Then, they were gone. He had lost Waltz's thoughts altogether. His emotions seemed to be making his gift harder to control.

They continued on with small talk until they finally reached Bernie's place. Waltz walked up the steps and turned back toward Stephen when he reached the top. "You coming?"

"Yeah, I'm coming Waltz. I..." Stephen paused on the bottom step, looking around. So many emotions hung in the air: fear, hurt, love, compassion, and more. He stopped to soak in Waltz's emotions again, stronger than his own. Stephen learned to subdue his own emotions, to bury them. Waltz, however, provided a steady flow of openness and honesty. "I never thought I'd see this place again," Stephen said. "You don't think he'll mind, do you?"

"No, he keeps my room for me. Not yours though." Waltz winked. "You'll have to sleep on the couch. No doubt all the other rooms are full up with homeless, as usual."

Waltz turned to knock on the door. He knocked again, and the door opened as the porch light came on.

On the other side of the threshold stood a tall, broad, elderly, bald black man, looking not so happy to find someone on his porch in the middle of the night.

"Waltz? What are --- is everything okay?" Bernie asked.

Waltz reached forward, took Bernie by the arm, and pulled him onto the porch.

"Perfect! Everything is perfectly okay!"

Bernie stood at the top, frowning down at Stephen. Stephen made his way up the steps.

"Hey, Bernie."

Bernie looked hard at Stephen. His jaw clenched in anger. "That's *Uncle* Bernie, and where have you been, Mr. Stephen Cross? Don't you know how much you worried two old men?" He pointed to Waltz. "And this poor fool been sleepin' in dat alley since you left!"

Stephen stepped up to Bernie. His figure towered over Stephen's five-foot-ten-inch height. "So, that means you care, since you were worried, right?" Stephen grinned. Bernie did not.

"Boy, don't get me wrong. I'm glad you're alright, and I'm gonna give you a hug. But you've got a lot of explaining to do. A lot of mending to do. You understand?"

"Yes, sir." Stephen looked at Waltz, who grinned and shrugged.

Bernie reached forward and picked Stephen up into a bear-hug, even tighter than the hug Waltz gave him. Then, he went inside, leaving the door open for the two to follow. Stephen entered last and locked the door behind himself.

❧ ☙

Stephen awoke on the couch the next morning. He opened his eyes and smiled at the change—being someplace familiar, being home. What Stephen did not mention to Waltz yet, was that he lived homeless over the past year or so. He wandered around, caught up in trying to deal justice, but never stayed in the same place long. He moved from hotel to hotel when he could, but often stayed on the street. While on the street, he grew paranoid, feeling as though someone watched him, not completely sure if someone really was, or if the lingering memories of others caused delusions.

When Stephen finally tore himself from the couch's comfort, he scuffed around the room, stretching as he went, and looking at old pictures on the walls. He saw the snow-covered yard and sidewalks through the window. Nothing else stirred outside or in. He walked over to the fireplace. On the mantel hung four stockings, two with the names Bernie and Bernard on the left and two more for Waltz and Stephen hanging to the right. Sparse decorations gave a quaint feel to the room; a garland on the staircase in the hall and a modest tabletop tree on the coffee table in front of the couch.

He ran his hand across the top of the mantel as he walked along, looking around the room. His hand brushed a framed photo, nearly knocking it off the mantel. He picked it up and saw an old picture of himself with Bernard, Bernie's nephew. Waltz took the photo of the two on a family trip to see the Superman museum in Metropolis, Illinois. Stephen still carried a smaller, worn version in his wallet.

"That was taken about a year after you moved in with us here."

Stephen looked across the room to see Bernie standing in the doorway to the kitchen and dining area. "Yeah, I remember." He took a closer look. "Did he end up going to that college down south? What was it? The one with two mascots?"

"Auburn."

"Yeah, that's the one. Auburn. Did he go?" Stephen stood the frame back up and turned toward Bernie.

"Yep. He graduates from veterinary school this spring."

"Man, that's awesome! Good for him."

"Yeah, his momma and I are real proud of him. You should go see Wanda. She'll be excited to know you're safe. They both will."

"Sure thing. I plan to. I'd like to get settled some first."

"So, you're staying with us a while?" Bernie raised his eyebrows in question.

Stephen thought for a moment, rubbing the back of his neck. When he realized what he was doing, he stopped. "Yeah, I plan to. I hope to. Truth is, I don't know. Waltz and I have some stuff to talk about, but I really want to."

"Well, if you want to, I don't know of anything or anybody that would stand in your way." Bernie turned and disappeared into the kitchen. Stephen heard him banging pots and pans. Stephen always thought Bernie's Southern accent to be amusing. Now it seemed only slightly out of place.

"Hey, what do you say we finish that conversation we started last night?" Waltz's voice came from behind Stephen.

Stephen turned to see Waltz walking down the hallway, alongside the staircase. His hair dripped from the shower he had just taken. His clothes looked nice, freshly pressed, but nothing new or fancy. "Most of the house isn't up yet. We can go downstairs and shoot some pool while Bernie starts on breakfast," Waltz suggested.

"Sure. That'd be good." Stephen missed the old house. He felt the shelter looked more like a small apartment building because of the size of it. Perhaps, it would make a good bed-and-breakfast. Bernie and Waltz continued to be the only full-time staff at the shelter for the homeless since before Stephen lived there. The downstairs floor held only a few bedrooms, two of which Bernie and Waltz stayed in. The rest occupied the top two floors. They converted the basement into a recreation area. He considered himself fortunate to grow up here, even though they frequently had homeless guests.

Stephen looked around the basement. The brown shag carpet he remembered now showed the wear of more than twenty years. The same tan leather recliners sat in the corners opposite the stairs. The paisley couch still rested along the wall and showed more than just his hot chocolate stains. The pool table rested in the center underneath the fluorescent lights. Pool sticks lay on the table. "Wow, nothing's changed."

"Feel like home?"

"Yeah, I guess. But look at this place." Stephen pointed to the outdated lighting and furniture. "Some things really should change!"

They both laughed as Stephen walked around the table to start racking the balls. "And air freshener wouldn't hurt. It smells mildewy."

Waltz took a sniff and shrugged. "You're probably right."

"So, what do you want to know? I'll be an open book. I owe you that. You've been a dad to me. I should have at least written you or something."

"Why didn't you?" Waltz asked.

Stephen felt hurt and mixed emotions radiated from Waltz. "At first, I was scared and didn't know what to write. After a while, it was embarrassment that kept me from writing, which eventually turned to shame."

"I understand, I guess." Waltz grabbed a stick and began to break. The crack of the balls echoed off the stone walls.

"Really?" Stephen looked for a good shot.

"Yeah, I ran once. I was in a situation not dissimilar to yours. Now, I wasn't having the type of issues you were having. But there was this woman. I had stayed a bachelor for so long."

"Wait. A woman?" Stephen gave his best sly grin.

"Yes, a woman. Now shut up and let me finish." Waltz winked before continuing. "I was forty years old when I met her. It was my birthday party, actually. Bernie introduced us. I had dated a lot. But I didn't really have time for a woman in my life. Not a serious relationship anyways. When I was younger, I was a ladies' man, not the gentleman I should've been."

Waltz looked across the table, then sank the five ball in the corner where Stephen stood. "She was so gorgeous. I had pretty much given up dating. I didn't consider it wise to start a family at the age of forty. But I had to say something to her. One thing led to another. A while later, she was talking about marriage and kids. For the longest, I just played it off. I really loved her." Waltz sighed.

Stephen heard the hurt in his voice. "What happened, Waltz?"

"I ran. Dummy me left a note. I had money back then. I could have given her anything. All she wanted was me. But I was a little paranoid then, didn't really trust anyone. I thought she might have wanted money. I couldn't see it—the love. Well, it wasn't long after that I realized my mistake. I wanted to go see her but kept finding excuses not to." Waltz paused and stared at the table.

"And...?" Stephen was impatient to hear the rest. He had never heard this story before.

"I eventually saw her in the park, just outside City Museum. She had moved on. I could see she was pregnant, and there was another man. So, I left without saying anything. But I vowed to never let my love of wealth get in the way of my life and God's plans for me again."

"So, what did you do?" Stephen had never given much consideration to Waltz having a life before they found each other.

"I gave it up."

"What? You gave the money up?"

"Yeah, I did. It took me a few years to really decide what to do with it. I kept a small amount, to take care of my needs and help me get settled into a new life."

"What about the woman?" Stephen asked.

"Whew, boy." Waltz looked at Stephen. "There was another man in her life. Years later, I learned that he hadn't stayed long. But it was too late for me to make amends. She'd passed away earlier that year."

"I'm sorry to hear that, Waltz." Stephen sensed something from Waltz, another emotion. "You still love her," he said excitedly.

"I never stopped."

Stephen paused for a moment, thinking about the story. "Wait a second. If you have money, why do you work here?"

"Work?" Waltz laughed. "I volunteer. I've always volunteered. I haven't had a paying job in a very long time. But the point is, I know a little about running. I get it. It's okay."

"Well then. I told you last night why I left. What more do you want to know?"

Waltz walked around the table, looking for his next shot. He already sunk three balls, not giving Stephen a shot yet. "Tell me about the boy that died. How did it happen?"

Stephen protested. "Waltz, I don't really want—"

Waltz held up a hand. "Stephen, you said you'd be completely honest with me. If you want my help, I need to know everything."

"Waltz, you don't understand. This thing I can do, it developed and changed. I'm not sure it's good. It seems alright, until I think about explaining. I'll sound like some kind of monster. I am a monster." Stephen knew he sounded frantic and worked to slow his breathing.

"Boy, I assure you. You are no monster. But I need to know what happened. I want the whole story this time."

Stephen sat on a stool. "There was this lawyer named Biggs. He defended all the wrong kinds of people. I had learned about him through others' thoughts. He was a bad guy, and in the pockets of some worse guys. I wanted to take him down. He was into prostitutes, drugs, and all sorts of stuff. I needed a way to get close to him. So, I possessed the kid's body, Tommy."

"You *what*?" Waltz missed his shot. "Is that really possible, to actually possess another person?"

Stephen got up and walked around the table as Waltz stood, staring at him. "Yeah, it's possible. It takes a lot of energy. It's not fun. I can feel the person's mind, but it's as if it's locked away. When they are freed, for them, it's like time is missing. It's hard for me to do, but sometimes necessary. If I have to implant thoughts into a mind, it can cause temporary mental issues, sometimes permanent ones. Anyways, Tommy was a runner for Biggs. He did small errands—delivering messages, picking up this or that. This kid could've had a chance to be better. I didn't want the mental issues for him. So, I possessed him, ensuring he would not remember anything."

"Okay, I guess. Go on."

Stephen leaned over the table, striking the cue ball, which sped across the table and sent the nine ball into the side pocket and the ten ball into the corner pocket.

"Nice shot!" Waltz scratched his head.

“Thanks.” Stephen looked around the table at the remaining balls. “I went to the apartment building where one of his women lived, on a night I was certain he’d be there. Tommy had scheduled the appointment. Sure enough, Biggs’s black Mercedes was parked out front. The people in that area of Chattanooga knew who he was. No one messed with him. I saw the woman look out her window as she drew the curtain closed. Afterward, I scaled the side of the building, using ledges, and protruding bricks. She was on the third floor, which isn’t really that far. I made it to her balcony and peered through a small crack in the curtains. I could see him sitting on the couch in his underwear, drugs scattered all over the table. She was standing with her back to me, feeding him pills.” Stephen wiped sweat from his forehead as he took another shot.

“I took pictures. There was enough there to make sure he went down. I emailed them from Tommy’s phone to a couple of news stations and the police. I had done it. There would be questions. At the very least, he would be finished as a lawyer.”

“What went wrong?” Waltz sounded more sad than curious.

“Before I got to the ground, someone had seen me—rather, Tommy—climbing down the building and started yelling. Biggs came out and saw me. When I got to the bottom, I ran.” Stephen shot again, sinking the fifteen. “I had made plans for Tommy to get away. I was going to leave him with a desire to flee and never come back.”

“But it didn’t work, did it?” Waltz looked angry, more than Stephen ever remembered seeing him. His fist and jaws clenched. His knuckles turned white.

"No, sir." Stephen hated to tell the next part. As he shot, his trembling hand sent the cue ball wide, just grazing the intended fourteen ball, and straight into the corner pocket. "When I turned and ran, I heard shots. The first shot missed. The second didn't."

Stephen collapsed, so weak that he fell.

"Are you okay? Stephen! What's wrong, boy?"

"I remember it all. Remember?" Stephen struggled to catch his breath. His heart raced, and he broke into a sweat. "I told you, I'd feel what he felt. Each time I access those memories, I access the feelings too. The greater the detail, the stronger the feelings. And they can be overwhelming."

Stephen slowed his breathing and grabbed the table, struggling to get back to his feet. "Each time, I relive death, the fear of it, the pain, and hopelessness. All of it. The body knows it isn't real. But the mind makes it seem real."

"And this is why you came back? Is this what you're needing help with?" Waltz helped Stephen to his feet.

"Only a small part, Waltz. It's so much more. I could turn it off. The pain, emotion, all of it. I used to do that from time to time. It helped me get done what needed to be done. I was doing a lot of good. But, with time, I started getting this feeling that something was wrong, seriously wrong. I'm not alone in this, Waltz. Someone or something has been following me, watching me, and it's trying to get to me. When I turn off the emotions, I feel it even more. It's like I'm drawn to it."

"We'll get this figured out, boy."

"How? How do we figure this out? I don't know anyone else like this. I looked when I traveled. I went as far south as New Orleans, over through Tallahassee Florida, up through Charleston, and settled in Chattanooga. Nothing. I'm alone."

Waltz let out a big sigh. "I can help."

"How? How can you help?"

"I've seen a lot on these streets and in life. I've seen things that most people would not understand and couldn't begin to grasp. I've seen this before. Not exactly like this, but close enough. I think I can help."

Stephen sat stunned, unsure if feeling relief was okay or not. *Are there really others like me? Really? Right here all along!* His strong emotional response caused him to throw his thought.

Waltz took a step back, grabbing his head. Stephen realized what he did. In his excitement, he lost control for a moment.

"Waltz? Are you alright?"

"Wow! That's quite a gift you have. You're really excited about not being alone."

"You heard that, huh? Sorry." Stephen reached to help Waltz back to the pool table to lean on it.

"Heard it, yeah. But I felt it too. I felt your emotion—the excitement, the confusion, and something else. You're worried." Stephen looked away from Waltz; he knew the rest. "You're worried that if you find others like you, they'll be monsters."

"Yeah, that's a real concern. Plus, how did I get this ability? Why am I different? Is it heredity or what?"

"Don't worry too much about it. We'll work all this out. I can tell you this: I believe that who you are, who you choose to be, will always be up to you, regardless of any ability. Freewill is one of the greatest gifts God has given man. The actions make the man. Or, in some cases, the inaction. You ask God for help, he'll give it."

"Thanks, Waltz, for understanding." Stephen sniffed. "You smell that?" His stomach rumbled at the smell of breakfast, unable to remember his last home cooked meal.

"Yeah, bacon. Smells like breakfast is ready. Let's go eat, son."

The two headed up the steps toward breakfast. Sitting around with Waltz, Bernie, and others who passed through, gave Stephen comfort. It allowed him to forget his troubles for a short time and focus on the moment—something he could not do for quite a while.

Stephen waited inside the old storage building behind the house. He looked around at some boxes they sorted through shortly after his return. Most sat covered with dust. Others got cleared a bit when Stephen looked through the contents. Light filtered through a small window and shone on a punching bag still hanging near the back and surrounded by more boxes and old furniture. His breath turned to fog, and his teeth chattered. He understood why they needed to be in the building away from the short-term residents. Still, that knowledge did nothing to take the chill away.

The door opened and Waltz stepped inside, locking the door afterward.

"Did you get a good breakfast?"

"Y-y-yeah." Stephen's teeth chattered.

"Good. You'll need your strength today. We've been working for weeks now, to help you control your gift."

"Is that what you call it?" Stephen rolled his eyes. "I feel like all we've been doing is torturing my mind, doing the same things over and over. Yes, I can read minds and even control others' thoughts. I don't think this is helping though. I think I've looked into all the minds in the shelter here, plus, everyone living between here and the next street over. Why can't we bring Bernie in?"

Waltz sighed. "I'd like to, Stephen. But things aren't like they used to be between me and Bernie. I don't know how to explain it. He's just not the same Bernie. Something's off."

"Maybe he just misses Bernard," Stephen suggested.

"I wish it were that simple. He's been beaten down by life. I don't think he and I would agree on this."

"But, Bernie—"

Waltz interrupted. "Let's just focus on this for now. Alright?"

Stephen reluctantly agreed.

"Hey, once we get you under control, you and I will need to have another talk. But, first things first." Waltz pulled up a stool and sat down. "Stephen, I believe the key to you controlling your gift is by coming to terms with it. You have a hard time differentiating your memories and emotions because you still try to fight them. So, they get all jumbled together after a while."

"You don't understand, Waltz. Some of these memories hurt. I don't want to feel them."

"I know." Waltz walked over to a box and dusted it off. He pulled out a ragged brown bear with brown glass eyes. "Remember him?"

Stephen nodded and smiled. He wanted to reach for the bear, but his desire to keep his hands warm in his pockets outweighed his attachment to the past.

"You had this with you when I found you. I couldn't get it away from you for months. It stayed in your room for years. You were seventeen before you asked me to put it away for safekeeping."

"Mom gave it to me." Stephen's voice cracked and sadness fell on him. He sniffed. Something about the bear called to him. Something forgotten. After all this time, Brown Bear still elicited a strong emotion. "She said that Dad had given it to her on their first date. It's all I know about him."

"I know. And you wouldn't let go because it eased the pain. Eventually you did. Once you accepted your situation, you were able to start healing. Right now, you need to be able to start healing."

Deep down, Stephen always knew it led back here, to her, his mother. Stephen worked hard, trying to remember details and pick apart memories. Stephen's abilities had increased since he returned. He heard thoughts from further distances and probed deeper into others' minds. However, he continued having difficulty separating his life from others.

"Okay, Waltz. What do I do?"

Waltz handed Brown Bear to Stephen. "You're gonna need this."

Stephen swallowed hard, knowing it would be very unpleasant.

"You need to remember Tommy."

Stephen's heart raced.

"We've tried everything else. You've read the entire neighborhood. Heck, I know stuff about people around us that I'd rather not know because of your ability. The control issue, I believe, comes back to your mind not healing after it's stressed. I think that may have something to do with Tommy."

"Okay, I'll try." Stephen sighed and closed his eyes. Thinking about Tommy made him feel sick at his stomach.

"Remember everything about Tommy. I think that once you are in someone's mind, you leave some type of imprint or connection. But I think they also leave an imprint on your brain, and that you're struggling to reconcile what happened with Tommy. I believe you have a lot more information in there than you realize. Once you understand it all better, my hope is that the problem will resolve itself."

Stephen saw Tommy, red shirt and blue jeans.

"Picture the first time you looked inside Tommy's mind."

The image of Tommy changed. He wore a black hoodie and blue jeans. Stephen observed Tommy leaving Biggs's place and followed him around the corner. He remembered getting into Tommy's mind looking for answers, trying to learn more about the operation.

Waltz's voice rang through. "When you got into Tommy's mind, did you see anything that you weren't looking for? Focus on the memories in the background, as though you are still in Tommy's head."

Stephen searched for anything that looked different. For a moment he thought the exercise useless. Instead, new thoughts began to flood Stephen's mind. He saw Tommy's girlfriend. He saw images of him with his friends at school. He somehow knew that Tommy had a mother at home that he took care of. He looked for Tommy's dad, finding only sadness. Tommy never knew his dad. Stephen understood this feeling.

"Now, remember the last time you saw Tommy. Remember how he felt."

An image of Tommy flashed in Stephen's mind. Tommy lay on the street looking at Stephen, fear still in his eyes. He fell only feet from where Stephen's body waited around the corner. Stephen experienced all the hurt, pain, and fear of the unknown that Tommy felt. This time, he remembered something new; Tommy feared for his mom. Who would take care of her? He wanted to hug her again.

Stephen gripped the teddy bear tighter. Tears fell like rain.

"Let it hurt, son. Let it hurt. You can't continue running from it. You have to own up to what happened and accept your part in it."

Stephen fell to his knees. "He wanted his mom. That's why I fought it so hard. I didn't even realize."

"Stephen, I was wrong. You weren't fighting Tommy's feelings. You were fighting your own."

Holding his bear, he looked up to Waltz, his eyes still filled with tears. "I miss her, Waltz. I thought I had forgotten about her. She seemed like a distant memory, someone else's life."

Waltz got to his knees and hugged Stephen. "You were hiding your own pain. It's okay now, though. You're not alone. And you don't have to forget her to be okay."

Stephen hugged him back. Tears streamed down his face. "Waltz, I never should have run away. I should have trusted you with this. I'm sorry. I thought it was all up to me. I remember when Mom got sick, she told me it was okay to be sad. But I felt I had to be strong. When she died, I didn't know what to do. The boys' home was horrible. I ran, just wanting the pain to stop."

"It's okay." Waltz held Stephen at arm's length. "Did you just remember all that?"

"W-what?" Stephen thought for a moment as he wiped his face clean. He remembered a memory long forgotten. He smiled. "Yeah, I did. I actually remember it all."

"That's great." Waltz smiled back. "You made a breakthrough today." Waltz stood up. "Listen, why don't we walk and see what else you remember?"

The two walked around the city for hours. Stephen recalled long-forgotten memories. He also told Waltz stories about people he encountered over the years. Separating his life from that of others became easier the longer they talked. Eventually, the temperature dropped too much, and the cold became unbearable. They backtracked their steps and returned home to get warm. After a successful day, it felt nice to be back hanging with the guys at the shelter and doing the day-to-day work, just like old times.

"Ahhh!"

The loud yell woke Walt from a deep slumber. He sat up. A faint glow from the light of the moon and distant streetlamps gave objects in the room discernable shape as he looked around, waiting to hear something again. Nothing seemed out of place. Sirens blared in the distance, setting off dogs down the street, but nothing troubling. Perhaps, he dreamed it.

"No, no!" Stephen yelled.

Waltz jumped from his bed and hurried down the hall toward the living room. As he neared, he saw Stephen asleep on the couch, tossing back and forth. *He must be dreaming.*

He approached Stephen cautiously, not wanting to startle him. Gently touching his shoulder, he felt what he assumed to be sweat covering his skin. Waltz whispered, "Stephen?" No response. He gave a more forceful shake. "Stephen. Wake up, boy. Wake up."

Stephen woke with a start and turned toward Waltz, before sitting up halfway. "Waltz? What is it?"

"You were dreaming. Quite loudly, I might add." He looked Stephen over and used his shirt to wipe the sweat from his hand. "Look at you, son. You're soaked. You alright?"

Stephen ran his hand across his forehead. "Yeah, I'm okay, Waltz. Just a dream. Every once in a while, I dream about Tommy. I guess the work we did yesterday stirred some things up a bit. Trying to learn to control and distinguish my life from everyone else's has been a little exhausting too."

"I think that's a good thing. Bernie says it best. If the boat ain't rockin'..."

Stephen interrupted with his best Southern accent, "It ain't a movin'."

Waltz saw movement in the hallway behind Stephen, and looked up to see Bernie standing there, looking sour.

"Sorry to interrupt, but I heard you guys in here. I just didn't realize I'd interrupt you pickin' at me." Bernie grinned.

"Awe, Uncle Bernie, you know I've always loved your accent. In fact, if I'd known that's what people in the South sounded like, I might have gone down there sooner."

Waltz chuckled.

"Yeah, yeah. Well, I sure do miss the South. The only thing I miss more than the South is Bernard."

"I wonder if he'll come back with that accent?" Stephen grinned.

Waltz chimed in. "Oh, he already has the accent."

"Well, since I'm up—and being made fun of—I'm a gonna go in the kitchen and fix myself some hot cocoa. I don't reckon anyone will be pickin' on me in there."

Bernie walked into the kitchen.

Waltz placed his hand on Stephen's shoulder. "Are you alright, boy?"

"Yeah, Waltz. I'm fine."

"Good. I'll leave you to sleep, then. Besides, I need to talk about some things with Bernie, you know. He's been asking questions about where we've been going."

"You mean when we work on controlling my abilities?" Stephen sat up, more erect.

"Yeah. He's seen the same stuff I have and all. He knows the same stuff I know. I'm just not ready to bring him in. This has become a sore spot for us."

"What are you talking about, a sore spot? Why can't we just tell Uncle Bernie? He'll understand. He could help."

"It's not that simple. But maybe soon. We'll see. Okay?"

"Okay Waltz, whatever you say." Stephen did not fully understand but accepted that Waltz wanted the best for him. "You know best."

"I don't know about that." Waltz sighed. "Why don't you lie back down now and get some rest. You'll need it today."

Stephen fluffed his pillow and rolled over as Waltz went into the kitchen, sliding the pocket door closed behind him.

Bernie stood at the stove with a pot on.

"Are you still making hot chocolate on the stove top? Haven't you learned to use a microwave?" Waltz patted Bernie on the back as he passed by, opened a cabinet, and got out two mugs before seating himself on the other side of the island countertop.

"Yeah, it just don't taste the same, Waltz. You know that." Bernie looked a little too serious, and a little silly, as he poured more milk into the pot.

"Yeah, I know. I just like giving you a ribbing from time to time."

Bernie chuckled. "Yeah! You and Stephen both."

Waltz smiled.

"So, that boy's got demons of some sort chasing him, huh?"

"You noticed."

"Of course, I noticed. It's been a while. But I still see the signs. Does he know? Have you been working with him? You ain't been telling me much."

"Yeah, I know. Sorry about that. I've been kind of stuck myself. I'm not sure telling him everything would be best for him right now. Plus, I think it's best that he just works with me for now."

"Fine, I get that. Too many cooks can spoil the broth." Bernie turned off the stove and began stirring the milk. "But you should tell 'em something, you know."

"Yeah, I agree. I think it's time, but I need to spoon-feed him. Honestly, I feel a little guilty for not telling him sooner. This life can be hard to grasp. He's already struggling with it."

Bernie poured the hot cocoa into the mugs. The aroma smelled wonderful. Waltz reached over and grabbed a couple of marshmallows from a nearby bag, then dropped them into his mug. "Two, right?" Bernie nodded and Waltz dropped two into his mug also.

"When did you learn about his ability?" Bernie asked.

"Well, I started sensing something when he was seventeen. But I couldn't understand it."

"I don't get it either. We know everyone, at least all the families. No one's missin'. Is it possible his family belongs to the other side?"

"Doubtful. You know it doesn't work that way."

"What if this is different? What if we *don't* know everything? What if something has changed?" Bernie took another sip.

Waltz looked at Bernie, considering the possibilities. After all, he knew Stephen should have no abilities. "I suspect something has changed. But I don't think that's it."

"Then what? Do ya think he's not part of a family, not one of the Mighty?"

The door slid open. "Who are the Mighty?"

Waltz and Bernie turned to see Stephen standing in the doorway with brow furled and jaw clenched. The door must have remained ajar after he entered.

"Uh-oh," Bernie mumbled as he got up, heading toward the cabinet.

"Well, now's as good a time as any. Have a seat." Waltz scooted a stool out from the edge of the island.

Stephen sat as Bernie placed a mug in front of him and proceeded to fill it with hot chocolate.

"Thank you, sir." Stephen sipped from his mug. "What are we talking about?"

"Uh-huh." Bernie sat down. "You're up, Waltz." Bernie sipped from his mug some more.

Thanks! Waltz worked his best sarcastic facial expression to show Bernie just how much he appreciated his support.

"Hey. You're handling this, right?" Bernie set his mug down, returning the expression.

Stephen frowned. "Wait, you heard that too? Bernie, you heard Waltz's thought?"

"Waltz, you wanna take it now?" Bernie asked.

Waltz cleared his throat. "What did you hear, Stephen, before you came in?"

"Hear? Oh, nothing. I just smelled the hot chocolate and thought a warm drink might help me rest."

Waltz turned to Stephen with a sigh. "Stephen, Bernie and I...Well, we're part of a group of people called the Mighty."

Bernie cleared his throat.

"Okay, fine, Bernie. Technically, we're retired, inactive."

"What? What are you talking about?" Stephen looked straight at Waltz, not turning away.

"One step at a time." Waltz turned on his stool to face directly toward Stephen, who still hadn't moved. "Do you remember King David and his men from the Old Testament?"

"Of course, I do. How could I forget? It seemed to be one of your favorite topics."

"Yeah, well. They were David's mighty men. Scripture records them by name and family. There were many. Among them were thirty that stood above the rest. Then there were three above them. Then, although not counted among the three, there was the chief of the three. The deeds of the thirty, the three, and the chief set them apart, along with King David, of course."

"Yes, Waltz, I said I remember."

"Well, their descendants continued to be the Mighty long after King David passed. They continued to serve the Lord. For their faithfulness and continued service, the Lord gave them various abilities, all of which fell into one of three classes: warrior class, priest class, and prophet class, symbolizing the Son of God—prophet, priest, and king."

"Let me guess—warrior class has unique fighting abilities, prophet class speaks for God, and priest class works to keep the others in communion with God."

"Well, it's not quite that simple. As Christians, we can all speak with God through Christ, so it's not exactly like that. But you're close. Warrior is simplest to explain. These have the ability to be great strategists, and yes, most often have some enhanced fighting abilities, such as strength, agility, and speed. Priests often act as shields, protecting the group from corruption, almost like a grounded center. They can also have a sense of when evil is present. In general, they desire to protect people. Prophets point the direction for the group. Their abilities focus on seeing what others can't, interpreting what is seen and heard, and they can often have other situational abilities that come and go as needed, like when Moses parted the Red Sea."

"Wait, seeing...Are you saying I'm a prophet? This is a little crazy, all of it!" Stephen pushed himself from the counter and began pacing the floor.

"I know it sounds that way. I assure you, however, it's the truth. Take a moment. You'll have questions. I'll answer them as best I can, one by one." Waltz observed Stephen, wondering what his first question would be. Stephen's eyes moved back and forth, as though searching for something.

Stephen stopped and looked at Waltz. "You said descendants?"

Waltz's heart sank. This was the one question that he thought would be most important to Stephen. It also happened to be the one question he could not answer.

"My parents were members of the Mighty?"

"Yes. As far as we know, one of them had to be. Usually it's the father. Most abilities are only passed through the male line. The women can have abilities, but it's usually the male that passes them along, and it is rare for Mighty families to intermarry."

"So, you don't know who my parents are?"

Bernie spoke. "We don't. We weren't even aware of your ability until recently."

Waltz glared sternly at Bernie for a moment before turning back to Stephen.

"Okay, what was that about?" Stephen looked back and forth between the two.

Bernie spoke again. “Well, it’s a ‘too many cooks’ thing.”

“No. Waltz should have told me sooner and didn’t. So, go ahead.” Stephen glared at Waltz. Waltz understood that Stephen felt betrayed, but he knew in his heart he did the right thing.

“Maybe you did the right thing or maybe not,” Stephen directed at Waltz. “Time will tell.” Stephen turned back to Bernie. “Go on, Unc.”

Bernie looked over at Waltz and waited. Waltz gave a nod and Bernie continued. “Well, the truth is, we aren’t one hundred percent certain you’re one of the Mighty.”

“Then what?” Stephen’s voice trembled.

“Well, sometimes, Mighty go bad. Those that do fall from their ranks are counted among Fallen, a group that has taken up the cause of fallen angels. They fall for any number of reasons. Ain’t one of ’em good reasons. But they fall nonetheless.”

“As far as we know,” Waltz interjected, “their children have never had abilities, none like yours. They are masters at deception and manipulation. Any abilities Fallen children have are used to deceive others. They are intelligent and ruthless. But no abilities like the Mighty.”

“As far as we know—” Bernie stated.

“Wait, you’re saying my parents could have been Fallen? That’s just great.” Stephen paced the kitchen. Waltz figured Stephen felt anxious but wondered what was going on in his mind.

“It’s not likely. The children of Fallen that I’ve met have been different from others, as if they don’t fit in with ordinary kids. As they grow up, they don’t fit into society like normal people.”

He stopped and turned toward Waltz. "When were you going to tell me?"

Waltz answered matter-of-factly. "Today."

"Really?"

"Yes. I had just discussed it with Bernie. I needed to know you were ready."

Stephen stopped and stared at Waltz. "Ready? How so?"

"We've been working on your mental control lately, which centers on controlling your emotions, allowing you to use them to fuel the gift, not to weaken your body. Some of your ability is tied very closely to how you're feeling or remember feeling at a particular moment."

Waltz got up and walked to Stephen, wanting to console him. He placed his hand on Stephen's shoulder, which Stephen shrugged off. "My boy, I knew all this would stir some deep-rooted feelings and hit you hard. It would anyone. Your ability is a very unique and powerful gift. If you weren't able to control it properly, well, you could have done some real damage. You only just broke through the barrier that kept you from moving forward."

"You mean I could have hurt you guys?"

Bernie laughed. "No, boy! You may very well be more powerful than these two old men. But we have enough experience to withstand a lot."

"Stephen." Waltz waited for Stephen to look at him. "There are innocent people in this house whose minds you could have destroyed with the wrong thought and without control of your emotions. You would not have known it until it was too late. Control is very important. If you'll focus hard enough, you'll find you can hear the thoughts of everyone else in the house at once, all twenty-eight others."

Stephen looked away for a moment, then nodded in agreement. "They're all asleep."

"And without control, they could all have been hurt. Your emotions have been key. Whenever your emotions have been heightened, your gift hasn't worked right, has it?"

Stephen shook his head, and stood there for a moment, looking at the two of them.

"Stephen, I needed to make sure you could handle this information and your gift before I told you. It would have devastated you if more were injured because of your gift.

Stephen turned and headed back into the living room. "You should have told me sooner, Waltz."

"You're probably right," Waltz said softly.

Stephen closed the door behind him. Waltz sat back down on his stool to finish his cocoa. Neither said much else, but they finished their drinks before saying good night.

The sun shone brightly, only occasionally blocked by a wandering cloud. A cool breeze blew from the north and rolled off the Mississippi. Stephen pulled his windbreaker tighter around his neck, following Waltz. He heard the excitement of kids and adults alike looking up at the grand arch that towered high above. A scent of spring carried on the breeze amid the surrounding gardens—nearing full bloom. The aroma of chargrilled steak from a nearby restaurant enticed his taste buds. His mouth watered. Business professional and casual shoppers filled the sidewalks on their way to lunch; some took a break from work while others ate before Friday shopping.

Stephen struggled to keep his mind on his training. He could not help but wonder about the conversation that took place in their kitchen a week ago.

What if my parents were members of Fallen? What would that say about me?

"I'm ready, Daddy." A nearby little girl's excitement caught his attention. *I'm really scared! What if we get stuck up there?* Stephen looked around to see her, pink jacket and pigtails.

So often what people said and what they thought were very different. Stephen learned that over the years. It made him want to distrust everyone. People are often untruthful with others, even themselves. How could *he* trust them?

"What do you hear?" Waltz paused for a moment before continuing. "Did you hear the little girl that just walked by?"

"I did," Stephen replied.

"She looked scared." Waltz continued. "But she said she was ready. What's the truth?"

"She's terrified—afraid of getting stuck at the top."

"Why do you think she said she was ready?"

Stephen turned toward Waltz, who faced into the breeze alongside Stephen. "I don't know. Does it really matter?"

"Of course, it matters. Why we do the things we do matters about as much as what we do. You have trust issues. With your gift, it's easy to understand why. You get to see the worst humanity has to offer over and over, until you begin to feel like you are the worst of humanity. So, I'll ask again." Waltz turned his head toward Stephen. "Why did she say she was ready? You have her emotions, not just in that moment but the moments afterward. What happened next?"

Stephen thought for a moment. He had heard something else. Closing his eyes and focusing on the memory allowed him to relive the memory in full detail. His memory paused, as though staring at picture, only with full feeling. Something hid underneath the raw emotions and thoughts. Something important. What was it?

Stephen turned his head back toward Waltz with excitement, realizing he had missed the point in her actions—selflessness. "She was trying to be brave for her dad."

"Go on. What else?"

Stephen continued. "She knew how much her dad wanted to go and how much he wanted her to be with him. She enjoys making him happy. She was terrified but wanted to be brave for him."

"Is that all?"

Stephen paused as excitement turned to sadness. "No. He's sick and she knows it. I don't think she knows how sick though. He has cancer, doesn't he?"

"He does. This will be their last family trip before he takes a turn for the worst. She'll be glad she conquered her fear in time. She'll give him a great gift before the end. She really isn't ready to go up that elevator. But she is ready to face her fear for him. Soon, she will be at the top of that arch, scared to death and in awe of the view."

"So, I should ease up on people? Is that the point?"

"Yeah, you should. You are kind of judgmental and have a tendency to come down hard on others and yourself." Waltz nodded back toward the city, and they began to walk. "This place is filled with people who do and think horrible things. But most people will never know this because they don't have your gift. They have to trust. And they get by just fine. We are all flawed. Your gift makes it hard for you to get close to someone. Still, you need to understand that the intent matters. You'll have to learn to be a judge of people, in a way, just as the prophets of old were."

"That's why I get the emotions too, not just the thoughts." It finally began to make sense to him. Stephen had noticed many times that people's words, thoughts, and emotions would differ from one another, never giving it much thought until now. "So, I can judge between them, to help in my actions and decisions."

"Well, less judging and more understanding. I don't think you were given the gift to be judgmental, but to understand."

"Okay. But what good is understanding if you don't take action? We've seen a lot these past couple of months, and you've had me sit by and watch, not intervene. What's the point?"

"Son, I want you to understand what actions do and don't need to be taken. Your answer has always been to use force. Either you want to force your will on someone or use someone else to force your will. I'm not saying that there isn't a time and place for that. However, that should be the exception, not the rule."

"Hmph. All this training and waiting—it's useless," Stephen sulked. He hadn't really shouted at Waltz since he'd come back, but he considered it. He felt a gentle hand on his arm but pulled away.

"Stephen."

He started walking through City Park, surrounded by sculptures of iron and concrete. They ranged from realistic depictions of historical figures to abstract renderings of who knows what.

"Stephen." Walt said louder than before.

He stopped near a large hollow head laying on its ear. He had not been yelled at since he returned. Stephen turned to see Waltz standing with his hands high on his hips. It reminded him of his childhood, how Waltz looked when he got mad at him and Bernard.

"Don't be like this sculpture over here. Yeah, it's a beautifully sculpted large head. But it's empty. You have a grand gift, meant for so much more than you now realize."

"Oh, yeah? Now you're saying I'm mindless!"

"The way you want to use your gift is." Waltz retorted. "Think back one moment to that little girl. You were in the moment, in her head. What drew you to her? Why did you pick her out to focus on? Think back, before you were fully in her head. What did you hear? What did you feel?"

"What's the point, Waltz? Just tell me." Stephen thought he was ready for the next step. He knew he was. This seemed a waste of his time, and it only kept him from doing what he felt needed to be done.

"Humor me!" Waltz said gently. Stephen heard the pleading in Waltz's voice.

"Alright, alright!" Stephen closed his eyes and went back to the memory. Concentrating, he heard the crowd as though he stood there again. He sorted through an array of emotions, all of which seemed quite ordinary. People felt excited, bored, sad, happy, distraught, and more—a plethora of emotions.

There! Something beckoned him. He barely noticed it at first. He strained, amplifying his ability. His palms sweated. Happiness and fear coexisted in the little girl. Still, he sensed something else, having missed it earlier.

A little sadness and accomplishment. The girl had accomplished something. But what? She had not gone up the arch yet. He strained harder. The feeling rooted deep and strong. Even the little girl did not yet understand the significance. But there it stood.

Stephen opened his eyes. "I thought she didn't know."

"She doesn't," Waltz stated plainly.

"I see. But she understands. She, deep inside, understands that something has been wrong with her dad. She wants to make him happy. They'd been there before, and she couldn't do it. They came back today so she could make him proud. She understands this could be her last chance. Somehow, she knows he needs this day as much as she does."

"Yes, this memory, this day—this is the way she will remember him long after he is gone. Do you understand now?"

"I think so. I'm just tired of waiting, of not doing anything." Stephen sat on a bench. Waltz walked over and sat next to him.

"You misunderstand me. I want you to do something, just as that little girl did. You need to do something, but not just anything will do. It must be the right thing."

As they walked back home quietly, Stephen thought about Waltz's words. The little girl's actions were small but so brave and selfless. How many times had he been selfish in his actions, wanting to be the hero, like in the Batman movies? But those were only movies, and this was real life. Maybe it was a little more complicated than going out and just beating up people until you've beaten up that single right person. Maybe his powers *were* also meant for smaller daily acts of kindness to have a profound impact on others and the world around them. Maybe, like the little girl, he should look beyond the concerns of his own parents and focus on what needed to be done.

⁂

"Stephen, let's go!" Stephen heard Waltz through the bathroom door but continued to drag a bit. He could not get the little girl out of his head from a couple of days earlier. He desired to be selfish and focus on who his parents might have been. He spent most of his life wanting to belong but feeling as though he did not. These new questions concerning his lineage only compounded his feelings of loneliness. He still could not shake the feeling that his parents might not be the most important thing to learn now.

I need to focus on and be in the moment.

Waltz yelled again. "Boy, hurry up!"

Well, I'd like to be in some other moment!

"Almost done! I'm coming!" Stephen opened the door and stepped out into the hall. He was wearing a plain black V-neck T-shirt, with blue jeans and black leather boots. "I'm ready, but I'm not dressing up! I trimmed my stubble and brushed my hair. I'm done."

"Fine, fine. Now grab your jacket and come on!"

"Waltz, I get having responsibilities," Stephen said as he struggled with his leather jacket. "I didn't expect to stay here for free, you know. I help here at the mission. I've been walking around with you downtown, handing out needed items and stuff. I think I do a heck of a job. I even enjoy the landscaping. But why church?"

"We help with the lunch for the homeless afterward."

"I can show up afterward, then," Stephen said as he stopped at the bottom of the porch steps. Waltz made it to the sidewalk, where he stopped too before turning back toward Stephen.

"My boy, you're lost, in more ways than one. I've been working with you on this gift. Truth is, if you don't find God, not a thing I teach you will help."

Stephen heard Bernie locking the door behind him. "How do you feel, Uncle Bernie? You've never been too vocal about God and Christ."

"How do I feel? Boy, I feel like you better listen to ol' Waltz there. He's done a lot for you. Pay him some respect." Bernie walked on past Stephen and Waltz, heading toward the church.

"What if I don't, Waltz? What if I don't find Jesus?" Stephen asked. "What then?"

"You'll eventually become a Fallen."

"You don't really believe that, do you? Do you really think I'd go bad?"

The two walked down the sidewalk, Bernie several steps ahead. "Stephen, you remember Friday's lesson?" Waltz asked. "The little girl?"

Stephen nodded.

"You'll learn to use your abilities to understand people, what makes them tick, how we're all intertwined and relate to one another. Likewise, you need to go to church to learn and understand faith. It isn't just about God and a person. It's about people, a family, a community, and trusting something you can't control.

We all play our part, just like the Mighty. Each member has his own gift. It all ties in, you see. Without it, faith, you are without hope."

"But I have you, don't I? You won't let me do anything too stupid." Stephen nudged Waltz.

"True, but I may not always be here. I'm getting up there. I'm sixty-seven, you know."

"Yeah, well, I'm gonna need you around a little longer. Besides, if I gotta sit through church, so do you. So, you can't go anywhere."

Stephen didn't really try to pay attention in church. His mind remained distracted with thoughts of his parents. What were they like? What did his dad look like? Which one had abilities and what were they? Once, he had noticed Waltz looking at him, smiling. He realized then that he needed to find another way to find out about his parents. If he started pressing Waltz about them, it might hurt his feelings. The last thing he wanted to do was hurt him again.

Church service ended sooner than Stephen expected. After meeting a few members, he went to the kitchen to join Waltz and Bernie, who worked getting lunch ready for the needy. They did this every Sunday. Stephen, however, felt a little awkward at first, which is why he worked extra hard to be useful. He really did want to help. Although he had been feeling more and more like he should be out there using his gift, he tried hard to live in the moment.

As people came in, Stephen tried talking to them and worked to make them feel comfortable. He took notice of an old woman that had come in. She wore a short-sleeved shirt. Stephen noticed how she shivered and how her sweater was worn thin. He set his mind on the woman, searching her thoughts.

It's so good of these people to do this for us. I wonder if it would be too much to ask if they have a sweater or jacket for my grandson at home. Stephen felt the woman's shame and reluctance. She had been without work for some time and tried many times to get a job. At her age, there wasn't much that people were willing to give her. Stephen continued to focus; he got a glimpse of a young boy with tan skin, brown curly hair, and large brown eyes. The boy and his parents moved back in with the woman. They all worked at the same place when it closed. The parents started new jobs, which paid far less than their previous jobs.

"Waltz!" Stephen motioned for Waltz to come over to where he was, near the end of the serving line. Waltz, who walked around greeting and cleaning up, quickly came over.

"Everything alright?"

"What? Oh, yeah." Stephen spoke softly and cryptically so that others wouldn't hear what he was *really* saying. "I just heard that elderly woman down there talking about her grandson. She seems really cold too. Don't you think we have some jackets and sweaters that might fit them? The boy is about nine and average size."

Waltz grinned ear to ear. "You're finally getting it, aren't you? You're learning to understand."

Stephen had not thought about it. He used his gift mostly out of boredom. He fidgeted with his apron and smiled back. "Yeah, Waltz. I suppose I am." Stephen started taking off his apron.

"Whoa! Where do you think you're going? I'll run back to the shelter and get the jackets."

Stephen frowned. He hoped running back to Bernie's would give him a break from church stuff. He tied his apron again. "Fine, I'll stay. You can go get the jackets."

Although he did not get away from the church, Stephen felt pleased. He used his gift to help, and in a way that Waltz agreed with. He watched the people as they came in. Each with new needs, so many that he could not do anything about.

After a while, Stephen noticed something seemed off. He was not quite sure what, but the feeling someone watched him returned. Having trained his senses somewhat, he separated his emotions, feelings, and memories from that of the others. He still felt them every bit as much, if not more than before, but he knew what belonged to whom. This feeling, though, felt much different—an intrusion. He looked around the room for something, someone out of place, someone that did not fit. Nothing. His head ached from the sensation.

Maybe that's all it is—a simple headache.

Stephen turned to a young red-haired woman passing by. His head hurt so badly, his vision blurred and darkened. "Ma'am, do we have something for a headache?"

"Sure. Uh, your nose! Oh, I'll get something."

My nose? Stephen grabbed his nose and blood ran between his fingers. His head hurt and throbbed, growing stronger with each pulse. He thought it might explode. "Waltz! Bernie? Hey..." Stephen's words trailed off as he plummeted.

"Stephen, you better be okay, boy. Waltz'll kill us both if anything's wrong with you."

Stephen opened his eyes and saw Bernie standing over him.

"You alright?" Bernie asked.

"I feel like someone very large punched me in the head. Other than that, yeah, I'm alright."

"Well, you better be thankful that young woman was helping out today. She grabbed hold of you when you started falling. She's a tiny thing. But man, she's stout. Kept you from hittin' your head on this hard flo'."

"*Floor*, Uncle Bernie. There's an *r* at the end." Stephen chuckled as he sat up.

"Fine, pick on me if you want. I'll just leave you lyin' there till Waltz gets back." Bernie slapped Stephen with a hand towel and walked off. One of the other men helped Stephen back to his feet.

"You sure you're alright?" the man asked.

"Yeah, I'm good. I don't know what happened. My nose started bleeding; maybe I stood up too fast. I've been organizing stuff on the bottom."

"Well, if you start to feel weak or dizzy, have a seat. Okay?" The man pulled over a chair.

Stephen nodded.

"Oh, and I'm Jack. If you need anything, just ask."

"Thanks, Jack."

Stephen noticed Waltz walking toward him in a hurry, navigating through the crowded room.

"Hey, Stephen. Bernie just filled me in. You okay?" Waltz seated himself on a chair close to Stephen and motioned for him to sit too.

"Yeah, I'm good. Waltz, I think someone else was here, like me. Like us!"

"What do you mean?"

"Well, I had that feeling that someone was watching me, like I used to get before I came back. But now that I'm more trained, I could tell what it was. Someone was trying to get in my head, maybe looking for something, trying to do what I do. Only, I was able to fight. I think that's why I passed out. I was fighting, but he or she is stronger than I am."

"I doubt they're stronger," Waltz stated as he looked around the room.

"What? Why?"

"Stephen, you have one of the strongest minds I've ever come across. I have some theories as to why. Now, they're just theories and could be completely off. But that's not important. If someone is getting into your mind, it's because the person is better trained. Most will spend years training as teenagers, learning simply how to control the most basic abilities."

"Who would want in my mind? I know very little of the Mighty. You won't tell me much."

"Yeah, and this is why, but I don't imagine they want information."

"Well, what do they want then?" Stephen snapped. He noted the concern on Waltz's face and felt the uneasiness grow inside his mentor's mind. All sorts of thoughts raced around inside too. Before Waltz had a chance, Stephen answered his own question. "They want me, don't they?"

"I'm afraid so." Waltz stood up. "Walk outside with me."

"Alright." Stephen got up and turned back toward the line he had been working at earlier. "I'll be back in moment. We're getting some air. Then I should be good."

Jack yelled back. "Sure thing, man. I got this."

The two men stepped outside, looking at those they passed by. Stephen could not help but wonder if it had been one of them that had attacked him in the building. He followed Waltz around the front of the church. Waltz stopped and stood there, looking up at the front of the building. "You see that?"

"What? The cross?"

"Yeah. It symbolizes a lot of things: hope, love, sacrifice, freedom, and the list goes on. I don't need to tell you about the cross. You've learned about Jesus since you came to live with me. But have I told you what the first thing I see is when I look at the cross?"

Stephen shook his head.

"I see choice. The Son of God chose to come down to Earth as a man to love us. He chose to refuse Satan, to live a sinless life. He chose to allow man, his own creation, to take his life. And in fulfilment of God's law, he chose to rise again."

Waltz turned toward Stephen. "Stephen, you were attacked because the enemy wants you. The Fallen have no good motives. Their goal is simply the destruction of man and to grab as much power for themselves as they can amass in the process. The members are deluded in thinking they can thwart God's plans. Satan has pulled the wool over their eyes. Soon enough, you are going to have to make a choice, my boy. You will have to either accept Christ or reject him. You can't walk through life without choosing a side."

"Why, Waltz? Why can I not just live my life? Why do I have to pick a side?" Stephen took a breath to calm himself. "It just doesn't make sense to me. I don't want to be part of this. Why can't I just live a good and decent life?"

"Well, how's that working for you so far? By not choosing a side, you *are* choosing one. And the results can be catastrophic for someone with your ability, not to mention for your soul."

"I'm just not sure I'm ready to buy into all this. Some of it still seems a little out there."

Waltz picked up a pebble and played with it in his hand. "Yeah, I get that. I wasn't so quick to believe all this either. I accepted Christ and all, but I was stubborn and continued to live a bit of a rebellious life when I was younger. I thought my gift made me weird. I didn't want to be a Mighty."

"Really? How did that go over with the Mighty?" Stephen found this curious. Waltz never gave any prior indication that he had done anything other than play by the rules.

"Not so well, at times."

"I bet with a gift like mine, you were able to read minds and steer clear of trouble though."

"What?" Waltz looked at Stephen, his face contorted. "Oh, no. I don't have your gift. I'm not a prophet."

"But the training, and the little girl?" Stephen was confused. How could Waltz see things and understand being a seer if he wasn't a prophet?

"I'm sorry. I've kept you in the dark a bit. I suppose I should tell you just a little more." Waltz tossed the pebble into a nearby flowerbed. "When we complete our training and fully realize our potential, we can come together with two others into a group of three—a triune. One group, three members—one from each class. Once that has happened, you're interconnected. To a very small degree you share the abilities of the others, for the purpose of allowing you to understand each other's abilities and burdens. Each ability comes at a cost. It's useful for each member to know and understand that. It helps them work as a team. For example, the emotions you get from others and constantly having to carry those around is a cost. If you don't control it, it seems you can lose yourself. The interconnectedness in a triune also helps you not only to protect one another but to train new Mighty."

"So, your triune's prophet can see thoughts, similar to me?"

"Similar. But I don't think the ability is as strong as what you're describing. You're still understanding your ability. But the things you're able to do already, without much actual training, is really amazing."

"So, who's your seer? Why don't you go do Mighty stuff?"

Waltz sighed. His demeanor changed. Stephen felt a sadness fall on Waltz. "A member of my triune became one of the Fallen."

Stephen felt sorry he asked. He kicked at a pebble, trying to decide whether or not to press or just let the matter go. Before he decided, Waltz continued.

"We never saw it coming. We tried to undo it, to turn Elizabeth back. She was our warrior. But it didn't happen. Not soon enough."

"She? Your warrior was a girl?"

"Oh yes! And a very good one. We were on a roll, doing all kinds of good. Before we knew it, she was a Fallen. One moment of weakness was all it took. After that, our triune broke apart. When you form a triune, your powers increase. You're stronger, more focused together. Well, we couldn't have a powerful warrior going around wreaking havoc. So, I got Bernie to help me dampen our gifts. Bernie was a prophet from another triune, but a close friend."

"Your prophet was okay with that?"

"No. But my job was to protect. And I did that. He understood but left the triune. Bernie took his place to help. He and I retired after that though."

"Did Bernie's triune take in your prophet?"

"Yep, he held onto his powers, and Bernie lost his, mostly. Like me, he basically lost his heightened triune ability. We're back to being normal Mighty."

"So, you are a priest and Uncle Bernie is a prophet. What ended up happening to your warrior?"

"The short story is that not long after she lost her powers, she got into some stuff–drugs and things. Several years ago, she straightened her life out. Almost as soon as she did, something happened to her that shook her up. I hear she kind of lost it. It's a shame she didn't straighten out sooner. She might have still been sane. Maybe the drug abuse damaged her. I don't know."

"Well, at least she finally made her choice, right?"

Waltz smiled. "Yeah, I guess she did."

"Couldn't you three form a triune? Get your powers back?"

"It doesn't work like that. Besides, we've been retired. And Elizabeth's bloodline was retired."

"What does that mean, her bloodline was retired?"

"When someone becomes a Fallen, the council of Mighty retire the direct bloodline. There's a ceremony and stuff. Basically, they can have no children—at least none with powers like Mighty. It's a curse handed down by the council."

"Is that why you never had kids?" Stephen asked before he thought. He worried he might have hurt Waltz's feelings. Waltz had never talked about not having kids and had avoided the subject when Stephen had been younger and inquisitive.

"That's exactly why I never wanted to have kids of my own. I felt any child of mine would be deprived of a proud heritage because I had failed to protect Elizabeth."

Stephen heard sadness in Waltz's tone. He placed his arm around him. "In the end, you didn't fail her though, did you?" Waltz looked at Stephen, who gave his best half-smile. "Besides, you got me for a kid. I guess you get to continue your bloodline—in a way."

"Yeah, I guess I do." Waltz walked toward the door. "Now, this bloodline needs to get back to work."

Stephen followed, understanding that was Waltz's way of changing the subject. "What about my attacker?"

"Well, there's really no way to track them at this point. We'll have to be vigilant. Besides, my guess is, whoever it was got hurt a bit. Your mind is strong."

Stephen turned his head away from the blowback mists of the bleach and water mixture he sprayed on the siding, an effort to remove the mildew growing on the walls of the shady side of the shelter. The weather had changed. The sun felt warm, and a spring breeze blew up from the south. It was a good day to be outside. From the top of the ladder, he saw the neighborhood. Many people in the area also worked on their houses and lawns.

The front door slammed, startling Stephen, causing him to grab tight to the ladder. The sprayer nozzle swung by his side after letting go of it. *Good thing I have this sprayer strapped on my back.* Although a month had passed since his mind was attacked, he still felt as though someone watched him, causing him to wonder if the feeling had ever really gone away.

He watched people come and go. Stephen knew they soon would sleep on the street again in warmer weather. A tall, slender man walked across the lawn toward the porch. His black hair hung long enough to brush the top of his collar. The man's goatee appeared neatly trimmed, and he wore what appeared to Stephen to be an expensive suit that the man didn't look at all comfortable in. He stopped and looked at Stephen.

"Excuse me," he called. "Is Mr. Stockton in?"

"Waltz, you mean? Yeah, he's in. You want me to get him for you?"

Before Stephen finished speaking, the gentleman was already walking toward the porch again. "No, thank you."

Stephen became curious. He climbed down the ladder, searching for the man's thoughts as he went. There were so many people inside, down in the recreation room, dining room, living room, and so on. He had a hard time singling out the stranger. He walked around the flowerbed and up to the porch just in time to see Waltz and the guest walking back toward him.

"Stephen," Waltz called out, "I'd like you to meet someone." They continued out to the porch. Stephen's clothes dripped from spraying. "This is Vincent, a friend of mine."

Vincent didn't appear much older than Stephen—late twenties.

"Nice to meet you," Vincent said, extending his hand.

"Yeah, likewise," Stephen replied. He looked at Vincent's hand and back up. "Oh, I'm covered in bleach. You really don't want to."

"Understood." Vincent looked around at the porch and yard. "Waltz tells me that you are the reason Bernie's shelter is looking better than it has in years."

"Oh, right. Waltz has been a dad to me, and Bernie's kind of like an uncle. I just came back in town. I grew up here. They've let me stay on the couch. So, I figured helping out is the least I could do."

Waltz nudged Vincent, who raised an eyebrow in return. "Ah, yes." He turned toward Stephen. "I would like to put you on the payroll."

"Oh, that's not necessary," Stephen replied.

"Actually, it is. Insurance will only cover you doing maintenance and repairs of this type if you are on the payroll. Plus, since we are a charitable organization, it would not look good to have a volunteer get hurt and not be able to pay his own medical bills. Besides, it could leave us open to a lawsuit. Which, as chief legal counsel for the shelter, I cannot allow."

"Well, okay then." Stephen grew excited. He hadn't had a job in some time. This could help provide a fresh start. "What do I need to do?"

"Come to my office tomorrow morning, between eight and nine o'clock. I will tell Patty, my assistant, to expect you."

"I'll be there." Stephen smiled at Waltz.

"Vincent," Waltz interjected, "I'll come along as well, so we can catch up."

"I look forward to it."

Vincent turned, walked down the steps, and crossed the lawn to a black luxury sedan parked on the side of the road.

Stephen waited until he felt Vincent was out of hearing distance. "He's sort-of odd, right?"

Waltz chuckled. "I guess. But, he's a good man."

Stephen sat in a high-back chair across from Patty's office early the next morning. He fiddled with his phone while Waltz talked with some other men down one of the aisles. He ran his finger across the face of the phone: seven-fifty-five. He focused on their emotions, just as Waltz instructed in their most recent training session. Something about one of the men felt off. He focused harder, searching the man's thoughts.

The man's name was Johnathan. In every way, he seemed ordinary, right down to his Van shoes and black thick-rimmed glasses. His emotions grew negative as they talked, but why? When the group broke apart, he walked by Stephen, who caught a glimpse of what troubled him.

"Hey! You're Johnathan, right? I'm Stephen," he said standing and offering his hand as a gentlemanly gesture.

The man adjusted his glasses before shaking Stephen's hand. "Nice to finally meet you. Waltz talks about you a lot." He pushed his glasses back up his nose, then swiped his brown hair from his eyes while glancing back toward Waltz. "By the way, most people call me Johnny."

"Oh, right! Sorry. Habit. People used to call me Steve, and I hated having my name shortened, especially without people asking me first. I mean, if someone really close to me did it, like gave me a nickname, that would be okay, but I feel like people take me more serious when they call me Stephen."

"Actually, Johnathan works. You know—no one gets that. If my name was Johnny, they'd probably call me John without asking. Thanks for understanding."

"You're welcome." Stephen looked down the hallway for a second. "I'm meeting with Vincent this morning. What time does he normally get here?"

Johnathan looked at his watch and pushed the brown shaggy hair from his face at the same time. "I'm sure he's already here. He's usually one of the first to get in. He's probably waiting on Patty. She ran to pick up some things. She should be back soon." Johnathan grabbed his keys from his pocket. "I've got to head to a meeting. It was nice meeting you."

"Yeah, you too."

The man turned to walk away but stopped. He turned back and asked, "How did you know Johnny wasn't my name?"

Stephen pointed to the laptop bag clutched in his new friend's left hand. It had the name Johnathan Friar embossed in the leather.

"Ah, gotcha. Well, I better get going."

Stephen waved and sat back down in his chair. He glanced back at his phone: eight o'clock.

He heard loud footsteps coming from the entrance. He turned to see a petite red-haired woman coming down the hall. He watched her with intrigue. She stepped with purpose; her head held high. She wore a knee-length black skirt and a blue blouse. She smiled when she seemed to notice Stephen.

Lost for words, he only smiled back.

"Here for your meeting with Vincent?" she asked as she walked over to her desk to put down a bag of supplies.

Stephen stood to greet her. Suddenly, he was caught off guard by her thoughts and couldn't help but be embarrassed. She thought he was cute.

"You look flushed. Are you alright?" The lady continued to put the supplies away.

"Oh, yeah, just a little embarrassed is all." Stephen realized he couldn't leave the statement like that. "W-Waltz always tells me to help a lady. I should have grabbed the bags for you. Sorry." He wasn't sure if she paid attention to his fumbling of words.

"Oh, nonsense. I'm used to it. There aren't many gentlemen around here," Patty replied, nodding toward the cubicles.

Stephen not only sensed her gladness at seeing him but that she enjoyed talking with him. As he intruded on her thoughts again, he saw that she especially liked his blue eyes. Stephen smiled. She liked his dimples too!

"Sorry, I'm Stephen, but I guess you knew that."

"Oh, right. I'm Patty. I'm the office manager around here, and Vincent's secretary." Patty began getting some papers together. She quickly picked up an envelope and a binder and set them on her desk in front of Stephen, knocking over a stack of papers in the process. "Sorry about that." Stephen helped her pick up the papers and placed them on her desk.

"It's not a problem." As he inhaled, he smelled her sweet perfume. He found everything about her attractive, the long red hair, emerald-green eyes, and even the few freckles on her neck.

After cleaning up the stack of papers, she handed him the folder. "You'll need this and a pen."

"So, number one aunt? Niece, nephew, or both?" Stephen leaned forward, taking a pen from her mug that read: "#1 Aunt."

Patty smiled. "One niece, Kaylin. And she's a handful. But I love her to death! You?" Patty sat down behind her desk. "Any nieces, nephews, kids in general?"

"Nah. I'm it. I don't know what you know about me. Folks around here seem to know Waltz pretty well. But, uh, my mom died when I was young. I don't remember much about her. I know *nothing* about my dad."

Patty looked back up from her work, her face very solemn. "I'm sorry. I didn't know the details."

"Don't be. It's alright. Waltz has been as good to me as any father ever could be to a son. I got a good deal when he took me in. It just felt right from the start. Don't get me wrong, it wasn't easy. We had struggles. But he's my family—he, Uncle Bernie, and Bernard—Bernie's nephew."

Patty smiled. "I'm glad they were there for you."

"Yeah, me too." Stephen turned to walk away but stopped. "Hey, what's the deal with Vincent? He seems a little odd to me. Do you like working for him?"

"I do. He's very efficient. He doesn't have you do a lot of wasteful stuff. But he does keep you busy. Some people find working for him hard. He isn't the most personable guy." Patty answered her phone as Stephen turned to walk back toward the chair. "Yes sir. They're both here. Hold on. Stephen," Patty called out to him.

He stopped and turned.

"They'll be right in," she told Vincent over the phone.

Waltz walked up. "I heard. Vincent's ready?"

Patty nodded. "Yes, sir."

“How many times do I have to ask you to call me Waltz?” he laughed.

“Ask many as you like, Mr. Stockton,” Patty replied with a smile.

“Well, let’s go,” Waltz said. “Everyone stays pretty busy here, and I don’t want to keep Mr. Vincent Abbott waiting.”

Stephen swallowed the lump in his throat. He wasn’t sure why he was nervous. He already had the job.

Stephen and Waltz walked down the hallway and knocked on the frame of the glass door.

“Come in!”

Waltz opened the door and walked in first. Stephen followed.

“Mr. Stockton.” A voice came from the right. “Thank you for coming. Mr. Cross, it is good to see you too.”

Stephen turned to see a large desk in front of an even larger window. Behind the desk stood Vincent in a navy suit and white button-down shirt, but no tie. “You too, Vincent!” Waltz approached and shook Vincent’s hand.

Stephen walked forward to shake Vincent’s hand. “Nice to see you again.”

“Please, both of you, have a seat.” Vincent motioned to a table and chairs positioned in front of a side window. He picked up a file, walked over, and sat opposite them.

“Stephen, yesterday you said you were planning to stay awhile. Correct?” Vincent began tapping a pen on the file in front of him, which made Stephen even more nervous.

“Yeah. I was away for a while. I guess you could say I wanted to give it a go on my own. I went to college for a time. I got about three years completed and decided it wasn't for me."

"What was your major?"

"Business..." Stephen hesitated. He realized this might be less nerve-racking if he knew what Vincent was looking for. He started to focus in an effort to hear Mr. Abbott's thoughts, but he heard nothing. He tried harder—still nothing. Stephen looked at Waltz, realizing the old man must have been blocking him from reading Vincent's mind.

Waltz smiled.

"How were your grades?" Vincent asked.

"I had a 4.0 GPA. What is this—a job interview?"

"Of sorts," Vincent replied. He opened the folder. "I run this place. It is a nonprofit organization that helps the less fortunate, including advocacy and other legal issues. The shelter is part of our charity. We are responsible for Bernie's operating budget. Waltz helped me out a few years back. So, I agreed to oversee the shelter too."

Vincent continued. "I walked by the shelter the other day and saw you working outside. You were tending the flowers. So, I went by the next day too. You were mending the gutters. The day after that, you were mowing. You, Mr. Cross, are a hard worker. That is very important to me. I could use more like you around here. I do not think, however, that the shelter's work will not keep you completely busy. There is some work you could do around here too. This old building has been renovated, but still needs some attention from time to time. We have a janitor, but he is older than he wants to admit. There are some things he can no longer do, or at least not alone. You would tend to both places. We offer benefits. And if you would like to finish that degree, we can also help with that."

"I want to make sure I understand." Stephen sat straight. "You want to pay me to do what I've already been doing?"

"Well, again you would have to come work here some too. Probably once or twice a week." Vincent slid the file over to Stephen. In it was additional paperwork to be completed, including a background check. "We just need a completed application and your signature to make it official."

"Stephen, it's a good offer, and Vincent is a fair person. They do a lot to help people too."

Stephen could read between the lines. Not only would he have a job that he could support himself with, but he would be in the perfect place to help others and to use his gifts.

"Okay, Waltz. I could use the money anyways. Besides, I love this building. I remember seeing it when I was a kid. It has a lot of history. This'll be fun." Stephen clicked the pen and completed the form, somewhat excited about earning some money of his own. He wasn't too sure about Vincent though. His face lacked expression, and his speech seemed overly formal. Vincent reminded Stephen of Lurch from The Addams Family.

"Good." Vincent took the pen and the application and looked at Waltz. "May I have a moment with Stephen?"

"Sure." Waltz got up headed to the door. "I'll just go talk with Patty a moment."

After he left, Vincent spoke. "Stephen, I am glad you are back. Waltz is a dear friend. I truly value his friendship more than any other. Why you left, where you went, is none of my business. I do not care. But you need to know that I expect a lot from the people that work for me. You seem like a hard worker. It would be less than fair, however, if I did not tell you that I want commitment from my employees. You hurt Waltz when you left, a man who loves you dearly, like his own son. He wants you to have a fair chance at life, regardless. He is a generous and forgiving man. I, on the other hand, am not as forgiving. I will be fair but firm. If you are anything less than dedicated to this job, you will be held accountable."

Stephen stared into Vincent's eyes, trying hard to see what was behind them, to what hid inside his mind. Vincent's tone of voice wasn't harsh, but very matter of fact. Still, he wanted to know more. Did Vincent have an agenda? What was his relationship with Waltz? Would Vincent really give him a fair shot?

Nothing. The harder Stephen tried, the more there seemed to be a wall between them. This agitated him. He figured Waltz was not wanting him to know what business Vincent and he shared.

Stephen spoke boldly. "You're right. My leaving, all of that, it's personal..." Stephen took a deep breath. "... and none of your business. Waltz seems to trust you. That's good enough for me. But don't think that my working for you gives you the right to nose into the relationship I have with Waltz." Stephen realized he had become a little too emotional. Waltz wanted him to have this job for some reason. "Look, if you don't want me to work here, don't hire me. But you'd be missing out on a good employee. And if you do hire me, I only ask one thing. Don't judge me before you get to know me. If you can't do that, again, don't hire me—and save us both the trouble."

Vincent's facial expression didn't change. Instead, he sat silent, looking at Stephen. Then he closed the file and got up, taking the file to his desk. He picked up the phone and dialed. "Patty, please come bring Stephen the information I asked for." Vincent put the phone back down and looked at Stephen. "It will take her some time to get all your information in our system. Officially, you start today. You'll pick up your check on Fridays."

Patty walked in and over to where Stephen sat. "Here is your laptop and a cell phone. This packet here explains our information policy. Basically, anything on either of these devices can be seen, used, or deleted by the company at any time, without your permission. This packet explains getting into your email and setting up your devices. Johnny sits outside. His number is listed here. He is our IT person, should you ever need him. Also, in here is a company directory of anyone you may need, Vincent and myself included."

"Thank you." Stephen looked at Patty. The sunlight shone through the window, causing her eyes to sparkle.

"You're welcome." She smiled and continued. "Checks are at my desk on Fridays, after one o'clock, but before four thirty. If I'm out, Vincent will have them. Any questions?"

Stephen shook his head. "No. I'm good."

"Great. You've got my number in there if any come to mind." Patty smiled again. "Welcome aboard."

"Thank you."

Patty turned and walked out. As she left, Stephen allowed himself to glimpse her mind—only what was on the surface. He seems nice enough. I better get him entered into payroll and have Johnny set up email and give him system access. I hope he stays around for a while.

Stephen felt calmer after having spoken with Patty. He glanced around the room. There wasn't much to see. A bookshelf, filled with what appeared to be legal books and journals, sat against the wall opposite Vincent's desk. There were no personal pictures on the walls though. No family or friends. It seemed odd.

"So, Vincent, do you just not like me or is it people in general?" Stephen's tone wasn't harsh but inquisitive.

Vincent's brows furrowed. "Why do you ask that?"

"Well, it's obvious you don't like me. But you don't have any personal pictures around here. In fact, the whole office setup says business. When I was traveling on my own, I met a lot of people and learned to read them. Your speech, your composure, your office—it's all closed off. My experience tells me either you don't like people or you're hiding something."

Vincent leaned forward in his chair. "Well, you are bold. I give you that." He got up and walked over to Stephen, then looked out the window next to the table where Stephen remained seated. "You see those people across the street? I do not know them. I may never meet them. Some people would wonder about them as they looked out the window. Me, I do not. I am a very focused, goal-oriented person. My ultimate goal here is to help and protect people who cannot do that for themselves."

He turned toward Stephen. "True, I do not like you. I do not dislike you either. Because, I do not know you. Waltz has been good to me. I have finally gotten my feet settled here. I had an unorthodox upbringing. I was schooled by private tutors at home, and I am not very well socialized. Waltz has helped me to get past that and to be who I am meant to be. I owe it to him to focus on that."

"Yeah, he has a habit of doing that—helping people be better than they are."

"As far as decor, I remain a private person who is not looking to make friends with employees. I am not what you call a people person. That is why I have Patty. She is really good with people." Vincent walked to the door and opened it. "Well, it was a pleasure speaking with you. Welcome to the team."

Stephen walked outside to find Waltz and Patty talking with each other. He couldn't help but wonder if there had been another reason Waltz had protected Vincent's mind from being read. Maybe he had been Waltz's attorney. Perhaps Waltz had secrets that he didn't want Stephen to know.

"Ah, there you are! You set?" Waltz turned toward Stephen.

"Yeah, Waltz, I'm ready."

"Good. I need to talk with Vincent a moment. If you don't mind hanging out here?"

Patty interjected, "I can show him around."

"Great." Waltz walked into Vincent's office, closing the door behind him.

What does he need with an attorney? Stephen tried to read their thoughts, but it was no use. He needed to continue his training.

Patty showed him around the building and introduced him to the various people. She also took him to the other offices on the lower level, which were separate businesses. He would be maintaining the entire building. The more they talked; the more Stephen felt this was the right place for him to be at this time. He had needed a place to establish himself, a place to belong.

As they ended the tour back at Patty's office, Stephen thought for a moment, wondering if he should ask Patty out on a date. *What the heck!* "Patty, would you mind getting lunch with me sometime? Nothing fancy or formal, just a casual lunch. I'd like to get to know you."

Patty blushed only slightly before replying. "Yes, I think I'd like that." She looked at her computer and began clicking and typing. Stephen's phone made a pinging sound. "There. I scheduled us for Wednesday, if that's alright. I sent you an invite."

"Vincent's efficient?" Stephen laughed. "Great, next Wednesday it is."

Stephen heard the two men talking and looked down the hallway to see them standing at Vincent's door. The two men gave each other a hug before turning down the hallway. Vincent looked uncomfortable.

Waltz joined Patty and Stephen in front of her office.

"Patty, it's always a pleasure speaking with you. I'm sorry it's been so long. Tell Vincent I'll call him next week, and we can have lunch." Waltz gave her a hug too.

"Yes, sir. I'll put it on his schedule."

Stephen gave a half wave to Patty. "I guess I'll see you Wednesday."

"Absolutely!"

"Wednesday?" Waltz asked.

"A lunch date," Stephen answered.

The two men walked back out the way they'd come in. Stephen glanced back at Patty. That whole experience had been a little awkward to him. Except for Patty. She was pleasant, comfortable, like he already knew her. Only, he didn't.

The clouds passed overhead, occasionally offering shade from the warmer rays of the sun as Stephen and Patty strolled along the walkways and paths. People talked and kids giggled in the background. The running water from a nearby waterfall and scent of flowers and bushes in full bloom made it a beautiful day to be at the zoo. The smell of smoked BBQ still lingered on their clothes as the couple strolled past a cotton candy vendor and up to the elephant's habitat.

"Man, I'm stuffed. I hope I wasn't too messy." Patty rubbed her belly.

"Not at all." Stephen chuckled. "I'm glad you dug right in. I wasn't sure how I was going to eat ribs with a fork." He smiled at her. "Pappy's BBQ wasn't there before I left. I wish it had been. I might have stayed."

"I know it's not really my business, but why did you leave and not tell anyone? Waltz seems like a good man and talked about you all the time."

"What all do you know about Waltz and me?" Stephen asked her.

"I know he's a good man. He raised you, kind of. But he's not your dad. Right?"

"Yeah." Stephen paused before continuing. "Are your parents still alive, Patty?"

"Mom is. Dad passed away last year—a heart attack. Mom's just now getting a handle on things."

"I'm sorry to hear that."

"It's alright," Patty said. "I'm healed for the most part. But what about you and Waltz?"

"I'm sure you've had a moment or two when you wished your dad was here to help with something, or answer a question, or maybe even to talk about whatever."

Patty's smile faded from her eyes before she managed the slightest smile with her lips and a nod. Her eyes looked sad.

"Well, just about my whole life has been like that. Mom died when I was eight, I think. I have no clue who my dad was or is. I mean, is he alive? Does he know about me? Would he care? Just knowing those answers would mean the world to me."

Patty interjected. "Did you go looking for him?"

"My dad? Nah. I wouldn't know where to begin. I think that knowing your parents helps give you a sense of who you are, where you come from, where you belong. You know?"

They stopped in front of the elephant exhibit where the waterfall flowed into a pool. A mother elephant stood there with her young, both getting water.

"See that baby elephant? If it was born and raised by something other than an elephant, I think it might have issues learning things, at least at first. For example, did you know that a baby elephant doesn't use its trunk to get water?"

Patty shook her head. "No, I didn't."

"Yeah, it'll dip its head into the water to drink."

"Really?"

"Well, that's what a Facebook meme said." Stephen grinned. Patty softly punched him on the arm. "Ha-ha. Hey now." Stephen continued. "My point is, you are who you are largely because of your parents. They say fifty percent nature, fifty percent nurture. Well, sometimes I feel like I'm missing the 'fifty percent nature' part. Waltz nurtured me, sure. But I left to try to figure out who I am—that is, who I want to be. I can't help but feel that who my parents were is an important part of making that decision. There was a part of me that I worried Waltz wouldn't understand. I wanted to talk to him, but I was afraid, I guess."

"Afraid of what? Waltz seems really nice." Patty gently pulled at a nearby leaf from a shrub planted around the habitat and fumbled with it.

"What if he didn't understand? What if the fifty percent that is nature was stuff he didn't like? Besides, Waltz has been really good to me. He's the only dad I ever had. The last thing I wanted was for him to think he wasn't good enough. It was stupid, I know. We've talked about it since I've returned. I think we're good."

"What brought you back?"

"A lot of things really. I had been able to make it on my own. That wasn't really what I was after. I really wanted answers, about me and stuff. Some I got; some I didn't. After that, I realized I needed someone to understand me."

"And Waltz understands you?"

"Yeah, more than I realized. I guess we're kindred spirits of sorts."

"Think you'll ever find him?"

"Find who?" Stephen asked.

"Your dad," Patty stated enthusiastically.

"Oh." Stephen looked down at the ground, not really having thought about it much lately. He did still feel like something was missing. Just knowing might be enough to fill that small void. "I don't know. I'd like to, even just to know who he was. Do I have siblings? That sort of thing. I used to get excited thinking about it. Now, I worry a bit that I wouldn't like what I found. Besides, I've come to realize that what's more important to me is not where I came from but having a place to belong."

"And you've found that?" Patty pushed a lock of hair back behind her ear and smiled, which somehow brightened her emerald eyes.

"I'm still looking for it. I know I won't find it by running away."

A small whorl of leaves blew by. Stephen looked up at the sky. Clouds moved quickly in. "We should probably get inside."

The distant sound of rustling leaves preceded shrieks as people began running by. Before the two could run, they found themselves in the midst of a downpour. They sought shelter under a nearby tree, which allowed them to keep most of the water out of their eyes, as large drops fell all around them.

They were drenched even though they made it under the tree within a few seconds. Hair dripped as well as clothes. It did not matter. They laughed and smiled.

Stephen could not help but notice how Patty's clothes clung to her form. *Wow, she's hot! Eyes up top,* he told himself. He saw that Patty noticed him too.

Wow! I wouldn't mind putting my hands on that chest. And look at those arms!

Stephen smiled even more at hearing her thoughts. The chemistry could not be denied. He wanted her, and she wanted him. It was not fair. Patty did not have this advantage. For the first time, he felt wrong about violating someone's thoughts—her privacy. *From now on, she's off limits.*

Stephen looked around for a way to get his mind focused on something else, then nodded at the rain. "I wonder how long this will last."

"I don't know. But it's a good thing Vincent let us take the afternoon off. I'd hate to have to go back to work like this. It's cold enough as it is in the office. The air blows right on me."

"Yeah, good thing." Stephen thought about the problems that might present but dared not mention them. He already heard some of the guys' thoughts concerning Patty. Many found her attractive, however, most lacked the confidence to approach her.

The rain died down. The newly formed puddles nearby shimmered from the combination of sunlight and ripples from the remaining sprinkles. People slowly emerged from their hiding places and soon filled the walkways once more.

"Hey, you wouldn't wanna swing back by the shelter with me, would you?" Stephen desperately hoped she would.

"Yeah. I'd like to see you in *your* natural habitat." Patty nudged Stephen with her shoulder. "But I'm soaked." She drew her lips to one side, her eyes thoughtful.

"We can throw your clothes in the dryer. I have some you might be comfortable in," Stephen suggested.

Patty smiled. "Sure, why not?"

Patty drove them back to the shelter in her beat-up little car. Once inside, Stephen grabbed a T-shirt and a pair of sweatpants from his room and headed down the hall to the bathroom.

"I threw something on the bed that I thought might be comfortable for you."

"Thank you," Patty replied as she ventured into Stephen's room, closing the door behind her.

Once Stephen changed, he waited outside the door. He expected to hear some comment from her by now, but nothing. The longer she remained silent, the more he worried, and searching for her thoughts was off limits. He waited until he was too embarrassed to wait any longer, wondering if she had perhaps already left.

"You okay in there?" he asked.

"Yeah, I'm almost done."

He felt relief at hearing her voice and the sound of her walking toward the door. The door opened.

"What do you think?" Patty smiled from ear to ear and appeared to be begging for a response.

"I think my Superman pajamas have never looked better!" Stephen grinned mischievously. "Only, what took you so long? And where did the sweats I laid out for you go?"

Patty, still smiling slyly, replied, “I had to dry my hair and put it up. And the sweats are still on the bed where you put them. They aren’t as cute as these I found folded in the top of the basket. I hope you don’t mind.” Patty batted her eyelashes.

“Ha-ha. I don’t mind.”

“Uh-hum!”

The two turned toward the living room to see Waltz and Bernie staring at them with inquisitive looks.

“Wow! You two look really odd standing there together,” Stephen laughed. “Waltz, Bernie, I believe you both know Patty.”

“Hello, Patty,” the two men said, nearly in unison.

“Hello, Mr. Stockton, Mr. Jackson. I hope you don’t mind, but we were at the zoo and got caught in the rain. Stephen invited me here to dry off and play some pool.”

“Now ya’ talkin’,” Bernie stated excitedly. “I’ll go rack ’em. Come on, Waltz!”

Stephen grabbed Patty’s wet clothes from his bedroom and took them down the hall to the dryer before heading downstairs.

When the two neared the bottom of the steps, Stephen noticed Waltz and Bernie had already racked the balls, pulled out a couple of stools from the closet, and sat, waiting patiently.

Bernie patted one of the seats between him and Waltz. “Come an’ have a seat, little lady. We don’t often get women around here. Mostly men come stay with us.”

“Yeah, I’ve noticed that over the past couple of years,” Patty stated as she sat.

Stephen walked up to the table. “I guess I’m breaking then?”

"Sure," Waltz said.

Stephen sent the racked balls flying. However, not a single ball fell in. "Well, who's up? We running teams? Me and Patty?"

"Yes and no." Patty stood up. "I'm not sure I'm ready to be teamed up with you yet. I've played with these two. I'll take Bernie here. You and Waltz can team up."

Patty looked around, choosing her shot. The game was on.

"So, you've been around here some over the past few years?" Stephen directed the question toward Patty.

"Oh, yeah," Waltz spoke up. "She's been here a time or two, on official business. When she realized we have a pool table down here, well, she came over to play, especially in the summers."

"I see. The guys clear out during the summer. But you guys still had someone to shoot pool with." Stephen turned to Patty again, seated on her stool. "So, how well did you get to know them?" He hoped she could not hear the concern in his voice.

Patty smiled. "Well enough to get some good stories of their beloved Stephen."

His concern, as it turned out, was well founded.

"Ah, really? What stories did they tell you? You know this isn't fair, right?" Stephen protested.

"Hey," Bernie interjected. "We didn't know you were coming back. It ain't our fault."

"Okay. Fair enough." Stephen felt his cheeks flush. "Nothing too bad I hope?"

"A few cute stories." Patty reached across and playfully nudged Stephen, who watched Waltz make a run on the table. "But mostly about how special you were. You sounded like a really good kid, helping them with the homeless and stuff. I believe you also had plans of going to college and being in business?"

"Yeah, that seems like a lifetime ago now, though. I did go to college."

"I know." Patty winked at Stephen. "I've seen your file."

"I can't shake the feeling that you know too much about me."

"Oh, I'm sure she does," Bernie said.

"Like how you used to wet the bed," Waltz interjected as he struck the cue ball.

"Really?" Stephen blushed from embarrassment. Already she knew so much about him—more than he wanted her to, and he knew so little about her.

"Yep," she said calmly. "I know that you always wanted a *real* dog too. You had an imaginary one. I know you had several crushes, all older, by the way. Let's see. Your favorite food was chicken teriyaki. You wanted to be a Ninja Turtle. Oh! And, you obviously love Superman."

"Wow! I can feel the love, guys. Truly." Stephen stood back up to shoot after Bernie missed his shot. "Well, I feel at a loss. I don't really know much about you. I guess you'll have to tell us something embarrassing about yourself. Eight ball, side pocket." Stephen sank the shot and smiled at Patty.

Patty got up and walked over toward Stephen. "If you want to know more about me, I guess you have to ask me out again." She leaned in real close to him, placing her face inches from his. "Excuse me, but I need to rack."

Stephen moved, but felt the romantic tension. There was something about Patty; familiar in a way, as if he should know her. After all, she did know a lot about him. She was not like any of the other women he had ever known. He truly felt at ease around her.

They continued to play until the dryer sounded. After Patty changed, Stephen walked her out to the porch.

"Stephen, I had a great time. To be honest, I didn't know what to expect. I'd heard a lot about you over the past couple of years or so. When you asked me to lunch, I already felt like I knew you. But you surprised me. I hope you figure out where you belong soon."

Before Stephen could say a word, Patty leaned forward and kissed him on the cheek. "See ya, Stephen. Don't wait too long to call me."

"Bye." Stephen barely got the word out before Patty turned and walked down the stairs, across the yard, got in her car parked on the street, and left.

Stephen heard the screen door creak open behind him and turned to see Waltz.

"Hey, Waltz."

"Oooh, boy. You're in trouble!"

"Huh? What do you mean?" Stephen asked, confused. His mind lingered on cloud nine.

"How many times did you read her tonight?" Waltz leaned against a post; arms crossed.

Stephen thought for moment. "None, I think."

"Uh-huh. Your mind was preoccupied with her."

"And?"

"Well," Waltz continued, "any guy that wasn't already head over heels in love with a girl would have thought to see how she was feeling about him."

"I didn't need to check that. She was having a good time. We both were."

"Yeah, but you're in love, Stephen."

"What? No way! I don't even really know her yet." Could I really be in love? She is amazing. I've never known a girl like her.

"Well, you may not know her. But she already has you wrapped."

"What if she does? Is that a bad thing? I'm getting better control of my gift. I'm able to keep my life separate from the memories. I'm settling in—you saw to that." Stephen slapped Waltz on the back. "Is there a problem?"

"No, no problem yet." Waltz turned to look at Stephen, who still stared down the road. "Relationships are hard for us, Stephen."

"You mean men?" Stephen asked, hoping that was what Waltz meant.

Waltz shook his head. "I mean us Mighty. You spend so much time building a relationship, while keeping a huge secret—one you know you eventually have to share. You hope she understands, that she's the one. You'll search for clues. But you never really know until you tell her."

"And what happens when I tell her?" Stephen began to understand.

"Yep. When you tell a girl who you are, what you can do, you have to face the fact that she may not accept it. Or worse, she may accept it and want you to give up being Mighty."

"Which we can't do—"

"Right. You have to be one or the other, Mighty or Fallen. It's a destiny that will seek you out, even if you don't want it."

Stephen dropped his head, searching his own feelings. Up to that moment, this had been the greatest night he ever remembered.

"You're forgetting something, Waltz."

"Yeah, what's that?"

"I still don't believe in this stuff. Choosing sides, Mighty or Fallen. I'll try to find my own way, if I have to. But I won't let either take something or someone away from me, if it comes to that."

"Stephen, all I'm saying is, don't move too quickly, okay? Be careful. Make sure you know her, the real her. Not your idea of her."

"Yeah, I get it. I've seen some crazy stuff in women's heads, and guys, when they're in relationships. I understand, Waltz. If it goes south, I'll have you to help me—you and Bernie."

Waltz put his arm around Stephen and gave him a gentle squeeze and went back into the house. Stephen stood on the porch, looking up at the stars for a while before going in. Looking at the stars made him ponder even more his place in all this. What if Waltz was right? What if God did all this? Where was Stephen's place? There were so many unknowns for him. Regardless, Stephen knew it was his life to live, and the choices were his. He knew he needed to keep training. It helped him. He knew Waltz wanted the best for him, and he knew he enjoyed his time with Patty.

The sun began to rise, giving the clouds hues of burnt amber, red, purple, and even navy blue. The birds lining the tops of the buildings and in the trees sang their usual morning songs. Traffic downtown stayed light, and Stephen figured it would remain lighter than usual. Many people prepared to take the Friday before Memorial Day off, getting an early start on their weekend trips.

The soda building, as Stephen liked to call it, appeared dark, only a faint glow came from the second floor, about halfway down the side of the building. Stephen knew that light came from Patty's desk. He expected it to be on since she always came in early, even on Fridays.

Stephen held a small bouquet—daisies and carnations—in one hand and a bag from a pastry shop down the street in the other. He wanted to surprise her with flowers and breakfast. They had been seeing each other for a little less than two months now and continued to grow closer.

Patty had started asking what Stephen did with his extra time when he and Waltz would go off together. He didn't lie to her, but he didn't really tell her anything either. Although they hadn't fought about it, he knew she was displeased. They had talked about it on the phone earlier this week, and he wanted to try to apologize before the weekend for being harsh with her.

He walked into the building, eager to see her, whistling a tune and his mind already focused on her presence. As he entered, he sensed that Patty was not the only one who came in early. Though Stephen knew Patty and Johnathan pretty well, he seldom spoke to the others. Seeing their thoughts tainted his view of some, and a couple even concerned him. Most, however, he simply shared very little in common with.

Alright, who else is here? Stephen listened for thoughts.

"Hey, Frank! Check that drawer. There's gotta be something somewhere." *There'd better be anyway.*

"Yeah, Chuck, just keep looking. We'll find it!"

Stephen heard them upstairs before searching for their thoughts. Not recognizing either of the men, he walked up the stairs, still focused on the strangers.

"Frank," one man yelled. "Check the girl. Make sure she's still out."

Stephen ran down the hall. Anger engulfed him, as he had caught an image of Patty lying on the floor, blood in her already red hair.

A familiar feeling of excitement and euphoria washed over Stephen like an alcoholic taking his first sip after a long dry spell. Too much time had passed since he hurt bad people. The control he learned since returning home would make this much easier than before. Could he risk setting the monster inside free?

"I see her here. We're good. Just keep looking."

*If she's hurt...*Stephen threw his thoughts at the men.

"You hear that?"

"Yeah, where did that come from?"

Over here! Stephen saw a large, muscular man standing near Patty's office. The other man remained out of sight, down one of the cubicle aisles.

"Frank!" The man's voice trembled. "I think we should go."

"Nah, Chuck. I see him coming down the hall. I can break him like a twig. You keep looking. I got this!"

Frank stood tall, more than a head above the cubicles. Stephen slowed as he approached him, knowing that Frank had no idea what he was in for. He sensed Frank's confidence in his large muscular frame. The man expected a short fight. Boxing had been more than a hobby when he was younger. Stephen didn't care.

I'm gonna enjoy this! Frank grinned, revealing a missing tooth.

No, you won't. Stephen smiled. Frank's facial expression changed to uncertainty.

Frank tried his hardest, punching and grabbing with all the skill and strength one might expect. Stephen knew every move before Frank executed it. Frank might as well have punched at the wind. Stephen played with him, smiling more and more with every punch he dodged.

That's enough! Stephen landed a hook to the behemoth's ribs.

Frank winced and swung again.

Stephen ducked, stepped to the side, and kicked Frank's knee from the side, forcing it to bend in a way knees are never meant to go. A near instantaneous loud pop evidenced the tearing of tendons and ligaments.

"Argh!"

He grabbed Stephen. "I've got you now!" Frank looked around for his partner. "Chuck! I've got him!"

Chuck came around the corner carrying a large stapler. "I see! You've got him, huh?"

"Yeah! I've got him," Frank panted.

Stephen laughed.

"What? Why are you laughing?"

Chuck spoke. "I think he has you, Frank. You and me." Chuck smiled as Frank's face again turned to confusion. Chuck swung the stapler and it came crashing onto the top of his head.

Frank fell unconscious with a loud thud.

"What? What did I do?" Chuck dropped the stapler.

"It appears you hurt Frank, Chuck." Stephen smiled.

"That voice. I know your voice. It's in my head. Why's it in my head? Get out!" Chuck clawed at his own head, then grabbed for Stephen.

"Good night." Stephen's elbow crushed the man's jaw. He watched, waited, and listened for thoughts as Chuck fell to the floor. The man hit the floor unconscious.

Stephen turned his attention toward Patty's office. She stood there with a blank expression. Stephen ran to her and attended a cut on her forehead.

"Patty, are you okay? You're bleeding. Sit down." Stephen helped her to a chair.

"I'm okay—just a little dizzy still, and my head hurts. I called the police. They should be here..." Patty's words trailed off.

Stephen grabbed a bottle of water from her desk. "Here, drink this."

She took a sip. "Stephen, I'm not sure what I just saw. Did the small guy turn on the bigger one?"

"Yeah, it looked that way. Lucky for me." Stephen looked back to the two lying on the floor. "Maybe that was his plan all along. I guess he thought he could take me next."

"Yeah, maybe." Patty grabbed her head. "Wait. What are you doing here?"

"Oh." Stephen smiled. "Surprise? I was bringing flowers and breakfast. I'm not sure you want either now." Stephen looked back over his shoulder. The flowers lay scattered in pieces, and the bag of pastries trampled flat.

They both laughed a little. Stephen grabbed her trembling hands.

"You're right. I don't. They look worse than me."

Sirens neared outside. The lights soon reflected off the buildings across the street. The sound of footsteps grew closer from down the hall and eventually filled the room.

"Police!"

"In here," Stephen boomed out for all to hear. "We're over here."

A couple of officers rushed over to where the two sat.

"We're okay. She needs to be looked at though."

Stephen barely saw around the corner to where Frank and Chuck lay. Several more officers checked the two men. "This one's just unconscious," one officer said.

"This one's gone," said another. The officers holstered their weapons and cuffed Chuck.

Only then did Stephen realize he killed the man. It was self-defense, but he had not meant to kill. His heart pounded deep within his chest.

"Sir...sir." An officer tried to get Stephen's attention. "I need you to come with me for a moment."

"Okay." He turned to Patty. "I'll be right back."

The two stepped to the side, away from everyone else. "What happened here? Did you do this?"

"Yeah, kind of." Stephen explained how he came to surprise Patty and found them there. "The big guy rushed me. I've studied martial arts. I guess training took over. But he managed to grab hold of me. Then the little guy turned on him!"

"Where was she?" The officer nodded toward Patty.

Stephen looked over. He listened to the other officer's thoughts, who asked Patty questions as he tended to her head wound.

"I'm not sure. When I looked up, she was standing only a couple of feet from where she is now. I ran to her and barely got to her before she fell. She was dizzy." The officer with Patty stepped away as the EMS workers arrived. "I need to get back to Patty."

"Sure thing." The officer smiled. "We may need to talk more though."

Stephen pulled out a business card. He never understood why Vincent had them printed. This was the first he had given out. "This has all my information. I'll be available whenever you need me."

As Stephen walked back toward Patty, he heard a ruckus behind him and turned to see the paramedic putting Chuck on a gurney. "Wait. Stop it!" Chuck yelled. "I didn't mean to. The voice made me. I couldn't get away from it. It's in my head. Get it out! *Get it out*!"

They wheeled the man down the hall toward the elevator. Stephen heard him yelling all the way out of the building.

When Stephen turned back around, he noticed how frightened Patty looked. He walked over and sat down next to her. "You okay? You look worried."

"I am. That man's a lunatic."

"Well, I'm here."

Patty punched him!

"Ouch! What was that for?"

"What did you think you were doing? You could have gotten killed!" Patty punched him again.

"Really? You're beating me more than they did."

She punched him several more times, yelling as she did, "It's not funny."

Stephen laughed hard and grabbed her arms. "Okay, you're right. It's not funny. I guess we're lucky the one guy was crazy. I knew you'd be here. I had to make sure you were okay."

Another paramedic brought a gurney over to Patty.

"Do you really have to take me on that thing? Can't Stephen take me?"

"Patty," Stephen said, "it's probably best, just in case. I'll follow behind in your car, if you don't mind me driving it."

Patty nodded.

"I'll follow you out and then meet you at the hospital. I'll gather your things here and let Vincent know what happened. Okay? I'll be there shortly. I won't be long."

"Okay." Patty grabbed Stephen and kissed him. "I love you!" Then they put her on the gurney.

She loves me? Should I say it back? What do I do? Crap! It's too late now. Stephen's thoughts raced. He wanted to listen to Patty's thoughts but felt he would be violating her trust. He walked alongside her, out to the ambulance.

"Patty?"

Patty put her finger up to Stephen's lips. "It's okay. I know you aren't quite ready yet. Something's holding you back. I just wanted you to know how I feel in case they did some serious damage to me."

"You're gonna be fine." Stephen smiled as he grabbed her fingers and kissed the top of her hand. "You're wonderful!"

"I know," she smiled. "Don't forget my purse and laptop."

Stephen waited until she was secure in the ambulance and both doors closed before he headed back to her office to grab her things. Near the top of the steps, he heard Waltz in the lobby.

"Stephen," Waltz called out as he hurried up the stairs, Vincent in tow. "Are you alright?"

"I'm good. Patty took a bit of a jostle before I got here. Two guys were trashing the place. If I had been here sooner, they wouldn't have touched her. I think she's okay, though. They took her to the hospital. I'm heading there now." Stephen could not help but feel protective of Patty.

"Be that as it may, you're okay?"

"Yeah, Waltz. I'm good."

"What happened in there?" Vincent asked, his attention divided as he looked down the hall to the covered body.

"I don't really know how to explain it to you. I was fighting with this big guy. He got hold of me. His partner came up and smashed him in the head with a stapler. Then, I knocked the other guy out."

"Strange." Vincent continued looking down the hall.

"It is." Waltz looked right at Stephen, his eyes glaring in disapproval.

Stephen shrugged.

"Excuse me a moment, gentlemen." Vincent said, excusing himself.

Vincent walked over to the sergeant giving other officers directions. Stephen could not make out what was being said. *I wish I could read him!* He looked back at Waltz, wondering why Waltz continually protected Vincent. *Is it a test?*

Vincent approached again. "Waltz, the officer is going to let me through to make sure nothing was stolen and see if I can tell what they were looking for. You can come with me."

"I'll come too." Stephen walked with them. "I need to get Patty's things for her."

"Great. Tell her we'll be by to check on her when we've finished here, will you?"

"Sure thing, Vincent."

Stephen hurried down the hall, back through the office to grab Patty's things after he cleared it with an officer. Then, he went out to Patty's car, eager to check on her.

∾ ∾

Stephen watched Patty wince with each stitch the physician's assistant made in her forehead. Though a curtain concealed them from anyone outside the room, he heard the occasional scream from somewhere inside the emergency room.

"I'm telling you, there's a devil in my head! He made me do it!"

Stephen smiled.

"What's that devilish grin about? This really hurts." Patty slapped Stephen's arm.

"Owwww!" Stephen chuckled. "I wasn't grinning at you. It's that piece of work down the hall. It felt good to knock him out!"

"Ah! You're the hero I heard about?" the attendant asked, glancing up at Stephen.

"Hero?" Stephen scratched his head. "I don't know about that. I just did what I had to."

"It's a shame about that other guy though," Patty said.

Stephen looked up at Patty, wondering how she could feel sorry for Frank. She had been attached, victimized, yet she felt concerned for them.

"Alright. That should do it." The attendant stood up. "I'll send a nurse in to get you checked out shortly." He exited the room.

"Don't get me wrong, Stephen. I'm glad you're okay. But he didn't have to die," Patty continued.

"Yeah, he could have not been stupid in the first place," Stephen protested.

"True. I guess that's what I'm saying. There were so many other options that could have ended with him living. The loss of life is always tragic. You don't agree?"

Stephen shrugged, not having given much thought to it yet. He only thought about how good it felt to finally use his gift to do some real good. Sitting there with Patty though, he felt something stir inside him, a familiar feeling that weighed heavily on him—guilt. Months ago, he would not have gone as far as he did. Tommy's death had devastated him. Why had he enjoyed the rush? Before today, he felt whole—complete for the first time in months, but not now. He had not intended to kill. But the man did die.

"You didn't answer me. Are you okay?" Patty looked concerned.

"Yeah, I'm fine. I was so worried about you, I, well...I didn't really think about either of them. Now that I know you're okay, I guess I see your point. But, given the situation, I'm glad things turned out as they did and that you're okay."

They sat quietly, waiting for the nurse. Patty's pain medication kicked in, making her eyelids droop. In the silence, Stephen considered her words until the nurse returned, and released Patty.

After sending Vincent a text, letting him know they had left the hospital, Stephen drove her home to her apartment, which was not far from downtown. He had not been to her apartment but a couple of times to drop off some things. On the walls of the living room hung pictures of her family. A couple more sat on a desk by the window across the room—a small economy living space with little room to entertain friends. Stephen helped her get comfortable before calling for a cab ride home. When he left, he noticed a picture by the door—a selfie of the two of them from their date at the zoo.

On the ride home, Chuck's screams still echoed in his mind: *"There's a devil in my head,"* played like a broken record. He could not help but wonder if that could be true. His emotions were in conflict with one another—pride in defeating them and protecting Patty, and sorrow for not having done more. On one hand, he felt the men got what they deserved; on the other, Patty struck a chord and he knew she was right. It *was* tragic. He also knew he could have prevented it. With his ability, he could have caused the outcome to be much different.

Stephen got out of the cab. He saw Waltz seated on the porch and knew a lengthy conversation waited for him. He dreaded it. He slowly walked up to the porch. He did not attempt to search the mind of his mentor; no sense in it. He saw that look on Waltz's face many times when he was younger. Based on his experience, Stephen knew Waltz would share in his own words exactly what he was thinking.

Waltz spoke in a gentle tone as Stephen cleared the top step. "Have a seat," Waltz said.

Stephen stood there looking at Waltz, pondering whether or not he should say anything, in an attempt to fight the coming onslaught.

"Please." Waltz patted the spot next to him.

Stephen sat down on the simple wooden bench, shifting his weight as he searched for the least worn spot in the already thin cushion.

"Stephen, I'm concerned—"

"You should be." Stephen turned to look at Waltz, his eyes welling up. The flood of emotion became overwhelming.

"Are you okay, boy?" Waltz faced Stephen, placing a hand on his shoulder.

"I don't know. I don't think so." Stephen wiped tears from his cheek. "I don't get it. I was doing good. I was in control of myself. What happened? And why did I enjoy it?" Stephen looked away for a moment, then back to Waltz. "You and Bernie had talked about me. Bernie thought I might have come from a Fallen. Is that it? Do you think that's what's wrong with me?"

Waltz laughed a tender, gentle laugh. "No, boy, I don't think that's what's wrong. You're going to be fine."

"How do you know that's not it? It could be, right?" Stephen looked at Waltz, desperate for any sign of hope.

"Listen to me. I know why this happened. And I know you are not the offspring of a Fallen. I can't get into it now, but soon we'll have a conversation about what I *do* know about your parents. It's about time you knew the truth. Trust me when I say it's not safe to talk about right now."

"Why isn't it safe? What's going on?"

"Stephen, when you were attacked, the pain was there because someone fought viciously to get into your head but couldn't. Your power is incredible. Now that you're learning to control its effect on you—your emotions, your memories, your recall of it—you've become a threat and have made yourself known to Fallen somehow. I've been able to feel it. They were looking for a way in and couldn't find it. You're learning too quickly. Your power is too strong."

"So, what happened?"

Waltz took a deep breath and slowly let it out before continuing. "Stephen, Patty happened."

"Wait. Patty? What? You've got to be kidding me. What does she—?"

Waltz cut him off. "How does she make you feel?"

"I still don't—"

"Stephen, answer the question. How does she make you feel?"

"Fine." Stephen sat for a moment thinking about the question. *How does she make me feel?* "Happy. Confident. She empowers me and makes me feel like I can do anything. She makes me feel good, not in the sense of just feeling okay but like I'm a good person. She makes me better."

"Good! Keep going. What else? Was there something new recently? A new feeling? Maybe you just felt it today. When those guys were there, how did you feel?"

"Well, I was confused at first. I guess I was angry."

Waltz grabbed Stephen's shoulders. "Stephen, use your recall. Relive the moment, the emotion. I know it'll hurt. But relive it. It's important."

"Okay, Waltz. I trust you."

Stephen closed his eyes. He saw the inside of the lobby, flowers in one hand, breakfast in the other. He smelled the warm pastry. He searched for Patty's thoughts. He felt the confusion, then...

"Fear." Stephen looked up at Waltz as tears fell from his eyes. "I was afraid. I've never been afraid before, have I? Even as a kid, I don't ever remember being afraid. She scares me. What if I lose her? What if something happens to her? I love her, Waltz!"

"That's how they got you. Fear. They used your moment of fear as a means to get in. Fear is a weapon of the Fallen. Stephen, I know you still struggle with believing this stuff. But you must come to accept it. They've planted a seed now. They'll continue to water it by growing that fear, nurturing it. It'll become the monster you're afraid of."

"I still don't understand."

"Okay, when they tried attacking you, Fallen wasn't trying to hurt you. They were trying to get in your head. They were searching for a way to control or manipulate you, but it didn't work. Now, they have an in, Patty."

Stephen threw his arms around Waltz. "We can fight this, right?"

"Yes, son, we can fight this. We will fight this together." Waltz squeezed Stephen tightly.

"Waltz?" Stephen backed away. "Why did I like it? The moment afterward, I enjoyed it. Why?"

"That's how they get you. It's like a drug; it's addictive. They take something away slowly and begin to replace it with something else, something to fill the void. We will face it though. We'll get you back on track. But I need to find some answers first. There's something off. I need you to be patient, just a while longer. We need to talk more tomorrow, okay?"

Stephen went inside, not wanting to talk to anyone else. He needed rest. It had been a long, rough day and all before lunch. Perhaps tomorrow would be better, brighter, but how long would it take for things to be back to normal. What was normal?

The next morning, Stephen clicked away on the computer keys while rain drizzled outside the window next to him. Surrounded by books with only the occasional passer-by, he found the solace he needed as he considered some of what Waltz had told him about the Mighty and the Fallen, but there had to be more to it. He refused to accept that this his troubles were the result of spiritual warfare, and if it was, what would that make him? Waltz told him he was one of the Mighty. However, he felt more like a monster than someone fighting for good. Waltz also indicated the night before that they had more to discuss, which is why Stephen left early to avoid another lecture.

Hoping to learn about the battle between the Mighty and the Fallen—the history, infrastructure, and more—he landed in the library.

Stephen typed his name: Stephen Cross, but the internet produced nothing but a couple of articles from the paper dating back to middle school, when he won some academic awards. He tried searching for Waltz under Walter Stockton and found an article concerning the shelter, Bernie, and Waltz. He continued searching and typed "mighty men of David." It returned scriptural references in 2 Samuel and 1 Chronicles, along with several sermons. Nothing he didn't already know. He saw various sites devoted to explaining who these men were and what could be learned from their exploits—nothing on modern day activities.

Next, Stephen searched "Fallen." A Denzel Washington movie came up in the search, which he recalled watching. He scrolled down to find more movies and books. He searched "Fallen" along with "scripture" and got several references from the Bible, but nothing helped. Then he searched "spiritual possession." Scrolling through, he found different theories on the topic; some of which looked to be obvious nonsense involving aliens from another galaxy.

Several sites showed many religions acknowledged spiritual possessions. In all cases they were thought to be the work of evil spirits, aliens, or gods. Stephen smirked, certain he wasn't any of those, though he knew something evil worked against him. The more he searched, the more aggravated he became—tapping his foot nervously, rubbing the back of his neck, and even allowing the occasional moan or sigh to escape.

"Really? Nothing?" He leaned back and scratched his head. "You'd think Google would have found something!" He watched the rain fall outside the window and a smile crossed his face as he thought back to the day he and Patty went to the zoo. A little less than a week ago, his life showed definite signs of improvement; no more attacks against his mind, nightmares came less often, and his relationships with Waltz and Patty flourished. He also continued to learn more control over his abilities in hopes of one day doing something worthwhile with them. In just a brief moment, however, he managed to take two steps backward. He no longer resided in Waltz's good graces and Patty was not safe because of their relationship. Now, he found nothing more about the Mighty or the Fallen.

There has to be somewhere I can go, besides Waltz. He considered going back to Bernie with questions, but he didn't, knowing Bernie would only redirect him to Waltz.

A gentleman walked by, laid a small booklet next to him and walked away. The brochure contained information about a ministry that helped the deaf. A cross adorned the front. He flipped the booklet over to find it came from one of the local churches.

"Sir!" Stephen called, receiving hushes from an attendant nearby. He stood and approached the man as he reached into his pocket. "Are you deaf?"

The man turned to look at Stephen. "No sir. I just volunteer to pass these out."

"Can I give you a donation?" Stephen pulled out a wad of small bills.

"Sure, thank you!" The man took the money and began putting it into a money bag.

Stephen looked back at the pamphlet and asked, "Do you know if the minister is at the church right now? I mean, does he have office hours during the day?"

"Yes, Pastor Buchanan is there during most of the day. In fact, I'm sure he's there now if you'd like to speak with him. You usually wouldn't need an appointment."

"Thank you!" Stephen shook the man's hand and ran outside, looking again at the pamphlet. *Hmmm, a cross. A choice...*

Seeing the cross on the pamphlet caused him to think about what Waltz told him about choices. As much as he might have wanted to, he just could not accept that he would have to make a choice to either follow God or become Fallen. He had seen so much evil. How could God let evil exist?

Stephen recognized the church. It was just a couple of streets over. He walked briskly in the rain, thankful of the slight drizzle as opposed to a downpour.

Wet, but not dripping, he arrived and walked inside the old stone church, looking around for the office. The church sanctuary appeared nice enough—old, beautiful wooden benches, high arched ceiling, and stained-glass windows down either side, but nothing grand like some of the oldest churches of Saint Louis. He heard the doors close behind him.

"Can I help you?"

Stephen turned to see a silver-haired man in a paint stained t-shirt and hole-riddled jeans standing behind him. "Maybe. I'm looking for Father Buchanan."

The man laughed. "Well, we don't use the term 'Father' here. I'm Pastor Buchanan."

Stephen looked the old man up and down again.

"Ah, don't let these clothes bother you, son. Today's my workday. I have some ground maintenance to do. I like to work with my hands. It keeps me honest, humble, and fairly active. What can I do for you?"

Stephen walked forward and shook his hand. "I'm sorry. You're just not what I was expecting. I'm Stephen."

"Nice to meet you, Stephen. Care to have a seat?" he asked as he sat a couple spaces in on the back pew.

"Thanks." Stephen sat next to the preacher. He thought for a moment before deciding just how to proceed. He looked into the pastor's mind and realized he was a good, honest man, and despite his appearance, well-educated and accomplished.

"Pastor, I'm curious about something that may or may not have origins in the Bible. It could be more myth or folklore than true religion. I've heard about something from a source I trust. But I'm not ready to believe what I'm hearing."

"Well, that's not very vague." Pastor Buchanan laughed.

"Yeah, I guess it is. I'm not sure I can share more than that."

"Well, are you afraid you shouldn't be trusting your source then?"

"It's not that, sir. I trust him with my life. But he's older and has always been a little zealous about things. I don't doubt most of what he's told me. I'm just trying to find the truth about its origins. I've found myself in the middle of a situation of sorts and truthfully don't know if I want to deal with it."

"Are you in trouble?" The pastor looked piercingly at Stephen.

"No more than anyone else, I suppose, if what I've been told is true. I mean, we all have the same choice to make when it comes to putting faith in God, right?"

The old man smiled. “In a way, I guess so. Is there something specific you want to know about?”

“There is.” Stephen took a deep breath before continuing, hoping he did not sound crazy. “What do you know about David’s mighty men?”

“Ah! David’s warriors? Well, let’s see. I believe there were about three hundred or so. Thirty were elite, David’s own guards, if memory serves. It’s been awhile since I studied the topic.” The pastor tapped the rim of his glasses, as if this helped him remember. “Yes, there were three that were mightier than the rest. There was one that was chief of the three. Of course, David was greater in battle than even they were. His bravery, faith in God, and righteous cause have never been equaled in battle, in my estimation. Is that what you were looking for?”

“Yeah, kind of. Now, what about a group called the Fallen?”

“Let’s see.” The pastor rubbed his forehead this time. Stephen listened in on his thoughts as he sorted through bits of information. *Lucifer was fallen. One third of heaven’s angels fell with him.* “Well, as for a group, there were the angels of heaven that fell.”

“Did David and his army ever battle fallen angels?”

“Interesting question. Not exactly.”

“Not exactly?” Stephen scooted closer. “What do you mean?”

“Well, I’m sure you know about David and Goliath, as well as the Philistines?”

“Certainly. Goliath was a mighty warrior, a literal giant, over nine feet tall. He was one of the three sons of Anak, descended from the Anakim.”

"Very good." Pastor Buchanan smiled, looking pleased and surprised at the same time. "Do you know where the Anakim came from?"

Stephen searched through his own thoughts for the answer. He knew it must be in there. With so much on his mind, he found it hard to concentrate. Still, he closed his eyes and focused to recall one of Waltz's lessons from childhood. "I feel as though it goes back to the flood of Noah's time."

"You are a smart one. In those days, the Sons of God left heaven and took the daughters of man and had children. As I'm sure you would agree, they found women to be beautiful. A superior race was born, warriors of renown. However, man became full of himself and forgot God. Those Sons of God were Raphaim or angels. Many believe they were fallen angels."

"Okay. Strange question," Stephen warned the pastor. "Could these two groups still exist?"

"You mean like giants and warriors?" The old man's face contorted in a funny sort of way, causing Stephen to chuckle.

"Not exactly," Stephen replied. "Is it possible that maybe descendants or even other people could have carried on the cause of these two groups?"

"Well, one group represents evil, the other good. So, I suppose there are many groups out there. But that's not what you're asking about, is it?

Stephen shook his head.

Pastor Buchanan remained silent for a moment, then sighed. "You're referring to two specific groups that still walk the streets."

Stephen nodded.

"Well, I've been a pastor in this area a long time. I've worked with the homeless a lot over the years. I've heard rumblings here and there about two groups fighting some kind of spiritual war. Once, I even heard those names from a man we were handing out blankets to and was later told by the same man to forget he said them. You're the first I've told. But that is all I've heard whispered inside these walls."

"So, they are out there? They're real?" Stephen looked at the man, locked his gaze, and read his mind for the answer, but was unable to get it before the man spoke.

"I know there is good and evil. I know we each fight that battle. I believe that some may be more involved in the fight than others. And, I know that there are people out there that believe these secret groups exist. Do I believe? Well, it doesn't really matter if I believe. Does it?"

"No, I guess it doesn't," Stephen replied. He got up to leave. "Thank you for your time, Pastor."

"Stephen." The pastor got up and walked him to the door. "If I was in a group of people like that, I'd want to make the right choices. The weight and consequences of such a group like that, if it exists, could be tremendous for us all."

"Yes, it would be." Stephen turned again for the door. He heard the pastor just before the door closed behind him.

"I'll pray for you, that you make the right choices."

The door closed, making a hollow, lonely clunk.

Thank you, Pastor. Stephen was not sure if the pastor received his thought.

He walked home as the rain poured down. Instead of relief, the answers he sought only added weight to his shoulders. It would be so much easier if this was all just the concoction of an old man and his friend. Instead, he accepted the truth in it—something evil waited for him, and he, somehow, managed to get caught in the middle of a war he did not want, and forced to make a choice concerning a spiritual battle he did not believe in.

As he walked along, he caught glimpses into the minds of people as he passed them. He saw cheaters, thieves, and all sorts of would-be sexual deviants. He wondered if people were worth protecting. He at least knew a few worth fighting for. Was he really the person to fight that kind of battle?

Passing a lady's boutique, he glanced in the window and caught an image in his mind. The man on the other side of the window plotted something evil. Stephen saw the images of the man asking the girl behind the counter out to dinner and slipping a little something extra into her drink. His wanted to take her back to a hotel, have his way, and leave her there wondering how it happened, feeling dirty and ashamed.

Not tonight! Stephen projected his thought.

The man's face changed from satisfaction to confusion as he looked around. He glanced out the window toward Stephen, whose thoughts burrowed deeper into the man's weak mind.

Come. Stephen planted an image of the man walking outside.

He did just that.

❧ ☙

The two sat in the hotel room, the same one the man planned to take the young woman to. Stephen managed to get the man there by merely directing his path. What he planned to do next would require all his strength and concentration. Stephen intended to take over the man's body, something he had rarely done. It only worked on the very weak—those whose lack of morals and self-control left them open to just about anything.

Stephen stared into the man's eyes. Sweat rolled from his forehead as the man's mind unfolded to him. Everything was there: his past, present, even memories and emotions long forgotten by the man himself. Stephen accessed it all. In an instant, he found himself staring back at his own body as it fell away from him onto the bed.

He sat for a moment in the man's body, getting acquainted with it. If felt different, slimmer and lighter than his own. He touched the skin of his arm. Like a hazy dream, he knew he touched it, and even felt it, but not the same as though touching his own body.

He looked back at his own lifeless shell lying on the bed. This too seemed strange to him. He got up, walked over to it, and repositioned his body into the most comfortable position he could. He did not want to be stiff later. Grabbing his arms and legs to move them, he felt them being touched; still connected to it, but weak and vulnerable.

Stephen walked into the bathroom and took a look in the mirror. The man had slick straight brown hair, brown eyes, and high cheekbones. He was what many women might consider attractive, though not as fit as Stephen. He sniffed, detecting a specific scent. Reaching into the inside coat jacket, he found a pack of cigarettes and tossed them in the trash can.

"Those things will kill you, man." His new voice sounded strange and raspy.

He reached in the man's pockets and pulled out a set of keys. He needed to speak with Waltz.

Stephen pulled up to the house in a 2004 Camaro, the kind that somewhat resembled a suppository. It rumbled loud and obnoxiously, much like the man's personality. Walking up the steps to the porch, he saw Waltz inside, sitting on the couch talking with one of the tenants. Stephen sat on the bench to wait.

After a few minutes, Waltz walked out to where Stephen sat.

"Can I help you?"

"I hope so." Stephen looked around. He never got used to looking through the eyes of another. Color was off. Edges were not quite as crisp either; like looking through dingy glasses. "Is there somewhere private we can talk?"

"Well, sure. I was just about to head around back to get stuff out of storage. Care to walk with me?"

Stephen got up, and the two went down the steps and around the back of the house.

"I'm Waltz, by the way."

"Yeah, I know. We've actually met," Stephen replied

"Oh, sorry. I'm usually good at remembering faces. I must be getting older than I thought." Waltz chuckled as they walked. "So, what can I help you with Mr.—?"

"I want to know more about the Mighty and the Fallen."

Waltz's face filled with confusion. Stephen sensed the internal conflict inside Waltz but nothing more, unable to focus his gifts when in another's mind this deep.

"What do you mean?" Waltz stopped and faced Stephen directly.

"Waltz, what is the extent of their powers? I feel like there's more to the story that I'm not getting." Stephen excitedly poured his thoughts out on Waltz. "I know we've talked about both and how the Fallen were once Mighty that fell. Their kids don't get the same type of powers but are versed in deception. But are you sure? Look at this, what I've done. I've literally possessed another person. Is this normal?" Stephen raised his voice. "Can others do this? You've asked me to make a choice about something I don't want to believe in. Because, if I do believe in it all—God, Satan, Mighty, Fallen, and a spiritual battle between them—then I must be one of the Fallen!"

Stephen looked at Waltz, waiting for an answer. Having gotten caught up in the moment, he forgot to tell Waltz who he was. Overwhelming emotion flowed out of him, both from his mind and the body.

Waltz stood motionless for a moment before his face turned to sadness.

"Stephen? Is that you, boy?" Waltz reached for Stephen's face, touching it slightly before Stephen reached and grabbed the hand. It felt strange.

"Yes, Waltz. It's me—or at least my mind inside this body. Sorry, but my emotions are much harder to control this way, and my thoughts can get away from me.

This isn't easy. I can only do it with the very weak-minded and for a short while."

"What's it like?" Waltz looked Stephen's new body over.

"It's kind of like a dream. The very first time I did it, I thought I was dreaming. It took me a day or so before I came to realize what had actually happened. I can feel both me and Freddy here. He's not conscious. He won't remember anything much. Anything he does retain will seem like a dream he'll soon forget."

"So, why did you do it?"

"I want you to see the fullness of what I am before you tell me whatever it is you want to tell me. I want you to know everything. This is it. Am I evil?"

"No, boy." Waltz smiled. "You're hurting, confused, in pain, and under attack. But you aren't evil, no more than I am." Waltz paused to look him over again. "I have to ask. Why Freddy? What did he do?"

"Oh! He's done lots. But it wasn't the past that caught my attention. I caught a glimpse of what he plans to do this evening, to take advantage of some young woman. He's done it before." Hearing Freddy's voice creeped Stephen out a bit. Different physical characteristics and strange physical sensations he had learned to ignore, but he continued to have the hardest time dealing with the different voices. It made his skin crawl, sending chills up his spine. "Brrr. Sorry, this voice is just creepy, but very much like the man. The things he's done to women—horrible. He'll never do them again though." Stephen smiled.

"Stephen, what do you have in mind?"

"Before, I would have done something to make sure he was caught and probably damaged beyond repair. It would've made me feel powerful. I realize now that there is an addiction to my powers, something that draws me to use them a certain way. But that's not my place. Is it, Waltz? That's not a choice I should be making."

Waltz smiled. "No, son, it's not. I'm proud of you for realizing that. What are you going to do?"

"Well, I've got access to his thoughts. I've called and reported it all to the police. What he planned with that girl; he's already done so many times. By the time Freddy returns home, still wondering where the last couple of hours went, police will be waiting for him. I gave them his license plate, auto info, driver's license, and physical description."

"And evidence?"

"Yeah, Waltz. I told them where to find the *trophies* Freddy here keeps, strands of hair, lingerie, ID's. He keeps them in a box in the top of his closet. A couple of boxes actually. They've been trying to find this guy for a while, I imagine."

Stephen glanced back at the car. "Well, I better go."

"Wait, how do you get back to being you?"

"Easy, Waltz. I just let go, like waking up from a dream. I just do it. But I've got to get Freddy here away from the shelter first. I think we'll go park in a no parking zone near his apartment. I'll wake up at the hotel a little tired, but I'll be fine."

The rain stopped.

"Stephen, meet me down at Kiener Plaza in a couple of hours. The clouds seem to be clearing out. We need to talk. It's only fitting we talk there. Okay?"

"Sure, Waltz. I'll be there."

Stephen walked toward the Camaro. He passed the front of the house, where he saw Bernie standing on the front porch with the door open, looking at the car.

"That yours?"

Stephen waved. "Yeah, kind of. I'll move it. See ya' later, Uncle Bernie." He smiled upon seeing the agitation in Bernie's expression. Then, he drove off to do what he said and make sure Freddy got caught.

He parked Freddy in a no parking zone, near a couple police officers, then rolled down the window to yell.

"Hey, you lookin' for me?"

Officers approached and asked him to exit the car. They checked his identification and immediately made him place his hands on the hood. Stephen released Freddy's mind after officers placed him in cuffs.

Stephen walked up and sat next to Waltz, who watched a group of children splash each other in the park. Other adults and teenagers sat around in the grass—some eating, others talking. In the distance, the melodious sound of an acoustic guitar carried through the air. Birds chirped and picked at the crumbs on the ground. The sun reflected off the ripples in the pool and occasionally created a rainbow in the mist that came from the white-water cascading down the stone steps where even more kids played. The Arch rose high above in the distance.

"Want to play, old man?"

"Nah. I was just sitting here thinking about you."

"Me?"

"Yeah, you weren't much older than them when I found you here. It looked different then. But it was here, right in the middle of this park."

Stephen tossed a small twig into the pool and watched it float away. "Yeah. Sometimes I remember better than others. But I *do* remember, thanks to you. I had run away, right to you."

Waltz laughed. "Yeah, you did. Even then you were a fighter. After your mom died, you went to a boys' home while they tried to find your relatives. You ran away and I found you. You were the saddest boy I had ever seen."

"I was what? Nine? Ten?"

"You were nine." Waltz put his arm around Stephen and squeezed him for a moment before letting go. "I used connections to get the boys home to let you stay with me. When they couldn't find a close relative, I applied for custody. You've been my boy ever since."

Stephen smiled. "And I eventually stopped being sad. The moment you found me, it felt right. Maybe because I wanted someone to care, and you seemed to be the only one to understand. My mom was gone. I never knew my dad. I had no other family—no grandparents, no uncles, aunts, no one. But you seemed to understand how lonely and sad I was. I bet it must have been strange for you—some strange kid just runs up and hugs you."

"Well," Waltz replied, "it was not what I expected. But I think I needed you as much as you needed me."

"You always wanted a son, right, Waltz?"

"Yeah, I did. I got one too."

"Sort of, I guess." Stephen paused. "I know it must not have been the same for you. I thought about calling you Dad a time or two. But I wasn't sure how you'd feel about it. I didn't want it to be weird or anything."

Waltz turned toward Stephen. "Boy, I would have been perfectly okay with that."

They exchanged smiles.

"Well, I guess now would be a good time to have that talk," Waltz continued.

"Oh, about the building, with Chuck? Or about Freddy?"

"Neither, Stephen. There's more for you to know about the Mighty and the Fallen."

Stephen straightened.

"Really? I'm ready?"

"You've been ready. I'm the one that wasn't ready. And there's more you should know about you."

Waltz turned sharply away from Stephen, looking in the direction of a large family nearby.

A pointed pain shot through Stephen's head and continued to pulse. "Waltz! It hurts! What's going on?"

"I don't know. Someone's trying to get in your head again. I can feel it. Dang it! I wish I had my old powers. Stay here. I'm going atop the rocks for a better view."

Waltz hopped up and headed toward the waterfall where kids played. He ran near the top and looked back and forth.

Stephen grabbed his head again and strained to see through blurred vision, trying to keep his eyes on Waltz. He could not concentrate. Trying to catch a mental image of his attacker made his head hurt worse. That did not keep him from trying, but whoever it was had more skill than Stephen.

Get out of my head! Stephen was not sure his mental outburst was heard in the attacker's mind. He tried to focus it toward the repeated attacks he felt. Regardless, it worked. The pain stopped immediately. He figured he definitely got someone's attention.

Looking around with clear vision, he finally spotted Waltz, who stood at the top of the waterfall looking at him. Stephen signaled he was okay, and both continue looking around. He ventured in the opposite direction of Waltz, hoping to see something, anything, that might give him an indication of the attacker's identity.

He heard screams. Felt fear and terror emanated from the people around. He focused, but only managed to get confusing fragments of images and strong, raw emotions. He saw many people and images of red. Was it red hair, a red shirt?

Waltz, where are you? Stephen ran back toward the pool, as an unexplainable feeling of dread continued to grow stronger the closer he got. Near the top of the rocks, he saw an old, frail body lying listless on the rocks. He ran up the falls and dropped next to the body. Blood poured from Waltz's head. He looked around for help, but people just watched, looking on at him in terror and disbelief.

"Waltz, stay with me, old man. There's more to tell me. You have to take care of me." He pulled Waltz up into his lap. The old man's breathing labored as blood flowed down the falls and swirled in the pool below. People rushed to get their children out of the water, but none offered to help. Stephen sobbed. "Don't leave me alone. Not again. I can't be alone."

Stephen looked around again. "Help! Please! Someone?"

He looked down at Waltz, listening for a thought. There was no more breathing. He felt Waltz's neck for a pulse—nothing. "WALTZ!"

Someone tugged at Stephen's shoulder. "Sir? Sir. Let me have him. I'm a first responder. Let me help."

Stephen looked up. Through the tears, he saw a man wearing rubber gloves holding some sort of kit stooped beside him. Stephen fell back, away from Waltz, listening for the man's thoughts.

Okay. Head injury. No pulse.

Another man in an EMS uniform rushed up. "What do we have?"

Stephen crawled further away, landing on his bottom. Listening to their thoughts, he heard a hopeless plea, *God, help him.* Waltz's thoughts had stopped. Stephen sat, water running over his legs, and watched the two men work from a distance, trying to resuscitate him. Seeing Waltz lying there, he knew he was gone

A third man arrived with a gurney. They loaded him onto it and trekked to the ambulance they had parked close by. Stephen continued watching in disbelief. He listened to the sirens recede as they drove away. It wasn't long before the sirens stopped.

People still looked on in terror. Stephen sat stunned.

"Sir, are you okay?"

A blanket fell around Stephen's shoulders. He looked around to see an officer, who tried to assist him to his feet.

"Let's get you out of this water, okay?"

Shocked and confused, all Stephen could manage was a nod.

"I'm sorry, but I have to ask you what happened."

How could he explain what happened? Stephen could not be completely honest with the man. He looked at the name tag, Nokes. He searched Officer Nokes's mind. *Decent man. Wife and two daughters. Hard worker. Cares about people.*

"We were just hanging, you know. Talking. He raised me. He's like my dad. I got a headache and went that way to get out of the sun. He came up here, to the top of the cascade. He's a people person, loves watching people and being around them. The next thing I knew, people were screaming. Then, I saw him. I ran. But I was too late."

"Was anyone near him?" Nokes jotted down some notes on a pad.

"There were kids playing up there. Parents sat nearby. But, no. No one was around when I got there."

"What's his name?"

"Walter. He goes by Waltz—he liked to dance when I was younger. He taught me to waltz right here in this park. But, sorry...his name is Walter Stockton."

"That was Mr. Stockton?" Officer Nokes looked toward the waterfall.

Stephen focused on Officer Nokes. The man's demeanor instantly changed. His shoulders slumped; his face appeared much sadder.

"You know him?"

"Yeah. I mean I've talked to him before. He comes down to help the homeless. He used to spend most of the tolerable nights in an alley a few blocks from here. He hasn't been there lately though. I stopped to check on him a couple of months ago. He wasn't there."

Officer Nokes looked back to Stephen. "You must be Stephen?"

"Yeah, that's me. He moved back to the shelter when I came back to town. I didn't realize he would stay on the streets when I left."

"Hey, hey!" Officer Nokes looked directly at Stephen. "None of this is your fault. He didn't have to stay there. He's a stubborn man. A very good man, but stubborn. You can't get down on yourself now."

"Yeah, I guess." Stephen wiped a tear from his cheek, but more continued to fall.

"Look, I need to talk to some more people and get with my partner over there. I'll be back in a bit, okay? I'll take you to the hospital."

"Yeah, sure. I'll be here."

Nokes walked away. While he and his partner took statements from bystanders, Stephen listened in on the people's thoughts, searching for what had happened. He heard all sorts of explanations. Many said Waltz simply slipped. One man said he might have been pushed. Stephen probed the man's mind, frustrated to find he had not seen anything at all. Then, he heard a thought in a child's mind. He looked around and saw a young girl talking to an officer. He was not close enough to hear her words. So, he focused on her thoughts more deliberately to hear the child's account.

He grabbed his head. It was like he was hurt. Then he just fell. And he was talking to himself. "Get out! I won't let you hurt him." That's what he said.

The officer dismissed the kid's words as the result of an overactive imagination. After all, none of the adults remembered seeing or hearing any of that, but the child stood closest to him when it happened.

Stephen realized that Waltz had been protecting him. Indeed, there had been a war raging all around him. He fought back emotions.

Finding another child who witnessed the tragedy, Stephen searched his mind too. He saw the same images: Waltz grabbing his head and talking to himself. This kid had not heard what was said but saw Waltz fall and the blood splatter. Both of them saw it, not sure what to make of it.

“Poor kids.” Stephen went back into their minds, isolating those memories. He was not sure how he knew what to do. Somehow it just seemed right, as though he had done it many times before. Like picking apples from a tree, he pulled at the most gruesome parts of the memory and locked them away in their minds where the memories would stay forgotten.

They’ll remember what happened, but without the horror. Besides, it might be safer if they never recounted the memory in detail to others.

The tears stopped flowing. He now knew what happened. Waltz died protecting him, and he was the only one who could do anything about it but had no clue where to begin. When he needed help, Waltz always knew what to do. Now, someone had taken Waltz from him. The sensible thing to do would be to call Uncle Bernie and see what he knew. Nothing about what happened seemed sensible though.

He reached into his pocket and pulled out his cell phone. Without thought, he called the first number on his mind. The phone rang. A familiar tone sounded nearby. He looked around as a gentle voice answered from the other end.

"Hey, babe! Where are you?"

He heard her, and not just through the phone. Patty was there. He scanned the crowd and saw her standing on the sidewalk, looking toward where the police tape now hung in place.

Stephen called out. "Patty!" He waved to her. Upon seeing him, she hurried toward Stephen, ducking under the police and sprinting by the people still being questioned.

"Stephen? What's wrong?" Patty looked around. "Where's Waltz?"

"What are you doing here?"

"What? Oh, I was supposed to meet Waltz down here. I have some papers for him. Something he and Vincent were working on. Have you seen him?" Patty placed her hand on Stephen's arm. "Babe, you're worrying me. Where's Waltz?"

"Something happened. I can't fully explain it. But he was hurt bad. Patty, he didn't make it." Stephen wrapped his arms around Patty, holding tight to her. "What will I do without him?"

Officer Nokes walked back over. "Stephen, I'm sorry to interrupt. But I'm gonna be a while longer. Do you have a ride to the hospital?"

"I'll take him." Patty looked at Stephen. "I'll take you. Are you ready?" Patty's eyes filled with tears.

Stephen sensed the emotional torment coming from Patty. She really cared about Waltz. He felt her hurting and forcing herself to be strong for Stephen's sake.

As they walked to her car together, they silently held hands. Stephen mentally prepared himself for the worst. Patty, despite a strong face, failed to contain her tears.

Stephen stood fidgeting with his tie. He had not worn a suit since he was a young boy. He remembered going to a couple of funerals with Waltz, but never for anyone he really knew. He could still hear Waltz say, "Over, around and through, then around, through and tuck. That's a half Windsor." Since learning to control his gifts better, even his own memories became more vivid and detailed, as though reliving each one while he recalled it.

"Waltz, why do people call you Waltz?" a younger Stephen asked.

"Isn't it obvious? I like to dance!" Waltz snatched Stephen up and waltzed around the room, his little feet dangling. The two filled the house with laughter.

A tapping sound at the door pulled Stephen out of the memory.

"Stephen, you alright in there?"

"Yeah, Bernie. I'll be out in a minute. I'm just trying to get this darn tie tied." Stephen pushed the tie down, smoothing it. He grabbed his jacket and put it on before opening the door. "I'm ready."

Bernie stood there; eyes red. Waltz's death took its toll on Bernie too. In the nights since his murder, Stephen heard Bernie in the kitchen, talking as if Waltz joined him for a late-night hot chocolate. Stephen did not listen though, not even to his thoughts. He did not need to hear Bernie's thoughts to sense the pain. His eyes showed it all.

"Stephen, I know that we haven't talked much the past few days. But I need you to know that I'm here for you, and I appreciate you taking care of all this. You probably know that Waltz took care of things for me for years. He helped me out a lot and kept me here doing what we both love: helping people. I'm not sure what'll happen with him gone. I've been lost. These past four days...they just don't seem real. More like a dream I can't wake up from."

Stephen wrapped his arms around Bernie's large frame. "We'll be okay, Uncle Bernie. One day at a time, right?"

"Yeah, we'll make it." Bernie sniffed. "Stephen, we do need to talk though, before the funeral. I know Waltz was going to talk to you about some things. I have no idea what about though. He could be a private person, but there are things I might be able to help you with, when you're ready."

Bernie appeared nervous as he rubbed the back of his head. Stephen got the impression there was more to the story.

"What is it, Bernie? What do you want to tell me?"

"Look, you know about how Waltz and I were forced to retire and stuff. But Waltz was still very well liked. Retirement wasn't really anything against him or me. It's just what needed to happen. And it became easier for us to stay away from Mighty after that. You know? We could have been around it, trained people or something. But we chose this life in the end. We both made our share of mistakes and figured this was best. Besides, I had Bernardo and he, eventually, had you."

"Bernie, I know all that. It's okay." Stephen grew concerned. He knew more stirred inside Bernie but did not know how to help.

"Some of them may come to the funeral. They may come to pay respects at the grave today. It's customary for at least a couple of ambassadors to be there, even when a Mighty has been long retired."

"Okay." Stephen puffed his chest up a little. "Well, thanks. I'll be prepared to meet them. They might be able to help answer some questions."

"No." Bernie raised his voice. "You don't understand. Waltz was well known. He had more contacts than most. At least one, as you know, became one of the Fallen. Fallen aren't allowed to be there. But because of his previous friendships, they'll be looking for any who are Fallen."

"Okay. Well, if there's trouble, we can handle it."

"Stephen, you still aren't getting it."

"What, Bernie? What am I not getting?"

"Waltz was your mentor and trainer. But with him gone and no decision made by you, they'll consider you one of the Fallen if they find out about you. They'll know you haven't made a decision."

"What? That's ludicrous! I'm no more a Fallen than you are." Stephen grew furious. No one would keep him from Waltz's funeral. "I'm going. I dare *anyone* to stop me."

"Well, they don't know about you, I don't think. But they might sense something. If you stay close to me, I think you'll be alright. I have enough juice to throw them off, like Waltz had been doing for you." Bernie smiled. "You sounded like him just then. He was bold like that. I think he'd be proud of you, ready to fight for him."

"Really?" Stephen smiled back.

"Yeah, really!"

He heard the clacking sound of footsteps coming from the front porch, followed by a couple of quick raps at the door. A tiny feminine silhouette appeared visible through the glass.

"Well, let me look at you." Bernie looked Stephen's suit over. "Well, you look right nice, don't you? Good thing too. You've got a pretty little woman out there waiting for you. It's still early for visitors. But I figured you wouldn't mind lettin' her in."

"Thanks, Bernie." Stephen looked down the hall to see Patty open the door and step through the doorway. "Yep. That'll make me smile every time."

Stephen walked to Patty.

"How are you holding up?" Patty gently smiled, which eased Stephen. She touched his cheek, looking into his eyes. She could not read minds, but she always seemed to know exactly what to say or do to help Stephen. The past four days she had been his pillar, as though when all his strength drained, her love alone held him firm.

"I'm gonna be okay." Stephen stepped outside with Patty. "Listen, there are going to be a lot of people there today. Many of whom I'll know. Some I won't. It may be a little overwhelming. I need to ask you something."

"Anything. You know that."

"Stay by me? Me and Bernie? Bernie needs me, and I need you. Will you do that for me?"

"For as long as you want."

Stephen smiled. "Careful, that may turn into a bigger commitment than you're asking for."

Patty smiled too. "Well, we'll deal with that if it happens."

Bernie joined them, hugging them both. "I guess it's about time, right?"

Stephen nodded.

The three of them made an odd trio walking to Patty's little compact car. Nevertheless, they were soon on their way to say their last goodbyes to someone who had made their lives so much better just by being around.

The sound of bagpipes closing another's funeral nearly drowned out the distant sounds of the city. The sun shone brightly. Only a slight breeze blew. Stephen noted how wrong it seemed for the weather to be so pretty, given the reason they were there. Despite the sunny day, a chilling darkness hung in the air. On the hillside, three men in work clothes, covered in sweat and dirt, properly secured the tent and chairs in their places. The side of the hill they worked on looked nearly empty, perhaps the newest part of the cemetery. Waltz's grave would be alone, solitary.

From underneath the shade of a tree, Stephen watched a funeral taking place not too far away, near the bottom of the hill. He allowed himself to feel their emotions and hear their thoughts which mimicked his own. An older gentleman cried into his son's shoulder as his daughter-in-law and grandson sat next to them. Stephen realized the road ahead held more pain and sorrow before healing. After listening to the man's thoughts, he felt some relief for himself as his heart broke for the man.

Stephen leaned toward Bernie, motioning toward the funeral. "No one should ever have to bury their child. I'd like to say I can't imagine what it feels like. But I now know *exactly* what it feels like."

Bernie patted Stephen on the back. "Today will be hard enough. Maybe you should stay in your own head, just until we get this day over with."

Stephen nodded.

Patty walked up from the bottom of the hill. Stephen could not help but feel comforted at the mere sight of her. Tension in his neck relaxed, as did his shoulders. For a brief moment, he even noticed how pleasant the warmth of the sun on his face felt. Today, if not always, she existed to be his angel.

"Vincent is on his way here."

Stephen stepped forward and kissed her cheek. "Thank you for everything."

Over the next several minutes, cars pulled up at the bottom of the hill. Stephen knew many of the people arriving. Vincent, of course, arrived as one of the first, along with Johnathan. The entire office showed up. Officer Nokes came too. Stephen nearly did not recognize him without the uniform. Jack from church, several other members, and even some of the homeless Waltz worked with came to pay their respects.

"You must be Stephen."

Stephen turned to see a distinguished-looking man standing in front of him. He appeared the same height as Stephen but older, maybe mid-forties, graying in his hair around the ears and in his goatee.

"Yes, I am," Stephen replied.

"Sam, how are you?" Bernie shook his hand.

Stephen saw that Bernie, although friendly, remained guarded.

"I'm doing well. How are you enjoying retirement?"

Sam sounded solemn and spoke with a strangely flat tone. Stephen tried to get a read on him, on his mind. At first, there was nothing. Stephen continued searching. After a moment, he felt pain buried beneath the layers of protection. Sam had cared for Waltz as a close friend and comrade.

"Well, it's not so bad. We get to help others in our own way."

"Yes, I've heard." Sam glanced at Stephen for a moment, a puzzled look on his face before quickly turning his attention back to Bernie. "Waltz and I hadn't spoken in over six months. He didn't tell me Stephen was back." He turned to Stephen again. "I apologize. I'm Samuel Jefferson. Please call me Sam." They shook hands.

"Thank you for coming." It pleased Stephen to see an old friend of Waltz had come.

Sam nodded. "It must be strange for someone to know you and you not know them. I used to work with

Waltz and Bernie a long time ago. On occasion, we would still talk. We kept in touch a couple of times a year. But I don't suppose he ever mentioned me."

"No, I'm sorry. He did tell me he had a former life but had given it up some time before he took me in."

"Yes, that's correct. He truly was a good friend. I'm sorry for your loss."

Stephen smiled. "Thank you."

"There's something I must ask of you, Stephen."

"Okay."

"There are a few others on the way, people who knew Waltz before he retired from his old life. Among our group of friends, we have many traditions for different occasions. We understand that Waltz left that life behind him. Still, we have one tradition I would like to ask you to allow us to keep, to honor him, and all the good he has done. It's a simple tradition. And it may seem odd. So, we would wait until everyone else is gone, if that's okay."

"What would you like to do, Sam? What's the tradition?"

Sam looked at Bernie, and then at Patty for the first time, before continuing. "We have a cloth, a shroud of sorts, that we would like to place on the casket. But there's a ceremony with it. The shroud has our coat of arms on it. Simply, it is a shield, a sword, and a stone. Each shroud is adapted to individual families. There is a specific one for him, a certain design and color scheme."

"Yeah, a sword behind the shield with the stone embedded in the middle." Stephen reached into his pocket and pulled out his flask, running his fingers across the emblem. "He gave this to me when I returned." He placed the flask back into his pocket. "That's it?"

"Well, we lay the shroud across his body. We each take turns saying a prayer or blessing for the departed and family. Then we will fold the shroud and pass it on to the next generation, the eldest child. As I understand it, he loved you very much. We ordinarily would only give the shroud to a blood relative. However, I can make an exception to honor the life he lived both before and after retirement, if you're willing to participate in the ceremony."

Stephen looked at Patty, then Bernie, allowing their feelings to unfold to him. Patty felt it was a beautiful gesture. Bernie had reservations.

"I'd like for Patty and Bernie to join me."

"Bernie is certainly welcome to join us. The others might frown on Patty joining us. She isn't family."

"Neither are you."

Patty interjected. "Stephen, it's okay."

"No, it's not, Patty." He looked at Sam. "Waltz loved Patty dearly. They had a great friendship. She helped to fill the void I left when I abandoned him. If you truly kept in touch, you'd know this. She *is* family." Stephen fought back the urge to look deeper into Sam's mind. He was not sure about Sam's motivation, but remained in control, knowing this was not the place or time to start trouble.

Sam looked down the hill. Four others approached dressed in similar colors and style. Stephen realized that Sam's attire was more than just a nice suit; it seemed a ceremonial suit, with what appeared to be a stone with a cross on his lapel.

Sam said, "Well, I suppose we'll have to make this exception as well. Please, allow me to inform the others before they present themselves."

"Thank you."

Sam nodded and walked down the hill to join the others near the bottom. He sensed some confusion but nothing more. After a moment, they approached Stephen—except for Sam, who went to stand near the tent, separate from the other guests. As they approached, Stephen noted that all but one looked to be around the same age, mid-forties. Two men, both neat in appearance and with darker hair led, while a woman with long blond hair that fell to her waist followed. Stephen observed the fourth looked younger, a man who did not appear to be much older than Stephen and about the same age as Vincent.

The first two men stopped in front of Stephen. They first looked at Bernie, then back at Stephen. "I'm sorry for your loss," one said with a thick German accent.

"Thank you."

"Waltz will be missed," the second man said, also with an accent.

"Yes, he will," Stephen replied.

"Pardon them, Stephen," the blonde lady said. "They don't get out much and have no manners. I'm Anastasia. These two are Adelmo and Derrick, brothers."

"Hi. I'm Alistair," interrupted the younger one with a Scottish accent. "It's great to meet ye."

"Nice to meet you all. I believe you all know Bernie. And this," Stephen put his arm around Patty's waist, "is my girlfriend, Patty. She and Waltz were close."

"Lovely to meet you." Anastasia gave Patty a gentle hug. "Listen, I apologize for Sam. He's really stuck on traditions for our society. And this is an unusual situation. I'm also aware of how Waltz felt for you all. We're happy to accommodate."

"Thank you, Anastasia." Stephen wanted to know more. "Sam said you were, I guess, old colleagues of Waltz's."

Stephen, what are you doing? Stephen heard Bernie question him.

I'm being normal, Bernie. The only reason for me not to ask would be if I already knew!

Ah. Right. Bernie replied.

"Yes, well, of sorts. We're part of a humanitarian group that works for the betterment of people. We don't like to bring attention to ourselves. The public likes to make a big deal about our type of organizations."

"Really?" Stephen looked at the four of them. "Why would the public have a hard time with your organization?"

Adelmo spoke up. "You know, it's much like the Freemasons and Shriners. They do good stuff for people."

Derrick interrupted. "Dah. But people question the secretive parts."

"I guess that makes sense." Stephen smiled.

"Yeah. Shame yer not related to Waltz by blood. You'd get to join us," Alistair chimed in.

The three looked at Alistair.

"What?" he shrugged. "It's true."

"Yes, well. I can see how our ways seem a little strange. But again, thank you for allowing us to have the ceremony. We'll go wait with Sam now."

They excused themselves and walked toward Sam, talking as they went.

Stephen felt anticipation and sadness crescendo. Turning toward the road, he saw the hearse parked nearby. He took a deep breath at the sight of what he dreaded. The scent of roses carried on the air.

Patty kissed him on the cheek. "I'll go sit."

Stephen, Bernie, Vincent, Johnathan, and two others from their church whom Stephen met only the day before, carried the casket to its final resting place. Then, Stephen and Bernie took their seats.

The ceremony was brief. People lingered afterward to talk with Stephen and offer final condolences. When the crowd thinned, the Mighty stayed. Before long, Vincent alone remained aside from the Mighty, Stephen, and Patty. He questioningly looked at the five people huddled with Bernie near the casket as he approached Stephen.

"Stephen, I need to talk with you. It is a matter of importance."

"What about? Is everything okay? You said Waltz had already taken care of the entire funeral. If there's anything else, I'll find a way to—"

"No, it is not like that. But it does have to do with Waltz. It looks like they are not leaving until everyone else does," he said, cutting his eyes back toward the Mighty. "So, we need to talk later, in private."

"Certainly. How's first thing in the morning?"

"I will see you then." Vincent turned to walk away, paused, and looked once more at the strangers. "Are you okay? They seem strange," he noted matter-of-factly.

Stephen chuckled at the thought. "Yeah, Vincent, we're good here. They're just some old friends of Waltz's from another life."

"Okay. See you tomorrow then."

Vincent walked away.

Stephen grabbed Patty's hand. "Let's do this." He and Patty walked over to Bernie and the five Mighty members. They stood together Sam reached into his suit jacket and pulled out the shroud, unfolded it, and laid it across Waltz's body.

"Stephen, the colors used in each shroud are unique to each family or bloodline in our group. This is Waltz's." Alistair continued, although getting disapproving looks from the German brothers. "Waltz was the last of his bloodline. After today, the black-and-white crest on this shroud will be forever lost to our organization."

"How often has that happened?" Stephen wanted desperately to know more.

"It has never happened before. In fact, our organization has been looking to this day with uncertainty. There will be all sorts of discussion, no doubt."

"And what's the name of the organization?" Stephen asked.

"I think that is quite enough information from the young Scotsman." Sam walked over to the two. "We are nearly ready to begin. Stephen, I understand he was like a father to you. For that, we have decided to allow you to participate. But we cannot divulge anything further. I'm sorry and hope you understand."

"Sure, I guess."

Bernie and the others took their places while Anastasia directed Stephen to stand at the head of the casket with Patty next to him.

"Patty, you technically aren't a participant. But you will be here with Stephen. If you'd like to offer a blessing, you'll do so just before him, before we present the shroud."

"Thank you."

"Patty, if you don't mind, I'd like for you to give the final blessing for me. That's not a problem, is it, Anastasia?" Stephen put his arm around Patty. "I want her to be as much a participant as me. We'll share the spot."

"I suppose we can do that. She will offer the blessing, and the shroud will be presented to you."

They each took their places around the casket. Alistair began, the first to offer a blessing. As he spoke, the shield started glowing red. Stephen watched, astonished. He opened himself to Patty's emotion, wondering if she saw the glow. Sadness. Following a gentle squeeze of her hand, he looked at her and smiled a little. She did the same. Nothing about her facial expressions made him believe she saw it too. For the first time, he listened to her thoughts in order to be certain. Her thoughts were only of concern for him. She hadn't noticed. For some reason, she did not see the glow of the shroud. He acted as though he didn't see it either.

The shield glowed even brighter through all the others' blessings. Adelmo spoke next, followed by

Derrick. Bernie's blessing was emotional but short. When Anastasia finished, she moved to one end of the casket, opposite Stephen and Patty. Sam offered his blessing for those Waltz left behind and asked God to watch out for them all, after which he stepped forward to the other end, next to Stephen. He and Anastasia picked up the corners of the shroud, then nodded to Patty, signaling for her to begin.

As Patty said her blessing, the glowing faded.

"Lord, we thank you for the time you gave us with Waltz. To many, he was a friend." She struggled with her words. "A friend and mentor. But to us," she squeezed Stephen's hand, "he was more than that. Waltz was family. He showed us how to truly love others. He taught us compassion and charity, and that one person can make a difference. Now he has gone home to be with you. We ask that you not let us forget the good he taught us, nor the sacrifices he made in life for others. In this way, we will honor him. Amen."

With Patty's final word, the shield ceased glowing.

Anastasia and Sam folded the shroud so that the emblem stayed centered on top. Sam approached Stephen, shroud in hand, and offered it to him.

"As the heir to this bloodline, we offer this shroud to you, to serve as a reminder of the honor this man brought to the family name. And although this bloodline has ceased, it will forever be recorded among our society as one of the greatest houses and Waltz as one of the most beloved and honored members to ever share our legacy."

Stephen reached forward and took the shroud. The moment he touched it, the rock glowed blue.

Immediately he felt excitement and confusion among the Mighty. He quickly searched for an answer, while concealing his excitement.

What's wrong, Bernie?

It shouldn't be glowing, Stephen. We thought it would only glow for a member of Waltz's bloodline with the symbol for their gift. It's giving you away!

No sooner had Bernie finished, Stephen noticed the members looking at him.

"What now, guys? Is the ceremony over?" Stephen played it off, as though he had not noticed anything. Before anyone could respond, the sword also glowed—yellow. Everyone turned their attention away from Stephen and back to the shroud. Everyone except Patty, who stood still, waiting patiently.

What now? he asked Bernie.

I don't know. This has never happened.

The shield, too, glowed again—red. One at a time, the symbols all changed to purple before fading back to the original white outlines.

"Guys, you okay? What's next?"

Sam answered. "Sorry, Stephen, it was a moment of silence. It is, after all, the end of a bloodline for us. We must be leaving now. As Alistair disclosed to you, we will need to meet to discuss what has happened."

They each passed in front of Stephen and Patty, giving them hugs before departing. Stephen wanted to listen to their thoughts, to try to understand what had just happened and what they thought it might mean. He sensed confusion and uncertainty. However, he was afraid they would sense him using his ability if he tried probing their minds for answers.

He watched as they walked away, leaving only Bernie, Patty, and him. It was not long before they left as well. It had been a long few days, with many more to come, and no Waltz to help him get through.

Stephen woke early the next morning; his body covered in sweat and his breathing labored. He sat for a moment, sorting through the dream that woke him; the first true nightmare in a couple of months. In the dream, he stood surrounded by darkness with no way out. With Waltz gone, he worried that the dreams would continue.

The clock next to his desk displayed 5:14 AM. He walked to the bathroom and splashed water on his face. The scars on his chest and back evidenced the rough times he had while he was away. The nightmare faded into the back of his mind, as most dreams do. He knew he had also dreamt about Tommy and Waltz, but the details already faded away.

He showered, dressed, and headed out the door.

“Where are you off to this early?”

Stephen turned and saw Bernie standing in the kitchen doorway. “I’m going to see Vincent. He asked me to stop by this morning. He said he needed to discuss something important with me.”

“What about?”

"I don't know, Uncle Bernie. It could be work related. Or it could be about Waltz. He's a pretty quiet and private person. He didn't say much at the funeral. I figure he wants to offer his condolences in private."

"Yeah, probably. He's a bit of an odd one, isn't he?"

"Yeah, I guess he is. You know, I never understood why Waltz liked him so much. He spent his time around people he thought he could help. It took me awhile to figure that out. The last few days I've thought about that a lot. Me, you, Patty, all his homeless friends, I suspect even those Mighty that showed up. But Mr. Abbott, I don't get. Maybe I will soon."

"Well, if you figure it out, let me know."

Stephen left and found his way to the office. As he walked down the hall toward Vincent's office, he heard Patty from behind.

"Hey, good-lookin'. What are you doing here?" She walked up and kissed his cheek.

"I'm not sure. Vincent wants to talk to me. You wouldn't have any idea what about, would you?"

"No. None. In fact, he was here before me this morning. He's sat in there with his door closed and hasn't said a word, other than to tell me to send you straight in."

"Well, okay then. I better get in there." Stephen kissed her on the lips—a quick kiss. "I love you. You know that, right?"

Patty blushed, only slightly. "I do. But it's nice to hear you say it."

Stephen walked down the hall, opened the door, and continued in. Vincent stood, looking out the window at the city. The sun had started rising, and red clouds lined the horizon.

Vincent turned and walked to stand behind his desk. “Please close the door behind you.”

Stephen closed the door and sat opposite Vincent.

“So, what’s this about?”

No sooner had Stephen completed the sentence than he realized that without Waltz around, he should be able to search Vincent’s mind. He focused in on Vincent’s thoughts with everything he had, searching for answers, but to Stephen’s amazement, he heard nothing. Vincent continued to flip through folders on his desk, completely unaffected and unaware of Stephen’s attempt. He tried again. *Give me your thoughts! Show me what’s inside!*

Still nothing.

“Stephen, I apologize for what must seem like secrecy to you. But this is a privileged conversation.”

Stephen focused back on the task in front of him, yielding his attempts to read Vincent’s mind. “Privileged?”

“Yes, as in attorney-client privilege.”

“What? I haven’t...” Stephen paused. “Waltz?”

“Yes, I handled many things for Mr. Stockton over the course of our relationship. This is the last thing I will ever do for him. I am both saddened and happy to do it.” Vincent turned his monitor around, so that it faced Stephen and placed the mouse in front of him. “Before I continue, there is a video I have been instructed to show you. I have not seen it and was specifically asked to remove myself from the room while you view it. Once you have completed the video and had time to process it, please call Patty and let her know. I will be right back in.”

"I don't understand." Stephen sat puzzled, not sure which was more disconcerting—the video or the fact he could not read Vincent.

"I believe the video will help to explain. If not, I will do my best when I return."

Vincent left. Stephen watched as the door closed. He sat in silence, staring at the monitor. On it, Waltz stared back at him, looking just as he had seen him less than a week ago. In the image, he smiled, looking happy as he most often did. Stephen wiped a tear from his cheek, grabbed the mouse, and clicked play.

"Stephen, if you're watching this, I've passed." Walter paused, took a deep breath, and let it out slowly before continuing. "I want you to know first and foremost that these past couple of months have been among the best in my life. I have been able to share a part of my life with you that I never thought I'd get to share with anyone ever again, let alone my son." Waltz paused again and smiled as bright as Stephen had ever seen him smile. "Hmmm, son. That's right. If you're watching this, we probably didn't get to have that conversation I so wanted to have with you. There is so much more you need to know. And I'm going to tell you as much of it as I can right now. But before I do, I must caution you. It's unfortunate, but you can't trust anyone right now. No one at all, except for Vincent. I can't explain why. But please believe me when I tell you that he is your friend and can be trusted.

"My boy, I'm sorry..." Waltz trailed off and sniffled as his eyes watered. "I'm sorry I wasn't able to tell you this in person, to be there for you. And I'm sorry I won't be there to be a good father and help you through the difficult times ahead." Waltz sighed. His expression saddened."

Stephen wiped a tear from his cheek, struggling to keep from weeping altogether.

"Stephen, the story I told you about the woman I loved is also your story. I didn't know it at the time, but the child she was pregnant with was my child—you. It was a few short years after my forced retirement from the Mighty. My head was not where it should have been, or I might have wondered. As it was, I saw her with another man and figured it was the man's child."

Stephen could not believe what he heard. Why had Waltz never said anything? He stared at the video, waiting for a punchline. Nothing. The story continued.

"When your mother got sick, she drafted a letter to be delivered to me when she knew she didn't have long. It took them awhile to find me. I had left the country to do some traveling. By the time the letter got to me, she had passed, and you had been placed in a home. I called the home and had all the legal documents sent, releasing you into my care. Your mom had also requested you be left in my care. She, too, did not tell anyone you were my child."

Waltz's demeanor changed. He wiped a tear from his face, leaned toward the camera, and continued in a more serious tone.

"Your mother was Mighty. You were raised outside the organization. Mixing bloodlines should cause you to have no powers. But somehow, you're different. It is important that you tell no one about this—not now. There are things going on in the darkness that involve you somehow. If the Fallen learn about you, well, I'm afraid of the battle that would follow. I don't think you're ready for it.

"After spending these last months together, I've realized that you are more like me than I could ever have imagined. But you are kinder than I was at your age, which comes from your mother, Layla." Waltz beamed. "You look just like her, except with my brown wavy hair and blue eyes. She was the only woman I ever truly loved. I wish I could tell you more. There is so much more for you to know. But now is not the right time. Eventually, you will uncover the full story on your own. As you already think of me as your dad, there was no harm in telling you that truth now. If the Fallen search your emotions, they won't find anything different than they already have.

"I know all this a lot to absorb. But there is more. I have left you everything. Vincent will give you all the details. I'm certain you'll do the right thing with it. After all, you've already shown yourself to be a very hard worker. Again, use Vincent's help. I've found him to be a great asset and friend.

"I love you, son. And I'm so very proud of the man you're becoming. Remember to love God first. Everything else will fall in line."

The screen froze with the image of Waltz and his smile.

Stephen wiped the tears from his face. It had hit him hard, seeing Waltz talk to him from beyond the grave, as though knowing his own fate. But to find out that he had been raised by his dad all along. *Does it change anything?* He reached forward and touched the screen.

Another tear trickled down his cheek, then another. As grief turned to anger, he slapped the arms of his chair before nervously running his fingers through his hair. He struggled to contain the conflicting emotions. Confusion ran rampant in his mind as his thoughts and emotions made his head spin. After several minutes, he realized the worst part—he couldn't tell Waltz how happy, mad, or confused he was about it all. He beat his hand against the desk. It hurt. Somehow the physical pain deadened the emotional pain. He hit it again and again. He sensed the concern coming from the others in the building. They must have heard him.

Someone knocked gently at the door. "Stephen?" Patty's soft voice carried some comfort. "Are you okay?"

He wiped away more tears. "Yeah, I'm good," he said, trying not to sniffle. "Can you get Vincent now? I'm ready."

"Yeah, I'll get him." Her footsteps faded.

It took only a moment before he heard another, distinctly different set of footsteps grow closer. Vincent walked in and shut the door behind him. "Well, to the matter at hand." Vincent took a seat behind his desk. He removed the flash drive from his computer and handed it to Stephen. "This is yours. I no longer need it."

Vincent adjusted his nameplate and a couple of other items on his desk that shifted when Stephen hit the desk. He opened a folder and handed a stapled stack of papers to Stephen. "After we finish, I'll need you to sign the last page. You'll receive a copy for your records."

"Okay." Stephen tried to act composed. He never considered that Waltz had much of anything left to leave him.

"Vincent, Waltz told me he left most of his wealth behind, keeping only a small amount to live off of. I had assumed he gave it to charity. What is all this?"

"Waltz did leave his wealth behind. He left it in a trust for you, allotting himself a small annuity payment to live on. Now that he's gone, there is no need for the trust. Everything is being turned over to you, as per his instructions. And it's quite a lot."

Stephen thumbed through the pages of documents. He found a parent company with several different subsidiaries. The company, Stockton Family Holdings, LLC, fully funded the nonprofit that Vincent's office oversaw. A property management company owned the building he sat in, the shelter, and many other buildings around St. Louis and more. The portfolio included stocks, bonds, multiple investment accounts, and a small restaurant franchise.

Stephen pushed himself away from the desk and shook his head. It was all so much to wrap his head around. Waltz really was his biological father and was very wealthy. He tried to process it all.

"Did you know?" He glared at Vincent. "This whole time, did you know Waltz was my dad?"

"Yes." Vincent's usually perfect and upright posture relaxed. "I learned years ago, when I started representing him."

"Did he explain why he didn't tell me?"

"He only ever told me that he felt guilty for not staying with your mom. He loved her and never forgave himself for leaving. When he learned of you, he did not believe he deserved to be your dad. That is as far as the conversation went." Vincent paused, but appeared as though there was more.

"That's all? Are you sure?"

"Yes. I know it hurts. But he did love you, as much as any father could love a son."

Stephen needed to sort this all out. He recognized that Vincent could not help him anymore than he already had. He pulled himself back toward the desk to continue thumbing through the papers. "Wow, there's a lot here. I guess I'll need to meet with a board or something?" Stephen continued flipping through the pages.

"There is no board. You are the sole owner."

Stephen stopped and looked up at Vincent. "What? I'm fully in charge? I don't know how to run a company. Heck, I don't know how to be rich. There's just so much crap going on." Stephen felt the tears welling up. "I just got back. I had settled in. Now, all this!" He wanted to break down and tell Vincent everything, about Mighty and Fallen.

"Waltz had faith in you, Stephen. He has good people at the heads of each of these companies. Not just good at what they do, but they're truly decent people. Waltz wouldn't have it any other way. I know they will help you, as will I. After all, you are the boss now."

"You'll take care of the introductions and informing them?"

"Yes." Vincent smiled. "I will inform them. And when you're ready, I will arrange a meeting with all the CEOs. I believe you will do fine. While there will certainly be business decisions for you to make, the biggest decisions will be about people—who to put where and doing what.

Who will you trust? Who will you take a chance on? You will make some mistakes. But it will be okay."

"Thank you, Vincent. To be honest, I thought you didn't like me."

"Really?" Vincent straightened up; a disappointed look flitted across his face before relaxing to his usual rigidness. "I guess I am not very good with people. I do not relate well to others. Please accept my apology for making you feel that way. We will be spending a fair amount of time together, getting all the documents straight and putting everything into your name. But you should know that I do like you. And I am glad I have gotten to know you. I did think you were a little arrogant at first. Well, you still are, but not too much."

Stephen managed a smile. "Yeah, I guess I can be."

"Is there anything you need at the present time?"

Stephen thought for a moment about what all this meant; the money, the businesses, the relationship. In a near instant, had become wealthy beyond anything he ever thought possible and could have anything he wanted, except for having Waltz back. He realized what he wanted more than anything.

"Time. I need time to take this in. Can we meet back here tomorrow morning, first thing?"

Vincent pecked at his keyboard. "My schedule is open in the morning."

~ ~

Rain drizzled on the sidewalk only a few feet away as Stephen waited on the steps. After having walked around the city the rest of the previous day and all night, he managed to find his way back and spend what remained of the night in the entryway of the soda building. He had gone to the places that held strong memories of Waltz; Blueberry Hill, the zoo, Gateway Arch, and more. Eventually he thoughtlessly found himself back at work. When morning came, it brought with it a desire to take whatever next steps waited.

"Stephen, you are here early. How would you like to start?" Vincent asked as he walked up the steps and unlocked the door.

Stephen walked inside with him, following him to his office. "You know, I wandered around the city all day yesterday, visiting some of our favorite places. The only place I remember calling home is the shelter. I don't remember much before that."

"Well, the shelter is yours now. That was Waltz's house before it became a shelter."

"It should stay a shelter." Stephen opened the office door for Vincent. "Can you have someone from the property management company call me? I'd like a place to call my own."

"Absolutely! I'll have them call you shortly."

"Actually, just have them come pick me up. I want one today."

"Okay." Vincent made a note. He then grabbed an envelope from his desk and handed it to Stephen. "You didn't sign the papers yesterday. Once you sign the back page, the envelope is yours. It's a personal credit card from the company for company expenses. You may also make personal purchases on it. You will have to pay the bill though. The company will reimburse you for business expenses as long as you keep the receipts and file the correct report. It has a one-hundred-thousand-dollar limit. We will need to discuss your accounts, holdings, and more in greater detail. I have set Monday of next week aside. Will that work?"

Stephen looked down at the stack of papers, flipped to the back page, and signed. "Monday will work."

The two wrapped up. Then he sat in Patty's office waiting for someone to pick him up. He explained to her that Waltz left him everything but said nothing more. There was no discussion about Waltz being his father. He desperately wanted to tell her. Even in death, however, he trusted Waltz more than anyone else.

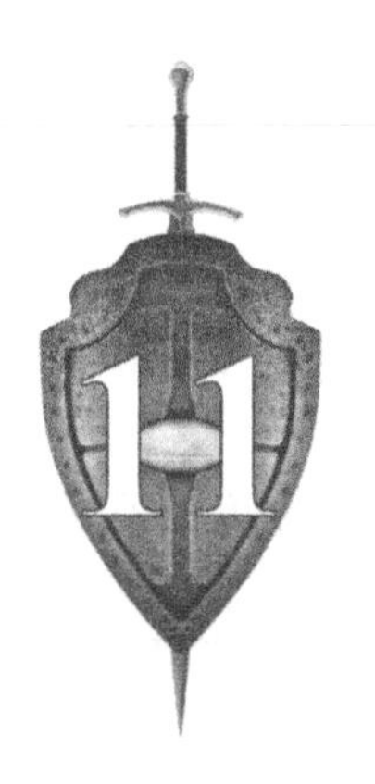

The night air sat stagnant, filled with moisture gathered from the nearby Mississippi and Missouri rivers. Streetlights illuminated the sidewalk while the stars and moon lit up the almost cloudless sky. Only a few, distant, and random sounds carried through the dark night. Most of the city slept. Stephen did not.

A few weeks had passed since Waltz died, and Stephen remained unable to sleep. His new apartment did little to comfort him. To ease his busy mind, he walked the streets at night—as he used to do—and worked on remodeling his new home, but he did not seek peace; he needed answers. A time or two, he thought he might try and contact the Mighty. Bernie, however, urged him to give it time, suggesting there might be other, less revealing ways to find answers.

The only other people Stephen thought might have answers as to who killed Waltz were Fallen. He knew what lurked in the dark; the worst sort of people, the kind with whom Fallen might associate. If the street held answers, he knew where to find them. He often found that people saw or heard things without realizing it—something that, to them, seemed insignificant. Sort of like when you run into someone that you should know and walk right by without giving them a second thought because you saw them outside of their usual surroundings.

Stephen walked in the darkness, the light evading him at every step as though unable to coexist with him. He sensed the homeless that lay around the city. Most slept, completely unaware of his presence. Occasionally, he came across someone that woke up just long enough to get a glimpse. No matter how hard they looked, they could not make him out. Stephen's control of his gift yielded new abilities. One he recently discovered allowed him to affect the minds of others within proximity in such a way that they couldn't really see him. Without something to remember, the individuals soon forgot seeing him at all. He saw what lingered in their minds; a distorted shadow of a man, as though looking through the bottom of an empty soda bottle in a dark room.

For several hours each night, Stephen walked around looking for an opportunity to find out anything he could about Waltz's death. He searched numerous minds. He found a few gang bangers, a pimp and his prostitute, and a couple of thieves, but learned nothing. As luck would have it, he saw something earlier today, from a client at Vincent's office. A young woman came to Vincent's office for legal help; concerned about a neighbor. Stephen sat in on random meetings to learn more about the nonprofit he now supported and heard her story.

The Mrs. Finney lived with a young daughter and caught the neighbor watching her a little *too* intensely. She went to the police, but the man had no criminal record, so they could not get involved. She came to Vincent asking if there was anything she could legally do to keep her daughter safe.

Stephen looked into her mind, wondering if there was something she was not telling them. He found she caught a glimpse of a second man she had not mentioned. Contrary to the image, her emotions, feelings, and conscious thoughts indicated she told the whole truth. Continuing his search, he saw more of the other man, talking to the first man. The lady's neighbor never seemed to acknowledge him, only occasionally reacting to him, as though he were somehow being controlled or coerced. The two of them often went into the backyard just after realizing she saw them. She had not seen any more because of the privacy fence and foliage that concealed them there.

After seeing the memory, Stephen realized this was the first evidence he had that Fallen might exist. He concluded the strange man somehow kept himself from being noticed, similar to how Stephen kept people from remembering him. He made note of Mrs. Finney's address so he could pay the man a visit. His nightly stroll took a detour from his normal route.

Stephen walked up the street, looking at the addresses on the mailboxes until he arrived at the man's house. There were no lights on as he stood in the darkness of night and listened for the man's thoughts.

You know I love you! That's why I keep you here, away from the world. I know you understand. I need you to help the others understand.

Stephen caught a glimpse of a woman dressed in a faded denim dress with long brown hair and no makeup. He searched for her thoughts and found out how horrible the situation was. Thoughts from more than one woman came into focus. He sensed fear, uncertainty, despair, and defeat. Then, he felt hope. One single girl remained hopeful that someone would rescue them.

Stephen went toward the privacy fence. The thoughts came from behind the house. He cleared the fence easily, focused on uncovering whatever waited on the other side. The thoughts and emotions seemed so jumbled and intense, he found it hard to filter through and fully understand the situation.

Inside the fence, Stephen noted a variety of garden plants and paths. A light shone from a detached garage in the back corner. He made his way over, careful to stay unnoticed while listening for any signs of trouble. There were none.

As he approached, he peered into a window. A curtain blocked most of the room from view. He saw only a few tools on the opposite wall and no evidence of anyone inside. Searching for thoughts again, he found them louder, more jumbled, and even more intense. He searched for the man's thoughts. He, too, sounded closer.

Stephen opened the door and entered the building. He barely looked around before realizing why the thoughts grew closer with no one in sight. In a back corner, a ladder stuck up out of a hole.

"I'll return in the morning with breakfast. I know you will all be excited to see me then."

The ladder shook as the man climbed it. Stephen walked over.

Never again!

"What?" The man looked down before his head snapped upward and his eyes locked on Stephen.

Stephen reached down and took hold of the man before the man uttered a word, jerked him up out of the hole, and slung him across the room. The wall shook as the weight of the man's body slammed into it. Several tools fell off the wall next to him. The man grabbed for the first tool he could reach, a hammer.

Come on, Dan! Stephen spoke to the man's mind, causing him to pause. *I said, come on!*

Dan charged and swung the hammer at Stephen, who sidestepped and disarmed him with an arm-bar hold before forcibly bending Dan's elbow the wrong way. The hammer fell.

Dan cried out in agony. He darted frantically around the room. Stephen saw various images in Dan's mind, looking for a way out; the door, a window, the ladder leading back down the hole. Stephen shoved him against the wall and stood between Dan and the door. Dan flopped to the ground and crawled back toward the hole; the only option Stephen left him.

That's right, Dan. You dug this hole. Now lie in it!

Stephen picked up the hammer and looked around. He listened for thoughts and heard only the women below and Dan; no mysterious stranger. He took hold of Dan before he entered the hole, lifting him to his feet.

"Don't!" the man pleaded, teetering on the edge of the ladder. "I'm sorry. I'll let them go."

Stephen searched the man's mind. Dan knew nothing of Waltz or the mysterious man from Mrs. Finney's memories. He dropped the hammer.

"Thank you. Thank you," Dan groveled.

Stephen pushed just enough for Dan to struggle against gravity pulling him into the darkness below. Dan lost the fight and his footing when his body fell to the bottom, making a loud thump and several cracks as it hit. Stephen listened but heard nothing. At best, Dan lay unconscious. He probed deeper. The pitiful excuse of a man remained alive. Stephen climbed down the hole.

Examining Dan, he saw a nasty cut on his head. He figured there were broken bones too but could not be certain.

Stephen found a light switch on the wall that illuminated the damp, smelly underground room. He walked through a doorway into another room with a small kitchen, table, bed, and television. It looked like a crummy hotel room, complete with sheetrock and a separate bathroom. At the far end stood another door.

Stephen opened the door. Inside were three cages, each with a bed and a woman. Each prisoner looked to be in her twenties to early thirties. Their similarities were striking, brown hair, fair skin, blue eyes, and dressed in denim dresses. Each looked a little too thin, but in otherwise decent condition, considering.

"Please, let us out," the one closest called out. The others stood up when they saw Stephen.

He took hold of the closest cage door and tried pulling it open. It creaked but didn't look to budge. He shook the bars. Nothing. "Where are the keys?"

"He keeps them on him. Just call the police," the lady said.

"Please, hurry," another begged.

Stephen walked out of the room and to Dan. "You're sick!" He roughly nudged the body with his foot, listening for the jingle of keys. He stooped down and found the keys in Dan's shirt pocket, then went back and freed the girls from their cages. Each stepped up to the open doorway, reluctant at first. He sensed their uncertainty and heard the questions in their minds.

"Look, you're free. No tricks. You need to hurry."

One of the women, who looked the youngest, stepped forward from her cage and wrapped her arms around Stephen's neck. "Thank you!"

Stephen searched their thoughts, finding memories of the other man.

"Where's the other man? Who is he?"

"There's no one else. Dan's the only one we see."

"I'm sorry for all this," Stephen replied.

The woman looked at Stephen as he reached deep into her mind and into the minds of the other two, burying any trace of himself in their memory. Instead, he implanted images of the youngest somehow managing to get the drop on Dan. He then planted a deep desire to run and find help in their minds. And they did.

Stephen looked around the room, knowing he did not have much time. He saw an image of another man in the mind of Mrs. Finney in Vincent's office, but he found no trace of anyone else, only a feeling of evil. Immense evil. The more he looked around, the more he felt it. Knowing the police would be there soon, he decided to leave.

As he walked away from the house, he saw flashes; images of a warehouse. Then he saw a sign: Stored Warehousing. He knew exactly where the place was. He remembered seeing it while picking up building supplies for repairs at the shelter.

Despite not finding the mystery man, he had a productive night. He felt he had done some real good and came away with another lead; one he hoped would lead to a Fallen. Stephen went home and tried to get in a nap before heading into the office. Even he could not go on forever without sleep.

The next morning came earlier than Stephen wanted. Morning sunlight filled his new studio apartment. Despite his fatigue, he managed to get up and prepare for work at the office. He usually enjoyed walking to the office. It was not far, and it gave him time to get himself prepared mentally for his inherited responsibilities. However, he began to realize that getting a vehicle of his own would be beneficial.

Stephen's phone buzzed. He had a text from Vincent. *I'm heading to the office. Want a ride?*

"That's good timing," Stephen mumbled as he typed, *Sure. Thanks.*

Stephen walked downstairs to wait for Vincent, only to find him already parked outside. He got in and closed the door.

"That was quick!"

Vincent smiled. "I was driving by and saw your light through your windows. It is already eighty-five degrees outside. So, I thought I would offer."

"Well, I appreciate it. Now, I won't be covered in sweat by the time I get to work."

The car pulled away from the building.

"Stephen, I have rescheduled your meeting with the CEOs of the various subsidiaries for next week."

"Okay...Why did you do that?"

"I notice how exhausted you are when you come to work. Losing Waltz has taken a toll on you, as it would anyone who lost a father. I also thought it would give us a little more time to continue going over the businesses."

"I guess I have been stretched a little thin with the business and remodeling the apartment. Still, I wish you would have talked to me about it first."

"My apologies. I know you are looking forward to the meetings. I am too. I am excited about the future of the company."

"Really? You don't feel like I'm in over my head?"

Vincent pulled the car into the parking lot at the soda building. "To tell the truth, I had concerns, but not about your ability. My reservations had more to do with the learning curve. I had anticipated the meeting with heads would have been more of a meet-and-greet. But you have shown interest in discussing the business in greater detail. That is a lot of information to absorb. And you are doing a remarkable job at it. Your knowledge, your business acumen, even your memory are superb. To sum up, you are going to *wow* them, as you have me."

Stephen managed a tired smile. “Thank you. I’m glad to hear you have confidence in me.” He yawned, which made him realize just how little sleep he had gotten. “I have been burning the candle at both ends. A week’s delay isn’t a bad idea. Besides, I have some research I’d like to do. Perhaps setting up one-on-one meetings would be best at first.”

“I think that is a wise decision. But we should go ahead and prepare some type of official company announcement and press release. Even the people in the office do not yet know.”

“Really?”

“Really.”

“Vincent, have Johnathan put something together.”

“Okay. But, why Johnathan? I was going to do it.”

“One, I’ll need your services elsewhere. Plus, you’re already busy with the nonprofit. Two, I’m considering a new position for Johnathan and want to see how he handles this one. I think he’ll do well.”

“What position?”

“I need a Chief Information Officer, someone to handle company releases and overlook information policies, securities, and more. I think he’d be good at it. But I want to give him a trial run.”

Vincent smiled. “Do you want to review the release? Or should I do it?”

“Have Patty do it.”

“Patty?” Vincent picked up his briefcase from the backseat. “Let me guess. You’re considering her for a new position?”

“Maybe. I’m not sure. We have this relationship thing going. I know she’s capable of more than she’d like to admit. I want to see if it's something she'd enjoy first. I don't want her to feel obligated because of me."

They got out of the car and headed into the building. The conversation turned toward the relationship between Stephen and Patty. Without fully understanding why, Stephen felt more comfortable with Vincent since Waltz passed. He always thought that Vincent had hired him because of Waltz. He now considered that Vincent may have hired him on his own, which helped him feel more at ease around Vincent, which seemed to be reciprocated.

Both continued chit-chatting as they walked into the building, up the stairs, and into the breakroom to get their morning caffeine.

"Did you guys see this?" Patty interrupted.

Both Vincent and Stephen stopped and looked up at the television, which displayed the morning news.

A picture of Dan shone on the screen as the anchor woman said, "This man is believed to have been keeping three women locked up in underground cages in his backyard. They escaped last night, one of whom reportedly beat him unconscious."

"Where was this?" Vincent stepped closer to hear Patty over the others chatting in the office.

Patty continued to stare at the television. "Not far from here, really. They said one woman had been there for almost ten years."

"Wait, I know that address!" Vincent ran out of the room, down the hall, and returned a moment later with a file.

"Mrs. Finney. She was in here yesterday, wanting to know if there was something we could do about her strange neighbor."

"Yeah, I remember her," Stephen said. "She seemed really concerned. Maybe she can rest a little easier now."

"Wow. That's strange, isn't it? She's here one day, and then this happens that night." Patty's face showed real concern.

Stephen thought for a moment, searching for a response that would throw off suspicion.

"Well, not really," Vincent replied. "It was only a matter of time. Out of all the complaints we and the cops get, imagine how many are founded. It happens, maybe not usually of this scale. But it happens."

"Yeah, I guess. It's just weird—and sad."

"Patty, why don't you contact her?" Stephen put his arm around her to comfort her. "Find out if there's anything she needs. Offer to put her and her daughter up in a hotel somewhere for a few nights to get away. Better yet, see if we have a vacancy in one of the luxury apartments downtown. Food, entertainment—whatever we can do to help. That little girl won't understand what's going on and doesn't need to either."

"Thanks, babe. I'll see what she needs." Patty took off.

Stephen turned back toward Vincent to see him smiling.

"What?"

"Just so we are clear, you truly are the right person to be running this company. A big part of what this company does is charity. You have the right heart for it. That is the kind of thing Waltz would have done."

Stephen smiled. "Thanks. But I sometimes still wonder if I'll live up to Waltz's name."

"Speaking of which, I've got the paperwork done." Vincent reached into his briefcase and pulled out several pieces of paper. "This is officially your company. Here is all your account information and such."

"Thank you." Stephen looked at the paper. He stifled back a tear and managed a smile as he held Waltz's legacy in his hands.

"I'll give you some space. I need to start on some things in my office anyways. Lunch?"

"Yeah, Vincent. Give me a shout then."

Vincent nodded and walked off. Stephen followed suit and went to work in his own office.

"Stored Warehousing, what are you?"

Stephen used his real estate business to pull county tax records, deeds, company information, anything he could find on Stored Warehousing. Within a couple hours, he had found that a local investment firm owned Stored Warehousing.

He picked up the phone and called Vincent. "Hey, I need you to call Rivers Property Investors, LLC, and get me a contact name. I'm looking at a property. We've got several companies in the area that use warehouses. It just makes sense to look at it. And thanks!"

Stephen hung up the phone, before Vincent got a full word in edgewise. His mind focused intently on the task as he continued to gather what research he could until lunch rolled around. Before long, Vincent stood in his doorway.

"Well, are you ready?"

Stephen peeked out from behind his monitor. “Yeah, I believe I am.” He grabbed some papers, a folder, and his backpack that he seldom used. “Let’s go.”

The midday temperature made any extended time outside unbearable. No clouds, no breeze, and no break in the traffic made walking across the street to Henry’s Grill torture. However, they managed it, thankful they didn’t have to go far.

Once inside and seated, both ordered a burger, fries, and a soda. Stephen pulled out his folder and looked through the papers inside.

“Is that research on Rivers Property?”

Stephen did not look up. He continued sorting through the papers. “Yeah. I want to have my ducks in a row.”

“Why the interest in warehousing? You have got plenty of other businesses you are trying to get a handle on. This might not be the best time to start a new business.”

“It’s the perfect time to start this business.”

“Okay. Why?”

Stephen set the papers aside and closed the file. “What? Do I need a reason?” Stephen snapped.

“I don’t doubt your abilities. I told you that earlier today. My function with Waltz was largely to question and advise. When the CEOs of the different businesses hear about it, they will likely question it too.”

“So, you’re trying to make sure I’m prepared and that I’ve thought this through.”

“In a word, yes.”

Stephen looked at Vincent. Intrigued by Vincent in general, he grew more annoyed each day that he could not read his friend's mind. He opened the folder and placed it in front of Vincent.

"We have at least four different companies in this area that are paying for warehouse space—a lot of it. Additionally, we could use some of the space to work out of and stage material for remodels we have coming up for various properties. It wouldn't be a bad idea to move the maintenance crew for our property company there either. They certainly could use the space."

"It sounds as though you've thought this out."

"I have. It came to me last night when I was up late. I'm certain there will be other benefits too."

"And you already have a space picked out."

Stephen smiled. "I do. This is the warehouse we're going to acquire. It's the only one Rivers Properties owns. It's older, which means it likely needs some work. And I see they have only about half of it leased."

"You got their records already?"

The waiter brought their food. Stephen grabbed a fry and chomped down on it.

"Ow! Hot! Hot!" He took a gulp of his soda. "I'll give that a minute."

"Yeah, you really should. They are always hot. Yet, you always burn your mouth." Vincent laughed.

"I'm always hungry," Stephen said before getting back to the subject. "I was able to find out that they are interested in selling. I approached them as a party interested in getting into warehousing and asked if they had any properties they might be interested in parting with. They brought this one up. The guy was a chatterbox. I'm looking at it later today."

Vincent swallowed his bite of burger. “Really? That was quick.”

“I try not to waste time.”

“Would you like me to come with you?”

“Nah, I think I’ve got this.” Stephen picked up his burger. “On second thought, there might be some legal issues to discuss. Come get me around three o’clock.”

~ ~

After lunch, Stephen found Patty waiting for him in his office.

“Uh, you don’t look happy. You alright?” he asked her.

“I’m fine,” Patty replied. “Are you okay?”

Stephen could not help feeling as though he should not answer but found it impossible not to respond. “Yeah, why do you ask?” He walked around to his desk and sat down.

“Well, you don’t usually skip out on our lunch dates.”

Stephen blushed and wanted to run and hide. He continued to love Patty more each day, especially since Waltz passed. He also knew how particular she could be about things not going as planned or, as in this case, agreed upon.

“I— I’m sorry, Patty.”

“Oh, I know you are. If I didn’t know you had a lot on your plate now—”

Stephen interrupted. “It’s not that. I’m not going to blame it on being preoccupied with Waltz.” Although that would have been a true statement. He realized that he had to move past that and accept responsibility. “I’ve been working on this business deal. I got a little excited about it. It would be my first big decision since taking over. You know? I just want it to go well. I was talking with Vincent about it at lunch. Here, look!"

Patty took the file and looked through it.

"I should have said something. Honestly, I've got to do better at remembering. I want you to know you're more important to me than that."

"This is a good idea." Excitement bubbled in her voice as she seemed to ignore his previous comment.

"You think so?"

"Yeah, I think so. I mean, the property will probably end up being more of an investment than you think on the front end. But it'll still be a good return. You've already got the parts in place to make this work. You'll just need to make sure you have the right people in place. And you'll need someone in charge of the warehouse business, someone familiar with logistics."

"You know, sometimes I forget you have an MBA."

Patty blushed.

"You sure you don't miss it, trying to climb the corporate ladder?"

"I'm sure. I like working for this company. I can trust that I'm working for people who make every effort to do the right things and who truly care for people. Most corporations tend to forget about people when it comes down to it. Some are better than others, I suppose."

"Okay. Well, I'll just have to keep you working for me then." Stephen smiled at her.

"Oh, don't think that smile is getting you out of trouble."

Stephen's smile quickly faded. "Huh?"

"You *do* need to do a better job at remembering. And you *will* make sure I know how important I am to you. And don't think you can buy me off, like you tried to do earlier this week when you took me shopping. That was nice and all. But if you want me to be happy, then make certain I'm not the last thing on your mind."

Patty tossed the file back to Stephen and stormed out. Stephen sat there trying to figure out how the conversation had gone sideways so fast. It only took a second when he realized he would never be able to. Instead, he went back to working on the warehouse. After all, he knew that this warehouse had something to do with the invisible man from the woman's vision.

Stephen and Vincent pulled up to the warehouse just before three o'clock. Looking around, Stephen recognized it. This was the place he saw in the image, the glimpse from the previous night. He listened for thoughts, trying to sense people nearby. He only sensed a few workers, a delivery driver, and the young man they were meeting, Jason.

"Are you sure you're interested in this place? It looks really run down."

"Yeah, I'm sure. At least it's not raining. Try to enjoy the sun, Vincent." Stephen chided, "You look kind of like a vampire."

Vincent glanced in the mirror. "Hmm."

Both got out of the car and went inside to meet with their contact. Once inside, they easily spotted him. A short red-haired man looked out of place as he clumsily thumbed through papers. When he noticed Stephen and Vincent walking toward him, he quickly got up to greet them.

"Hello. I'm Jason Smith."

They all shook hands. "I'm Stephen. We spoke on the phone. This is Vincent Abbott, my associate and legal adviser."

Jason shook Vincent's hand and he continued standing there holding his papers with an awkward grin on his face.

"I'd like to get started," Stephen insisted. "Can you show us around?"

"Oh, right," Jason's hands shook as he pulled at the papers again.

"Are you alright?" Vincent asked.

"Yeah. I'm sorry. This is my first deal flying solo, and this place kind of creeps me out. As you can see, it's largely vacant. We used to own several warehouses but have sold all but this one. We've had a lot of interest, but we just haven't been able to make a deal. Which is surprising."

"How so?" Stephen asked as he walked and looked around, the other two in tow. Exactly as Jason already stated, the building sat largely vacant. Two bay doors stood open as a couple workers loaded crates into trailers on the farthest end of the warehouse.

"Well, the others sold quicker. In fact, this was the first one we wanted to sell. And it's quite a deal, at what we're asking now."

"Have you received any feedback from the other potential buyers?" Vincent inquired.

Stephen heard Vincent and Jason as he walked a distance away from them, looking for anything that might give him a clue as to Fallen's involvement. On the opposite side of the building, a finished wall separated a space from the warehouse, with no discernable door.

Stephen walked toward the area, curious to know what was on the other side of the secluded space.

"No, not really. That's strange too. We've even been set to close, but the potential buyers backed out at the last moment."

Stephen sensed another presence, different from the others he already felt. He searched through the thoughts. One man thought about a card game later. Another man mulled over his work. Jason's mind lingered between his conversation with Vincent and an attractive woman he met with earlier. Of course, Stephen still could not read Vincent. A feeling of immense hatred pulled at Stephen's senses. He saw images of someone with plans to set off a bomb. He believed this might be the man who influenced Dan. He dove into the man's thoughts and found images of the girls and Dan's place. The man manipulated Dan for years. With Dan caught, the man's mind turned to other sinister endeavors.

"What's in here?" Stephen motioned to a door he found around the corner on a back wall of the room.

"Ah. That's a part of the warehouse that was renovated into office space. It's leased to a club or support group of some sort. The door locks from the other side."

"I've seen enough."

"You have?" Jason's tone hinted at disappointment.

"I have. Vincent will draw up the paperwork. He can get with you later today to schedule the closing this week."

"This week? Stephen, you haven't talked to the bank yet. These things take time," Vincent said.

"Why would we talk to the bank, Vincent? We're paying cash."

"Uh, gentlemen, we haven't discussed price yet."

"Well, the last offer you tentatively accepted was what—five hundred thousand?"

"Yes. But," Jason put his paperwork away in the briefcase, "inflation and such."

"What, do I seem too eager?" Stephen glared at Jason.

"Well, you're wanting to do this in a hurry, and that means extra costs." Jason smiled.

"Sir, that is not how we conduct business." Vincent sounded irritated.

"I've got this, Vincent. It's okay." Stephen turned to Jason. "How much?"

"Seven hundred and fifty thousand."

"Done. Vincent—"

Jason interrupted. "Plus, a hundred thousand handling fee."

Vincent tugged on his arm. "Stephen, we should leave."

"No." Stephen stepped toward Jason. "Jason is going to agree to the original five hundred grand I offered, which is fair."

"What?" Jason laughed. "Why would I do that?"

"You would do that to keep your wife from finding out about the affair you've been having with your son's babysitter."

Jason's face turned pale.

"I make it a habit to know about the people with whom I do business. I am fair. But I will not be cheated or taken advantage of, Mr. Smith. Do we have an understanding?"

"Yes sir."

"Great. Vincent will send you the paperwork. I want to close by the end of the week. Vincent, is that doable?"

Vincent stood silent, a blank expression on his face.

Stephen became irritated. "Vincent? Is it doable?"

"Oh, yes. It will be a lot of work. But we can make it happen."

"Good. It's time to go." He turned to Jason and shook his hand. "It's been interesting meeting you."

The two men walked back to the car. Stephen heard Jason's thoughts, trying to rationalize what just happened and figure out how Stephen knew about the affair. When they got in the car, Vincent smiled at Stephen.

"You know, I had almost forgotten about the years you spent on your own. You, sir, are good at this."

Stephen smiled back. "Thank you."

"But," Vincent continued, "how did you know about the babysitter?"

"I called his office this morning. They told me he was working from his house today. I looked him up, wanting to meet with him immediately. Guess who opened the front door."

Vincent shrugged.

"The babysitter. Her blouse was on inside out, and he was in the shower. I asked her to have Jason call me."

Stephen felt pleased with the meeting overall. He had confirmed something strange going on in the warehouse, and he had helped his company to venture into a new business that he expected to be very profitable. He felt bad for not telling Vincent the truth. Vincent trusted him. Stephen grew concerned that Vincent would eventually figure out that there was more to Stephen's story.

❧ ❧

Stephen patiently waited a few days until the weekend arrived. Determined to find out who was responsible for Waltz's death, he worked to make sure they closed on the warehouse before the weekend. The warehouses closed Friday evening and stayed that way until late Sunday night. It created the perfect opportunity for him to find out what hid behind that closed door.

Good thing it's not raining. Stephen walked around the corner to where his new motorcycle waited and slung his leg across the bike, seating himself comfortably on his cruiser. Looking up, he saw what few stars the city lights allowed. The moon, however, shone as bright as ever. Breathing the night air in deep, he tried to relax.

Sirens in the distance wailed, growing louder and louder, eventually screaming by Stephen before they faded again.

"So much for relaxing."

He put on his full-face helmet and fastened the strap. His bike rumbled beneath him—a low menacing growl. He loved the sound. It reflected the way he often felt inside. He twisted the throttle. The bike roared as he raced away from the curb and down the road, heading toward the warehouse. His mind raced nearly as fast as his bike with thoughts of what he might find. He had faced many people in the past, conquering each, for good or bad. This might end up being the first time he stood opposite someone else with powers. What would the stranger's power be? Would he be powerful? Would he know Stephen was coming?

Stephen sped along, turning up and down roads, carefully navigating the streets. When he came within a couple of blocks of the warehouse, he pulled into an alley. That part of town remained mostly dead in the middle of night. He hurriedly walked toward the building, staying constantly tuned in for the thoughts of anyone who might be nearby. The closer he got, the more he sensed that someone occupied the warehouse.

Stephen stopped at the door he entered with Vincent only a few days ago. He tried the door–locked. He stepped back and looked for another way in. A few windows sat along the top of the building, some already open. Unable to reach them, he walked around the building, hoping to see an open door or bay. Eventually, he came around to what he assumed was the door to the office space. He searched for thoughts, trying to determine if it would be safe to enter.

Stephen could not hear through the door. However, he could access the thoughts of two men and pull their conversation straight from their minds.

What happened with Dan?

I don't know! Things were good. He was indulging himself. Someone must have gotten wind of what was going on and done something about it. I don't believe for one minute that one of those women freed herself and the others. You think the Mighty could have been involved?

Stephen smiled at the name, Mighty. He had the confirmation he wanted but continued to listen to their thoughts. Digging deeper into their minds revealed that the first man gave the orders and the second followed, like a soldier.

Possibly. It doesn't matter though. We'll have to continue with the next plan. You just need to make sure no one stops it. Are they ready?

The second man paused. Stephen sensed hesitation, even remorse. This man had reservations about his actions.

Yes. They're ready. I only have one more piece to put in place before the bombing. I need to be able to get them past security. I've found the security team working the event. I just need to pay Officer Nokes a visit and make sure he won't be in the way.

Something churned inside him. Stephen knew nothing of the men inside, except that they planned to hurt more people. He could not let anything happen to Officer Nokes, and he certainly could not let them plant a bomb. The situation blew up bigger than expected. This misadventure started in hopes of finding Waltz's killer. Instead, he stepped right into the middle of something he wanted nothing to do with. He saw only two options: walk away and try to live a normal life or stop the bombing and make himself a target for Fallen.

That *is* what started all of this. Fallen already targeted him for some unknown reason, and Waltz got caught in the middle of it.

Stephen grabbed the doorknob. It turned easily. He grinned upon realizing they had left the door unlocked.

That was not the smartest thing you could have done, fellas!

Stephen busted through the door to see two men looking at him with confusion on their faces, their thoughts having echoed his own.

Both men were average size and appearance. Neither looked notable or special in any way. The man to Stephen's left, however, looked to be the same man in Mrs. Finney's memory, talking with Dan. His slight build and shaggy brown hair gave him away. Stephen glared at him, paying little attention to the larger man.

A desk, a table, and some cabinets made the space look like any other office. It looked all wrong, though. Boxes stacked on one wall looked too neat, staged. No pictures hung on the walls. No phone, no computer. Only a few chairs pushed away from the desk and table made the room look used at all. Whatever they used the room for, it had nothing to do with running a business.

The man on the right spoke. "Who are you?"

Stephen laughed but only in his mind, which he projected into theirs. As he laughed harder, he sensed fear rise in the smaller man, who remained silent.

"I asked you a question!" the larger man said.

"Who am I? I'm the one who taught Dan a lesson. I'm the one who held a great man in my arms and helplessly watched him die."

"You're Stephen?" The first man looked at the other man and back to Stephen. "You aren't supposed to exist. You're Waltz's *adopted* son. But you have powers!"

Stephen smiled. "Yes, I do!"

"I see. You're one of them, aren't you?"

"Not quite," Stephen replied.

The man lunged at Stephen, who easily moved out of the way, knocking the man's head into the door frame. He heard the attack in the man's mind before it happened.

"You know, there's a reason they call me Rebound." The man stood back up, his head bleeding, but the bleeding slowed until only a small cut remained. "You aren't the only one with powers!"

Stephen looked around for the second man. He had disappeared.

Rebound came at him again. This time, Stephen planted his foot straight into the man's stomach, knocking Rebound back against the door. Stephen searched Rebound's thoughts for a way to quickly end the fight.

Rebound came again. Stephen tried to evade but failed. Rebound struck him across the jaw. Stephen fell to the ground as a jolt of pain shot across his face and down the side of his body. The assailant picked Stephen up and threw him across the room. The desk squealed as the weight of Stephen's body crashed into it. He crawled around to the other side. It served as a temporary barrier between him and rebound.

A moment's delay allowed Stephen to find a weakness in his formidable adversary. The man's will was too strong for Stephen to control the body. Stephen projected thoughts and images into the man's mind. He stood up as a body lunged past him, missing him completely.

"What? I saw you!" Rebound turned for another pass, swinging wildly, missing the mark each time. "How are you doing that?"

I read minds. I can also project my thoughts. You see what I want you to see.

"Cute parlor trick. But that won't stop me."

Wrong. I've seen your mind. I know your secrets.

The man continued to struggle, swinging and kicking, making contact with objects in the room. He never touched Stephen.

Stephen landed an elbow to the man's jaw. Rebound fell into a filing cabinet. He stood up, but slower, his chest heaving with each breath. His face turned red with anger. That's when Stephen felt it, fear.

"The more tired you get, the slower you heal. Your battery is draining."

The man charged Stephen, missing him and falling over the desk instead. Rebound staggered to his feet, his breathing labored. "You know, Waltz didn't have to die. He was really out of the picture. But there's a bigger player now, one that wanted him gone. Now I see why. Waltz died because of you. You're strong."

"Who ordered his death?" Stephen dove into his thoughts, trying to see the bigger player. A sharp pain pulled Stephen from Rebound's mind. "*Argh*!" He looked down at Rebound. The man lay on the floor, foaming at the mouth. Stephen checked him and found a couple of cyanide capsules.

Looking down, watching his answers fade, Stephen grew furious. He had been so close to getting answers. He stood still, shocked by what he witnessed. He looked around and remembered the other man disappeared. The door leading into the warehouse was not open, which might not mean anything to someone with abilities. He listened for thoughts. The other man waited outside to see the result of Stephen's skirmish. Stephen ran out the door he entered moments earlier, looking from side to side, hoping to see someone in the shadows. Nothing.

He listened for thoughts again. The man stood close, looking right at Stephen, but he was invisible, a powerful gift. The man's mind, however, was weak. Fighting as hard as he could, he could not keep Stephen from forcing his will on him. His body instantly appeared on the other side of the street.

Stephen walked across the empty street. He kicked the side of the man's knee, sending him screaming to the ground.

"How does it feel to be helpless?" He kicked the man again, only in the ribs. The crack of the ribs breaking echoed down the street. "Waltz was helpless. He didn't have his old powers anymore. But you killed him!" Stephen grabbed the man's head and thrust his knee into his face. Blood flew.

The man fell, motionless. Stephen grabbed him by the hair again, raising him to his knees.

"Stephen, stop, mukker."

He recognized the voice. Without turning around, Stephen searched the man's thoughts and confirmed his identity. "Alistair, you don't understand—"

"That this bloke had something to do with Waltz's death?" Alistair interrupted. "Yeah, I understand. But I can't let ye kill him for it. Ye knew Waltz better than anyone. What would he want?"

Stephen stood over the man; his hair still clutched in his hand. He squatted down to face him. "What happens to him? A jail can't hold him. He has the ability to make himself unseen."

"No, a jail can't hold him. We have something that can, though."

Stephen let go of the man's hair and stood back up.

The man fell forward to his hands, panting heavily as he spoke. "Thank you, Alistair."

"Shut up, Matthew." Alistair glared at him.

"Wait, you know him?" Stephen turned to Alistair, who wore plain, casual clothes, not the ceremonial garb he saw him in last.

"Yes, he was my friend."

"I was a friend of Waltz's too!" Matthew tried to rise to his feet.

"I said shut up, Matthew!"

Stephen turned toward Matthew and knocked him to the ground. No thought, no emotion, only instinct. The body hit the ground with a dull thud. Alistair reached to grab Stephen but was too slow to restrain Stephen's fierce blow.

"Don't worry, Alistair. He's alive—barely." Stephen turned back toward the Scotsman. "You need to explain what's going on, why you're here."

"Well, I suspect ye already know who we are."

Stephen nodded.

Alistair continued. "And ye know who they are."

Stephen nodded again.

"Then the answer should be bloody easy to figure out."

"You've been tracking them?" Stephen asked.

"Aye, I have."

"Well, you've done a poor job. Didn't you see what was in the news?" Stephen asked.

"I've been the only one able to track them, except for *you*, of course. Ye see, my gift is to see images of the future, or possible futures. And they're only short glimpses, just enough for me to figure out where to go, usually. The closer I get to a situation needing attention, the more detailed the glimpses become. People, places, sounds; they all become clearer. Matthew here, however, has the ability to seem invisible, by altering the mind's ability to process seeing him. He can do a similar thing with his voice. The weak-minded won't recognize hearing him, but the words seep into the subconscious."

"So," Stephen asked, "you couldn't see him either?"

Alistair smiled. "Ye are a smart one."

"Your flashes, or premonitions, didn't make sense without him in them."

"Keep going, please."

"Me?" Stephen looked to Matthew, then back to Alistair. "You first saw him when I did."

"Bingo. Well, almost. The images take place twenty-four hours before what I see actually happens. I wasn't sure who you were, only that someone had seen Matthew. After that, I headed this way to stop him."

"Did you see me?"

"About twenty-four hours ago, yes."

"So, you know about me?"

"Honestly, mukker, I haven't the slightest. I don't understand how ye got involved."

"It's probably best that you don't, not right now anyway." Stephen turned to walk back toward his bike.

"Stephen?"

Stephen paused, looking back over his shoulder at Alistair.

"I understand ye not wanting to trust me. You don't know me yet. Something Waltz taught me was to find someone to confide in with everything, a mukker, a friend. You know?"

"Can I trust you not to tell anyone about me?"

"It's not my secret to tell." Alistair grinned.

Stephen continued to his bike, saddled up, and rode back toward his building with the stars and moon still shining brightly above, knowing he would sleep a little easier tonight.

Bernie stood in the middle of a largely empty studio apartment. Stephen watched Bernie walk around, first sliding his hand along brick, then looking at the exposed beams overhead. He walked over to the window, which ran nearly the length of the room. The sounds of the large overhead ceiling fan and the echoing of footsteps filled the air.

"Well, it took me a month to the day to get all the work finished. What do you think, Uncle Bernie?"

"I think you should have come by more often."

"Yeah, yeah. I know. You've been worried about me. I get it. But things have been mostly good. I've been dealing, you know."

"Yeah, I know." Bernie turned toward Stephen. "You did a fine job. Did you put the kitchen in yourself? Or was it already there?"

"Oh, it was there. But I basically scrapped it and started over. It was outdated."

"And these hardwood floors—beautiful!"

"Thanks. I had some help installing them. But I picked them out and did a good portion of the work on them too. It's hand-scraped wood."

"Has Patty seen the place yet?" Bernie continued looking around.

"Nope. She saw it the day I picked it out. But that's it. There's plenty of space here. If I ever need to throw up a wall, there's room."

"Like a nursery?"

"Whoa! Hey! Slow your roll. I was only thinking about acoustics, aesthetics, and stuff."

Bernie laughed. "How's work?"

"Good. I've met with all the company heads. They're decent enough and smart too. They've been helpful. But Vincent was right. The biggest part of my job is people, settling issues between people, dealing with people's complaints, and so on. Vincent handles all the legal stuff for me. The decisions though, they're all on me. It's a lot."

"You and Patty?"

Stephen smiled. "We're doing really well. She's going back home to spend time with her family for the Fourth of July."

"Speaking of which, are you coming over for the Fourth?"

"Sorry. I can't. Vincent invited me to go with him to his mom's. She lives in Kentucky. It'll be a long weekend. We're leaving tomorrow night and will be back Tuesday."

Bernie pulled up a stool and sat at the counter next to Stephen. Stephen saw he had something on his mind.

"Bernie, what's bothering you?"

"I don't know. There's just something about that guy that just don't sit right with me. Ah, maybe it's nothing. But he's strange."

Stephen chuckled. "Yeah, he's odd. He was homeschooled. He had private tutors and was basically kept at home. He wasn't socialized very well growing up. Vincent's a little different and knows it, but he's getting better."

Bernie still looked worried. Stephen chose not to press the matter.

"Where's Bernard been?"

"What?" Bernie shifted in his seat as though it suddenly became uncomfortable.

"Well, he's out of college now. I hoped he'd be at Waltz's funeral."

"Yeah, that would've been nice. But I haven't heard from the boy. After college, he went to Europe for the summer. Said he'd call when he got back, probably next month."

"Bernie?"

"Yeah?"

"We haven't really talked about Bernard much. If this Mighty stuff is a family thing, where does Bernard fit in? Does he have a gift? Does he know?"

Bernie rubbed the back of his head and appeared think for a moment. "Sometimes this stuff skips family members. They don't get the right gene or somethin'. I can't say I fully understand that part. Usually those members still find themselves working in the organization. Not all of the Mighty have gifts. In fact, there are more that don't than do. They're sort of like foot soldiers and support. They're very important.

Bernard's mom wanted to wait to see if he developed a gift. After losing my brother, she didn't want Bernard involved unless he had to be."

"So, he knows nothing about it?"

Bernie shook his head. "We never told him."

"That's his heritage. Don't you think he has a right to know and make that choice for himself?" Stephen struggled with the thought of not being able to share all this with Bernard. He also understood Waltz kept the truth from him to protect him. "What if his abilities were latent and didn't show up until later, like mine?"

"Stephen, it's alright. He doesn't ever need to know."

"Not need to know, you're kidding, right?" Stephen got up and paced the floor. "I've come to realize that I'm in the middle of something big, like it or not. I know why I was kept in the dark. From what I understand, there was no reason to keep Bernard clueless. At least after he turned eighteen, someone should have told him. He needs to know."

"Stephen, you can't talk to Bernard about it."

"Oh, really? I can't?" Stephen stopped and stared Bernie down. I don't believe you get to tell me what I can and can't do. Unless you think you can stop me.

"Hold on a second, Stephen. What the heck is that about? It's not like that at all."

Stephen breathed a deep sigh, and his shoulders drooped as he walked over to the window.

"Stephen, did something happen?"

"The nightmares are back."

"Ah. That's what's got you on edge."

"Yeah. They're affecting my emotions a bit. And that's not all. I've been having a new one, of sorts. I'm in the darkness, and someone is there with me. Whoever it is doesn't say a word. But I can feel him. I feel hatred. When I realize that I'm in my own mind with someone else, I wake up. Each time, I feel the hatred more clearly, like I'm getting tuned into it."

"Well, I was afraid that more stuff would start with Waltz gone. Running into the Mighty at his funeral didn't help. Waltz was concerned with people finding out about you for a reason."

"Yeah, and what reason is that?"

"Stephen, if you continue to learn to control your powers, there's no telling what you can accomplish. Your power is greater than you know. Powers range."

"Yeah, I know. You guys told me this months ago. There are the classes. Then, it's different for each person. No two are exactly the same."

"Right. But most people's powers are more subtle."

"What do you mean?"

"Okay. Let's say that someone else had your ability. You know how you get a sense of people—their emotions, their moods and such—just by being around them? Well, that would be the extent of the gift for most people. Stephen, what you can do, the things you're capable of, they're nearly unheard of. Waltz wasn't one to brag, but he was very powerful too. That's how he retained some abilities. After disbanding the triune and retiring, he should have had little to no power left. He should only have been able to train you by telling you, not showing you. But you are stronger than even he was. And I think there's more to learn about you and your powers."

"Why didn't Waltz tell me? I mean, he told me I was powerful but not like that."

"Waltz was one-hundred-percent Mighty, even after. He never wavered in his conviction. Not all of us are like that. I'm more along the lines of balance. I feel if either side became too strong, it would be game over for us all. Stephen, I believe you are strong enough to do what no one before you has done—walk your own path. I don't think you need us, any of us. Both sides should feel threatened by your existence. You could choose to let Mighty and Fallen fight it out on their own."

"If what you told me is true, Bernie, I can see why I upset the status quo. I'd exist outside the rules."

"No, son. You'd *make* the rules!" Bernie got up and walked over to place a hand on Stephen's shoulders. "Listen, I can see this is upsetting you a bit. I know it's different from what Waltz might have said. I'm not saying he lied. We just saw things differently." He looked around. "Hey! You have a nice place here and are doing well for yourself. I'm proud of you. I know he would be too. You did a great job."

"Thanks." Stephen lost his excitement. "Look, I need to tidy up a bit before Patty comes over. And you've given me a lot to think about. How about we talk more when I get back from the weekend?"

"Yeah, that's a good idea. Love ya, kid."

"Love you too, Uncle Bernie."

Stephen walked Bernie to the door and stood at the top of the steps until Bernie disappeared. Afterward, he went back inside and did just what he said. Stephen tidied up by putting away a few tools that were still out and cleaning the place again, one more time. All the while, Bernie's words played over and over in his mind like a broken record. Stephen laughed to himself at first, thinking about how powerful he could be. His thoughts quickly turned to focus on the fact that Waltz might not have told him everything. He mopped vigorously as old emotions bubbled to the surface. He soon remembered, however, that Waltz's message spoke clearly about that, saying there was more for Stephen to discover. Waltz also cautioned him to be careful in trusting others, but Bernie made sense.

What did not make sense to Stephen was why Bernie disagreed with Waltz so much but kept Bernard's heritage a secret too, like Waltz did with him. The relationship Waltz and Bernie shared looked stranger each day. Yet, they remained Stephen's family through the years.

By the time Patty showed up, Stephen settled on continuing as he had been, taking one day at a time. Patty, on the other hand, moved full speed ahead. When she arrived, she immediately took to suggesting decorations and new furnishings. Her excitement gave him a new focus. She loved his choices of color and materials, and even suggested various plans for their future. He only objected strongly on one item, expanding the kitchen area.

"Where's your mind at?" Patty asked

"Huh?" Stephen turned from the window to face Patty.

"I've been talking about how excited I am to finally get to go spend some quality time with my niece, and you're just not here."

"Oh, sorry. Bernie was here earlier. He laid some stuff on me. Not a big deal really."

"Well, it seems like a big deal." Patty stepped closer. "You've been a little distant lately. I know Waltz's passing has been hard on you. But you've kind of distanced yourself some."

"I'm sorry. I've been working on this place and trying to figure out what I'm doing with the company."

"Yeah, I know. It's just that I want to help. And I don't want distance. I want to get closer. I love you, Stephen. I'm here for you. And I can help."

"I just need a little more time to get *me* settled. I promise. Let me do that, and I'll let you help. Some of what I'm dealing with, you can't help. I don't even know how to help myself. It's one day at a time. Besides, I hope getting away with Vincent will be a good de-stresser."

"I have noticed you two spending more time together lately." Patty grinned slyly. "Should I be worried?"

"Ew! No!" Stephen laughed. "Waltz trusted him."

"I know. He's been helping you get grounded with the business. I see all the paperwork and notes from your meetings, remember?"

"Oh, yeah."

"Well, I better get going. You need to pack for the trip before it gets too late." Patty grabbed her purse from the kitchen counter, looked around the room, and stopped at the bed. "Perhaps we could go shopping for furniture when you get back."

"Sure, sounds good."

Stephen walked Patty to the door and kissed her goodbye. He lingered at the door while she headed down the steps.

"Have fun, babe!"

"I'm sure I will," he replied.

࿐ ࿐

Stephen stood surrounded by darkness. As much as he tried, he could not see anything else in the room with him. He knew someone was there, lurking in the dark. He felt a presence. His powers gave him a confidence and boldness that most could never experience. Searching the room with his mind, trying to see the only way he could, he sought out the other's identity.

Who are you? Why are you hiding from me?

He waited. Nothing. He tried again.

I know you're there. You can't hide from me forever. If you really knew who I am, you'd answer me!

Slowly, ominous laughter echoed, softly at first. It continued growing louder and louder, until Stephen's head hurt from the noise.

Stop it. It continued. I said, stop it!

The laughter stopped. Stephen knew he had hurt whoever was lurking nearby.

A voice rang through the darkness. I know who you are! We'll continue this later.

For the first time, the person spoke to him, but Stephen did not recognize the voice. He could not even be certain it was male or female. He knew what the voice wanted to say, though he never heard it speak.

He woke with a jolt in the passenger seat of Vincent's luxury sedan.

"Are you okay?" Vincent asked.

Stephen looked around and rubbed his head where it stuck to the window. The sunset shone as bright as ever from behind them. Tall trees passed by on either side as the car clung to the twists and turns in the road.

"Yeah, I'm fine." Through a break in the trees, he saw they road along a ridge with only more trees, farmland, and scattered houses. "How long was I asleep?"

"Long enough."

Stephen sat up from his slouched position. "So, are we close?"

"Yes, we're nearly there." Vincent kept his eyes on the road ahead. "Who were you talking to?"

"Huh? Oh, in my dream? I'm not sure." Stephen changed the subject. "Why did you invite me to your mom's?"

"I noticed that you have been staying away from the shelter. I guessed it has something to do with Waltz. I did not want you to be alone. Besides, it will give us an opportunity to get to know each other better." Vincent grinned as best he could. It still looked awkward.

"Well, thank you." Stephen looked back out the window. "We are sleeping in separate beds, right?"

Vincent rolled his eyes. Stephen noticed how uncomfortable jovial banter made Vincent. He decided to keep working on him.

Through the woods a large lake appeared as they continued down a gravel road. It reminded Stephen of his travels while he had been away. He often stayed at a campground to get away from the noise of other people's thoughts and emotions.

"How long is this road?"

"Well, this driveway is pretty long. Fortunately, we are here."

They rounded a row of spruce trees and a large Victorian home appeared. Primarily stone, it looked more like a castle to Stephen than a house. The lawn looked neat, but the shrubs needed shearing. Parts of the house had ivy growing up the lower walls. A few shingles on the roof looked to be missing.

They parked around back, where a woman with long, unkempt black hair and wearing a yellow nightgown came down the steps to greet them as they parked. She wore no makeup and did not seem overly concerned about her appearance. She wore no shoes.

"Stephen, I forgot to tell you something about my mother. She is a little crazy. She nearly lost her mind several years back and has been on the mend ever since."

Stephen nodded. He felt compassion for her, having seen for himself inside the minds of mentally disturbed people. He even caused it a time or two. It was never pretty. Thoughts ran rampant amid emotions that overwhelmed, but Stephen understood. He related it to how he felt when he first returned to Waltz, before he learned to control the memories, emotions, and sort through the ones that did not belong.

The two approached Vincent's mother. She looked familiar to Stephen, somehow. Perhaps the fact that he came so close to being like her, or that the guilt he felt for driving others insane weighed deeply. Regardless, he empathized and felt compassion for her. He remembered very little of his own mom, and only imagined what it must be like for Vincent to see her suffer.

"Mother, how are you?" Vincent set his bag down and gave his mother a big hug. It was the first gesture of grand emotion Stephen had witnessed of Vincent.

"Good, good. How's my boy?" She seemed fully of energy.

"Fine, Mother." Vincent motioned to Stephen. "This is my friend I told you about—Stephen."

Vincent's mother turned to greet Stephen but froze for a moment. A look of confusion fell on her face. Just as quickly, the expression left, to be replaced by a whimsical smile.

"Stephen, very nice to meet you." Stephen reached forward to shake her hand. "No, No. Give us a hug." She threw her arms around him. Overwhelmed with compassion, he returned the hug, sensing something terribly wrong inside her.

"Stephen, my mother, Marie," Vincent said.

Marie started up the stairs back toward the house. "Well, come now. Don't be slow. Bring your things."

The two grabbed their bags and followed her inside.

Stephen followed Vincent into a large living area. A grand open fireplace sat positioned in the middle, a family room to one side and an activity room to the other.

"This is a beautiful home." Stephen ran his hand along the stone accents on the wall. "Just gorgeous. You grew up here?" he asked Vincent.

"I did. I had the finest tutors but seldom left the grounds. I remember going out when I was much younger. After Dad left, we did not go out much—not until I became an adult."

"If you didn't go out much, how did you get what you needed—groceries, packages, clothes, and stuff?"

"Vincent! It is very good to see you home, sir!"

Stephen turned to see a butler standing in the doorway they just entered. "Ah, help. Of course! How silly of me."

Vincent grinned sheepishly. "Phillip, it is very good to see you too. This is my friend Stephen. He will be staying with us for the weekend. Will you please have his things taken to his room?"

"Gladly, sir. Which room will Stephen be staying in?"

Vincent looked at Stephen for a moment. "Put him in the 'Big Blue' room. He will be comfortable there."

"Right away, sir." Phillip grabbed the bags and disappeared back the way he came.

"Where'd your mom go?"

"She went straight toward the kitchen, probably to see how Anna is coming along with dinner."

"Anna?"

"Yes, Anna, the chef."

"Oh, of course, the chef," Stephen kidded.

Stephen continued walking around, looking on in amazement at the grandeur. He never saw such high ceilings in a house before. The wood and stonework looked exquisite, each perfect in craftsmanship and placement. Through an archway he saw a lovely wooden staircase located just inside the front entrance. "Do you mind if I have a look?" Stephen motioned toward the staircase.

"Not at all."

As Stephen entered the foyer, he noticed a large crystal chandelier hanging above him from a ceiling that opened up to the second floor. The staircase ended in a balcony that encircled the chandelier.

Beside the staircase stood a table with a few picture frames displayed on it. Stephen walked over and picked up one of the photos. “Look at this. It’s little Vincent Abbott.”

“Yes, I was a bit chubby then.”

“Nah. Most every kid has a little baby fat that lingers.” He picked up the next frame. “Your mom?”

“Yes, several years ago before she had her meltdown.”

“She’s gorgeous!”

Stephen held the frame closer. He knew he recognized her. His eyes widened, taking in the gravity of his present situation, as he fumbled with the frame.

“Uh, Stephen. You are staring a little too long at my Mom.”

“I-I know her. Or, rather, I met her.”

“What?”

“It was years ago. I...uh...before, when...when she was like this.” Stephen handed the picture to Vincent.

“That’s not possible.”

“It is. She was in St. Louis.”

“I remember she used to go to St. Louis when I was younger. She stopped when Father left us. However, she did come see me there about five years ago, not long after I began practicing law on my own.” Vincent placed his hand on Stephen’s shoulder. “She was starting to get out more, trying to enjoy life again.”

Stephen looked at Vincent, trying to hide the pain he felt. Sweat formed in his palms, as his heart ached. Here he stood, facing a wrong of his own making.

"How did you meet?" Vincent paused. His expression changed as he appeared in thought for a moment. "She started losing her mind right after her visit. Did you see her then? Did something happen?"

"It's more complicated than that, much more complicated. I bumped into her, literally. Besides, it's in the past now."

"There you are, boys. Vincent, I do hope you've been a hospitable guest." Marie walked over to them and looked down at the picture in Vincent's hand. "How gorgeous. What a lovely young lady. Vincent, are you seeing this young lady? You must bring her over."

"No, Mother. This is you when you were younger."

"Oh, right. I certainly was lovely." She passed by and continued walking into the next room. "Dinner will be ready soon. Please see Stephen to his room so he may freshen up." She disappeared again.

Vincent continued, "I apologize, Stephen. My mom can be a handful at times. Are you certain you are still okay staying with us?"

"I'm certain." The two started up the stairs. "Vincent, there is more to the story, much more. Waltz told me to trust you above everyone else. I'm willing to do that. But I think your mom is right. Let me relax a moment, freshen up, and we'll talk."

"Agreed. It was a long drive. You must be exhausted from all that sleeping." Vincent grinned. Stephen followed him to the room. They met Phillip on the way.

"I was just coming for you, sir."

"I'll show him the way, Phillip."

"Yes, sir." Phillip continued on.

They arrived at a door. "Here you go."

"Big Blue?" asked Stephen.

Vincent nodded.

Stephen opened the door. As he walked in, he looked around and laughed. Moments before, he worried about how to explain everything to Vincent, including the full truth of what happened between him and Marie. Laughing felt good. He laughed uncontrollably and let go of the stress. For now, he felt better.

"Patty told you about the pajamas." He barely got the words out while catching his breath. He took a deep breath to calm himself and walked further into the room. A large quilt hung on one wall. It displayed Superman flying through the air with the American flag as the backdrop and the words, "He wages a never-ending battle for truth, justice, and the American way." Stephen read it aloud. The comforter set, curtains, lampshades—all of it portrayed Superman. The blue walls, gold trim, and red curtain paled next to the red and blue furniture, with gold accents.

Vincent laughed. Stephen turned with a start. "I don't think I've ever heard you truly laugh." It was a loud, easily distinguishable laugh. After a moment, Stephen asked, "What is the deal with this room? It's great!"

"It was mine when I was younger. I loved it so much that when I got older, I asked for another room and kept this just as it was."

"It's incredible."

"It is. And, we have something in common." Vincent motioned to Stephen's things on the bed. "I will leave you to freshen up. We can talk in a while." With that, Vincent left.

The relief brought by the Superman-themed room lasted only a moment, as Stephen's thoughts shifted back to Marie and the torment she lived in ever since their encounter five years ago.

How do I explain that her situation is my fault?

Stephen listened for thoughts in the house, trying to take his mind away from the conversation sure to soon take place. He heard all but Vincent and Marie. Her mind appeared guarded but not in the same way as Vincent's. His remained locked behind an impenetrable wall. Hers, however, appeared to be just beyond reach, as though his power extended only so far before failing to find her.

Stephen lay on the bed staring at the ceiling, his eyes trained on the propeller-powered Superman circling overhead. Slowly, he drifted off.

Stephen stood alone and surrounded by black once again.

Hello? I know you're there. I can feel you. What do you want?

No response, nothing. Something hung in the air that Stephen did not want to accept. Something familiar, yet foreign—fear. He felt the fear of others time and time again, but not his own fear. He feared so little. Why did he feel it now?

"Stephen?" Vincent's voice rang through the darkness.

Stephen sat up, ready for anything or anyone. He looked around to find he was still surrounded by Superman. Vincent stood in the doorway.

"Sorry I startled you. Dinner is ready." Vincent seldom showed emotion. Stephen, however, noticed the slightest frown.

"I...I must have dozed off for a moment. I'll be right down."

"You must have." Vincent looked at Stephen's bag, still packed. "You must have been tired."

Stephen looked at the bag. "Yeah, I don't even remember lying down."

"We will be waiting. At the bottom of the stairs, take a right. You will see us." Vincent closed the door as he walked out.

Stephen leaned forward, placed his face in his hands, and massaged his temples with his fingers for a moment. "Well, let's get this over with."

Stephen found the dining room with no trouble. Someone had prepared three place settings at a grand table meant to entertain many more. Marie and Vincent sat at the far end, with Marie at the head. Vincent sat to her left and an empty seat and place setting to her right. He looked at the empty chairs. He knew of at least two servants in the house. "What about the others?"

"Stephen, so glad you could join us. My boy, Vincent, just got home. Have you met Vincent?"

"Uh, yes, ma'am." Stephen looked at Vincent, not sure what else to say.

"Please, come sit. The food is ready to be served." Vincent motioned to the empty seat across the table. "The staff eat elsewhere."

Stephen pulled the large sliding doors closed, walked over to the doorway behind Marie, and closed that door too.

"What are you doing?" Vincent asked.

"We need to talk in private."

"If it is that important, we should probably step into a more private room." Vincent moved to get up.

"No. It concerns her too." Stephen looked at Marie. "You *do* recognize me, don't you?"

Marie's smile of oblivious bliss changed to sadness as she looked up at Stephen. Their eyes met. She quickly looked to Vincent. "We should eat now, so we can have dessert."

"Stephen, what is this about?" Vincent asked.

"Vincent, you're gonna think I'm crazy. I believe your mother is the way she is now because her mind was pushed in a way it never should have been pushed. Something unexpected happened to her the last time she was in St. Louis—me."

"You are beginning to worry me. What are you talking about?"

Stephen sat in the seat across from Vincent. "In Waltz's video to me, among his last words was the remark that I should trust you. Vincent, I'm about to trust you with something I have only ever trusted one other person with—Waltz. First, I have to ask you to trust me. I have to make this right."

"Stephen, I do trust you."

"Good." Stephen placed his hand on Marie's shoulder. "Marie, I'm sorry. I never meant to hurt you."

Marie looked at Stephen. *There you are.* He accessed her mind.

Stephen looked inside, searching. Her thoughts sounded fragmented and scrambled. She remained afraid and confused. *What is out of place? Show me what isn't right.* He saw flashes of memory and experienced brief emotions that made no connection. *Show me when we first met. I know you remember.*

Stephen stared at a younger version of himself through Marie's eyes. They stood at the edge of the water in Kiener Plaza. The eighteen-year-old Stephen wore dirty old clothes with holes in them. It looked just as he remembered—only, from Marie's perspective. He bumped into her and heard her harsh thoughts.

Lazy child. Dirty. He should be in school, learning to be productive. I'd hate to support another one on unemployment.

The face of his younger self looking back at him turned from surprise to anger. His eyes glowed a brighter blue. Stephen sensed a hatred and anger that he had not known in a long time. He felt an uncontrollable urge for Marie to throw herself in the pool, which he did. Lifting herself out of the pool, she looked back at his younger self. Marie's mind filled with loathing and self-hate. She pulled at her hair and clothes. "Meaningless, cruel," she said. "What's the point? Hide at home. Vicious world."

That's it. I made you hate yourself. The feelings I felt toward you, I embedded in you.

Stephen reached and placed a hand on the side of Marie's head, then cradled it. He needed to search through the memories again, go further. Flashes of various memories continued to go through his mind. Marie shook and groaned.

"Stephen, what are you doing?" Vincent grabbed hold of him, trying to pull him away. "Let go of her."

His efforts proved useless. Stephen and Marie were linked. Nothing could pull them apart.

In her memories, he saw Marie as a younger woman, in a wedding gown. In front of her, he looked at the face of a young man with black hair and brown eyes, much like Vincent, only not. The man smiled with such love and adoration for her.

"Elizabeth Marie Cohen, I will love you until I die."

Stephen pulled back out of Marie's mind as more images flashed through his. He sat looking at her. A single tear ran down her cheek. Stephen wiped it from her cheek with his thumb, releasing her face to hold her hand.

"I'm so sorry. I was a kid. I didn't know." A tear ran down Stephen's cheek too.

"What just happened?" Vincent's voice quivered as he stood next to Marie, looking at Stephen.

Marie turned to Vincent, placing her hand on his. "Mr. Stockton here just saved me." Marie smiled.

Stephen and Vincent looked at Marie, then to each other. Stephen wondered how she knew he was Waltz's son. He tried to think of something to say, some explanation to discount what she said. He wished he could see Vincent's mind. He turned back to Marie. "Actually, my last name is Cross."

"Nonetheless, you are his son." Marie smiled at him.

"How? What?" Vincent pleaded.

"You mean how did he save me? Or, how did I know he was Waltz's son and the last of his bloodline?"

"Elizabeth Marie...you were the one from Waltz's triune that fell."

Vincent sat back down, mouth half open, looking back and forth between the two.

"Vincent, don't act so surprised. You grew up with the stories, son."

"But Waltz? He was one of the Mighty? And part of your triune?"

"Yes, son. He's the protector who tried to make me see reason. When he failed, he did what was needed."

"I thought that was nonsense." Vincent looked on for a moment. "So, you really had powers and lost them—"

"—and," Marie said, "finally came to see reason when I was no longer drunk with the allure of it all. You were just a toddler then."

"So, how did Stephen fix your mind?"

"Young Stephen inadvertently caused my issues as he had never been taught about his powers. Being the child of two Mighties, he shouldn't have powers at all. However, his powers awakened in a very strong fashion when he heard my thoughts. My thoughts made him angry. Only, what he couldn't know was that my thoughts were directed at some other young man, not him. The child was rude, a lazy delinquent." Marie looked at Stephen. "You bumped into me at the wrong moment."

Stephen sat stunned for a moment. "I...I didn't know." He looked at Vincent and continued. "I filled her with hatred for herself, making her crazy. To be honest, she's incredibly strong to have survived like that." Stephen wiped a tear from his face. "I can't tell you how sorry I am."

"It's okay. You didn't know about your powers. None of us did. If we had known, Waltz would have trained you, and it wouldn't have happened." Marie turned to her son. "Stephen took the hatred and replaced it with a memory I had long lost, a memory of your father on our wedding day."

"Before my father turned full-on bad?" Vincent leaned in toward Marie. "Was he kind then?"

"Very." Marie smiled. "I thought I could help him, to keep him from becoming one of the Fallen."

"Wait, your dad was one of the Fallen?"

"He is still." Vincent lowered his head. "He left when Mom changed and renounced the ways of the Fallen."

"Well, now I know why you're special," Stephen retorted.

"What are you talking about? How is he special?" Marie asked.

"Vincent has powers."

"That is impossible. The child of a Fallen does not have powers, let alone the child of two." Vincent recounted from memory.

"Vincent, you're finally wrong about something, because you do have powers. Besides, your mom here isn't exactly one of the Fallen anymore."

"But Dad is." Vincent donned a confused expression.

Stephen shrugged. He did not know very much about Mighty or Fallen and assumed there must be an explanation.

"What powers? What has he done?" Mary looked surprised.

"Your son, Vincent, is the only person I have never been able to read."

Marie looked at Vincent with amazement. "You're a protector, a priest."

"Excuse me?"

"She's right," Stephen said. "It all fits. That's one of the reasons Waltz trusted you so much. He knew you wouldn't tell anyone about me and that no one could extract the information from your mind." Stephen stood quickly, sending the chair crashing to the floor. "Wait! How did Waltz help you get started?"

"He got me to go out on my own and help people."

"There has to be more to it. Think, son." Marie grabbed Vincent's hand.

Vincent leaned back into his chair. "Meditation..." he mumbled.

"What?" Stephen and Marie asked in unison.

"I was not fitting in at the firm. I was doing very well, but not fitting in caused me to feel stressed. Waltz began talking with me and convinced me to have a Bible study with him. Sometimes we would spend a moment quietly meditating on what we had read or the day in general. On particularly stressful days he would have me picture a wall around me that kept everything else out. After a while, nothing got to me anymore."

"The wall. When I would try to read your mind, it felt like running into a wall." Stephen laughed. "All this time I was working with a protector and never knew it."

They continued to talk that evening and throughout the weekend. Marie explained that she understood what happened around her the past five years but was unable to process or respond to it in a normal manner. Vincent never suspected anything. He always believed the Mighty and the Fallen to be tales. Stephen picked Marie's brain for stories about a younger Waltz and made plans to help Vincent further train his gift. Before long, the weekend ended, and it the men packed for St. Louis.

Stephen loaded their bags into the trunk of the car as Vincent said goodbye to his mother.

"Stephen, don't think you're getting out of here without a hug." Marie walked around the back of the car with Vincent as Stephen closed the trunk.

"Walter would be so very proud of you." Marie threw her arms around Stephen. "Doing what you did was not easy. Sharing yourself with us and healing my mind the way you did is not something many Mighty would have done." She stepped back and held Stephen at a distance. "You aren't alone. You'll always have family here. As for the Mighty, it's a journey you'll have to take. I can't make it for you. And, I can't give you shortcuts. I have faith you'll get there though. When you do, I'll tell you anything you want to know. But I don't believe you'll need me to at that point."

"Thank you. I think you've given me more this weekend than I gave you. You should come and see Bernie."

"No." Marie walked only a couple of steps before turning back to Stephen. "Bernie cannot know about me. No one else can. I'm better off if they still think I'm crazy."

"Why?" Vincent asked.

She grabbed Vincent's hand. "If the Mighty know, it won't be long before your father finds out. I don't want to chance him trying to find you—not now."

"Okay, Mother. No one will know."

They hugged one more time. Marie stood on the steps and watched them drive away.

"Well, are you ready to get back to the city?" Stephen looked at Vincent, who appeared more serious than ever.

"Vincent, are you okay? You know I can't read your mind, so help me out." Stephen's attempt at humor went unnoticed.

"I need your help, Stephen."

"Sure. With what?"

"I have to find my father."

Stephen protested, "What? Your mom said—"

"She's afraid of him. She wants no one to know because of him. I remember him being abusive to her before he left. I want her freed of him."

"Okay. I'll help you. But you have to help me find the person responsible for Waltz's death."

"Deal."

"What's your father's name?"

"Anthony Abate."

The rest of the ride home remained mostly silent; they chatted very little, but Stephen's mind went back to his task. The weekend detour had been great. Yet, a daunting task waited for him in Saint Louis. Plus, he now had to help Vincent find *his* father as well.

Stephen sat on the couch in his apartment, looking out the window as the rain pounded against the glass. He did not mind it. In fact, the sound soothed him. It helped to ease all that lingered in his mind. A week ago, he made Vincent a promise to help him find his father. He hadn't a clue as to where to begin.

He carried so much weight on his shoulders—finding the person responsible for Waltz's death, training Vincent, and helping to find Vincent's father. Not to mention the choice that had been looming over him ever since he first learned of the Mighty: follow the Son of God and join them or risk being rejected, even hunted, as one of the Fallen.

A door opened and shut. The sound of heels crossing the hardwood floor echoed in the spacious room. A warm touch relaxed his tense muscles as soft hands rubbed deep into his shoulders and neck. It felt good; exactly what he needed.

"You're very tight, Babe." More than the rain, Patty's voice soothed him and melted the troubles of his mind. "Has the office been that stressful?"

Stephen turned and pulled her over the couch into his lap, laughing as she slapped his bare arm. "I guess I just have a lot on my mind. Waltz's death has been hard." He had not thought much about his business—another weight on his shoulders.

Patty grabbed his chin and kissed him, lingering just a moment.

"I needed that," he said with a smile.

"There's more where that came from," Patty replied.

Stephen leaned in for another kiss. Patty pushed him away. "But not right now. We have to get going. So, get up and put a shirt on." Patty stood and walked back around the couch to grab her purse from the floor.

"Why won't you tell me where we're going?" Stephen protested as he snatched up a shirt and stuck his arms through the sleeves.

"If I did, it wouldn't be much of a surprise, now would it?" Patty turned to Stephen and dusted off the shoulders of his shirt. "Really? You couldn't have pressed it?" She gave him a look.

"Okay, it's that kind of surprise." Stephen walked over to the closet and grabbed a dry-cleaned shirt still in the plastic. "You didn't tell me I needed to dress nice for the occasion."

"Fair enough. Please hurry." Patty fiddled with the handle of her purse while he grabbed a clean shirt from his wardrobe and changed.

He grinned. "This better?"

"Much." She smiled. "Button it, and let's go."

The two rode in Patty's small beat-up car, heading downtown. Stephen attempted to find out what secret she kept the entire way. He did not like surprises. Patty, however, proved better than most at keeping secrets and refused to say a word. They parked downtown, near Gateway Park, and walked away from the arch. It was not long afterward that Stephen realized where they were going.

As they approached Kiener Plaza, mixed emotions began to fill his heart. He experienced so much in this park. Waltz found him, his gift awakened, and Waltz died all in this same spot. On top of that, he spent countless hours playing there as a kid and helping Waltz hand out necessities to the homeless. It seemed that all the good that had taken place here sat in the shadow of Waltz's death; forever marred.

Stephen noticed several people grouped together underneath a covering of umbrellas. As he and Patty approached, he recognized Vincent, Johnathan, and several others from the office. "Hey, guys. What's going on?"

"Stephen." Johnathan stepped forward. "We know this place meant a lot to you and Waltz. He told each one of us on multiple occasions how fond he was of this very spot. Where we're standing is the spot where he found you. We can only imagine that this place has just as much meaning for you as it did Waltz."

Stephen held back his emotions no longer. Tears ran down his cheeks. Patty wiped them away and pulled herself close to his side.

Vincent spoke next. "We want to bring some joy back to this place—not only for you, but for the many lives

Waltz touched." Several people that lingered nearby joined the group. "In this gathering, you will find people that were homeless whom he sheltered, hungry whom he fed, even imprisoned whom he visited. Waltz was a light to this world, showing just how brightly one light can shine in the darkness."

The group in front of him parted. In the center stood a small tree and monument. On the monument was inscribed:

In honor of Ian Walter "Waltz" Stockton

He let the Light of Christ shine ever so brightly.

Isaiah 9:2

"The people walking in darkness have seen a great light;

On those living in the land of darkness a light has dawned."

"Stephen." Bernie stepped through the crowd. "Waltz will be missed. I know he was your light. He helped you in so many ways. Now it's time to find your own path. I hope this will help you do that."

Stephen hugged him tight. He sometimes forgot how big Bernie was, until he hugged him. Bernie squeezed him back.

"Thank you," Stephen said as he moved back to Patty's side. "Thank you, all." Stephen raised his voice for everyone to hear. "Waltz's death was the hardest moment I've endured. And you're right—this place has meant a lot to me over the years. Waltz dying here tainted those memories." He turned and looked at the arch, lit and standing high above the rooftops. "Just as the Gateway Arch stands as a sentinel, forever guarding the memory of those who left their homes, and even families, to expand westward, this monument will stand to remind others of a man who devoted his life to loving others and spreading that love. It will remind me to be more like him, to stand boldly for what I believe in, and never waiver."

Vincent went and stood next to Stephen. "Now, we ask you all to join us back at the office, where we will have refreshments. And you'll have an opportunity to look at plans for a new kitchen for the homeless that will be built in Waltz's honor."

As the crowd dispersed, Stephen lingered. He stared at the monument. He thought it a nice gesture, even though it would not bring him back. A small, gentle hand squeezed his shoulder.

"Babe, are you okay?"

"Yeah, I'm fine."

"You don't seem fine." Patty paused for a response. Nothing. "You haven't really talked to me much about this past month. I know this has been hard for you, but I'm here. I can help."

"I wish that were true." Stephen turned to face her. He realized by the look on her face that what he said hurt her. "Patty, there are some things I need to keep to myself right now. I can't explain it. I'm sorry. I'm not going to lie and tell you nothing's going on. You deserve better than lies. But I can't tell you about it, not right now. I've just got a lot on my plate, stuff you really don't want on yours yet."

Patty tried to interrupt, but Stephen did not let her. "I know you'd gladly help me. And maybe you could handle it. It's stuff I don't want you to have to handle yet. Someday, maybe."

Vincent walked up. "Sorry to interrupt. Patty, would you mind if I drove Stephen back to the office? I need to talk with him briefly about something sensitive."

"No, not at all." Patty quickly kissed Stephen on the cheek. "I love you."

Patty walked to her car, leaving the two men standing in the rain.

"No umbrella?" Stephen asked.

"No, I loaned mine out."

They walked to Vincent's car as the rain turned from a drizzle to a downpour. Water dripped from their clothes onto the car's leather seats. Stephen tried to find something to soak up the water but had no such luck.

"It will be fine," Vincent said with a smile.

Stephen sat, quiet. Vincent started the car and waited for an opening in the traffic.

"We haven't really spoken about my dad since we got back," Vincent said.

"I know. I've been thinking about it."

"I figured as much," Vincent replied. "I want you to stop."

"What? Why?"

"I am not ready yet. I need training and to learn more. And I need to help my friend. My father has waited this long; he can wait longer."

"Are you sure?"

"Very sure. It was not fair to throw more on you. I know I can count on you when the time comes. Right now, you need help, not a distraction."

"Thank you."

"Thank me by training me." Vincent pulled the car away from the curb. "Do you have any idea where to start?"

"Unfortunately, I do. We need help, someone we can trust."

"You want to tell Patty?"

"No," Stephen snapped. "Eventually, yes. Not now though. I was thinking of someone like us. I believe I know a person we might be able to trust. I'll need to meet with him and question him, if he agrees."

"Call him then."

"That's the problem. I don't know how to get in touch with him. He was at Waltz's funeral, and he found me again later."

"How do you know you can trust him?"

"I don't, not one hundred percent. That's why we need to meet. But I have a feeling that if I couldn't trust him, I'd already know it."

"How so?" Vincent asked.

"I think the Mighty would be knocking at my door."

"Why not Bernie? Can he help?"

"I don't think he wants any part of this life anymore. He keeps cautioning me not to trust them—the Mighty. He might be right. But for now, at least, I don't see another option."

"I guess we better see what we can do to locate..."

"Alistair," Stephen replied. "But first, we have guests to entertain."

It took about ten minutes to get to the office. Vincent pulled into the parking lot at their office, and they made their way upstairs to join the others. Vincent made it a point to talk with people, something he committed to getting better at. Stephen shook hands and strategically moved through the crowd looking for Patty. He spotted her auburn hair easily and caught up to her in front of the plans and model of the kitchen. She was explaining it all to a blond-haired gentleman, whom he recognized immediately.

"I see, lass."

"I hope you're not here to try and steal my girl." The two turned and faced Stephen. "Alistair, I'm really glad to see you." Stephen reached forward to shake his hand.

"How ye doin'?" Alistair asked, his Scottish accent thicker than before.

"Good, and you?"

"I'm guid."

"I was just showing Alistair the plans for the homeless kitchen," Patty said.

"And?" Stephen looked at Alistair.

"Ye need to make sure the telly has footie." The three of them chuckled. "Stephen, I need to speak with ye for a few, if'n Ms. O'Connor can spare ye."

"It's fine, hon. There are plenty of people here I need to talk with anyway."

"Thanks." He motioned to Alistair. "This way."

The two walked back to Stephen's office. Stephen closed the door and motioned to a couple of chairs in the corner. "Please, sit." After an awkward moment, Stephen broke the silence. "You're accent is thicker than before."

"Yeah, it is. I've been back to Scotland. It always gets a bit thicker when I go home."

"Makes sense." Stephen tapped his fingers on the small table. "What are you doing here? I'm glad to see you and all. In fact, I was wondering how to get in touch with you. But why are you here?"

"Well, ye know 'bout me gift, how it works."

"Yeah, you see visions a day before it happens, and they guide you."

"Well, yesterday I had a vision of you and me sitting here. So, I came."

"Hmmm. Do you know why?"

"No clue. But just this morning I had another vision. I saw you, Vincent, and myself together. I'm guessing ye told him about your abilities."

"I did. Do you know why?"

"No. I just know that I need to be there tomorrow. If I have a vision with me in it, it serves as a suggestion. In other words, it's telling me that this is what needs to happen."

"Alistair, I need to go into your mind."

"What? You can do that?"

"Yes, it's my gift."

"You're a seer, a prophet?"

Stephen nodded.

"But I thought ye were a warrior."

"Why would you think that?" Stephen asked, sitting up a little straighter.

"Just the way ye handled yourself the last time we met." Alistair appeared in thought for a moment before shaking his head. "No matter. You need my permission to see inside my mind?"

"No," Stephen replied, "not at all. But I respect you. So, I'm asking. I need to be able to trust you. To trust you, I need to see inside your head. I'm leaving that decision up to you."

"If I say no?" Alistair asked.

"Then the vision you had this morning will be nothing more than that—a vision."

"I see. Heid doon, arse up."

"Excuse me?" Stephen did not understand.

"It's a Scottish expression. Translation, get on with it then." Alistair grinned.

Stephen looked into Alistair's mind and began searching. So much knowledge about the Mighty and the Fallen rested on the surface of Alistair's thoughts. However, Stephen searched for something that would show him Alistair could be trusted. He saw Sam and Anastasia sitting in a room with several others he did not recognize, although Alistair did. These people made up The Council of the Mighty, twelve in all. The room looked to be adorned in brilliant blue and purple tapestries. The council sat at a crescent shaped table covered with a red cloth. Council members wore white robes, each with a medallion hanging from a necklace and pendant on the collar that signified their class. Each had large colored cuffs around their wrists, signifying a hierarchy. Only Sam wore gold-colored cuffs. They questioned Alistair about Matthew.

"Yes, I had help."

"And who helped you?" Sam asked.

"I apologize. I cannot tell ye," Alistair replied.

"Why not?" a man with a French accent asked.

"I had a vision of today. All the questions were asked, and I refused to answer questions concerning this person."

"Why should that matter? We are the council," another demanded in a slavic accent.

Alistair looked at the man seated at the end. He appeared younger than the other members but older than Alistair.

"Novak," Anastasia chimed in, "when Alistair's visions include him, they serve as a recommended course of action, the way things should happen. It goes very badly when it doesn't happen the way the vision indicates."

Sam spoke up. "It's true. I believe most of the members also know this to be the truth."

Several nodded.

An Asian man next to Novak stood. "It's clear to me that the questioning is over. I believe we have all the answers the Lord intends us to have...for now."

"Thank you, Xiang." Alistair kneeled down and bowed low to the ground.

The council stood and returned the gesture with modest bows.

Stephen withdrew from Alistair's mind.

"You kept your word. You didn't tell," Stephen told him.

"As I said, it's not my secret to tell. Besides, I've not had visions that would make me think yer the enemy."

"Thank you."

"Stephen, I need to be honest with ye though. If ye ever do become the enemy, if ye don't make the right choice, the council will know. Ye have a choice to make. I sense that ye are still struggling with it. I get vague, fuzzy images of you in the future. They become clearer the closer they get. I like you. I hope ye make the right choice."

"I understand." Stephen walked over to his desk, then jotted something on a piece of paper. "This is my address and phone number. Meet us there tomorrow."

Alistair walked to the door. "Don't need it, mate. I saw it in me vision." He grinned and left Stephen holding the note.

Stephen wadded the paper and threw it in the trash can. "I should've figured."

The next day, Stephen, Vincent, and Alistair sat in Stephen's living room staring at one another in awkward silence. Vincent sat on the couch, while Alistair and Stephen sat in chairs on the other side of the coffee table. Lightning flashed outside the windows, and thunder echoed in the apartment.

"So, should we eat lunch first?" Stephen broke the silence and pulled out his phone. "I can order pizza."

"Probably not a good idea."

"Why not? I *am* hungry," Vincent interjected.

"Sometimes this type of training can make the uninitiated, well, sick."

"I'll order after a while." Stephen set his phone on the coffee table.

"Good idea," Vincent agreed.

"You're welcome, fellas." Alistair looked to Vincent. "So, yer a priest."

"Apparently so."

"But ye don't really know anything about using your powers."

"Correct."

"Stephen, show me what ye know."

"Show you?" Stephen gave him a puzzled look.

"Yeah. You and I, we're seers. Our gifts come from the mind. We can share things mentally. Where ye might damage some without any powers, or cause discomfort for someone with other powers, sharing thoughts or ideas with someone else who has mental powers should be harmless."

"Interesting. I'll give it a try." Stephen entered Alistair's mind and thought about all he knew of Vincent's gift, which was not much.

"What?" Alistair looked at Vincent, a confused look on his face. "That doesn't add up. Yer parents are Fallen."

"My father is. My mother is reformed. She was largely impacted by him. Eventually, he left."

"Amazing," Alistair exclaimed. "Don't worry, I won't tell a soul. It's not my secret to tell." He looked back to Stephen and smiled. "I guess we should get started. I think we should start with teaching him how to control the gift. Ye see, right now, he seems to have built some type of constant protection. Possibly, it's instinctual. For example, Stephen tries to read you and the wall goes up." He turned his chair to face Vincent. "Vin—can I call you that?"

Vincent shrugged while rolling his eyes. "Sure."

"Vin, I want ye to focus on the wall, meditate like Waltz had ye do. Only, when I tell ye, imagine the wall going down. Stephen is going to look inside your mind. I want ye to allow him to. Stephen, focus on his feelings while ye are in there. Got that?"

Stephen and Vincent both nodded.

Vincent closed his eyes, and his breathing slowed. After a moment, Alistair asked Vincent to lower the wall, then motioned to Stephen.

"It's down. I can feel him without entering his mind. I've never been able to sense him before."

"Can ye see inside?" Alistair sat on the edge of his seat.

Stephen tilted his head. "Yes, I can. Vincent, you don't have to be nervous."

"Vincent's nervous, huh?" Alistair's eyes roamed, as though looking for something. "Here's what ye do. See if ye can calm his nerves. Like ye shared yer thoughts with me, see if ye can gently share yer feelings and emotions with him, establish some type of link."

"I think it's working. Vincent, how do you feel?"

"Strangely, I do feel much calmer, even though I can feel you inside my mind. I am being affected by it. I cannot say how exactly."

"Vincent, you have a little bit of the dark side, don't you?" Stephen jested.

Stephen jerked back, knocking his chair to the floor. Alistair and Vincent both jumped to their feet. Alistair rushed to help Stephen up.

"You alright, mukker?"

"Yeah, I'm fine." Stephen dusted himself off. "What the heck was that?"

"Sorry, I panicked," Vincent said.

"What are ye panicking for?" Alistair looked at Vincent sternly.

"It's alright, Alistair," Stephen said. He still felt some type of connection with Vincent, although unable to see inside him anymore. *You alright? I know you're scared and what you're scared of. You don't have to be.*

Vincent nodded.

"Alright, what's going on?" Alistair looked back and forth between the two.

"He forced me out, but we're still connected somehow. If I throw my thoughts at him, he can still hear them."

"Either of ye want to tell me what bloody happened?"

"Go ahead, Stephen—tell him." Vincent sat back down.

"I saw something in Vincent, while searching for emotion. Fear. He...uh...he's afraid he'll fall, like his parents did. I saw the fear. It's holed up in his mind. Others' fears tend to be rampant. His is contained in a small area."

"Because he's a priest. Priests rarely turn. Their abilities instinctively protect them from emotions and thoughts that might hurt or weaken them. The ones who turn do it because they lose faith or simply want to be evil. It's extremely rare."

"Well, I say we take a small break, let Vincent relax again." Stephen went over to the kitchen and took glasses out of the cabinet. "I don't keep much to drink aside from water and juice."

"Water," Vincent stated.

"Same," Alistair added.

Stephen filled three large glasses at the faucet as the other two men made small talk. With the water running, he was not able to hear much, only a loud boom of thunder followed by laughter. Grabbing the filled glasses, he turned to rejoin them.

The room plunged into darkness. Stephen stood in the silence, surrounded by darkness, yet again. Something was not right. Not only could he feel another presence, but prickles of pain spread across his chest and arms.

Where are you? What do you want with me, Fallen? Stephen waited for an answer.

After only a moment, he heard a faint whisper echo.

You...

You can't have me. I'll find you and stop you, Stephen replied.

Join us...

NEVER. Stephen projected his thoughts with force. He felt the presence withdraw only for a moment. The pain in his body continued growing, making it harder to focus.

Emotions of fear and loneliness flooded Stephen's mind, causing him mental torment he had not felt before. *Stop it.* He tried to be more forceful with his thoughts, but the pain continued to increase. Through darkness, he heard a familiar voice.

"Ye have to, Vincent. It's the only way." Alistair paused. "Do it now!"

Stephen opened his eyes to find himself lying on the floor, Alistair and Vincent knelt beside him. His shirt felt wet from the water that spilled. His face hurt, and shards of glass lay scattered across his now scratched hardwood floor.

"What happened?" Stephen slowly sat up, his body still hurting. He saw a fair amount of blood on the floor beneath him. Shards of glass stuck in his arms and abdomen.

"Ye'll need stitches," Alistair informed him. "Nothing seems to be too deep."

"What happened?" Stephen glared at Alistair.

"Ye were attacked by one of the Fallen." Alistair glanced at Vincent, then back to Stephen. "Vin had to take a crash course in protecting someone else. He put up a wall around you, effectively kicking the other person out."

"Thank you, Vincent."

Vincent nodded.

"They want ye, don't they?" Alistair helped Stephen to his feet. "Has anything like this happened before?"

"Yeah, kind of. Someone tried to get into my head when Waltz was alive. Unsuccessfully, I might add. Waltz never said it, but I believe he kept them out. The attempt was painful. After he passed, I've had a couple of visions, like dreams. I'm in the dark, but someone is there with me. Waltz had told me before he passed that they'd found a way in, a weakness."

"Anything more?" Vincent asked.

"This isn't the first attack since he passed. Each seems to invade further into my mind. But this is the first time I've been awake when it happened. I don't know how to stop it."

"We'll get this figured out. I promise. For now, we need to get ye to the hospital." Alistair looked at Vincent. "Will ye drive?"

"I will bring the car to the door." Vincent walked toward the door.

"Call Patty, please," Stephen said. "If we don't tell her, she'll kill me. Your hard work will have been in vain."

Vincent smiled and pulled his phone from his pocket as he disappeared through the doorway. Alistair helped Stephen walk out and down the stairs, where Vincent waited with the car door open. Once all three were in, they hurried to the emergency room.

~ ~

Stephen lay on a bed in the hospital room wearing a hospital gown wrapped around his waist exposing several shards of glass sticking out of his torso. "This sucks," Stephen exclaimed with slurred speech while looking at his chest.

Vincent and Alistair sat nearby. Alistair continued to chuckle as Vincent merely looked at the shards, occasionally shaking his head.

"Oh my." Patty hurried through the door, to Stephen's side. "What happened?"

"Vincent didn't tell you?" Stephen looked at Vincent, dumbfounded.

Vincent shrugged.

Patty looked back at the shards. "He said you were hurt and needed stitches but were okay. He didn't tell me you looked like a pincushion."

"Well, uh..." Stephen searched for an explanation, but the medication made his thoughts fuzzy.

Alistair helped get him off the hook. "Stephen was getting us some water. We'd been hanging out, talking, ye know? On his way back from the kitchen, he flattened out."

"Yeah. When I fell, I must have fallen forward. The glasses broke—and, voila, I'm a porcupine, but on the front side."

Patty gave him a funny look before continuing. "Are you hurting?" She grabbed his hand.

"They gave me a shot. I don't feel much right now." Stephen flicked one of the longer pieces of glass sticking out. "See? Nothing." He found it hard to focus as the painkillers coursed through his system.

Alistair and Vincent chuckled.

"Oh! You two think this is funny, do you?" Patty's eyes lit up as she glared crossly at them. Both men straightened up in their chairs.

"No, yes...uh, maybe?" Alistair looked at Vincent for help.

Vincent simply shook his head.

"No to the hurt part. But funny to the drugged-up part?" Alistair's face contorted as though he also felt severe pain.

Patty stormed out. Stephen heard her calling for a nurse as she walked down the hallway.

"I think Alistair and I should go. I believe Patty can take care of you from here. The wall is up. Ye should be safe."

"Thanks." Stephen gave them two thumbs up and tried his hardest to smile as they walked out the door.

Eventually, Patty came back in and sat with Stephen while a doctor pulled glass from his body. He received stitches in half a dozen places and had bandages all over when he left the hospital.

Stephen awoke on his couch. He was not sure how he had gotten there. His mind still felt numb, and his memories fuzzy. The storm had passed, with little more than drizzle tapping against the windows.

Stephen grunted as he sat up. "That stings." He counted at least six areas with stitches. Additionally, bandages covered much of his arms and body. He sniffed the air. The aroma of bacon began filled his nostrils. He turned toward the sound of sizzle and saw Patty preparing plates.

She looked at him. "Great timing! How are you feeling?"

"Hmmm, s-sore," Stephen managed as he tried to find a more comfortable sitting position.

"Well, you'll have to take it easy until you're healed." Patty brought the plates and drinks over, then set them on the coffee table. "It took them awhile to get the glass out. The doctor said you may still have very tiny shards just under the skin in areas. Over time, they'll itch and come out on their own. You'll want to be mindful of that. And, you'll need to buy some more drinking glasses."

Stephen looked again at all the bandages, wondering just how many shards were still there. The sudden urge to scratch overwhelmed him as his fingernails lightly scraped across some of the smaller bandages.

Patty slapped his hand. "Don't scratch."

"Okay." Stephen chuckled. Patty looked cute whenever she got cross with him. His attention turned back toward the plate of food in front of him. "Biscuits, gravy, bacon, and eggs. You really are a keeper. I must have been out cold," Stephen managed as he scarfed down a forkful, only then realizing how hungry he was.

"You were. I tried to be quiet. That's hard to do with the echo in this place." Patty took a small bite. "So, are you ready to talk now?"

"Sure, babe. What about?" He shoveled another bite.

"I thought we could start with what's going on with you."

Stephen continued eating, not giving it much thought. "Like I said, I just passed out."

"Not that." Patty said, a concerned look spread across her face.

She got Stephen's attention. He sat his fork and plate down, concerned with where the conversation might go.

"Well, kind of that and more," she continued. "You've been distant. I get that Waltz's passing has been hard on you. I do. And I'm glad that you and Vincent are getting closer. But secret meetings, Alistair from Waltz's 'secret society' of friends." She made quote marks with her fingers, "and now the glass. I love you—"

"I love you too," Stephen replied.

"Wait." Patty waved her hand as though magically stopping Stephen with it. "I'm not done. I love you. And I trust you. But there's more going on than you're telling me. I don't like that at all."

Stephen remained silent. He did not dare interrupt again.

"I'm willing to give you a little more time to figure out what you want from this relationship. I think we could have something great together. If that's going to happen, you've got to trust me. If you don't want to tell me the truth, don't tell me anything at all. I know you well enough to know when you're being less than honest."

Stephen sat motionless. His heart raced. He wanted to tell Patty everything. What would she think? Could he really trust her? Would she believe him? Worse, what if she believed him and wanted nothing to do with it all? That too familiar emotion—fear—arose up in him. Could he make her stay? Of course, he could, but by doing so, he would lose her forever.

"So, I want to know. What's going on?"

Stephen said nothing. He felt defeated.

"I see. At least you aren't lying to me. I said I'd give you time to figure it out." She grabbed her plate and took it to the kitchen. "I'm gonna go. I need to do a load of laundry at home. I'll be by this evening to check on you. I love you." Patty remained poised.

Stephen, however, could not help but feel the tension, nervousness, and concern she hid on the inside. It only compounded his own emotions. He grabbed her wrist as she walked back past the couch toward the door. "I love you, Patty." His lips pressed against her knuckles. She stroked the back of his head and left.

Steam continued to rise from the food on Stephen's plate, but he no longer felt hungry. Instead, sadness loomed. The more he thought about it, the angrier he got until his plate of food became a flying mess that splattered against the brick wall. As quick as it came, the anger left, leaving him all alone.

For a month, Stephen wondered if he and Patty would be able to make it work. He talked with Vincent and Alistair. Both agreed that telling Patty anything was a bad idea and would only put her at risk. He tried everything he could think of to get past their problem. He put flowers on her desk early one morning, to find them in his trash can after lunch. He bought chocolates and had them delivered to her house. They were on his desk the next morning with a note that read "I don't like chocolate...today." Despite having Vincent, Alistair, and even Uncle Bernie to talk to, he never felt more alone.

Outside his office window, he watched people walking below. He tapped into their thoughts to share their happiness and feel how the warmth of the sun pleased them. It could not have been a more beautiful day outside. This made his personal suffering hurt even more. Even in the office, people seemed to be in a better mood.

"Hey, Boss."

Stephen looked at the doorway to see Johnathan entering. He also looked cheerful, wearing a bright blue button-down. "Oh, hey, Johnathan. What's up?" Stephen tried to sound chipper too.

"I was just wondering if you've read the press release for the warehousing business."

"Yeah. It's good."

"Great. I still need you to officially sign off on it."

"Oh, right." Stephen sifted through the papers on his desk. He grabbed a pen and signed the bottom of the release. "Here you go. Hey, I thought Patty was signing off on these now."

Johnathan hesitated. "She told me you could do it. Oh! You haven't given me anything yet on the organizational structure for the warehouse. I know you've been working on it. But the renovations are almost done. I'll need to announce the officers soon, so we can start getting operations up and running."

"Yeah, I know. We're almost there. You'll have it by the end of the week."

"Okay. Thanks, Stephen."

"You got it."

Stephen could not get his mind back on work. Patty dominated his thoughts. He loved her but remained aggravated, wishing she could understand. The closer his proximity to her, the more agitated he became. Being near her but unable to talk with her, touch her, or hold her made him sick to his stomach. Knowing that she worked just down the hall only served to make the agony worse. He grabbed his keys and helmet and headed down the hallway.

"Will you be out the rest of the day?"

The sound of her voice irritated him even more, absent of its usual sweetness. "Yes." *How can she just sit there working?*

He hurried down the stairs and out of the building to his motorcycle. He hopped on and sped away. The wind racing by seemed to take away some of his troubles. The warm sun soothed him. Like a river following its natural flow, he ended up back at the shelter, where Bernie sat on the front porch.

Walking up to the porch, he felt as though Bernie's judgmental eyes burned a hole right through him. He sighed as he sat down next to him on the bench.

"Hey, Uncle Bernie."

"Hello."

"I'm sorry I haven't been around much. I've had a lot on my plate."

Bernie did not answer him immediately. For a moment, the two simply sat watching the birds in the yard. "One of my dearest friends in the world is gone. I was beginning to feel like I'd lost you too."

"Unc, you haven't lost me. I've just been trying to find my way. I've called you a couple of times and left messages."

"Yeah, I know." Bernie gave Stephen a hug. "I've just missed you, is all. How are things with you and Patty?"

"Funny you should ask. We're kind of fighting, I guess."

"What about?"

"Mighty and Fallen stuff."

"What? You told her?" Bernie sounded agitated.

"Calm down, Uncle Bernie. No, I didn't tell her. That's the issue. She knows something's going on, and that I won't tell her what that something is. She takes that as a sign of trust issue. I trust her. I...I'm just concerned for her safety."

"If you want my opinion, you definitely shouldn't tell 'er."

"Really?"

"Nope. You've only been seeing each other a few months. Fact is, you really don't know her yet, do you? Besides, women shouldn't be pushy like dat. A man's gotta have his space. You can't let her control you."

"I don't think she's trying to control me. I think she just wants to be closer to me."

"Maybe. But boundaries need to be set early."

"Yeah, I guess." Stephen got up to head inside. "I'm getting a soda. You want one?"

"Nah. I'll come in with ya though. It's cooler inside."

Stephen walked inside and straight to the kitchen, where he popped open a soda and sat on a stool.

"So, you been lookin' for Waltz's killer?" Bernie asked.

Stephen nearly choked. He grabbed a couple of paper towels and started wiping up his mess.

"I'll take that as a yes. You know, Waltz was well liked. But he had enemies too. Heck, we all do. We've all done something we aren't proud of to someone that remembers it. I know it hurts, and Waltz deserves justice. But maybe you should let it go."

"Why would I do that?" Stephen knew Waltz and Bernie stood on opposite sides of the fence on occasion. This suggestion, however, upset him.

"One, I don't want you to get hurt. Two, you should be trying to find out about you, your roots. Dat's what should be important to you. Let the Mighty and the Fallen sort their stuff out without you."

"I know all I need to know about my roots." Stephen hesitated, realizing he almost revealed his true relationship to Waltz. "I know you're worried about me. You care about me a lot. Thank you. But it's time for me to start being my own man, the right way. That means not running."

The two sat silent for a moment before Stephen spoke again. "Hey. I'm gonna go to the building out back and go through some of my old stuff. Why don't I buy dinner? You got any guys staying here? I'll have something ordered for them too."

"Nah. The weather's still pretty. It'll be another month before we really start seeing people come in and stay. Go do whatcha gotta do. I'll fix dinner tonight."

Stephen went out the back door and around to the small storage building where he and Waltz first started his training. Walking in, he remembered his many lessons with Waltz in the deep of winter. He found an old football mixed in with the other sports equipment. He came across all kinds of things from his childhood that Waltz had kept; mostly trophies, ribbons, and certificates. He had been a fair student and participated in as much as time allowed. Near the back of the building hung a dusty punching bag he had not used since high school. Memories of him and Waltz working on the bag together flashed in his mind. *I'd forgotten about this old thing*.

He jabbed at the bag and dust flew. He waved the dust away and punched again—first a jab, followed by a cross. He landed a right hook on the bag. The chain snapped. "I guess it's an old chain." Stephen chuckled.

In the back corner, a box marked as Waltz's stuff sat covered with more dust than any of the other boxes. He opened it carefully, the dust so thick it fell to the floor. Inside lay newspaper clippings from around the world, where bad stuff happened or had been stopped. He had no doubt these had to do with the Mighty. Underneath, he found pictures. He recognized a younger Waltz and Bernie. A photo of Waltz's original triune sat among them: Waltz, Marie, and Sam. They looked happy.

He stopped. The last picture in his hand featured Layla, his mother. He had never had any pictures of her, and he understood why. No one could know about him. He stared at the picture, making note of the red hair. He had nearly forgotten she had red hair, much like Patty's.

Stephen boxed everything up. He would have it all moved tomorrow. He closed the building up and locked the door. He had the only key.

He headed to his old room, hoping to nap until dinnertime.

Stephen dreamed about Tommy, who stood outside the apartment building again. The woman came to the window and he saw something he had forgotten. He climbed up to the balcony and looked in. There she stood, the woman with red hair. Next, Stephen found himself back in the church with Waltz, helping to feed the homeless and needy. His mind hurt, just as before. Someone helped him, a woman with red hair. Finally, he found himself at Kiener Plaza. He recognized the day. He looked around and knew what was about to happen. He had to stop it. Running through the crowd, someone caught his eye—a red-haired woman. He turned back toward Waltz. It was too late.

Stephen awoke, jumped to his feet, and looked around, disoriented. Instead of the park, he stood in his old room, his chest heaving. Grabbing a picture of Patty from his chest-of-drawers, he ran his fingers along her red hair. “Patty?”

He sat the picture back down, opened the door, and walked down the hall to the kitchen. He found Bernie had finished cooking.

Bernie frowned. “Hey, hey, hey! What wrong? You look rattled.”

Stephen’s heart still raced. “I had another dream.”

“A nightmare? What’s going on?”

“You don’t understand. It was more like a memory. I remembered Tommy, the boy that died. I remembered being attacked in the kitchen. I remembered Waltz’s death.”

“Stephen, why are you so shaken up? Calm down.”

Stephen leaned on the counter. “You don’t understand...Red hair!” he shouted. “A woman with red hair was at all three! I couldn’t make out any faces. But after Waltz died, Patty was in the park.”

“Are you suggesting that Patty—”

Stephen interrupted Bernie. “Uncle Bernie, I need you to think. How did Waltz meet Patty?”

“Through Vincent.”

“Did she already work for Vincent before Waltz met him?”

“No. She was the first hire Vincent made though. She showed up the day he moved into the building. She helped him carry stuff from his car and asked for a job.”

"Was Waltz there?"

"Of course. Waltz helped Vincent move."

Stephen paced the floor. His thoughts ran wild before turning back toward Bernie. "Last question: Do you know if she took time off two weeks before I came back?"

Bernie's eyes shifted back and forth for a moment before locking on Stephen. "Yes. She was gone for a couple of weeks, visiting some friends. What's this about?"

"Patty was in the park when Waltz was killed. She found me shortly afterward. I'm remembering details I didn't before. Uncle Bernie, do you think it's possible she...Patty is one of the Fallen?"

Bernie scratched the back of his head. Stephen watched, waiting patiently for an answer. "The girl always seemed special. I always thought there was more to her. But this?" He shook his head.

"Uncle Bernie?" Stephen glared at him.

"Yes...it makes sense. She could be responsible."

Stephen sat silent. He knew the truth now. Bernie revealed it to him. As much as he did not want to believe it, the feeling of betrayal confirmed what he just saw. "I need to go."

"Stephen, you have to be careful. You know people are gonna be after you."

"Yeah, I know. Don't worry. I know who I can trust." He walked around the counter and gave Bernie a hug before leaving.

Stephen rode his motorcycle to the apartment, where he sent Patty a text asking her to come meet him for dinner. He explained in the text that he was not able to talk at the moment but did need to speak with her. Then he called Vincent and Alistair and explained everything. Last, he ordered pizza.

⁂

Stephen, Vincent, Alistair, and Patty sat in the living room eating pizza. He sensed they all felt awkward. He also sensed Patty's uncertainty. Looking into Patty's mind would have been all too easy. But he did not.

They sat quietly; only the sound of chewing broke through the silence. The light outside faded with each passing minute. Through the window shades of red, orange, purple, and dark blue lit the horizon.

Patty broke the silence. "Okay, this is a little weird. What am I missing?"

No one spoke up.

"Stephen, I thought just you and I were going to go out for dinner. I don't mind Vincent and Alistair, of course, but I feel like you three are keeping something from me. Is this a joke of some sort?"

Stephen took a sip of his soda before setting it on the table. "You know how you wanted to know everything?"

Patty nodded her head.

"Well," Stephen continued, "I'm gonna give you that opportunity. First, I'm giving you full disclosure. You're going to hear some things that will seem strange and impossible."

"What are you talking about?" Everything about Patty—her voice, facial expressions, posture, and mannerism—showed concern. She even shifted uncomfortably in her seat.

Stephen knew in his heart that Patty could not be the one responsible for all this—the trafficking, the planned bombing, Waltz's death. It simply did not make sense.

"Patty, I need to know if you trust me."

"Of course, I do. What's going on?"

"Are you hiding anything? Is there anything in your life that you wouldn't want me to know about, or see?

"No, nothing..." Patty's facial expression changed from concern to curiosity. "What do you mean *see*?"

Stephen gulped down another swallow. "If you trust me, I'll show you."

Patty nodded slowly.

Stephen did what he never wanted to do; invade Patty's mind. He searched the deepest corners. Nothing remained hidden from him. No doors. No walls. Her mind opened to him in a way no one else's ever did. He saw her life, past and present. Her thoughts felt warm to him, much like the sun had been earlier that day. He withdrew.

"Just as I told you guys, she's good."

Vincent and Alistair looked at each other; confusion flooded their faces. Patty sat quietly.

"Guys? Give us a moment, will you?" Stephen stood up as the two men moved across the room to sit at the kitchen counter.

"What just happened? What was that about? What do you mean, 'She's good'?"

"There's a lot to explain. In time, I will answer your questions as best as I can. For now, I'll cover the big stuff."

"Okay? Should I be scared?"

"Yes." Stephen sat on the coffee table in front of Patty. "This will sound crazy."

"Well, get it out already." Patty's words whipped out. She looked worried, almost in tears.

"There are people in the world with abilities that others don't have. I'm not talking about athletes or scientists. I'm talking about other kinds of stuff. These people are engaged in a war between good and evil, dating back more than two thousand years."

"Are you serious?" Patty's voice got loud. "You think this is a joke, right? If you don't want to trust me, why don't you just tell me it's over?" Patty grabbed her purse and made for the door.

Stephen stood to his feet. "Why haven't you told me about Brandon?"

Patty froze, her hand on the knob.

Vincent and Alistair made their way to where Stephen stood.

"Who is Brandon?" Vincent questioned, looking at Stephen.

Patty let go of the knob and turned toward the others. "How do you know about my brother?"

"You have a brother?" Vincent asked.

"I had a twin brother. But he died when we were younger." She locked eyes with Stephen. "How did you know about Brandon?"

I saw him in your mind. I can see your memories, hear your thoughts, and feel your emotions. Please don't be afraid, he pleaded.

Patty's eyes widened. She did not say a word.

"Did he just do his thing?" Alistair inquired.

"He did," Vincent replied.

Patty walked to Stephen and threw her arms around him.

Alistair's face contorted as he scratched his head. "I wasn't expecting that."

Vincent shrugged.

Patty pulled away. Stephen, now confused, was not sure what to say. "Uh...what?"

"That was beautiful." Patty rubbed Stephen's arm and held his hand.

"Most people get freaked out when they hear me inside their head."

"Oh, that was weird, no doubt. But I could feel you." Patty bit her lip for just a moment. "You're scared that I won't love you. And you love me so much."

Stephen smiled. "I am. And, I do." He had not meant to share his emotions. He felt so strongly for her that he had not been able to fully conceal them.

"This is a lot to take in though. I need to sit back down."

They all sat back in their original spots.

"So, you can read minds and use telepathy?"

"Yes, among other things."

"There are others that can do this too?"

"Yes, and no. There are others with abilities, each somewhat unique to the individual," Stephen explained.

"Why now? Why are you telling me now, when you wouldn't before?"

"Well...I...I...umm." Stephen did not know exactly how to answer her.

"Stephen, if ye don't mind," Alistair chimed in, "I'll take this one."

Stephen sighed with relief. "All yours."

"Stephen has been having visions of a sort. Someone has been invading his mind. We aren't one hundred percent certain why. But we believe that whoever it is may be responsible for Waltz's death."

Patty gasped and quickly covered her mouth. She looked at Stephen with watery eyes.

"Unfortunately, it gets worse. The person killed Waltz to get to Stephen. Remember my friends from Waltz's funeral? We are part of a group called The Mighty, which dates back to the mighty men of King David. It's our heritage, passed from generation to generation. These gifts were bestowed upon us to fight a group called Fallen, so named for the Nephilim—fallen angels. They want power and control over God's creation."

"Why are they after Stephen?" Patty asked.

"There's a lot we don't know about Stephen. His bloodline is in question. We keep a close track of all the bloodlines and their children. Stephen is unaccounted for."

"What does this have to do with me?" Patty enquired.

"Stephen's last vision had memories of previous events, including Waltz's death. This time, the memories had a new detail he had forgotten: a woman with red hair, whose face remained hidden. And you happened to be in the park the day Waltz died."

Stephen felt the hurt and anger rising up in Patty as she realized the implication.

"Wait. You think I had something to do with any of that?" She glared at Stephen, as though warning him to choose his words carefully.

"No, Patty, I didn't." He tried to hold her hand, as she pulled away.

"He is telling the truth," Vincent interceded. "But someone else suggested that the vision could be pointing to you as the culprit. That someone is one of The Mighty, so we really had no choice but to eliminate the possibility."

"I knew it wasn't you," Stephen pleaded.

Patty looked at Stephen. He saw her glaring eyes soften. "I believe you."

"Patty, you aren't going to like the next part," Stephen replied.

"What do you mean?"

"I need you to stay away from me for a while, to make it appear that we had a falling out. I'm hoping it will draw someone out."

"No. I'm not leaving you."

Stephen knew all along this would be the hard part. He learned Patty could be obstinate. This was not going to be easy.

"You need to. You could get hurt. Being away from me is the best place for you. Aside from that, they need to believe we had a fight. Go stay with your niece, Kaylin. I'm sure she'd love to spend time with you. Just don't go back to your apartment."

"But—"

"No buts. I need you to leave. I can't do what I need to do if I'm worrying about you." Patty looked hurt. Her countenance saddened. "Look, I know you're a strong woman. This isn't about being strong. This is a battle that you have no clue how to fight. I'm not sure I do, but it's my fight. You'll distract me from what I need to do."

"Fine," Patty said softly but pouting. "But who's going to take care of you?"

"We will," Vincent said.

"What—Vincent gets to stay?"

"Vincent is..." Stephen looked at Vincent, who understood and nodded. "Vincent is one of us too."

"Oh, of course he is." Patty grabbed her purse and headed to the door. Deja vu.

"Patty, I love you."

Patty turned back to Stephen and kissed him on the lips. "I love you too."

Then, she left. The door stayed open and Stephen listed to her footsteps disappear down the stairs.

Stephen did not like leaving things like that with Patty but knew the risk if she stayed. Besides, he had a plan.

"It's okay, Stephen. We will take care of her." Alistair paused to listen as Stephen spoke on the other end.

"I know. I can't help but worry," Stephen replied. "Patty's important to me. Tell Vincent to keep me updated. Alright?"

"Aye. Relax, Stephen. She'll be fine. And Vincent knows to call ye back in a couple of hours. We'll talk later." He ended the call and handed the phone back to Vincent—seated beside him in the driver's seat. "Ye know we're in trouble if anything happens to her, right?"

Vincent smiled and sipped his latte. "I do. But do you?"

"What do ye mean?"

"When I let Stephen in my head, I saw something I did not understand at first. But I do now. Stephen has not accepted Christ. He is not truly a Mighty."

"I know. But he isn't one of the Fallen either. He'll have to make a choice soon. I feel it coming. I can almost see it."

"Will you be able to see his choice?"

Alistair looked at the moon. The moon looked very clear, unlike Stephen's future. So many things needed to go right for this to end well. He looked across the street to see Patty through the window of a modest house. Kaylin sat with her. The neighborhood looked quiet, but for how long? If they failed, Patty and Kaylin would be hurt, and Stephen, lost forever.

"The way my gift works is that I see possible futures based on choices that have already been made."

"If the choices are made, how are they only possible futures?"

"Possible, because once I see them, I am able to introduce new choices, creating new decisions. And I can always change my own decisions."

"So, your visions change."

"Occasionally. I seldom see the end result. When I do, yes, they have changed. What I see are often suggestions. See the moon? See how it becomes more defined and brighter as the sun goes down?"

"The closer you get to the vision, the clearer it becomes."

"Yes. Twenty-four hours is usually the point when I can see something clearly. It may lead to something else. But that's usually when a specific vision becomes clear. Everything else is more like a feeling."

Patty left the room for a moment. The two men watched and waited on the edge of their seats until she returned with cups for her and Kaylin.

"I need to stretch my legs." Vincent got out of the car and stood on the sidewalk. Alistair joined him. "You saw a vision of us watching over Patty, right?"

Alistair nodded.

"Do you know what happens?"

"I don't." Alistair grabbed a leaf from a nearby plant and played with it. "I just know I need to be here. That's what I saw shortly after she left yesterday."

"But there's something you're hiding."

Alistair looked away from Vincent. How could Vincent know there was more to his vision? "Yes, there's more. I don't know what happens. I just know it's bad."

Vincent looked back to the window, seeing Patty and Kaylin. "Bad how?"

"I don't know. We'll just have to wait and see."

"Until then, cheers." Vincent swallowed the last drop of his latte and chunked his cup in a trash can.

The tops of the buildings blocked out the setting sun as Stephen walked down the sidewalk toward Waltz's memorial. As he approached, he saw Bernie waiting on him. It had been little more than a day since he last spoke with Bernie about Patty. He dreaded the conversation ahead. If only he knew what the truth was, it would be much easier.

He held two milkshakes in his hands; a half-full chocolate and a vanilla.

"I got you a vanilla milkshake, Uncle Bernie, from Crown's. It's a little runny, but still good."

"Thanks, Stephen." Bernie took a sip. "That right there's good, real good." He took another sip. "I'm glad you asked me to meet you here. It's good to make sure we remember him together."

"Yeah, it is..." Stephen responded half-heartedly. His thoughts focused on the task ahead as he stood there looking at Waltz's memorial.

"Are you gonna drink the rest of your shake?"

"No, Unc." Stephen did not want to talk to him, but knew he had to.

"What's wrong, Stephen? I haven't seen you like dis in a while." Bernie turned to Stephen. "Is it Patty?"

"Kind of."

"Listen, I know you love her. But with dat dream you had; you need to let 'er go. I'm afraid she's trouble for you, boy."

"What if she isn't?"

"If not, then you don't need her caught up in all this craziness. But I think we both know she's the cause of what's been going on with you."

"How did you do it, Bernie?" Stephen snapped. He cut his eyes at Bernie and glared as though trying to burn a hole through him.

"Do what?" Bernie shrugged, before taking another sip.

"How did you get into my head? How did you plant those images of a red-haired woman in my memories?"

"Now hold up a sec, boy." Bernie placed his hand on Stephen's shoulder. Stephen knocked it away.

"I know your tell. It's the same as mine. When you lie in poker, you can't help but rub the back of your head. That's why you suck at it." Although Stephen raised his voice, no one paid them any attention.

Bernie's facial expression changed from concern to fear. He took a step away from Stephen. "Stephen, calm down. People don't need to hear this."

“Does it look like they care?” Stephen motioned to the numerous people that passed by them. “They don’t care. I’ve seen to that.”

“You’re using more and more of your ability.”

“Don’t change the topic. Why did you do it? *How* did you do it?” Stephen shoved Bernie, who back-peddled several steps. “Why did you kill Waltz? Why are you framing Patty?”

“Stephen, I didn’t...” Bernie yelled. He fell to one knee and grabbed his head. His face twisted in pain. “It hurts! Get out of my head, boy.”

You want me out? Tell me the truth. Stephen could have pulled the truth free himself but wanted—no, needed to hear Bernie admit it.

“I can’t. You don’t know what’s going on.” He fell to both knees, tears evident of the torture Stephen inflicted on his mind. “Please, Stephen, don’t,” Bernie panted and fell forward onto one hand.

“Tell me, or I’ll lock your mind away in this torment for the rest of your life.”

“Stephen—”

“No, I trusted you. You and Waltz raised me. He trusted you.”

“No, he didn’t.”

Stephen stopped. “What?”

Bernie breathed deep during his moment of respite from the onslaught. “He didn’t trust me. He knew something was wrong. That’s why he seldom stayed here when you were gone. He stayed in the alley, knowing I wouldn’t go there.”

“What does that have to do with anything?”

Bernie looked up. Blood trickled from his nose.

“Dat’s where my brother, Will, died—Bernard’s dad. I can’t stand the sight of dat alley. He was Mighty, but he should’ve listened. He was supposed to wait for help but didn’t.”

“He was supposed to wait for Waltz?”

“Yes. I swear, I never held a grudge against Waltz. It wasn’t his fault. I never would’ve hurt Waltz. You gotta believe me.” Bernie sobbed. “You and he are family.”

“Why the lies about Patty? Who are you hiding?” Bernie lost control and Stephen saw it in his mind. A brief glimpse. “No, no, no.” Stephen pulled at his hair with both hands. “Why-why him?”

“They got to him. He’s one of the Fallen, Stephen. They deceived him. Waltz helped Marie come back from the darkness. I want to help him.” Bernie pleaded with Stephen. His sobs barely discernible from words. “He’s been family to you, Stephen. He’s the only close blood I have left. I can’t lose him like I lost Will. Dat would kill Wanda.”

Stephen paced back and forth for a moment before squatting down to face Bernie. “You want to help Bernard?”

Bernie nodded.

“Then you’re going to tell the Mighty everything.”

“I covered up the truth. You don’t know what they’ll do to me,” Bernie begged.

“Whatever it is, I know it won’t be worse than what I will do to you, if you don’t.”

Vincent looked at his watch. "Eight-fifteen, almost time to call Stephen. Do you think I could go ahead and call?" he asked Alistair.

"We should have one more look around the block before we call."

"Is everything alright?"

Alistair sensed something different but did not know what. "I can't say. It's almost time for whatever is going to happen."

"Okay, then. You go to the right. I'll go left."

"I think we should stay together," Alistair suggested.

"I do not. We can't let anything happen to Patty."

"Ye haven't been trained. How are ye gonna fight if ye have to?"

"With all that I have." Vincent replied.

"Alright. If ye see anything, call me." Alistair stared at Vincent until he nodded.

The two men went their separate ways down the street. Alistair glanced back a time or two at Vincent. He could not help being concerned for him. But Vincent had been right. Patty was the reason they were there. Before long, Alistair rounded the corner, and Vincent continued out of sight.

As Alistair walked on something felt terribly off. He paused to listen. The night sat eerily quiet. He scanned the shadows for movement. Nothing. Already halfway to the corner of the block, he moved on. Soon the feeling accompanied a hazy vision of someone beating Vincent. He could not make out a face in the darkness. A streetlamp in the distance allowed him to see Vincent's sedan in the background. Then the vision was stopped.

Alistair raced around the corner to the next street over. No Vincent. He continued running down the street hoping to see Vincent round the corner in front of him. Turning the next corner in full stride he spotted two men scuffling. Alistair ran as fast as he could.

Vincent lay on the ground with another man on top of him. The assailant tried to get up and run down the street in the direction of Kaylin's house. Vincent grabbed his leg.

"Stop," Alistair yelled.

The man kicked Vincent a couple of times and broke free. Alistair arrived and tackled him to the ground. The man was stout, like running into a brick wall. Alistair managed to get to his feet quickly. He looked at the man. Standing face to face, the man was much taller and broader than Alistair, but the Scotsman moved quicker. He kicked one of the man's legs. He dipped but did not fall. Instead, the man growled.

Vincent yelled, "Bernard, stop."

Bernard turned and looked at Vincent. "Sorry, Vincent. I can't." He grabbed for Alistair, who slapped his hand away and spun around behind the man for a chokehold.

Vincent pulled his phone from his pocket and dialed. "Yes, there is an emergency. My friend and I are being attacked—"

"No," Bernard screamed as he flung Alistair to the ground like a rag doll. Then, he seemed to fade from existence, as though dematerializing right in front of them.

"What?" Vincent pulled the phone away from his ear and lay flat on his back. "Where did he go?"

"Projection," Alistair panted, trying to catch his breath as he rolled to his side.

"He...he was somewhere else?" Vincent asked, struggling to speak.

"Yes and no. He duplicated himself. He can only keep it up so long." Alistair struggled to his feet and walked over to Vincent. "Now, let's get you cleaned up." He bent toward Vincent. "Vin? Hey!"

Vincent lay motionless. Alistair checked for a pulse. The dim street light shone enough to see Vincent's face; beat up and covered in blood. Alistair had not realized how badly he had been hurt until now. He grabbed the phone.

"Hello, are ye still there? The man's gone. But me friend is unconscious. I need an ambulance."

It seemed an eternity to Alistair, as he waited for the ambulance. It finally arrived and loaded Vincent into the back. The EMTs tried to reassure Alistair of Vincent's condition, though he detected an uneasiness in their voices.

Additional responders looked over Alistair; only minor bruising but a busted rib. Still, he declined going to the hospital. Once the ambulance left with Vincent, he ran down the street to Kaylin's house and beat on the door. Patty answered.

"I need you to come with me," Alistair told her.

"What's wrong?"

"Vincent's on the way to the hospital. I've got to call Stephen. But I need ye to come with me now."

Patty's hands shook as she grabbed her keys and told Kaylin she'd call her later to explain. She drove them to the hospital. Alistair, however, had the worst job of all—calling Stephen.

❧ ☙

Stephen and Bernie sat in silence at Stephen's apartment, Bernie's demeanor that of a scalded dog. Stephen told him not to speak until he said otherwise.

Eight-thirty came and went with no phone call. Stephen grew concerned. The more time that passed, the harder he glared at Bernie.

"Has something happened?" Stephen asked.

Bernie did not say a word.

"If you know something, you better tell me."

"I don't know." Bernie barely spoke louder than a whisper.

The phone rang. Stephen snatched it up from the table. "Vincent? Is Patty alright?"

Alistair spoke on the other end. "She's fine, mukker. She's driving."

"Driving? Where are you going, and where's Vincent?"

"He should be at the hospital by now. It's a long story. EMS assured me Vincent will be okay. He was unconscious when they took him. Some bloke attacked him. I jumped in. He was pretty big, very strong, and was projecting his body. Once Vincent called 911, the attacker vanished."

Stephen did not understand. "Projecting? W-what?"

"He duplicated himself, probably for only a short time. The actual person was somewhere else."

"Do you have any idea who he was?"

"Vincent yelled a name. Any idea who Bernard is?"

"Yeah." Stephen fought to remain calm. "I know Bernard. Let me know what you find out about Vincent when you get there. I'm gonna see if I can find where Bernard is."

Stephen hung up.

Bernie said, "Stephen, listen. I—"

"I don't care what you want to say. Instead, you're gonna tell me where to find Bernard."

"I can't do that." Bernie straightened. "I can't tell you where Bernard is. He's confused. He's my blood."

"You misunderstood. I wasn't asking." Stephen pulled thoughts, memories, and emotions from Bernie's mind. Bernie struggled hard against it, his guard already up. However, Stephen overpowered him.

You'll only make this more painful if you struggle. So, go ahead. Struggle.

Stephen started locking onto memories of Bernard. Soon, he heard conversations. Bernie and Bernard argued about his decision to become one of the Fallen. An image of Bernie and Bernard's meeting became clear, with a statue of Chuck Berry in the background.

"Delmar Loop."

"No. Stephen, listen to me. If you go, one of you will die. You'll kill him if he's by himself."

"By himself?" Stephen snapped.

"Yes. There's someone else that's been pulling his strings, controlling him. He needs help."

"Who's the puppet master?"

"I don't know. I know he's powerful. If he's there, they'll kill you. You can't go."

"I think you underestimate me. First, we've got to make sure you don't have a chance to warn him."

Stephen went back into Bernie's mind and locked it away, leaving him fully aware of what went on around him, but unable to respond in any meaningful way. Bernie sat there catatonic, a prisoner inside his own body. Only Stephen held the key.

Eventually, the Mighty would have to know. They would come get Bernie and take him, just as Alistair took Matthew and Rebound's body somewhere else. He did not know where that was, nor did he care. By the time they came to take Bernie, it would be over. Stephen would gladly free Bernie's mind. In spite of it all, he still loved his Uncle Bernie. When inside his mind, Stephen felt Bernie's pain in losing Waltz and even more pain in losing Bernard.

Stephen, Patty, and Alistair waited in the room when Vincent regained consciousness. Stephen and Patty sat together on a small couch while Alistair paced the floor. Monitors beeped a steady rhythm, a good sign.

"Stephen," Patty said. "What are you grinning about?"

He nodded toward Vincent. "He's dreaming. I can hear it."

She slapped his arm. "Stop."

"Okay," he chuckled. "I just wanted to check on his mind is all. It seems pretty normal. I think he'll be fine."

"Hey, mukkers," Alistair's hushed tone carried a hint of excitement. "I think he's coming to."

Vincent moved a little and grunted. He opened his eyes and looked around the room.

"Hey, buddy. You okay?" Stephen quickly went to Vincent's side. "Don't try to do too much."

"Aye, ye took a guid beating, ye did." Alistair stood at the foot of the bed.

"Is...Is Patty..." Vincent sounded raspy.

"I'm here. I'm okay." Patty grabbed his hand from the other side of the bed.

Vincent looked at all three, then back to Alistair. "You look like crap. Have you seen your face?"

They all chuckled.

"So, ye have to nearly die to get a sense of humor, eh?" Alistair chided back.

"I need some water," Vincent said.

Stephen grabbed a cup from the table next to him, poured water from the pitcher, and added a straw. "Here you go."

"How long have I been out?" He sipped from the straw.

"A few days. You were touch and go for a while. Several broken bones, a cracked skull, and bruised organs." Stephen moved the tray table so that Vincent could reach it. "We were worried."

"Yeah, Vin. Ye guid now though. Right?"

Vincent looked weak and paler than usual. Stephen felt Vincent's disappointment. Vincent dreamed that a pretty nurse awaited him. What he woke up to looked much different.

Stephen assured his friend. *Don't worry, buddy. There are a couple on this floor. I'll let them know you're awake.* "I'll be right back," he told the others. "The nurses need to know he's awake."

Vincent smiled wide.

"Did I just miss something?" Patty asked Vincent.

"I think we both did," Alistair replied.

Vincent did not say a word but continued smiling.

The nurse came and checked his vitals, asked him how he felt, and recorded everything on his chart. When she left, he questioned them about what happened.

"You mean you don't remember?" Stephen asked Vincent.

"No, not a bit."

Alistair chimed in. "Do you remember that we were watching Patty's house?"

"Vaguely. Stephen was concerned that someone might try to go after her."

"Wait, I don't understand," Patty interjected. "Why would someone come after me?"

"Stephen?" Alistair looked at him.

"After you left, I was concerned that whoever was responsible for my visions might hurt you, or even try to kill you, to keep me from knowing the truth."

"And you thought I was in danger too?" she pointedly asked the other men.

Vincent grunted as he sat up more. "Alistair had a vision."

"It's true. I did," Alistair said. "I saw Vincent and me watching ye and yer niece. I saw a struggle and blood. I wasn't sure what would happen. I just knew we needed to be there for the best possible outcome."

Patty massaged her scalp. "I'm not sure if I'll get used to this. But, please, go on."

Alistair picked up where he left off. "We took another look around the block, before calling Stephen to check in. We were supposed to meet up on the other side of the block. As I neared, I felt something was wrong. I even got flashes of images, which is something new. I rounded the corner thinking he should be coming around the corner on the opposite side. When he didn't, I hurried toward his side. I got there when the two of them were struggling."

"By the look of your face, I owe you my life."

Alistair grinned. "Ye do. I have to say though, for someone without training, ye put up one heck of a fight, against a trained warrior too. In fact, ye called 911 before ye passed out. That's when he left. It saved my life too. So, I guess we're even."

"Any idea who it was?" Vincent asked.

"You really don't remember anything, do you?" Stephen stared at Vincent. He knew Vincent's heart would break to find out Bernard was the attacker.

"Yeah, mukker. You recognized him."

"I know him?" Vincent queried.

"We all do, Vincent. Well, you, Patty, and I do." It pained Stephen more than anyone to know the truth. He hesitated to say his name. For the first time, he accepted the likelihood that he had to fight his only real childhood friend and brother. "Bernard."

"What? No." Vincent's eyes widened.

"I confirmed it with Uncle Bernie. He's been protecting him. Bernie didn't mean for all this to happen. But he didn't want to lose the closest person he had to a son."

"What about Bernie?" Vincent's voice still sounded tired and raspy.

"I locked him in his mind. He's with the Mighty now."

Vincent's stomach rumbled so loud that everyone could hear it.

"I'll go see about breakfast. You need to try and eat something." Stephen walked outside the room while

Alistair and Vincent continued talking. Patty followed behind.

"Hey," Patty called out to him before he had gone too far. He stopped, and Patty joined him. "I know how close you two were when you were younger. Waltz and Bernie told me stories."

"When I found out it was him, I was so angry. I think it didn't really settle on me that I would have to fight my oldest friend. This sucks so bad." Stephen hung his head, looking at the floor. His mind raced with all the good times the two shared as kids—playing in the water, throwing the football, and even double dates. They had done so much together.

"Maybe you should let the Mighty handle this one."

"No," Stephen replied quickly. "He's my family, my responsibility. I'll do whatever needs to be done."

"At what cost though? What will it do to you?"

Stephen did not answer. He only kissed her cheek and continued to the nurse's station. He told Nurse Chelsea that Vincent asked for food. He knew Vincent preferred dark-haired women. He saw that in the brief time he spent in Vincent's head.

Stephen's stomach rumbled too, and he remembered a St. Louis Bread Company not far from the hospital. The city had plenty of them. Stephen found it funny that something as simple as the name St. Louis Bread Company gave him comfort. It signified home. Anywhere else, people called it Panera Bread. He walked to the nearest one and ordered two coffee drinks, several bagels, and a half-sweet tea for Patty.

When Stephen returned to the hospital, the nurse had already seen Vincent. She had also checked his vitals and taken care of all the necessities, food, drink, and helping him to the bathroom. Alistair and Patty looked concerned yet relieved when Stephen finally walked in the room. Vincent smiled.

"I brought food. I couldn't let Vincent eat in front of everyone and leave us to starve."

"Thanks." Alistair got up and grabbed a coffee and a bagel. Stephen handed Patty hers.

"Sorry, Vincent. They want to monitor what you eat for now. So, you're stuck with hospital food." Stephen sat the bag down out of Vincent's reach.

"Not a problem."

Stephen took a bite from his bagel when he realized Vincent continued to stare at him. "I thought it wasn't a problem."

"The bagel is not a problem."

"Okay. What is?"

"I want you to wait to go after Bernard," Vincent stated, still staring at Stephen.

"What? Why?"

"He's powerful. He took on two of us and won."

Stephen gave Vincent a questioning look.

"Fine. I know I am not a fighter. Still. It was too easy for him. Plus, if he is of the warrior class, that means whoever got into your head is helping him. I'm a protector. Let me help protect you."

"I can't do that, Vincent. This is my fight. Someone is after *me*. Besides, if there is any chance of saving him, it has to be me."

Vincent motioned to Alistair and Patty. "Can you two give us the room?"

Alistair stood up. “Uh-oh, Patty. I think Stephen’s in trouble.”

“Nah, it’s just a lover’s spat,” she joked, as she followed him outside.

“Stephen, I did not want to say anything in front of them. But, when you and I connected, I saw things. And right now, I am too weak to protect you. You need me.”

“What did you see?”

“Well, Mr. Cross, I saw that you still need to make a choice, the one Waltz tried so hard to get you to see. Do you not get it? This is real, all of it.”

Stephen walked over to the window. The building’s shadow covered the rest of the rooftop below. The sun still filled the sky with light. Short sleeves and shorts provided evidence of how warm it remained.

“Stephen, I saw the struggle inside you. Somehow you feel you do not deserve what God has to offer you—forgiveness. And that is true. None of us deserve it. Just know, your choice will either allow God to transform you into the man Waltz saw you could be or turn you into the monster you fear you already are.”

Stephen said nothing. Just the mention of his own last name reminded him of a conversation he had with Waltz in front of the church. “I see choice,” he heard Waltz say, as though speaking from the grave.

“Yeah, I have to make a choice. It’s my choice to make though, right?” Stephen turned to look at Vincent. “I’ve got to do this. I didn’t kill Waltz. I didn’t beat you nearly to death. But it happened because of me. What if you die the next time, huh? What if it’s Alistair, or...or Patty, God forbid? I’ve got to do this. But I don’t like the idea that things are black and white, good or bad. There's a lot of grey in the world too."

"I know. I am simply reminding you of the real fight, the one inside you. I think you have used what has been going on around you to distract you from it. Maybe that *is* what they truly want, for you to default to their choice."

Stephen stood silent. There was nothing else to say. Vincent might have been right. They both knew it. His mind raced, looking for anything that would give him hope. "I have to go see someone."

"Who?" Vincent tried to sit up more.

"A friend, I think. I'll see you soon."

Stephen stepped outside and saw Patty and Alistair waiting. "You heard?"

"Didn't everyone?" Alistair patted him on the back.

Stephen looked at his girlfriend. He felt her worry. She had every right to feel that way. "I love you, Patty."

"I love you too, Stephen."

"What? Ye don't love me?" Alistair held his arms out as though expecting a hug.

Stephen grinned. "Does anyone?" He turned and walked away.

It did not take Stephen long to get where he needed to go. He looked up at the familiar church. A track led him there the first time. This time, he ventured there because of words from a friend. The sun sat in the sky, somewhere between the western horizon and the zenith. The cross of the steeple cast a shadow on Stephen as he approached the doors. As expected, he found the church doors unlocked. He walked in.

"Pastor Buchanan?" Stephen looked around. The church appeared empty. He turned toward the doors to leave when no one answered. He was not sure what he hoped to accomplish anyway.

"Leaving so soon?" The voice came from behind him.

Startled, he turned to see the older gentleman walking through an archway near the front of the church. The sight looked familiar—worn overalls, raggedy T-shirt, and work boots.

"No, I...uh..." Stephen was not sure where to start.

"You want to talk about something. But just like before, you are of two different minds."

"Kind of, yeah." He realized Pastor Buchanan had an uncanny aptitude for reading people.

"Did you find out what you wanted about the Mighty and Fallen?"

"Yeah, at least, I suppose I did."

The old man played with the rim of his glasses. "So, you're here about something else."

"I am."

"Why don't you sit?" Pastor Buchanan sat on the pew and motioned to Stephen.

"I...uh..."

"Just sit." The preacher seemed a little forceful. But it worked. He sat. "What about that friend of yours, the man that raised you? You aren't asking him for advice?"

"I can't."

"Ah. That was his funeral I saw you at."

Stephen looked at him, surprised he remembered him.

"Surprised? I seldom forget a face. I'm sorry to hear he passed."

"Thanks." Stephen needed to find an answer but was not sure what the question was.

"The last time we spoke, you seemed nearly as burdened as you are now. Did you make your choice?"

Stephen looked at the floor. "No, I still haven't made a choice. I guess I'm not sure that a choice needs to be made. This battle between God and Satan, Lucifer and Christ—why should it concern me? Why can't they just hash it out and leave me, all of us, alone?"

"James four, verse seventeen. Do you know it?"

Stephen shook his head.

"I'll paraphrase it for you. If a man knows to do good and doesn't do it, that is evil enough. Stephen, we were put here, from the beginning, for the purpose of serving God. He also made us stewards of this world he has given us. If we do not recognize His authority first, then why would people want to take care of anything? Look at the world today. It seems more and more like it's falling apart. So many people simply do what they want, believing they alone decide what is good in their lives. That doesn't make it so. They simply ignore God, believing the lack of choice causes Him to not exist."

Stephen shifted in his seat, searching for comfort. "So, their refusal to make a choice is a choice."

"You've got it."

"I'm not sure if I'm ready for it."

The pastor patted him on the shoulder. "I'll pray that you're ready before it's too late, then."

"Thank you, Father—sorry, Pastor Buchanan."

"Anytime."

Stephen got up and walked out the door, not sure if he would see him again. He got onto his motorcycle and rode to Delmar Loop. He walked the loop for most of the morning, hoping to catch a glimpse of a memory, or to hear a thought that might tell him where Bernard hid.

Around noon, he went into a convenience store to grab a snack. As he stood in line, strong, raw emotions of hurt, despair, and self-pity filled the atmosphere. He looked around, unsure of what he might see. Seated near the entrance, he took notice of a young man, barely of college age, not who Stephen hoped to find. Still, the young man intrigued him.

The man got up and walked down the sidewalk. Stephen paid for his snack and soda and followed behind. As the man entered an apartment building, Stephen waited a moment and entered the building too. *Something's off,* he thought.

People came and went as he made his way up the stairs and down the hall. He listened for thoughts, trying to find him. Pain hung in the air, like a strong scent. The young man felt alone. His girlfriend left him a couple of weeks ago. His parents recently passed from injuries in an auto accident, and he had no real friends to lean on.

Stephen rushed to a door and beat on it. “Hey! You in there, man?” He beat on the door again. The door opened.

“Hey, bro, I think you've got the wrong apartment.” The young man's stringy black hair nearly covered his puffy red eyes.

“No, this is the right place.” Stephen pushed the door open and went into the living room. In the middle of the floor lay a rope, one end tied to the balcony, the other, a noose.

"What are you doing?" the young man shouted.

"Look...Brandon, right?" Stephen thought about the memory of Patty's brother.

The man nodded; a confused look washed over his face. "D-do I know you?"

"No, you don't. Listen, I saw you outside the market. You looked like you could use a friend. I wanted to talk to you, but you took off. I had a bad feeling, so I chased you down."

"Yeah? You wanna hang and be buds then?"

Stephen thought about how stubborn he had first been with Waltz. "Look, I get it. You don't know me. But I was an orphan. I had no dad, and my mom passed when I was young. This man took me in after I ran away from a boys' home. It changed my life. And he recently died. I get it if you don't want to talk to me." Stephen pulled his wallet out. Inside was the folded pamphlet he'd gotten the first time he'd met the pastor. "Talk to Pastor Buchanan. He's a good guy. I don't go to church there. Still, he's easy to talk to." He pointed to the rope. "This is not a good choice. Things can get better." Stephen snapped the rope from the balcony.

Brandon dodged as the snapped end whipped by him. He looked blankly at Stephen, over to the balcony, and back down at the pamphlet. "Thanks." He took the pamphlet. Then he grabbed Stephen's wallet.

"Hey!" Stephen complained and grabbed the young man's wrist.

"Whoa, take it easy, man. This picture..." Brandon pointed to a picture in the wallet, a smaller version of the one that rested on the mantel at Uncle Bernie's. It showed Stephen and Bernard when they were kids. "I swear this is the same."

He handed the wallet back to Stephen, hurried into the kitchen, and pulled something from off the door of his fridge. "Yeah, I thought so." He walked back to Stephen with a picture in his hand. "I had a roommate, a really quiet guy. Other than clothes and stuff, this was the only thing in the apartment that was his. See?" He held up a picture identical to the one in Stephen's wallet. "Bernard left a couple of days ago. He said he had to go."

Stephen did not know whether to be excited, worried, or sad. He had found where Bernard had been staying. But did the picture mean that pieces of their old friendship remained, or was it simply a picture of a target?

"Did he say anything?" Stephen asked.

"Not really," the boy replied. "He seemed a little worried though. I guess you know him?"

"When we were younger, like family. I heard he was living here now and came to find him. Guess I was too late."

"Yeah, I guess so."

Stephen handed Brandon a card. "Hey, if you see him around, call me, will you? And if you need to talk or just want to hang, call me."

Brandon smiled. "This has been weird. But I can do weird. I think I might give this church guy a go. Maybe you'll hear from me afterward. You know, to let you know how it goes."

"I'd appreciate that." Stephen turned to walk out of the apartment.

"Hey, how did you know my name?"

Stephen tried to come up with something but stood stunned for a brief moment before eying his deliverance. He pointed to a school folder in the middle of the floor. The man's name rested across the top, Brandon Teague.

"Oh. For a second there I was beginning to think you were some kind of mind reader."

Stephen laughed. "That would be something, wouldn't it? See you around."

He walked out the door, then closed it behind him. He listened for the kid's thoughts, then smiled once he knew that Brandon had changed his plans. The odd turn of events gave the young man hope that someone cared what happened to him.

Delmar Loop got hotter as the day went on. The crowds seemed to grow. Stephen actually considered an apartment in the loop right after Waltz died. This day trip made him very glad he had decided against it. Although he considered himself a people person, he both liked and needed his space and privacy.

After a few more hours, he realized that he was not going to find any new information on Bernard's whereabouts. He made his way back to his motorcycle and called Patty along the way. "Hey, babe."

"Is everything okay?"

He barely heard Patty for all the noise around him. "Yeah, I'm heading back. I didn't find him. He's moved. How's Vincent?"

"Good. They're letting him go home in the morning," she replied.

"That's great. Listen, I'm gonna head back to the apartment. It's been hot out here. I need a shower. See you in the morning?"

"Yeah, that'll be fine. I love you."

"Love you too." Stephen hung up. He pulled his helmet on and started the bike, taking one look back in the direction of Brandon's apartment.

Where did you go, Bernard? But no one answered.

Stephen opened the car door. Vincent placed his feet firmly onto the ground. The cane also pressed firmly against the concrete as he made his way to his feet. Although Vincent continued to recover a little more each day, he seemed frail and less confident than when he left Stephen's apartment just over two weeks ago. As long as Stephen had known him, Vincent always held his head high, until now. His feet shuffled, his shoulders sagged, and his smile awkwardly drooped.

Vincent paused at the entrance to the building.

"What's wrong, Vincent?" Stephen asked.

"I know pride is a sin. While I have never considered myself a proud man..." Tears formed in the corners of his eyes. He wiped them away. "I'm finding that, perhaps, I was wrong. This is," he motioned to the cane and the bruising still on his face, "is hard. Others will see me as weak."

"Maybe," Stephen admitted. "Patty, Alistair, and myself, more than anyone else, will continue to see you for the hero that you are."

Vincent wiped a stream from his cheek and blew his nose with a handkerchief from his pocket. He nodded. "Thank you."

Together, they went up the elevator and down the hall. Vincent looked pitiful. He always dressed nicely. The aluminum cane, however, looked out of place.

Stephen accompanied Vincent to his office and opened the door. "Surprise!" the staff yelled in almost unison. Vincent jumped, then smiled. Everyone showed up early to welcome him back to the office.

He turned to Stephen. "You knew about this?"

"Yes, I did." Stephen grinned.

"Hey, Vincent." Johnathan patted him on the back.

Vincent grunted.

"Glad you're back. Perhaps Stephen won't mope around the place now. You should have seen him this past week. It was depressing."

"Oh, I know," Vincent replied. "He was horrible at the hospital. Then, I told him he had to stop coming to the house when I was released. He made me want to come back to work."

They laughed.

One at a time, they all told how much they missed Vincent and how glad they were that he was okay. Stephen came to realize that they were mostly decent people. He saw things inside each that he did not like. For the most part, however, each person worked hard to be better than their struggles. Lying to them about what happened to Vincent proved harder than he thought it would. He did not like it, but thinking a car struck Vincent had to be much better for each of them than knowing the truth.

Patty came by last. She kissed him on the cheek and gave him a light hug. “We’re glad you’re back.”

“Thanks, Patty. It is good to be back at work. Can you get me up to speed?”

“Sure. But I think Stephen wants a word first. I’ll be back when you two are done.” Patty left, closing the door behind her.

Vincent looked at Stephen. “You want to talk?”

“Kind of.” He pointed to a long, wrapped box on the desk, which seemed to have gone unnoticed.

Vincent walked over to the package and unwrapped the box with meticulous care. He did not tear the paper except around the tape. With the scissors from his desk, he cut the tape holding the box closed and opened it. His eyes brightened a bit to see his gift.

“It is very nice. You did not have to, though.” Vincent pulled a cane from the box.

“I hope you like it. It’s Italian, made from beech wood. The handle is real silver.”

“I love it.”

“You said you may be using a cane for a while. You deserve something with style. Besides, I feel responsible for what happened to you.”

Vincent whacked Stephen’s arm with the new cane.

“Ouch. What was that for?” Stephen said.

“We talked about that. It is not your fault. I am a man and make my own choices. I would do it again and likely will. After all, I am a protector.”

“You’re really taking this whole priest-protector thing to the next level.”

Vincent sat down behind his desk. “You do not really understand. I know you have doubts about the Mighty and the Fallen. I also know that you still feel a bit like a monster sometimes. You are not quite ready to take your place. For me, I had hoped that the stories were not true."

"Really?" Stephen sat across from him.

"Mom was one of the Fallen. Dad, too, is one."

Stephen realized what concerned Vincent. "So, you've been worried all these years, that if it was all true, you would become one of the Fallen."

Vincent took a deep breath, then slowly let it out. "It was such a relief to know that I got to choose my own fate. And I have made my choice. I made it years ago, a choice to serve Christ and do good. So, you see, my burden has been lifted. What about your burden?"

Stephen wondered for a moment which burden he referred to. Was it the choice, or could Vincent sense his conflict over hunting down Bernard? He picked up a pen and fussed with it.

"I don't know. You're right, though. I still feel like a monster sometimes. That boy died because of me. Waltz died because of me. You nearly died. I don't feel worthy."

"I am not saying you have made no mistakes. However, you did not kill either of them. Someone else made that choice." Vincent paused for a moment. "Something else is bothering you."

"Bernard. What if it comes down to one of us killing the other? He's like my big brother. When I came to live with Waltz and Uncle Bernie, some kids down the street picked on me. Bernard stood up for me. He was always there, helping me to get by. My senior year, he delayed going to college to be there for me and watch me graduate. What if Bernie's right, and someone else is controlling him?"

"I have not known you very long. However, what I do know of you is that you are always trying to do the right thing. I think you merely overthink the solution sometimes."

"Really? How so?" Stephen asked.

Vincent's fingers tapped the top of his walking stick. "You have been looking for someone to oversee the warehouses, right?"

"I have."

"I think you already know who you want to run it."

Stephen halfheartedly shrugged and nodded at the same time. The decision proved to be more complicated than he would have preferred.

"So, why has no one been named?" Vincent questioned.

"I see your point," Stephen relented.

"Do you? I believe you have a solution, a good solution. But I also believe you see or perceive issues or problems where they might not exist."

"You know, I really want to be successful, to make Waltz proud in the way I handle this business. What if I'm not as good as I want to be? What if that person isn't what I expect?"

"Stephen, you are one of the brightest men I have ever met. And you are a diligent and committed worker. But that's not always enough. Where's your faith?"

"My faith?" Stephen raised his voice only a bit.

"Yes. You're good with people. But you aren't very trusting. You gave Johnathan a promotion, and he's done very well. But you continue to have him bring every little thing to Patty for approval first. You need to have faith in your decisions. Have faith in the people you put in those positions. Above all, have faith in God to see you through it all."

Stephen tossed the pen into the box. "You sound like Waltz."

Vincent smiled. "Thank you."

Stephen stood and headed toward the door.

"Where are you going?"

Stephen stopped with his hand on the door. "I'm going to offer someone a promotion." Then, he left. He walked down the hall, past his own office and into Patty's.

Patty looked up as Stephen entered. "Is Vincent ready for me?"

"Yeah, but I need to talk to you first."

"Can you walk with me?" Patty grabbed a file and started walking toward Vincent's office. Stephen followed alongside her.

"You know, I've got the warehousing business ready to go."

"Yeah, I've been following it. But you haven't named someone to oversee it yet. What's with the secrecy?"

"What do you mean?" Stephen replied.

"Well, I haven't seen you do any interviews here. I haven't really noticed any phone calls either. I assume you've been keeping interviews and stuff off the radar."

"Oh, no. I know who I want to head it up. You."

Patty froze after having opened Vincent's door. She let the door close back. "Me? You're joking, right?"

"No."

"I can't do that." Patty chuckled.

"Hear me out. You have a master's degree in business. You've been highly involved in this business at a very high level."

"I've only been an assistant," Patty interjected.

"Only? You know all the right connections to get this business up and running. You know all the other businesses and their needs. You understand logistics. You've helped Vincent to make sure all the right people were hired in this office from the very beginning. You have more than proven you are capable."

"What if I fail? You'll have lost a lot of money. I'll be jobless."

"First, you won't be jobless. You can have your old job back. Second, I've looked at the history of this company. There have been failures. This wouldn't be the first. We will survive if it fails. Last, I will not accept 'no' as an answer."

The door opened, and Vincent stuck his head out. "Is everything okay?"

"Yes." Patty turned to Vincent. "I'm sorry, what?"

"Am I to guess the 'yes' was not meant for me?" Vincent asked.

"Correct. Patty just accepted a promotion." Stephen knew she and he made the right decision. Patty had more than proven her abilities. She only lacked confidence, which Stephen could help with. Although he worried that this would affect their relationship, he understood it did not have to have a negative impact.

"Patty? I figured you had someone in mind. I did not think it was her." Vincent opened the door wider and motioned for them to join him in his office. Once inside he patted her on the back. “Congratulations. I know you will do wonderfully.”

“Really?” Patty did not sound so sure.

Vincent smiled.

Patty’s eyes widened. “Oh my. I’ve got work to do. I need to start hiring my team and getting to know the warehouse workers.” She handed the folder to Vincent. “All your updates are in there.” She hurried out the door, her shoes making tapping sounds as she hurried to work.

“Find me a new assistant too, please,” Vincent called out. “Well.” Vincent turned to Stephen. “What’s next?”

Stephen pulled his wallet out and found the picture of him and Bernard. “I’ve got to find him now.”

“You two look close in the photo.”

“Oh, we were. That was a great day. We were in Metropolis, the home of Superman.”

“Yeah, I recognize that museum there, in the background,” Vincent replied. “It had the Bat Boat and all kinds of Hollywood props.”

“What do you mean *had*? They closed?”

“Yeah, it was some time ago. I go there every year for the Superman parade.” Vincent smiled.

So did Stephen. They shared a love for all things Superman.

Vincent grabbed the photo. “You know, it is strange that he left this photo.”

“What do you mean?”

“Well, that Brandon guy told you that Bernard had taken all his belongings, right? Why did he not take this? Still stranger is why did he leave this behind knowing you are after him?”

Stephen snatched the photo out of his hand. "I've got to go." He hurried out of the office, leaving Vincent standing in the doorway. "I'm taking the company truck," Stephen called out.

He ran down the stairs and straight to the truck, and then headed to Metropolis, Illinois. He felt Bernard left the photo on purpose wanting Stephen to find him. Perhaps Bernard had been forced to attack Vincent, and really wanted Stephen's help, or maybe Bernard meant to set a trap. Either way, Stephen understood that he needed to go.

The truck beeped; it needed gas. Stephen pulled into a gas station to fill up. He Googled Metropolis on his phone for directions. *Three hours. I don't remember it being that far.* He went inside, grabbed a snack and a drink, giving him time to think. Would he just show up? How far was he willing to go? He considered calling Alistair for a moment.

No, this is a family problem. I need to take care of this myself.

Stephen set his phone back to Google Maps. It notified him of construction along the way. The trip would take longer than he thought. He got back into the truck and headed for the home of Superman to find his Fallen brother.

Construction traffic caused standstills for part of the trip. Stephen arrived in Metropolis late that same afternoon. Under normal circumstances, the expected three-hour trip would have been tough enough. With construction, the weight of the trip's purpose, and all the emotions that accompanied it, the five-hour drive taxed Stephen in every way.

The hot sun did little to help his mood. The last five hours tormented him. He thought about a strategy for facing Bernard, as well as a potential puppet master. He worried about trying to find some way to save his oldest friend. On top of that, he felt rumblings in his stomach.

Metropolis did not have much of anything of interest except Superman. He parked his truck in the square, where the fifteen-foot-tall bronze statue of Superman stood in all his blue, red, and yellow splendor. Seeing it again somehow brought a smile to his face. A family stood at the base of the statue while someone took their picture. Each family member wore a different Superman T-shirt.

On the corner across the street stood the Superman Museum. Stephen remembered enjoying walking around inside the small building with Bernard. The Americana Hollywood Museum was not far from there. Still, he needed to eat and rest.

Stephen walked into a small shop in the square to grab a bite. He sat in a booth near the back of the shop and looked over the menu.

"Hey, hon. Can I get you something to drink?"

Stephen looked up to see a young woman waiting for a reply.

"Yeah, sure. I'll take a water."

"Okay. Are you ready to order? Or do you need a minute?"

"I'm ready." Stephen put the menu away. "I'll have a chicken sandwich."

"You want mayo on that?"

"No, thank you." Stephen replied quickly.

"How about fries?"

"That sounds good. Thanks."

The woman scribbled on a pad and walked away.

Stephen pulled the photo from his wallet. He felt simultaneously nervous and relieved that this fight might finally come to an end. He needed closure for Waltz, and he really wanted to be able to help Vincent find his father. Vincent continued to be understanding of all that took place; a true friend.

The waitress placed the cup of water on the table.

"Your food will be out in a minute."

"Thanks." Stephen went back to looking at the picture.

"Hey, that boy there in the photo--" she pointed at Bernard, "that's not Bernard, is it?"

Stephen turned his attention to the woman. "Do you know him?"

"Well, yes and no. He comes in here sometimes. He's friendly enough but doesn't talk much. I think he carries that same picture. The other kid, that's you?"

"Yeah, we grew up together."

"I always wondered who that cute little guy was." The woman smiled at Stephen.

Without meaning to, he glimpsed her thoughts. She thought he was even cuter now. Stephen fidgeted in his seat. He felt her looking him over.

"Do you happen to know where he lives?" Stephen inquired.

"Nah, I think he comes and goes. He stopped in here yesterday morning for a bite. So, I think he's back in town. If you tell me where you're staying and give me your number, I'll pass it along when I see him."

Stephen peeked inside her mind again. She wanted his information, but for other reasons.

"You know, he's already told me where to meet up with him. I'll just wait until then."

She shrugged. "Okay. If you change your mind—"

"I know where to find you," he finished.

She winked at him and walked back to the kitchen. At least he confirmed this was in the right place. He sat there waiting on his food. He listened for thoughts as people went by. Nothing appeared to be out of the ordinary. Many of the people who walked by were locals, going about their daily schedules. Occasionally, a Fort Massac tourist or Superman enthusiast wandered by, their thoughts filled with excitement.

"Here you go. Can I get you anything else?" The waitress continued smiling at him in a way that made him fidget some more.

"No, I'm good, thank you. But here you go." He handed the woman a twenty. "You've been kind. Keep the change."

"Thanks, hon."

Stephen grinned to himself as the waitress walked away, grateful Patty was not on this trip. Otherwise, he would have had to pull her off the woman. The mental imagery made him chuckle. He shoveled down his food and left.

He made his way down the street, toward the museum pictured in the photo. He walked up to the green painted rock out front, a nearby sign advertised it as Kryptonite. He held up the photo one last time. He stood in the same spot they had stood together about fifteen years prior.

He looked around. No one appeared to be watching. He took hold of the fence and hopped over it. He jumped it easier than expected. Walking to the door, however, took forever. Each prop, sign, or structure in the lawn could be used for concealment. He peered this way and that, searching for anything out of place. But how would he know? His heart raced. When he finally reached the front door, it was not locked. Stephen took a deep breath and entered.

Memorabilia from various movies lay covered in dust, but not all. Some items clearly showed the layers of dust had been recently disturbed. The only light came from the windows behind him. The air smelled stale and made his throat itch.

"Bernard?" he called out in a raspy voice. Clearing his throat, he tried again. "Bernard? I'm here." He heard movement near the back of the building. "I want to talk. We're brothers. We can work this out. Just talk to me."

Moving slowly toward the back, his eyes slowly adjusted to the dim light. Movie props abounded. He passed a life-size Lara Croft, Rhett, Scarlett, and even Jack Sparrow, until he could go no further.

"Dang it. Where are you?"

"I'm here."

Steven whirled around to see a large dark figure standing next to a Mr. Spock replica, between him and the door. "Bernard. What's going on? Where have you been?"

Bernard said nothing. Stephen tried to read him but met resistance. He debated forcing the issue, but did not want a confrontation, if avoidable. "So, did you want me to come here to fight or what?"

"I didn't want you here." A sadness exuded in Bernard's voice.

"Then why am I here?"

Bernard said nothing.

Stephen knew he made a mistake. Something about the situation was not right. Reaching out with his mind revealed one other person. Someone else hid nearby. In searching deep, Bernard's thoughts revealed sorrow.

I never intended for this. I'm sorry, Stephen.

"Bernard, this doesn't have to happen. We can leave now and fix this."

"Do not be mistaken," a man's voice said from the darkest corner. "Bernard is devoted to the cause. He understands what is at stake."

Stephen looked, but saw no one around. Then, he looked at Bernard, not yet ready to believe Bernard had willingly chosen to be Fallen.

"Really? What's at stake, then?" Stephen asked.

"All of it," the voice replied. "Victory is within our grasp. And as fate would have it, you are the key."

"How can I be the key? I barely know anything." Stephen continued looking around. The voice now seemed to come from all directions.

"Yet, you have power beyond anything we have ever experienced."

"Show yourself. Let's have this conversation face to face." He searched for the man's thoughts. Locking onto his thoughts proved difficult.

"You want to meet me? Let me show you who I really am."

All light slowly faded from the room. Methodically, darkness filled every corner from the back of the building to the front, until all light had been snuffed out. Stephen felt alone and suffocated. Trying to escape only proved the situation to be desperate, as he ran into object after object. Things crashed and collided with every move.

He tried to find the mind causing all the trouble. *Where are you? Why can't I see?* He continued looking for a way in.

"There is nothing to see—no light, no hope."

Stephen searched harder. *Let me in.* The harder he pushed, the harder the voice pushed back.

"This can all stop, Stephen. It can all end. What have the Mighty done to help you?" the voice taunted.

Stephen felt around, finding something sturdy to brace himself against. "Alistair helped me. He's one of the Mighty."

"How has He helped? You still haven't found the answers you seek. He sees the future but was conveniently absent when Vincent was attacked. The Mighty should have found you sooner. Waltz should have told you about your gift sooner. He had suspicions before the gift fully manifested."

"You're trying to twist everything," Stephen yelled.

"I'm trying to show you who the Mighty really are. We could have ended you long ago. Instead, we've watched you. We've followed you since New Orleans to see if you are worthy to join us."

"Join you?" Stephen snickered. "Is being crazy a requirement for the Fallen or just exclusive to you?"

"If you don't join us, there remains only one option. Die."

"*Argh*!" Pain shot through Stephen's head as though his brain were being torn apart. "Stop it," he cried out.

"The pain only stops if you join us."

"Then kill me and get it over with."

"No. You will die slowly." The voice sounded pleased.

The pain continued to grow. Stephen never experienced anything like it. It spread throughout his extremities, sending him falling to the floor in agony. His arms and legs drew up. His fingers disjointed. Every muscle in his body pulled tighter and tighter. Tendons and ligaments popped as they continued to draw taut.

"You already know what it means to be Fallen. Tommy, Chuck, Rebound, they're all your doing. Accept being Fallen and the pain stops. The rush of adrenaline, the high you get from using your power, can remain all the time. Deny it and you will die a most horrific death."

"Please, Bernard. Help me." Stephen called out to him, pleading for help. No answer. "I can't do this." Small tearing sounds preceded shocks of pain throughout his body. "*Argh*!" The sound died as it left his lips, swallowed by the darkness. His heart ached.

Stephen struggled with the thought of death. The pleasure he got from using his ability tempted him. Bernie often hinted that the Mighty were not always right. Stephen needed to make a decision. He knew he could not stand the pain much longer. Still, he did not want to die. He did the only thing left to do, utter his last words.

"Lord, Jesus, help me. I-I am Fallen." Stephen gasped for air as the pain increased. "Take my life and let me die."

The pain dissipated and light crept back into the room. Stephen felt strength return to his limbs, gaining control of his muscles once again. He worked his way to one knee and steadied himself before rising to his feet.

"What are you doing? How are you doing this?" the voice yelled.

Stephen looked around, confused as to what was taking place. He was not doing anything.

Light continued to grow brighter and fill the room. At first it seemed to have no source. Shadows and dark spaces ceased to exist. Before him, the bright image of a man appeared. Stephen dared not look at his face. Instead, he threw himself to the ground in awe. His entire being understood that he was in the presence of holiness, and he responded the only way he could—in reverence and adoration. In front of Stephen stood a man dressed in a flowing white robe.

"I'm not worthy," Stephen called out.

"Do not bow to me. I'm a servant, like you." The sound of the man's voice pierced Stephen's very soul. "He is worthy enough for you. Stand, Stephen."

Stephen raised himself and saw the man pointing to the source of the light. He saw the image of God and his Son seated on thrones.

"What happened? Am I dead?"

The man smiled. "No. You put your life in God's hands. The Father and Son answer all who call on them."

"Is this a dream?" Stephen still wasn't sure what to make of it.

"More like a vision. This is happening outside of time. When we are done, you will be returned to the same time and place you left."

"Will I die?"

"Only if you choose not to act."

Stephen paused for a moment before continuing. "Who are you?"

"I am Areli, an angel of sight."

"You say I need to act, but what can I do? I don't fully understand my power yet."

"Stephen, in your weakness, He is strong. God has strength that will be enough and take care of you when you are unable to."

"What do I do or say?"

"Don't worry about that. When the time comes, you will know the answers."

"So, that's it?"

"No. You are here for a different reason." Areli pointed again—only this time to another vision. "Look over there. What do you see?"

"It looks like there are two armies. One appears to be made up of demons and evil creatures. The other looks like an army of God."

"Yes. The release of these armies means a final chance for man to choose. There will be devastation like never before. Only a third of mankind will survive. The atrocities will be great."

Stephen turned away. He did not want to see more. The thought of two-thirds of humanity dying made him sick to his stomach.

Areli pointed again. "Now what do you see?"

Stephen turned his head back to look again. "I see two more armies. One is dressed like the Mighty; the other appears to be Fallen."

"The Fallen seek to conquer the world, so they think. In truth, they seek only to destroy all goodness, such as hope, faith, and love. They are responsible for so much that is wrong in the world. They'll take anything and turn it toward evil. When they make it so that man cannot turn back, the evil army will be released, setting the tribulation into motion. The world has been so close before. Many times, the Fallen have risen to almost complete power over man. The Mighty has always fought them back. Now they are stronger than ever. New challenges are rising among them. Their strength and numbers are greater than the Mighty know. You are essential to fighting them, to giving man more time."

Stephen thought for a moment before asking, "That's why you helped me?"

"No. I helped you because you made a choice. You chose to serve Christ, giving him your life, not knowing where that would lead you. That choice has allowed you to be Mighty. You expected death but gained life. You waited late in the game to do so. Still, you did it. I'm showing you all this so you will understand your role."

"What do I need to do to fight them?"

"It's simple: do good. Love man and do not withhold compassion or justice from anyone. Follow the Way wherever it leads you." Areli walked away. Light faded and Bernard wove into view again.

"What do I do about this?" Stephen motioned toward Bernard.

"You will know. God's instructions are written upon your heart."

"What if I mess up?"

"There is no *if*. You will. But that's okay. He forgives you." Areli faded out of view. The room returned to darkness.

With the vision completely gone, Stephen realized he still lay on the floor, writhing in pain. Only now, he believed he had the power to stop it.

Enough! Stephen sent a shockwave of mental energy out in every direction. The darkness ceased, and the room returned to being dimly lit by the light coming through the windows. His muscles and joints ached. However, the immense pain subsided. He jumped to his feet, wincing and fighting against the pain and numbness that lingered in his body.

"I knew I was right about how powerful you are. It's a shame you won't join us. You have to die now." Light entered through a side door behind Bernard as someone ran out. The door closed.

Another Bernard slowly materialized in front of Stephen, next to the original.

"That's a neat trick. Where'd you learn that? *Star Trek*?" Stephen listened for thoughts and felt for emotions. Only Bernard remained; his emotions buried deep inside. "Ah, it appears your friend left Bernard. I think he's scared."

Both Bernards approached Stephen. "I'm sorry, Stephen," they said in unison.

"I am too. I still love you; you know."

One of the Bernards swung at Stephen. He easily evaded the first attack. Back and forth, Stephen fought with them. One sent him flying into the Elvira booth. He jumped up and sent a Bernard soaring into a Superman display. He tried to take control of one but did not have enough time to focus. The faster he moved and countered, the harder they punched and kicked.

Bernard kicked Stephen into an Adam West Batman replica.

Looking at the Batman mannequin, he said, “You know you got me started in all this, right?”

He dodged a flying Jack Sparrow head just in time for it to crash into Robin.

This has to end.

Stephen ran toward a Bernard, jumped, and kicked him square in the chest. That Bernard fell into the other one. Both crashed to the floor—the opportunity Stephen needed. He focused and found Bernard’s trigger. One of them disappeared.

Bernard looked around frantically. “What happened? Where did he go?”

“He’s where he belongs, right back in your head. And you can’t let him back out.”

Bernard ran. Stephen felt his fear. He chased after Bernard. Out of the door and across the lawn the two ran, Stephen nearly matched him step for step. Bernard bounded over the fence. Stephen followed. Bernard looked back as he lunged into the passenger seat of a black car. Stephen closed in, but not quick enough.

“Go! Go!” Bernard yelled. The car sped away and he turned toward Stephen, eyes wide. *How in the world?*

Although Bernard escaped, Stephen felt pleased. He faced Bernard and uncovered the truth. A puppet master did exist. Most important of all, he made a choice. Even with a new weight on his shoulders, the pending fate of man, he managed to find relief in a new sense of purpose. Waltz's death, though important, appeared such a small thing when compared with the path ahead. Waltz would be proud.

Stephen walked to the truck and headed back to St. Louis. He sent Patty a text, telling her he found Bernard and would explain everything when he returned. He passed construction on the other side of the road, so he expected to be back for a late dinner. The three-hour drive home gave him the time he needed to process everything.

Alistair returned to the Mighty to report what happened and that Bernard joined Fallen. Stephen sent him a text, telling him he faced Bernard and was fine.

As he thought about the events that transpired, he realized the success he achieved. In his burst of mental energy, he received an echo back from the mind of the voice. He echoed fear and pain. Whomever the voice, he now feared Stephen, and nursed his own wounds.

As for Bernard, Stephen locked the gift of projection away inside Bernard's head, in a deep hidden place, that he knew Bernard himself would not think to look—Bernard's first memory of Stephen.

Stephen drove back to his apartment. A beautiful array of colors filled the sky, leading the way back to St. Louis. Buildings cast shadows throughout the city. The sun set earlier now, and the cool winds of autumn blew. Though sore all over, Stephen enjoyed the ride with his windows down.

He thought about Bernard and the voice, as well as Areli and the vision shown to him. Everything Waltz tried to teach him was true. He understood being one of the Mighty alone would not stop the army of the Fallen. The battle starts with what the individual man encountered each and every day. Waltz worked so hard to teach Stephen that same thing the last few months he lived.

Stephen limped up the stairs and into his apartment. To his amazement, Patty, Vincent, Alistair, Sam, and Anastasia sat on the couch, all looking at him as he walked through the doorway.

“Hey.” Patty ran to him and kissed him. “I’m glad you’re back. I was worried.”

"Is it over?" Vincent asked as he limped his way to Stephen.

"Yes, and no. I'll explain in a moment." He looked at Alistair. "How did you beat me here? You just left town."

Alistair smiled. "Ye can't guess?"

"Your visions, right?"

Alistair only grinned.

"And you brought a couple of familiar faces. I thought it wasn't your secret to tell."

"They didn't come with me!" Alistair replied.

Sam spoke up. "Stephen, we are aware every time a choice is made by someone who becomes one of the Mighty. Imagine our surprise when we saw Alistair already here. I can only surmise he has been aware of your gifts."

Stephen noted that Sam looked just as uptight and uncomfortable as he did at Waltz's funeral. "By we, you mean you two or the entire council?"

"The entire council," Anastasia chimed in. Her voice continued to be as gentle as Stephen remembered. Her presence added an air of elegance to the conversation. "But we will talk about this and more later. Sam and I are here on behalf of the council, to welcome you to the family and answer questions when you are ready. There is a process of sorts."

Holding Patty's hand, Stephen made his way over and pulled up a couple of chairs for himself and Patty. She squeezed his hand and gave him a look of concern. Her thoughts focused on Stephen and his well-being, nothing else. *I'm good, Beautiful,* he assured her.

She smiled back and nodded.

"It appears we have matching limps," Vincent joked. "Care to use my cane?"

"No, thank you." Stephen eased onto the chair.

"We could wait somewhere else and give you a moment with your friends." Sam offered, though Stephen sensed Sam did not really want to.

"But," Anastasia said with a smile, "we would appreciate staying to hear what happened."

"I don't have a problem with you staying," Stephen quickly replied. He did not want to hide from them anymore.

Sam got straight to the point. "In that case, Mr. Cross, what happened?"

"That's a good question." Stephen thought for a moment. On the way home, he processed everything that happened in Metropolis. He learned some things. Yet, he developed more questions. "I made a choice and have questions. I'm guessing you want more details than that though."

Sam and the others sat quietly. Vincent looked uncomfortable, shifting in his seat. Did they know about Vincent? He searched Vincent's mind. He could not get in at first. Then, the wall fell. Immediately, he knew Vincent had let the wall down.

Do they know about you?

Vincent replied, *I don't know.*

Stephen decided to tell the tale without giving anything away concerning Vincent. "Where would you like me to start?"

Sam started to speak, but Anastasia interrupted. "To be fair to everyone else, let's start with what happened while you were gone. We can discuss any questions we have later."

"I followed Bernard to Metropolis, Illinois," Stephen began.

"Bernard?" Sam looked at Anastasia. "At least now we know why he's been missing."

"Wait, you didn't know about Bernard?" Stephen found this curious.

"No. We only recently began wondering if he had gone missing. It's not unusual for our people to be away for a while, especially if they aren't on a mission. They have lives to live. We try not to interfere more than we have to. And only the council and a few others knew Bernard. His missions were sensitive."

Stephen was not sure what to make of this new information but continued. "You may or may not know that Bernard is...was like a brother to me. My hope was that I could save him. Bernie felt Bernard was being controlled by someone else. Turns out, that's partly true. I found him at a closed museum. Someone got into my head. I only heard his voice. There was so much pain and darkness. I was dying. Somehow, he caused my muscles to stretch to the point that they started tearing. My head was the worst. I've never experienced such pain. It was as though I was hurting in every way possible. Worse, I never saw him. He hid in the darkness."

"Wait." Sam looked serious. "Why was he in Metropolis?"

"We went there together when we were younger. There's a fifteen-foot Superman. It's cool. There's a Superman museum, and—" Stephen saw that no one, except Vincent, appreciated the Superman information.

"Anyway, he used it to let me believe he still cared about me like a brother. Maybe inside he still does. I don't know. My guard was down, and the plan worked. They wanted me to join them. When I refused, the man said the only other choice was to kill me. Everything went dark." Stephen's speech slowed as he remembered the incident and began to relive the emotions as well. "The light slowly left the room. I was alone. Feelings of despair and helplessness took over. I was angry, which only seemed to help his cause. After I fought with the pain, I started accepting that it was over for me."

Patty squeezed Stephen's hand. He looked at her and saw tears welling in her eyes. Realizing how hard it must be for her to hear, he smiled at her and kissed her hand before continuing. Knowing she supported him gave him strength.

"When I realized I couldn't win, I asked God, Christ, to save me. It was more than a physical need. But as I was dying, I was suddenly aware that I deserved death. I asked God to take my life. I just wanted him to give me a merciful death. Instead, time stopped, and light crept into the room. But it continued to grow until I was surrounded by light, which emanated from God's throne. The pain was gone."

Stephen heard a gasp. Looking around, he noticed that the entire room was locked on his words, eyes wide.

"Ye saw...Him?" Alistair asked.

"Yeah. But I figured that was usual for one of the Mighty."

Alistair looked at Sam, who looked at Anastasia. She slowly shook her head. "There is nothing normal about that."

"Well, an angel, Areli, proceeded to show me a vision concerning the Fallen and the Mighty. The Fallen's actions, if unchecked, would result in the Tribulation. My job—well, our job—is to hold them back, giving people more time to accept Christ. He wants as many people saved as are willing to accept."

Stephen got up. Cotton mouth set in from all the talking. He hobbled to the kitchen to pour a glass of water as he continued.

"After that, I knew what to do. I sent out a wave of mental energy. It only affected people with gifts nearby, disrupting them. Bernard was the backup plan. We started struggling. I fought two versions of him. He kept me too occupied to use my gift, until I caught a break. I locked his projection ability away. Our gifts are mostly mental, from what I can tell. So, I moved his to a different spot inside his mind. He immediately realized what happened and ran."

"That's when he got away, I assume." Sam sounded certain.

Stephen took a sip and made his way back to his seat. "Not exactly. I chased him over the fence. I would have caught him too, but he got into a car. I could tell another man drove. That's about all though."

He sensed confusion. The feeling came from Anastasia. He looked directly at her. "Why are you confused? What am I missing?" She said nothing. Sam's facial expression indicated to Stephen that indeed, something was up. "Look. I don't mean this as a threat. But you're hiding something from me. Do either of you know what my gift is?"

Again, neither said a word. Alistair, however, spoke. “They do not. They know yer powerful. In fact, yer one of the most powerful Mighty any of us has ever known. When someone with a gift gives his or her life to Christ, the council is made aware. And for a brief moment, they can sense the strength of the individual. I’m not on the council. But I have heard some talk about it.”

Sam glared at Alistair.

“What’s the problem? He’s one of the Mighty.”

Anastasia did not look away from Stephen when she spoke. “You know he still has to go before the council.”

“Yeah, I know. I also know that’s a formality. Right?”

Vincent and Patty remained quiet, only looking back and forth between the four of them as though watching a doubles tennis match.

“Look, I won’t hide anything from you about me. I only ask that you do the same. With my gift, I could pluck the information from you. I’d rather not.”

“Warriors’ abilities, like all others, differ from person to person,” Sam said. “No doubt, you discovered what Bernard’s is. However, all warrior class have some level of speed and strength greater than your average person.” He looked around the room, then back to Stephen. “You should *not* have been able to keep step with Bernard unless you are a warrior.”

“I was right,” Alistair exclaimed. Everyone looked at him.

“Right about what?” Patty broke her silence.

“Stephen is a sensitive.” Everyone stared blankly at Alistair, except for Sam and Anastasia.

“A sensitive?” Patty continued.

Sam took over. "Sensitives are Mighty who have gifts in two classes. It's very rare. They have a primary class. The second skill set is muted, not quite as strong as it might be if it was their primary talent."

"I'm not certain that's it, though." Anastasia leaned forward in her seat. "Stephen, Waltz knew about your gift?"

Stephen nodded.

"How did he classify you? Alistair says you're a prophet class," she stated.

"Yes," he replied.

"Hmm." Anastasia looked at Sam. "This is curious. Waltz would understand how to classify someone. Based on what we've heard, I'd classify him as a warrior. I'm guessing Waltz had passed before he had an opportunity to know the warrior-like gifts. Sam, how about you?"

"I'd classify him as a warrior, indeed." He looked at Stephen. "I'm guessing there is more to your gift than fighting and running fast." Sam glanced at Vincent and Patty. "Do we need to have a more private conversation?"

"Sam," Anastasia said, "can't you see how close they all are? Please don't be rude." She smiled at Patty.

Stephen sipped his water to wet his throat. Explaining his gift to Waltz seemed so strange not long ago. He found himself having to explain it more and more. Talking about it came much easier now. He now understood just how little he actually knew. He thought he was just a fast person and never considered for a moment it was an ability. So, instead of trying to explain his gift, he told them of all the recent instances when used his gifts, careful to leave nothing out. He started with Waltz teaching him how to control his gifts.

They learned of his involvement in capturing Matthew and Rebound, and in setting the women free. All of which led to preventing a bombing. All hung on his words, amazed when he explained how he actually took control of a person's body, depending on the person. He told them everything, except for Vincent and Marie. Stephen said nothing of his time with them over the July Fourth weekend.

No one asked questions. They remained silent the entire time Stephen spoke. Only distant noises in the background broke the silence on occasion. When finished, Stephen waited for a response. At first there was none—only quiet. All waited for Sam or Anastasia to say something.

Alistair spoke first. "I know I'm not the most experienced here. But it would help to know Stephen's lineage. Sam, do you think we could figure it out by looking into the genealogical records at the Enclave?" He looked at everyone else. "The Enclave is sort of like a base for us."

"Alistair," Sam said, "that's a good idea. We'll need to sort that out before we can continue this conversation."

Anastasia stood. "I apologize. It may seem strange, but we really do need to sort out his lineage before we can continue. There are still many questions that need to be answered."

"Waltz raised him," Patty objected. "Doesn't that matter?"

"We mean no offense, and while the council may decide to allow Stephen to take up the line vacated by

Waltz's death, we first need to determine where he came from."

"But—" Patty said.

Stephen gently squeezed her thigh. He turned to face her. "It's okay, Patty."

He took a deep breath. "I know where I come from. Waltz warned me not to tell anyone while the Fallen were still after me. I believe he knew they wanted me. The truth would have only made them want me more."

"What truth?" Patty asked.

Stephen faced the group. "I am the son of Ian Walter Stockton and Layla Isabel Taft."

"That's not possible." Sam leaned back in his seat. For the first time, Stephen noticed his stoic appearance fade.

"What's not possible?" Alistair appeared confused.

Anastasia walked to the window and looked out toward the city.

Patty did not say a word. Stephen listened for feelings and thoughts from her. She was torn, hurt that she had not been made privy to the truth but understood that there was something larger at play. It made her mad, and Stephen knew well enough to tread softly.

"I should have seen it." Everyone turned toward the window where Anastasia stood.

"I'm sorry, but say again?" Sam sat up.

Anastasia turned to face the group. "I should have realized it, that you were their son—Layla's and Waltz's. I knew them both. I remember the night they met. It was Waltz's birthday. He had retired from service after sacrificing his triune in an attempt to save one of them from being Fallen. Layla retired a few years later. That must have been when she realized she was pregnant. She kept you a secret."

"It's not possible." Alistair stared at Stephen. "You shouldn't have any powers. Crossing bloodlines is discouraged to keep from shrinking our numbers."

"It does make sense. Both Layla and Waltz were sensitive to the warrior class." Sam paused. "This gives the council a few new questions to consider. Two Mighty have never produced a child with power."

"I've told you everything I know," Stephen stated. "You understand why Waltz kept me a secret?"

Sam nodded. Over by the window, Anastasia remained silent.

"Waltz knew that it was important no one knew about me. *I* didn't even know until after he passed. He left a video file with Vincent for me."

Anastasia rejoined the group. "Sam, we should go see the other council members."

"Agreed. Stephen, I know you must have questions. After we meet with the council, we'll be back. Alistair will stay here with you, just in case we need to get in touch before we return."

Stephen rolled his eyes. "Let me guess—he's actually a security detail?"

Sam smiled. "Do you think you need one?"

As they left, Sam opened the door for Anastasia. Before he walked out, he looked back at Stephen. "We won't be away long." Then, they were gone.

Stephen scanned the room. He imagined they all wondered the same thing: How would the council respond to all this? Even Alistair did not seem sure what to make of it all.

"I'm sorry I couldn't tell you two about Waltz being my dad."

Patty threw her arms around him. "It's okay."

Alistair paced by the windows in the conference room. Lightning lit up the room, and thunder rattled the building. Stephen looked at the lights as they flickered a moment. Alistair had not left Stephen's side since the incident in Metropolis. For the past three days, he had been Stephen's shadow, even preventing Patty from having any meaningful conversations with Stephen. Basically, he turned into Stephen's bodyguard.

Stephen waited in anticipation. He was not completely sure why Sam and Anastasia had gone back to meet with the council. Quizzing Alistair did not produce any results. It was clear he did not know anything either. Stephen longed for answers.

The conference room phone rang, and Stephen answered. "Yes?" He listened to Patty on the other end. "Will you walk him over? Thanks."

Alistair stopped pacing.

"Sam is here," Stephen told him.

Alistair took a seat next to Stephen.

Patty opened the door and Sam walked in.

"Thank you, Patty." Sam's voice gave no indication of his mood.

"You're welcome." Patty smiled and winked at Stephen before she closed the door.

Stephen felt good seeing him. Besides learning what took place, he hoped Sam's arrival meant Alistair would stop following him everywhere. Sam seated himself across from Stephen and Alistair.

Sam spoke first. "Stephen, I should start by telling you how surprised the council was at discovering you had a gift. You were a very well-kept secret. Your mother gave you the last name Cross, which was her mother's maiden name. She wasn't one of the Mighty, which kept you off our radar. We've never had a Mighty with the last name Cross. You are the first and have now been recorded in Waltz's bloodline. And of all your family's bloodline, you are the last, Mighty or not."

Stephen had always felt alone on some level. Finding out he had no family left scared him. "Wait, was my family targeted?"

"We had never considered it until recently." Sam sighed. "With what we do, sometimes people die. Your bloodline has a history of being bold and fearless, sometimes even reckless. Several of the last ones to die out were due to age or illness. It was not until Waltz's mysterious death that we realized it could have been part of something larger. Only then did we search for members of his bloodline to find they were no more. Your vision confirms our fear. Somehow, the Fallen realized your family would be instrumental in stopping them in the future and took drastic measures to see that doesn't happen."

"All my family killed because of me?" Stephen tried to process the revelation. He did not know what to do with this new information. Should he be happy he was alive or sad to be alone? Guilt built at the realization of how many must have died because of him. "Should I be concerned?"

Alistair remained quiet as Sam continued. "We think you are safe for now. They obviously knew you were important. But they underestimated your power. Greed kept them from killing you early on. They likely wanted you to join them, thinking that would secure their victory. Based on what you told us of the vision, they would have been right. What they could not have known was just how much like Waltz you turned out to be. Being attacked by the opposition opened your eyes and heart to what is right. They thought it would harden you. But you are compassionate and kind, like Waltz. It softened your heart to be open to God's call."

"Yeah, I guess it did. Waltz made sure I was brought up right. When I discovered this gift, I first felt like a monster. It made me question God."

Alistair chimed in. "What about the council? What did they have to say about Stephen?"

"Of course, they all want to meet him," Sam replied. "Stephen, we have protocols, rules we go by. There is training that would help you reach your potential. Aside from that, you live your life, making a difference. At times, there are larger problems that may require a group effort. Mighty may be called upon then. The decision to respond is always up to you. Training at Enclave has a lot to offer. There are records that can give you information about your family history. Each bloodline has its own trove where historical artifacts, personal belongings, and various items are stored. Only blood relatives can open the doors. You are the only one that has access to yours. I believe there are a lot of opportunities for you there. There is much we don't understand about you. Perhaps we can learn together."

Questions floated around in Stephen's mind, and he wanted answers. "Answers, huh? Can you answer some questions for me now?"

Sam smiled. "I will try."

"The shroud that was placed over Waltz's casket—why didn't the stone light up?"

"We discussed that while I was with the council. They are probably still discussing it, among other things. There are several hypotheses. The truth is, we really do not know. Please understand, you are different, more special than any Mighty since the time when these gifts were bestowed upon us. I'm sure they are searching the archives for clues. I've studied them more than most, and I don't believe the answer is there."

"Okay, then." Stephen thought for a moment. He did not expect to be a mystery to even the council. "Am I a Sensitive?"

"Only training will confirm. There are some who believe you are actually a warrior, based on the information you gave us. The mental abilities you've described can be used as a weapon or to a strategic advantage. However, it doesn't explain your vision, or being able to share thoughts. You said Waltz indicated you are of the prophet class. The council needs to know more. Waltz was a skilled trainer, having trained even

Alistair many years ago. He almost instinctively would know a person's class, even before seeing their skill."

The idea of going to Enclave intrigued Stephen. He figured he would meet the council sooner or later. But to see his family's trove and learn more about his skills and the history of the Mighty excited him.

He turned to Sam. "One more question. When I told you I was Waltz's son, your physical reaction seemed greater than the others. Why?"

Sam dropped his head. Stephen sensed the sadness build in him. "Stephen, I was the Prophet in Waltz's triune. He and I were close once. Knowing you were his son and that he never told me forced me to see just how betrayed he must have felt." Sam sighed. "When our warrior- Elizabeth fell, he did the only thing he knew to do. As a protector, he surrendered the triune's powers to get her away from the drunkenness of it. I'm sure you know what I'm talking about."

"Yes," Stephen replied without hesitation. "Using the power feels good. It makes you want to use it more."

"Right. That's why we teach restraint. Elizabeth had none. She didn't see the harm. The council admonished her. She didn't like it and ended up falling."

"It was more than that," Stephen replied.

"You know the story?"

"Yes. She fell in love with a Fallen named Anthony Abate. That wasn't known until later. Waltz never gave up on her."

"I do know Waltz never gave up; but I did. I didn't know about Mr. Abate, though." He stared into space for a moment. "Anyway, I left the triune. Bernie agreed to take my place and surrender his power as the triune's prophet. What we didn't know was that in surrendering our power for a just reason, we would have kept our original powers. Waltz kept his, as well as Bernie."

"Bernie kept his power? What was it?"

"Bernie's ability is similar to yours. But he can see only someone's subconscious. He's very limited."

Stephen felt betrayed. Dreams take place in the subconscious mind. He realized Bernie implanted the dreams and nightmares in his mind. And at some point, Bernie joined Fallen.

"Where is Bernie?"

"At Enclave. We also hold some of the Fallen there; in a place we call the Catacombs. It's well guarded, and all powers are dead there, in a way. You'll have to see it for yourself to understand."

Stephen looked at Alistair. "Do you have any questions?"

"Nah. I know what Enclave's like. And I know what the council is like. Sure, the individuals have thoughts and ideas about things. But it can take the council a bit to decide on something collectively."

"Well, then, I'll be ready—"

The door burst open. Vincent stood in the doorway; cane in one hand, the other still holding the door. Strands of hair hung in his face, not his usual neatly kept appearance. "Sorry to intrude, but I do not wish to hide any longer."

The three looked at Vincent as one might look at a crazy man.

"Vincent," Sam said, "what are you hiding from?"

Vincent took a deep breath before replying. "You," he stated. "Stephen and Alistair can confirm that I am Mighty; a priest. Only, I did not know it until recently."

Sam laughed. "That's impossible. We know when all become Mighty. We do not know about you."

Stephen spoke up. "Sam, very simply, how does your notification system work?"

"Well, there is a scroll—the Scroll of the Chosen. Children of the Mighty are recorded on the scroll, and their names disappear. When they have both awakened and chosen Christ, their names reappear. After the funeral, because of the shroud, we wrote Stephen's name on the scroll, just in case. Vincent Abbott, however, is not listed on the scroll. You would have to be born to a member of the Mighty to have your name written in the first place."

"Can you tell if his name was ever written on the scroll?"

"We do keep a record of all Mighty children. Even though some aren't chosen to have gifts, many still fight the good fight alongside us. But I did check when we returned to the council. I checked on Patty too. I did not want any more surprises."

"Well, surprise. Elizabeth Marie is my mother."

Sam's eyes widened. "Elizabeth's son? But who's your father?"

"Does it matter?"

"I guess it doesn't, at least not now." Sam stood and walked past Vincent through the door, pausing to look at him one more time. "Excuse me a moment."

Stephen heard him talking in the hallway but could not make out the conversation. After a moment, he returned.

"They wrote your name on the scroll. It disappeared and reappeared instantly, signifying that your name is recorded as Mighty. We would like you to accompany us to Enclave also."

Vincent and Stephen smiled at each other.

"You'll need to pack your things and be ready to leave tomorrow. Alistair, you know where to meet."

"The airport?" Alistair asked.

"No, the other place."

"Oh." Alistair looked surprised.

"What other place?" Stephen asked.

"He will show you tomorrow," Sam replied. "But I must go. Until then."

Sam left in a hurry as Patty walked in.

"Did I just hear Sam say you guys are leaving tomorrow?"

"Uh, yeah. We're going to meet the council. If that's okay? Stephen realized his mistake in not talking with Patty about it first.

"You were planning to tell me, right?"

"Of course. I was going to come see you right after the meeting. Actually, I was going to ask you to check on my apartment for me too. I had a key made for you, just in case." Stephen pulled a key from his wallet, hoping it would save him.

Patty smiled. "Really, you want me to have a key?"

"There's no need for you to knock when you come over. Just come in. I don't know how long we'll be gone. But I'll let you know what I find out."

"You better. No secrets."

"None. I'll also have my laptop and cell phone for business stuff."

"Not a problem. Johnathan and I will keep both of you up to date." Patty kissed him and walked away. "See you tonight."

"Tonight?" Alistair asked.

"Yes, Alistair, tonight. We have a date planned. And I'll expect you not to tag along, unless you bring a date."

"A double date, huh?" Alistair smiled. "I might be able to manage that. Yer place?"

"No, not my place. Pappy's, six o'clock."

Stephen left, wondering what Enclave would look like. The opportunity to learn more about his roots nearly overwhelmed his mind. It had been a long time since he had any hope of knowing more about his family. The mere possibility meant the world to him.

Both Stephen and Vincent left early to pack. Stephen packed light, not knowing what to expect. A few articles of clothing littered his bed as he stuffed clothes into a duffle bag. Before long, the time came to pick Patty up for their date.

Stephen got up early the next morning and dressed in comfortable clothes for the trip; raggedy jeans and an old long-sleeve T-shirt. He felt like a kid again, getting ready for the first day of school. As time neared for Alistair and Vincent to pick him up, he grabbed his things and went outside.

The streets remained quiet as the eastern sky showed signs of brightening. The stars faded and the slightest hint of blues snuck into the sky, soon followed by reds and oranges.

Stephen waited outside the apartment as Alistair pulled up. Vincent already sat in the car dressed in his usual business attire. Stephen shook his head before rethinking his own clothes, but it was too late now. He opened the rear door, threw his bag in, and sat down behind the driver.

"Guid mornin'."

"Shut up," Stephen grumbled.

Vincent chuckled. "I think he is a little cross with you."

Alistair looked in his rearview mirror. "Nah, I can see he's a lot of *Cross*."

"I'm glad you two are enjoying yourselves."

Alistair pulled off. "Are ye still upset with us? We didn't know she would leave early."

"We thought she would see the humor in me being Alistair's *date* last night," Vincent added.

"Guys, we really needed some time to talk alone, without either of you."

"I'm sorry. Alright?" Alistair said. "I really didn't think she'd be that upset."

"I'm just lucky she was hungry, or she might have left as soon as she saw you two doofuses." Stephen leaned back in his seat and stared out the window. "So, are we going to pick up Sam?"

"No," Alistair replied. "We're on our way to meet him."

"Where is Enclave?"

"He will not say," Vincent interjected before Alistair could speak. "I tried already."

"Okay? Are we driving there?"

"No," Alistair replied.

"Flying?"

"No." Alistair sounded irritated.

"What then?" Stephen continued.

Alistair smiled. "Ye'll see soon enough. We'll be meeting with Sam in about forty minutes."

The rest of the drive remained quiet. They left early, well before rush-hour traffic. Stephen thought about Patty and how disappointed they both had been not to be alone together. Until then, he had not realized how much he missed being alone with her. Even still, he recognized how good it felt to have friends.

"Are we going to Fort Belle Fontaine?" Vincent's question got Stephen's attention.

Stephen sat straight and looked around as they crossed over train tracks, leaving suburban houses and entering a rural area, where pasture and forest dominated the scenery. "It looks that way. Why are we meeting here?"

Alistair remained silent and parked the car. Sam waited at the bottom of the steps to the fort. Stephen looked around. "How did he get here?"

"Ye'll see in a moment."

The three men got out of the car and made their way to Sam. Vincent and Stephen carried their bags.

"Gentlemen, are you ready to meet the council and see Enclave?"

Stephen and Vincent looked at each other and shrugged.

Sam smirked. "Follow me."

As he turned to walk up the steps, a red mist appeared, getting thicker and thicker. Sam disappeared in the mist.

"Ye two better get going," Alistair encouraged. "It won't last long."

Vincent and Stephen walked up the stairs into the red mist.

Stephen looked at Vincent. "What's supposed to happen?" He barely made out his shape.

"I do not know," he replied.

They continued walking until they exited the red mist. Somehow, they no longer stood in St. Louis. Instead, the two looked up at a fifteen-foot-tall statue of Thomas Jefferson.

"Are we in the Jefferson Memorial?"

"Yes." Sam's steady voice floated through the air. He stood against one wall.

"Vincent? Do you see what I see?" Stephen asked, looking back and forth between Sam and the statue.

"Yes. I see the resemblance," Vincent agreed.

Sam's ceremonial attire resembled the clothes Jefferson wore. He pulled a medallion from inside his shirt. As it started glowing, a door appeared and opened in the wall next to him. "Follow me."

They walked through the doorway and down a spiraling staircase that descended thirty feet or more. Soon they stood in a small chamber in front of two large stone doors. Above the door rested words in a language that Stephen did not understand. "What is that?" he asked.

"It's Latin," Sam answered. "Beatus vir qui non abiit in consilio impiorum et in via peccatorum non stetit, et in cathedra pestilentiae non sedit."

Vincent translated. "Blessed is the man that walks not in the counsel of the ungodly, nor stands in the way of sinners, nor sits in the seat of the scornful. Psalm 1:1."

"You speak Latin, Vincent?" He continued to surprise Stephen.

"I had private tutors, remember?"

The doors opened.

"Gentlemen, it's time." Sam motioned toward the opening.

The two followed Sam through the doors. Stephen expected only one thing on the other side: to be awed.

Stephen walked to the middle of a large empty room. The walls, made of stone, were decorated with tapestries depicting various acts of King David and his mighty men. On one side hung a tapestry of the young shepherd boy, David, being anointed by the prophet Samuel. The tapestries circling around the room depicted various scenes. On the wall across the room and to the far right, the first scene showed David's battle with Goliath, then the three mighty men drawing water from a well for their thirsty king, followed by Jashobeam and his spear that killed three hundred in one battle. In front of Stephen hung depictions of Eleazar and the sword that clung to his hand during battle succeeded by Shammah defeating an entire Philistine encampment. Many more hung on the walls and continued around the room. The last tapestry showed Benaiah helping Solomon secure the throne after King David's death. Between the last tapestry and the first stood a long table in the shape of a crescent raised above the floor on a stage-like balcony, with what appeared to be twelve thrones behind it. Stairs led up on either side.

Vincent walked around the room, looking closely at the tapestries.

"Is this the council chamber?" Stephen turned back toward Sam, awaiting an answer.

"No. This is what we call Solomon's Hall. The council chambers are smaller. This room is more like a courtyard and serves many different uses."

"I did not think this looked like what I saw in Alistair's mind." Stephen turned, looking around the room.

"How old are these tapestries?" Vincent asked.

"They are not as old as you might expect, Vincent." Sam walked over to him. "This is only the cavern for North America. There is one in each continent, Antarctica excluded, and a smaller one in the Middle East. Each is called Enclave. Plus, the world headquarters is in Rome. Each continent has two representatives on the council except for Australia. We *do* have a presence there though. But because of their close ties with Great Britain, they are represented by Europe."

"Are all the council members here now?" Stephen joined the other two men.

"Not all. But they will be here tomorrow. Before you two meet them, I want you to look around and make yourselves welcome."

Vincent turned to Sam. "Will we see our families' troves?"

"Not just yet."

“Why not?” Stephen thought this seemed odd, since he alone could open the trove for his bloodline. What was the big deal? Why keep him from it?

“There will be all kinds of different things in your families’ troves, many of which will have great value to you and the Mighty. However, some may also have value to the rest of the world. And while these items are yours, there are guidelines we strongly encourage everyone to follow concerning certain types of items. Once we have gone over this with you, you are free to explore your trove. Stephen, many of the regulations will not apply to you, as you are the only one left in your bloodline.”

“Wait,” Vincent exclaimed, “you mean the items are not fully mine because I have family that is Mighty.”

Sam looked at Vincent, his face like stone. “You do. You will come to know them in time.”

Vincent smiled. Stephen felt his friend’s surprise and happiness, which made him happy too. He also smiled.

Stephen turned his attention back to Sam. “I want to see Matthew and Bernie.” He realized they must be nearby.

“Why do you think they are here?” Sam asked.

“I don’t imagine you would willingly take Fallen to the world Enclave or whatever you call it. So why not here?”

“You can see them after you get settled and meet with the council. Keep in mind, the cavern that holds them nullifies all powers, unless you are chosen as a guardian. So do not worry about their abilities.”

“Do I look worried? Why do you think they’re here?” Stephen grabbed his bag. “Has anyone been able to unlock Bernie’s mind?”

"No," Sam replied.

"If you want, I'll fix it," Stephen stated with a grin. "That would be helpful to the council."

Vincent tapped Stephen on the shoulder. "Already making friends. See, you *are* a real people person."

"Someone's here," Stephen said.

A door opened opposite where they entered. An attractive young woman entered. She wore a long black robe, which made her braided lock of blonde hair appear golden. She looked serious and held her head high. She wore the same type of medallion that hung around Sam's neck. Now that Stephen saw it clearly, he recognized it as the emblem of the Mighty.

Sam held his hand out to her. "This is Shannon, my daughter. She will show you around and try to help you get adjusted. I have responsibilities to which I need to attend. I'll check in on you later."

"Are your eyes purple?" Vincent asked her.

"They're only contacts," she said through a half smile.

Stephen felt like a spectator for a moment. He could not help but feel a spark between them, which started the moment Vincent saw Shannon enter the room. Looking at them, he thought they would make a cute couple. He sensed another strong feeling in the room coming from Sam—a need to protect. He, too, noticed their interaction and did not like it.

"So, your daughter is one of the Mighty?" Stephen asked Sam.

"Yes. However, she has no abilities. The robes tell you which class. Blue is for prophets, red for priests, and yellow for warriors."

"Black," Shannon interjected, "is for soldiers." She smiled. "You'll notice subtle differences in our robes. On my collar," she pointed, "is a spear. It means I am skilled at combat. And I often help to train in combat. You don't need abilities to make a difference."

"No, you don't," Vincent said.

The two grabbed their bags and followed Shannon down a hallway, which resembled a cave more than an underground building. Lights ran along the top and bottom of one of the walls.

"Shannon, what do you know about us?" Stephen wondered how informed the members were.

"Not much. The council will have to meet you to complete their inquiry before we are fully briefed. I know that you weren't raised as one of the Mighty—either of you. That's kind of a big deal. Other than that, not much."

"Big deal?" Vincent wondered. "How so? What does that mean?"

"Being one of the Mighty is something that is usually automatic. When abilities present themselves in the early years, kids are brought in and trained. After they complete their training, there is testing and a ceremony, more a formality than anything else. Everyone has a place here. After all, we're kind of like family, with relationships between our families going back more than three thousand years."

"And us?" Stephen asked.

"You'll go before the council. They'll question you and search your hearts to determine if you will be members of the Mighty."

"What do you mean *determine*? I made a choice to serve," Stephen stated.

"Yes, you may have. The council needs to know they can trust you before accepting you as a member. Being Mighty grants access to information, tools, and resources that not just anyone should have."

Stephen continued to press for answers. "But some Mighty fall. What makes us different?"

"From what little I know," Shannon replied, "everything."

Stephen and Vincent looked at each other and exchanged confused looks.

"Here." Shannon stopped and motioned with her hand. "Your rooms are through this hallway, first and second doors on the right. I'll give you two a minute to drop off your bags. Meet me back out here for a tour."

The two men walked to their rooms, which seemed to Stephen little more than sizeable hotel rooms. In addition to the bed, the room consisted of a bathroom and a small sitting area. He dropped his bag on the bed and went back to Shannon. When Vincent joined them, they began their tour.

The place had the overall appearance of a high-tech underground castle. They saw a formal dining hall, treasury, guard armory, recreation and fitness rooms, and the council chamber. The library, however, left Stephen in awe. It contained more books than Stephen had even seen in one place. The cedar from the bookshelves filled the air with its aroma. Gold and silver sconces illuminated the rooms. Their footsteps echoed in the silence. A large winding staircase stood in the center, and open to each level. The biggest chandelier he had ever seen hung in the center, made up of what he assumed was multi-color crystal.

"How much does all that crystal weigh," he asked.

"Those aren't crystals," Shannon replied. "They're gems."

They met several others, all of whom cordially greeted them. People acted eager to meet them, though not all excitement appeared positive. Either way, Stephen and Vincent were a common topic of discussion. Stephen felt much uncertainty from others wanting to know more. None dared to ask.

Stephen's own emotions heightened, making his mental abilities harder to control. He unintentionally picked up fragments of thoughts from others, most of which were harmless. However, he picked up one thought about Vincent that he found interesting.

He's kind of awkward in a cute sort of way...

The thought belonged to Shannon. Stephen grinned at Vincent, who responded with a questioning look.

The day went by quickly. They saw only the tip of the iceberg, which was a lot. Stephen knew he wanted to be a part of it all. For the first time, he found himself surrounded by others like himself. He even imagined Waltz down there with him, and wondered what Waltz used to enjoy doing there to pass the time in his youth. For the first time in awhile, he realized again how little he knew about Waltz's younger days.

The next morning Stephen found Vincent waiting outside his door. They walked together, both too nervous to say much. The realization that they would soon stand in front of the council gave them reason to feel both honored and concerned.

After they finished eating, they lingered at the table. Although they looked for her, Shannon did not join them for breakfast. Everyone kept their distance. Each person seemed unsure how to respond to them, except for one.

"Hey."

Stephen turned to see a man with shaggy brown hair, wearing a deep-yellow robe standing behind him and Vincent.

"Hey," Stephen and Vincent replied.

"I'm Edge. We didn't meet yesterday. I'm a trainer here."

"Warrior class, right?" Stephen remembered the yellow color from the shroud.

"Yeah, that's right. I am a warrior. That's not what I teach though." He pointed to what looked to be a scroll on his color.

"Let me guess," Vincent said. "History?"

"Not just that. The history, regulations, and protocols of the Mighty. They're intertwined. You'll see."

"What makes you so certain?" Stephen asked, looking around at the others. "The council isn't."

"The council won't have a choice. They'll have to welcome you. You'll see soon enough. But I've got work to do. I just wanted to see you before Shannon took you two away." Edge nodded toward the door. "Here she comes now."

Shannon walked toward them. She looked different, dressed in regular clothes—blue jeans and a solid-black blouse.

"No robes?" Stephen asked.

"I'm not training today, so they aren't required."

"Well," Vincent said, "I think you look very pleasant in street clothes."

She smiled. "Thank you, Vincent. Now, are you two ready?"

They nodded.

"Follow me then."

They dropped their remainders in the trash and walked down the hallway toward the council chamber as Shannon gave instructions.

"You'll go in individually. Like you, each council member has some ability and falls into one of the three classes. Suffice it to say, they will know if you tell them the truth or not. They will ask you questions. Again, this is usually a formality, only not with you two. You have nothing to fear though. When they are done, you will either be offered a chance to train with the Mighty, or you will be asked to go home."

The two men looked at each. Stephen heard Vincent's thoughts. *Stephen? Are you nervous?*

Stephen wiped sweat from his brow and nodded.

They stopped in front of the chamber doors, where two guards in yellow robes stood waiting. One opened the door.

"Vincent, you and I will go first." She looked at Stephen. "When they are ready, I'll come get you. Don't worry, priests are usually the quickest."

Stephen waited outside for what seemed like hours. The longer it took, the more he paced. He desired to use his ability to see the minds of those inside, but he restrained himself, afraid they would know. Both of the guards watched him closely but refused to say much of anything. He looked at his phone. Only thirty-two minutes had passed. The door opened. Shannon stood just inside.

"They are ready."

Stephen walked inside.

"And Vincent?"

Shannon smiled. "He'll be here as long as he wants."

Vincent walked past on his way out. "Good luck. And try to play nice."

Stephen looked around the room. In the middle was a single seat—for him. On one side stood the large table he saw in Alistair's mind, the council members seated on the other side of it. Anastasia and Sam sat in the center. Opposite them, numerous names covered the stone wall. At the top it read, "The Mightiest of Acts."

"Your father's name is up there."

Stephen recognized Anastasia's voice. He turned back toward the council.

Anastasia continued. "When he sacrificed his triune's power to bring Elizabeth back from darkness, it nearly killed him, and it would have killed any ordinary person. It earned him a place on that wall. You should be proud of him."

"I am. I only wish I knew this side of him."

The faces in front of him were the same he had seen in the vision. He recognized Novak, who sat next to Xiang at the right end of the table.

The man on the opposite end spoke with a slight British accent. "Stephen, it's a pleasure to meet you. Allow me to first offer my condolences. I knew Waltz. He was a good man."

"Thank you," Stephen replied. The man looked slim, though the robes made it hard to completely tell. He did, however, appear to be older than the others.

"I am Charles. This lovely lady to my left is Sabine, from Paris." Sabine smiled and nodded. She had long brown hair and a nice smile. Charles continued. "Next to her are Julien, from Venezuela, and Daniel, from Brazil." Both waved. Stephen nodded. "Then, there is Mugisah, from Rwanda, and Rania of Egypt." Mugisah's dark skin was a stark contrast to his robe. Anastasia and Sam sat between Mugisah and Rania, which seemed to be the head seats. Rania made no facial expression, only nodded. "The two after them are Zachariah, from Israel, and Joash, also from Israel." Two older men with long white beards nodded, although Zachariah's was whiter. Stephen couldn't tell if they were smiling or not. "Last, we have..."

"Novak and Xiang," Stephen interrupted. Except for Sam and Anastasia, all the members seemed surprised. Anastasia, however, seemed to find it amusing. Sam did not.

"Stephen," Sam sounded annoyed, "to be clear, we are going to ask you some questions. We need you to be completely honest. We will know if you are not."

"I will be." Stephen felt anxious again. However, he sensed the same from the council members. He took his seat as the council members watched, and he waited to begin.

Xiang spoke up first. "Stephen, please tell me if the account you gave Sam and Anastasia is accurate."

"It is. I omitted information concerning Vincent. It wasn't relevant to what happened. Nor was it my story to tell. But what I told them is true."

"Impossible." An angry-sounding voice with a French accent came from the opposite end of the table. "He is obviously lying."

Xiang spoke up. "Sabine, you know my gift. He is not lying."

Sam spoke up. "Council members, we are not to discuss this without completing the examination. You all know this."

One at a time, they asked him questions about his childhood, relationships, Waltz, his time away, and even of the past several months. No part of Stephen's life remained private. He poured it all out to them: his feelings of loneliness, Tommy, the addictiveness of having powers, and more.

Three hours later, the council opened discussions among one another. They hid nothing from Stephen. Emotions heightened and tempers flared. Stephen sensed a myriad of emotions; fear, anger, love, and compassion being chief among them. Fierce discussion broke out before they reached a decision, which Sam delivered.

"Stephen, the council would first like to recognize and apologize for the hard life you have had. Were you taught sooner, perhaps much of your pain could have been avoided. That being said, we also understand why you were not taught and do not fault Waltz. You are unusual. He had no reason to think you would have abilities of the Mighty. The council would also like to recognize the service you have performed. You have identified those responsible for Waltz's death. For that, we are grateful."

Sam continued. "For a person to be allowed in the order of the Mighty, a council member majority vote is required. A tie vote is not enough to pass. The council's findings are this. You are honest and brave. You are also drawn to the feeling of power and vengeance. You are compassionate. You are also extremely dangerous. You are loyal. Yet, you often seek to satisfy your own needs first." Sam looked around at the council. "How say you, Council of the Mighty?"

Xiang spoke first. "Yes." Seated next to him was also a yes, followed by two votes of no.

The voting continued and Charles voted yes, while Sabine said no. Anastasia and Sam voted last. Stephen sighed in relief. Voting had stopped even at five for and five against. His fate rested with the only two members with whom he had any type of relationship.

"Yes." Anastasia smiled at Stephen.

"Stephen." Sam paused. "I must vote no."

The room spun. Stephen could not understand what just happened. Even Anastasia looked shocked and spoke heatedly with Sam. Council members, once again, talked heatedly back and forth.

"Quiet," Sam shouted. "You all know that our decisions are not to be challenged. That is why we all sit equal to one another."

The door opened and twelve guards rushed in.

Startled, Stephen jumped to his feet.

"We are not done. Why are you interrupting?" Sam yelled.

A man in a red-hooded cloak strode into the room. Immediately, the council murmured among themselves. Stephen watched, still unsure as to what was happening. He looked at Sam. The surprise on Sam's face told Stephen that this was not expected. Stephen searched Sam's mind.

"Who is David?" Stephen yelled.

"Not who. What." The man under the hood boldly answered. He stood before Sam, facing the council. "You reject him, when you yourselves have forgotten protocol?"

Immediately, the council members filed out from behind the table and stood opposite their chairs facing the man. Following Anastasia's lead, they knelt.

The man turned toward Stephen; his face hidden. "Stephen, Sam wasn't one-hundred-percent truthful in what he told you. The council's findings are final only when required. It was David who chose his mighty men. Today, David is a title among the Mighty, given to someone named as the most honorable of the Mighty. And the single person holding that title may choose anyone to be a member of the Mighty. The council is meant to act in his absence to alleviate the burdens of being David."

The man stepped forward to Stephen, who also fell to one knee. The David removed his hood and placed his hand on Stephen's shoulder. Stephen looked up, amazed, recognizing a friend he least expected to see.

"Pastor Buchanan?"

"Rise, Mighty Stephen."

Stephen stood.

"But..."

Pastor Buchanan shushed Stephen. "There will be time for questions but not today." He turned to the council. "How dare you? You are charged with the care of all the Mighty. Yet, because you fear his power and don't understand it or him, six of you chose to exclude him out of purely selfish motivations. You may tell yourselves that it was for the safety of the Mighty. That, however, would be a lie. Here," he motioned to their seats, "you sit as equals, all twelve of you. Some of you, however, could not stand the thought of someone who was not equal with you, someone more powerful than you all. What are you afraid of? Do you not trust God above yourselves? If the council cannot be trusted to bear witness, then these twelve guards will. Stephen is Mighty."

Stephen barely heard The David's words as he stood stunned at what had taken place. All this time, Pastor Buchanan had been right there. He wanted to be upset, but couldn't, realizing that the preacher had told him what he needed to know in order to make the right choice. When Pastor Buchanan finished, Stephen felt thankful, and honored.

Sam stood. "The council recognizes the decision of The David as law."

The David continued. "Stephen has done what this entire council has been unable to do. You have sent people to find out about this enemy in the shadows. None have returned except him."

Anastasia grabbed a piece of paper from the table and took it to each member, who signed it with a signet ring, using a wax seal. She handed it to Pastor Buchanan, who did the same. The wall behind the table rumbled.

An opening appeared after the last seal had been affixed. She walked over and placed the scroll in the opening. The wall sealed itself closed.

"The matter is settled. Welcome, Mighty Stephen." She approached Stephen and hugged him. "Waltz would be very happy."

"Thank you."

Shannon escorted Stephen out of the room.

"Your dad doesn't like me?" Stephen asked in a raised voice.

"Honestly, I'm not sure what that was about. He spoke very highly of you to me."

Stephen looked over her mind. She told the truth, which made what just happened even stranger.

"So how is it that you became our escort?" he continued.

"I asked. After hearing what Dad and Anastasia had to say about you two, I wanted to meet you."

"Any idea why Sam voted no?"

"None. But he must have had a reason. I don't think it's as simple as fear. Dad's not a selfish man."

"Yeah, I was surprised." Stephen stopped. "Will I have issues here, because of the mixed vote?"

"No. No one will question The David's choice, especially now that it's recorded."

"Who is the enemy he talked about? What do you know about him?"

Shannon shrugged. "I don't know, exactly. We know someone has been out there evading our attempts at finding him. We've managed to capture a Fallen or two that know little bits, just not enough to put a complete picture together. This is the first time we've had someone actually confront him and come back with information. Before, we only heard unsubstantiated rumors."

Stephen turned and ran back into the council chamber. The David and the council members did not seem to notice him at first and, instead, continued discussing something among themselves.

"Who is the voice in the darkness?" Stephen spoke loudly, ensuring everyone heard him.

They all looked at him and silence filled the chamber. Those with their backs to him, turned toward him. He sensed displeasure with his intrusion.

"Maybe you feel like you don't owe me answers. But I disagree. Someone killed Waltz, is after me, and has blinded a family member of mine. Who is he?"

"We don't know." Pastor Buchanan approached Stephen. "We've only heard whispers. There were some who came close to him a few years back, only getting to people under him. That's how we know of him. Afterward, we sent others to gain more information. He's powerful. Bernard was the last one we sent. None have returned."

"But I returned." Stephen still found it odd to speak with Pastor Buchanan inside of Enclave.

"Yes, you did. I believe you shocked them—Fallen. They didn't expect you to be so stubborn." Pastor Buchanan smiled. "I know you have more questions, but now is not the time. You have answers waiting for you that are more important than this, at the moment. When you're ready, you'll need to begin training."

Stephen knew exactly what Pastor Buchanan meant. "They have hunted my family nearly to extinction. I want to be a part of ending this threat. My life and future are at stake."

The preacher nodded.

Stephen returned to Shannon, who waited in the doorway. They left again to go track down Vincent. Their family troves awaited them both.

They marched to the recreation room. Vincent sat in the corner reading a book.

Stephen called to him. "You almost done reading?"

Vincent hurriedly set the book down and stood. "You had me worried. What took so long?"

"I'll tell you on the way," Stephen said.

"Where are we going?" Vincent asked.

"I want to see my family's trove room. Don't you want to see yours?"

On the way, Stephen relayed everything to Vincent as Shannon nodded occasionally in agreement. He finished as they arrived at the Chamber of Bloodlines. A large stone door stood before them.

Shannon stopped. "I'll leave you two here. Your doors will open for you when you say, 'Blessed is the man.'"

"That's it?" Stephen asked as he walked into the chamber, the stone doors opening for him.

Hundreds of doors lined the walls, all the way around the room and up to the high ceiling; all carved from stone with the same insignia in the middle that rested on the shroud. The air hung damp and cool but smelled surprisingly fresh. A large chandelier hung from the ceiling overhead in the center of a dome—painted to show the scene at Christ's crucifixion. One of the doors opened, and a teenage boy with purple hair wearing a blue robe came out. He wore headphones and bobbed his head as he walked past them.

"Blessed is the man." A door opened directly in front of Stephen. He walked in.

On the wall opposite the door he saw the Stockton family tree, which appeared to be scorched into the stone wall and wrapped around the corner. Looking at it, he saw hundreds upon hundreds of names and dates as he followed it around the wall. Eventually, he came face to face with the truth. A fact carved in stone that he hoped to be wrong. He saw Waltz's name, birthdate, and the date of his death. Beside his name was a shield, the symbol for protectors. A sword appeared next to it, his sensitive class. He touched Waltz's name. Layla's information appeared, glowing bright, next to Waltz's, along with a stone followed by a sword. Stephen backed away from the heat and watched as his name appeared underneath them, along with his birthdate. But no emblem appeared. *Curious*, he thought. But the truth remained. Stephen was, indeed, the last surviving member of his family's bloodline.

He looked around for what seemed like hours. There was a lot to digest. There were weapons, armor, cloaks, books, scrolls, paintings, musical instruments of all types, and more. He knew there would be time to discover the significance of it all later. After a while, he wondered about Vincent and what he found in his own family's trove. As he approached the door, it opened back into the room. Only, it did not open in the same place.

He found Vincent waiting with Shannon.

"Did you look in yours?"

"Yes. It was interesting." Vincent smiled. "I will look at more later. I know there are rules and do not want to mishandle anything."

"Did your door...?" Stephen looked back.

"Change?" Shannon asked. "Yes, they do. The doors are not tied to any specific trove. The trove is tied to the person."

"There was no information about my mom's family in there. Where would I find out about her side?" Stephen asked.

"That would be in her bloodline's trove. We'll have to find someone in that bloodline to let you in."

"Wait." Stephen tried not to get excited. He had not considered his mother's bloodline would be different. Could he still have family? "My mother's bloodline?"

"Yes," Shannon smiled. "You can only access one, and Stockton is your bloodline. However, someone from Layla's bloodline may be willing to show you around. I'll see who I can find. I don't think anyone is presently at Enclave."

Stephen hid his excitement. He had family after all, however distant they may be.

Shannon next led them to the Catacombs, where Matthew and Bernie stayed locked inside barred rooms. Stephen went to both of their rooms, looking through the bars. Solid stone made up the other three walls. A guard control center sat in the middle of the sector. Matthew refused to look up or talk to Stephen. Bernie remained in a near catatonic state, barely able to feed himself.

In the end, he saw all he wanted to see. The time came for them to go home and make preparations for a longer visit. Stephen and Vincent discussed it. Both agreed they needed to learn more.

Sam took them back home the way they had come—by mist. Being around Sam felt strange now. A tension between Stephen and Sam kept any real conversation from taking place. Stephen tried to look into Sam's mind to understand. But something blocked him.

They arrived back at Fort Belle Fontaine, where Alistair waited.

"Stephen, wait a moment please." Sam stepped in front of him.

Vincent went on ahead without them.

Sam continued. "I can't explain everything now. Maybe one day. I want you to know I voted no because I felt it was the best way to protect you. If the Fallen learned we voted no, they might not see you as a threat any longer."

Stephen glared at Sam. He felt the veins in his neck bulge as blood pumped through and his heart raced. "When are you people gonna learn?" He poked Sam in the chest. "I don't need you to protect me. All I've ever wanted—all I still want—is family, people I can trust and who trust me." He nodded toward Vincent and Alistair. "They are my family. Patty is family. I thought...It doesn't matter."

Stephen turned and walked away. As he reached the car where Vincent and Alistair waited, he turned around to take one more look at Sam. He saw only the dissipating red mist.

The time came for Stephen to make a decision. A week seemed an eternity to him to consider going back to Enclave. But it gave him barely enough time to make all the necessary preparations, which he did not do. Vincent decided he needed to go and made plans for others to fill in at the company—one in legal, another to head up the nonprofit. Stephen straddled the fence up until today. He knew that returning had to be the right thing to do but worried about Patty. He decided a visit to see Waltz would help. The fresh air and sunshine could not hurt either.

Birds sang in the distance as Stephen and Patty made their way up the hill. Their melody helped Stephen to realize that life continued, even for Waltz. Stephen placed a single rose on the top of the headstone. *This stone doesn't tell the whole story*, Stephen thought as he stood at the grave, Patty by his side.

"You know, there were three sides to him—father, philanthropist, and Mighty. I'm just starting to know him."

“So, you’re going.” Patty sounded sad. He could not be certain if it was because she thought of Waltz or him leaving.

“Yeah, I have to. There is so much more I don’t know, not only about him but about me.” Stephen wanted so badly to take a peek inside her head, to see what would make her feel better. But he had promised her he would never do it without her permission.

“How long?”

“I don’t know. I’ll be able to come back at times. I’ll still be available by phone, email, or Skype. They have some tech there that’s very impressive.”

Patty turned to Stephen. He expected to see sadness. Instead, he saw an all too familiar mischievous glint in her eyes.

“Patty?” Stephen barely got her name out when she could not hold it in any longer.

“I’m coming,” she blurted out.

“You’re what?”

“I’m coming with you.”

“Wait, you can’t. I mean, you’re not...” Stephen did not finish a sentence without getting raised eyebrows from Patty. “What makes you think they’ll let you come?”

“*Shannon* doesn’t have abilities.”

“She was born into it, Patty. You can’t just—”

“I don’t care. If they won’t let me train, I’ll do something else.”

“No.” Stephen knew he had to be stern.

“I have good people in place to run the warehousing unit. I can head it up from anywhere. Plus, I can look at expanding to the East Coast while we’re there.”

“What if something happens to you?” Stephen implored.

“Really? What if something happens to me?”

Stephen realized too late his mistake.

“You’re the man that gets so angry when people try to protect him,” Patty started. “Mr. ‘I don’t need protection.’ You don’t want something to happen to me so I can’t come? Tell me, babe, when’s the last time that worked for you?”

“Well, uh...” Stephen stumbled in his greatest weakness, arguing with Patty. “It’s not really my decision, I get that. But it’s not yours either.”

Patty’s face turned sour with disapproval. But he knew she understood. The council would have to agree. She dug deep into her purse and pulled out her phone.

“What are you doing?” Stephen scoffed.

“I’m calling Anastasia.”

Stephen thought conversation to be cute to this point. It quickly turned one-eighty. He, nor the council, could risk her safety. He knew the council would not allow it. Or would they? He watched her search through her phone, her smile growing brighter by the second. Did she know something he didn’t? He rubbed his temples, an effort to relieve the sudden headache so he could think. “You’re what? When did you get—”

Patty stuck her hand in the air, motioning for Stephen to be quiet.

“Anastasia? Hey, thank you for taking my call. I have a question. Am I allowed at Enclave?” Patty paused. Stephen heard Anastasia talking, though not well enough to make out anything she said. “Right. Okay.” Patty nodded as she twirled her hair with her free hand.

"I'd like to learn more about the Mighty. Stephen is very important to me. You all are. I want to help, if I can."

"What's she saying?" he asked.

Patty held her hand up again. "Okay. Thank you. Yes, thank you. See you soon." Patty put her phone back in her purse.

Stephen waited impatiently as Patty took her time. "Alright already, what happened?"

"She's on her way to your apartment."

"Why?" Stephen tried to hide his skepticism.

"It's possible for me to come. But she needs to talk to us."

The couple arrived at Stephen's apartment and waited for Anastasia to arrive. Neither said much on the way over. He silently hoped the obstacle for her to follow would be too great. Patty cheerfully hummed certain she too would go to Enclave.

As they waited Patty worked hard making dinner for the three of them. She whistled, hummed, and even sang as she worked. Stephen watched her from the other side of the room, dreading either answer. A "no" or "yes" might possibly lead to Patty getting hurt. Reading her mind became more and more tempting. But he resisted.

After a couple hours, someone knocked at the door. He opened the door to see Anastasia waiting with a smile. She showed up with near-perfect timing, as though she waited outside the door for dinner to be ready.

"Hello, Stephen," she grinned.

"Hello," he said. Seeing Anastasia dressed in casual attire–jeans and a T-shirt–caught him off guard. Stephen's gaze lingered over her clothes.

Anastasia glanced down and back to Stephen. "Right. I've always been in more formal attire. Well, this is a visit to a friend, nothing official."

He motioned for her to come in.

Anastasia walked toward the table. "Patty, it smells delicious."

Patty turned off the stove and darted over to hug Anastasia.

"How are you?" Patty asked, smiling.

"I'm well. How are you?" Anastasia replied in her usual tender voice.

"Good, thank you. I'm glad you offered to come."

"I hope I can help. Stephen," Anastasia continued, "what is your position on this?"

"W-well." Stephen thought fast. "I want Patty safe. I fear her helping us and coming to Enclave will endanger her." As hard as he tried, he did not even convince himself.

"Let's sit at the table." Patty motioned to the kitchen. "Dinner is ready."

It did not take long for Patty to dish out the spaghetti and garlic bread. Stephen enjoyed it when she cooked, especially when the food was not burnt.

"Let's cut straight to the point," Anastasia said. "Patty can come."

"Really?" Patty and Stephen spoke simultaneously, though Patty appeared more excited.

"Yes. The fact is, she may be in danger. The Fallen want to get to Stephen. Patty, you are a great weakness for him. The Fallen would try to exploit you if they could. The council learned in questioning him that being alone is his greatest fear. Losing you would devastate him. For now, you will be safest with the others."

"What about training?" The excitement in Patty's voice sounded childlike.

"I'm sorry. You may learn certain things, but you cannot train."

"Never? No fighting? Nothing?" she asked.

Anastasia grinned. "That depends on Stephen, in a way."

"Why me?" Stephen protested.

"Since she was not born one of the Mighty, the only way she can be allowed to train is to marry one."

Stephen felt the blood leave his head. The room spun as his head felt lighter and lighter. He loved Patty but had not considered marriage. He felt Patty's gentle hand on his arm.

"Babe, it's okay. I'm not there yet either. I'll be fine with learning. Besides, the business will keep me busy."

Stephen breathed again. His heart slowed, and his temperature returned to normal. The room slowed and came back into focus. "I love you, Patty."

"I know you do. Just don't forget it." She gave him a playful scowl and turned back to Anastasia. "Is there some process I have to go through?"

"No. But there is a downside." Anastasia's tone turned somber.

"Downside?" Stephen joined the conversation again.

"Yes. If you two don't get married—that is, if you break up—Patty's memories of all she learns in the caverns will be taken from her. It will be as though it never happened. We are unable to take the memories obtained outside. But we are able to track memories of the uninitiated while they are inside and remove them, if needed."

The three sat in silence for a moment. Stephen understood the reasons. If a normal person ever got in somehow, they'd need a way to keep them from revealing the Mighty. Patty's silence concerned him most.

"Patty?"

She did not acknowledge Stephen. "All my other memories would remain?"

"Yes, all of them. You'll only forget Enclave—where it is and everything you learned inside. Any trips back home, you'll remember."

"How do you do it—take the memories?" she asked.

"We developed technology for Fallen prisoners. We have sometimes removed certain memories and released captives back as spies or to spread false information. Now, we often use it for diplomatic reasons. We have been known to coordinate with authorities. However, it is safest for them not to remember certain details."

"So, it's a machine that removes the memories and not someone's ability?"

"Yes." Patty looked at Stephen then back to Anastasia. "Okay, I'll do it. But I'd like for Stephen to do it with his ability, if it ever comes to that."

Anastasia did not answer right away but sat looking at the two for a moment before speaking. "If that time ever comes, I agree to give you the option as to how you want the memories removed. Afterward, we would have to verify that it had been done."

"Then, I want to go. I want to try to be a part of your world." She squeezed Stephen's hand. He squeezed back.

After dinner, Patty grabbed a suitcase from her car. She already packed her clothes. Stephen threw his clothes in his duffle bag. The three of them took a cab to Fort Belle Fontaine. Alistair and Vincent sat, waiting on the steps.

"Two bags, mate?" Alistair laughed. "Ye're more upkeep than I would have thought."

"This one's mine," Patty said.

"Whoa. What?" Alistair stood to his feet. "She's coming?"

"I saw this coming a mile away," Vincent said, as he stood. "It is funny, however, that you did not."

"Really?" Stephen walked over to give Vincent a hug and whispered, "You should have given me a heads up, then."

Vincent patted him on the back and smiled. "Not a chance."

"She can't bloody come with us. She's not one of the Mighty."

"I can and I will," Patty told him.

"Do you know what will happen if you two don't work out? It's not a vacation spot," Alistair warned.

"They'll take my memories," Patty replied.

"Anastasia told ye?"

"Why wouldn't I?" Anastasia demanded of Alistair.

"I just figured she wouldn't be going if she knew." Alistair replied, slowly backing away.

Stephen noticed that Alistair was more upset than he had been. He did not need abilities to know what that was about. “Who was she?”

Alistair’s shoulders drooped and his head hung. “Victoria. We were engaged. She got down there and...” He shook it off. “Let’s just say she couldn’t handle what she learned. I’m sorry, Patty. Ye’re a fair bit tougher than she was. Ye’ll be fine, right at home, I imagine.”

“Thanks.” Patty hugged him.

The five of them walked up the stairs together, disappearing into the mist.

Epilogue

Twelve months to the day passed since Stephen last visited Waltz's grave with Patty. He knelt alone as freshly fallen leaves blew by on the cool wind. He did not look the same. His hair had grown longer, and the neatly trimmed stubble gave him a more mature look. He no longer looked like a young man trying to find his place in the world. Instead, he wore the ceremonial dress garb of the Mighty.

"I hope you're proud of me. It's not what I thought it would be. I had expected excitement, battles, constant action. But I'm finally beginning to understand what you told me when we first started training. Being one of the Mighty isn't about saving the world in grand gestures. It's about helping people to be saved. Sometimes that means physically fighting the Fallen in face-to-face conflict. Most of the time, it means being there for others, making a difference in everyday life for everyday people."

Stephen stood and looked around. He saw only one other person, just down the hill. He listened to the man's thoughts.

I'm sorry. I just don't know what to do anymore. I've tried everything.

Stephen turned back toward the grave.

"It's been good talking to you, Dad. I've got to go to work."

Stephen walked down the hill to where the man stood and waited to be noticed by him. The man's head hung low. After a moment, he looked up.

"Did you know my brother?" the man asked.

"No, I didn't. Sorry," Stephen replied.

"Oh." The man paused a moment, embarrassed. "I apologize, but should *I* know you?"

"Sorry, no. I just recognized you from the funeral."

The man looked confused.

"My dad was buried up the hill the same day as your brother. I remember seeing you. I know your pastor though, Pastor Buchanan. He's a good man." Stephen smiled warmly at him.

"Y-yeah, he is. He's a really good man."

"Listen, I know it's none of my business. Have you ever had something that you knew you had to do, although you weren't sure why or even how it would turn out in the end?"

The man's eyes appeared to soften. "It's funny you ask that. My life has seemed like a series of those types of events lately. Why do you ask?"

"Because I'm supposed to tell you that I'm here to listen if you need to talk."

"I'm usually a private person, but..." The man looked back down at the grave and then around the cemetery before continuing. He sighed. "I've been trying to change my life. I learned some time ago that the people in my life don't think very highly of me. I've been trying to change the way they see me. I don't want something horrible as my epitaph."

"Hmm." Stephen thought for a moment. He listened to the man's thoughts and dug deep. What he saw amazed him. Tom wrestled with his own personal angels and demons. "Tom, don't try to change other people's opinions. You can't. Don't worry about what others think of you. It doesn't matter. Just focus on each day and the person you want to be that day. Any more than that can be overwhelming. When it becomes too much to bear, and it will, give it to God. He will gladly take it from you."

"That sounds like good advice." Tom smiled. "Thank you."

"And, if I may offer one more word of advice? Love God first, then love others. It may seem silly but trying to change the way others think of you sounds selfish—not that you mean to be. Instead, if you focus on being kind to others and ask what their needs are, I suspect everything else will fall into place."

"Yeah, I suppose."

Stephen turned to walk away.

"Wait," Tom yelled. "How did you know my name? Are you an angel too?"

"No," Stephen called back as he continued walking. "I'm just a man who is running late for a wedding."

The Adventure Continues In

Prologue

Pastor Benjamin Buchanan yanked his red cloak off his shoulders, tossing it across the large table where he and the council members had often met in years past. He glared at the head councilman, Sam, who stood tall stroking his goatee, his black hair flowing over his white robe. "What on earth were you thinking?" Pastor Buchanan barked.

Sam showed no expression and remained silent.

"Sam, I *am* wanting an answer. I trusted you to keep me informed and manage things while I was away. When Stephen and his abilities became known, I told you how important he was to us. I'm certain he's the key to defeating Fallen in the coming battle. You know the stakes."

Sam nodded. "I know. If Fallen wins, the Beast will rise to power and the Tribulation begins. Time will have run out for humankind. But we've never lost."

"Don't be so foolish," the pastor shouted. "We know it will happen one day. But it doesn't have to be this time. If we win, it should set them back another twenty years, maybe more. Now, I want an answer for your actions.

Why didn't you vote for Stephen to join us here in Enclave?"

"Pastor Buchanan, you have known me for years. Please believe that I thought it was the best way to keep Stephen safe. Though I respect your wisdom as the David, I believed that if we rejected him as Mighty, perhaps Fallen would not see him as a threat and leave him and his friends alone."

"Sam," the David replied, "that was foolish. Stephen is more special than anyone knows. Waltz knew that, which is why no one, not even the boy himself, knew Stephen belonged to Waltz's bloodline until it was necessary."

Sam looked thoughtful for a moment and stroked his goatee once more before asking the question Pastor Buchanan knew would come. "How long have you known about Stephen?"

Pastor Buchanan sighed. "I've known since the day Waltz learned he had a child—the day he saw Layla and realized she was pregnant."

He knew Sam and the council would not like having been kept out of the loop, especially when Stephen's powers emerged. But his deep friendship with Waltz over the years had all been in an effort to protect the young boy until the time came. He had watched from a distance in anticipation, but never interfering in Waltz's relationship with Stephen.

"Waltz found out and came to me for advice. He wanted to be with Layla and the child. I went to Oracle. Oracle showed us the boy would grow to be different and would have great power. We also saw we had to hide him. So, I used my power of protection as a priest to shield him from detection, which also hid his power from himself, until he turned eighteen. Waltz had his own memory altered so that he would not remember the child Layla carried was his. Waltz received Layla's letter nine years later, explaining she was ill and that he was Stephen's father. That's the moment he learned of Stephen for the second time. Waltz immediately returned, hoping to talk with Layla. That poor man never stopped loving her."

Pastor Buchanan, realizing he had gotten lost in his thoughts, looked back at Sam. "Cancer took Layla before Waltz had received the letter. He found Stephen and raised him, never telling him the truth."

"I thought Oracle was a myth," Sam said.

"No, not a myth, Sam." Pastor Buchanan waved his hand, dismissing the idea. "Oracle is very real, and very hidden. I was told Stephen would have two mentors, and both would be priests. He also said the second would finish what the father had begun." The old man anxiously tapped the table with his finger. "That's when we knew what had to be done. Waltz had to forget Layla was pregnant. It was the only real way to protect Stephen."

"You are the second mentor," Sam asserted. "This means you *must* see this through."

The old man chuckled at Sam's growing comprehension of the situation. "Yes. It falls to me to watch out for him and help him grow. Waltz was always a mentor to Stephen. Stephen only became aware that Waltz was his biological father after Waltz was killed."

He played with the rim of his glasses and continued. "We worried when Stephen disappeared. But when he came back, we knew it was time for him to know the truth. Waltz worked to help him learn control of his gift. Still, we knew Stephen would need more help. That's why Waltz had already been working with Vincent, although Vincent didn't realize it. Waltz knew Vincent's mother was Elizabeth Marie. He also sensed Vincent was a priest. So, he made sure that Vincent and Stephen spent time together and developed a friendship. Stephen needed a priest to help keep him centered. Waltz and I both knew his time was drawing near."

"So, you two arranged their friendship?"

"No, absolutely not. Waltz only arranged the introduction."

"And Patty?" Sam asked.

"Patty was not planned. Their relationship happened as normally as anyone else's might." He looked up and noticed another council member had entered, an elderly gentleman near his own age. "Charles, his friendship with your son, Alistair, was also happenstance."

"That's good to know. Alistair has a bright future ahead of him. Stephen is on a different path. I don't want Stephen to be a stumbling block to Alistair."

"Rest assured, their meeting had nothing to do with me," the David offered. "Their friendship is genuine."

Charles smiled and nodded. "I didn't mean to intrude, Benjamin—I mean, David. But, some of the elders have arrived. They'd like to know what has happened."

"We'll be out in a moment," Pastor Buchanan replied.

Charles gave a nod and left the room.

Pastor Buchanan shook his head. “Charles and I go way back. But sometimes I think he’s a little too involved in Alistair’s affairs.”

“What about Bernie and his nephew?” Sam continued. “Did you know they had fallen?”

“No.” Pastor Buchanan tried to control the emotion in his voice. He had helped to train Bernie when they were both younger. He remembered feeling pride watching Bernie’s nephew, Bernard, join the Mighty. “Waltz sensed something strange, more and more, after Bernie’s brother died years ago. He took it hard and became distant. I thought that’s all it was. We both knew Bernie worked to keep his nephew from this life. At some point, however, Waltz stopped trusting him. There was never any suspicion of Bernard. He and Stephen grew up together. They were best friends before Stephen ran away. Bernard’s involvement in Waltz’s death was a surprise to us all.”

“Do you know what class Stephen falls into?” Sam’s voice cracked. “He clearly has abilities of both prophet and warrior classes. Which is his primary and what is he simply sensitive to?”

“Sam, old friend...” The David snatched his cloak from the table. “He’ll need to be tested to know for sure. Now we should go.”

Together the two walked back out into the open meeting room. The David looked around at the council members, giving no recognition to the elders just yet. “I know there are reservations about Stephen. He is different, much more than any of you know. Half of you voted against him being Mighty. But he should be treated no different than any other descendant of the bloodlines that has chosen to follow Christ. His defeat of Bernard and whoever is pulling the strings is only temporary. Now that they know he will not join them, we can expect they'll want him dead. As the angel Areli showed, Stephen is the key to giving humanity more time on this earth. If we fail, the Beast *will* reign.

"Stephen's friends are important too. Alistair needs to be sent to the field to find out what he can. We all must help him and remain vigilant. Stopping Fallen from influencing the human world from the shadows is no longer good enough. If they win this battle, they'll finally step out of the shadows, bringing the darkness with them. Their attempt to wipe out an entire bloodline was a bold move. Stephen's battle with Bernard was only the beginning."

Pastor Buchanan threw the cloak of the David around his shoulders as he left the room. "God only knows what's coming next."

Stephen walked down the corridor located beneath the streets of Washington DC, eager to begin combat training. Fragments of history, rules and regulations, and structure of the Mighty continued to swim around in his head. He hoped a demanding workout would help clear his mind. Since he made his choice to serve as Mighty, a soldier of God in the fight against Fallen, he hadn't seen any fighting at all, much less had the opportunity to engage in combat.

A group of teenagers passed by as he neared the training wing, which did little to detract from the humbling knowledge that all the other students, apart from Vincent, were much younger than him. It didn't bother him too much. Still, fitting in and finding his rhythm had been harder than he had expected. He was so distracted: by his much younger classmates, Waltz's death, Bernie's imprisonment, Bernard's whereabouts, and even his relationship with Patty. He found it hard to stay focused, especially because he was the one responsible for the fate of the human race. What did they expect him to do? How could he defeat Fallen when he hadn't even been able to save Waltz?

"Hey! Stephen!"

Stephen turned around at the sound of the familiar voice. Edge, a lanky man about Stephen's age, stepped from a room into the hall, wearing his usual gold-colored uniform, which signified warrior class. Stephen waited for his history teacher and friend to catch up.

"Hey, Edge. How's it going?"

"I can't complain. I saw you walk by and thought I'd take the opportunity to catch up some. I mean, you and Vincent don't really have downtime, having to double up on normal class time."

"Yeah, I guess so. We don't have the luxury of time that our younger counterparts do." Stephen nodded toward the next group of kids walking by. A taller teen with dark skin waved at him. He waved back.

"I've been wondering how you feel about everything." Edge shifted his dark, shaggy hair out of his eyes as they continued walking toward the training room. "I know you're barely getting to some of the more exciting stuff, combat and ability training, but how's everything going?"

"Let's see." Stephen grinned. "I've been underneath DC here in Enclave for the past six weeks. I know almost no one, except for Patty and Vincent. I'm still getting use to the idea that I'm a descendant of King David's mighty men from the Old Testament. My best friend from childhood is now a Fallen..." Stephen sighed and scanned the area. "There is a bright spot in all this. I look around, and even though he's gone, I feel closer to Waltz.

I know him better now than I ever did while he was alive."

"How's your girlfriend doing?"

"She's good. I was concerned she might not fit in. At the moment, she seems to be fitting in better than me. She spends hours in the library reading up on Mighty history. They let her take a couple classes. She's soaking it all in. And Pastor Buchanan has gone out of his way to make her feel welcome. Considering he's the David and all, it says a lot about how much you all care for each other."

"But?" Edge said.

"I really like her. What if she decides she can't handle all this? It's kind of a big deal."

"I see your point." Edge nodded. "How's Vincent?"

"He's better. In fact, he should have started his combat training this morning too. But I think he's adjusting well. I have, too, honestly." Stephen smiled.

A group of preteen girls giggled as they walked past the two men.

"Although I sometimes feel silly sharing classes with kids. Well, I guess the older teenagers aren't so bad. I connect better with them." He thought for moment. "Eh. Really, they're all great kids. They grow on you. Everyone else has been nice enough. Most are inquisitive, but not too intrusive. I still find it hard to concentrate knowing what all's out there."

"Yeah, I bet. The kids don't really understand that yet."

"That's a good thing. They still get to be kids."

Edge was just as friendly and personable in class as he had been when they met, just before Stephen and

Vincent went before the council to learn their fates. “Hey, Edge. When we first met, you were so certain that I’d be Mighty, as though you knew. The council tried to keep me out. It was tie vote. I mean, it was a real possibility that I wouldn’t, right?”

Edge nodded.

“Did you know something the others didn’t?”

Edge stopped in the hall. “You don’t know?”

“Know what?” He knew Edge had warrior abilities, so it couldn’t have anything to do with powers. He shrugged.

“I thought someone would have told you.”

“Vincent and I haven’t really had time to talk with anyone outside of class, other than Patty and a few other students.”

Edge started walking again. “My last name’s Buchanan. The David is my pap.”

Stephen stopped walking. He had known there was something familiar about Edge. Now he could see the resemblance. “Pastor Buchanan...is your grandfather,” Stephen said aloud, as if saying it made more sense than hearing it.

Edge smiled and started walking again. “Yep. But I don’t flaunt it. We’ve been really close since Dad passed, several years back—”

Stephen interrupted. “Fallen?”

“No. Cancer. Anyway, he sometimes tells me stuff that I have to keep quiet. But I figured a little reassurance wouldn’t hurt.”

Stephen stopped at a door on the right. “So, you knew all along that the David would welcome me as Mighty?”

"I had just heard from him that morning. I rushed down to meet you and Vincent. Pap says you're more special than you realize."

"I should probably speak with him again."

Edge patted him on the shoulder. "You will, when the time is right."

Stephen nodded to the door. "Well, this is me. I know you're the history teacher, so I mean no offense. But I'm glad I can finally start some *real* training. I've been cramming so much information about Mighty and Fallen, I need this break—this release. It's been all study and no fun. This should help get me energized again."

"Combat training, huh?" Edge grinned.

"Yeah, Vincent should be in there now. I thought I'd stop in a little early to catch the end of his session." Stephen chuckled, thinking about Vincent trying to fight. "Wanna join me?"

"Nah, I need to go to the library. But let me know how it goes." He patted Stephen on the back and continued down the hall.

Stephen tapped the emblem of a sword on the wall next to him. The door opened. He walked inside and immediately heard grunting, followed by what sounded to him like pads smacking. He stood in a small observation area. Several feet in front of him, the room opened into a larger, mat-covered training room. Dummies and punching bags lined one wall. Another held various weapons. In the middle, a very tired and sweaty Vincent waved, just as he got clobbered in the head by a smaller Asian man.

Stephen winced as Vincent fell to the floor.

"I think that's enough."

Stephen looked around the corner to see Shannon standing just inside the training room.

“Vincent, who were you waving at?” She turned toward Stephen. “Oh.”

Stephen chuckled as Shannon walked out to help the Asian man lift Vincent to his feet.

“Do-Yeong, you were supposed to go easy on him,” she snapped.

“I was. He was doing well until he lost focus.”

“It’s okay, Shannon.” Vincent stood and walked in Stephen’s direction. “Mr. Kim is correct. I should have stayed in the fight.”

Vincent pulled up a chair next to Stephen and took off his gloves, helmet, and chest protector. Stephen looked Vincent over from head to toe. He had never seen Vincent covered in sweat. He noted a small spatter of blood on his red training clothes. The white trim made the blood more obvious. Vincent’s jet-black hair dripped with sweat, as did his neatly trimmed goatee.

“You need to make sure you drink lots of water,” Stephen said.

Vincent nodded toward the far end of the observation area at a gallon jug of water sitting with his walking stick, which Stephen had given him as a gift, and a duffel bag.

“Yeah, that should do it.” Stephen chuckled.

Based on Vincent’s labored breathing, the training session looked to be a good cardio workout, but Stephen didn’t expect it to be more than that. His ability to read others’ thoughts had proven to give him an edge in past fights.

Vincent grunted and winced as he continued to take off his sparring equipment. He smelled musty, or perhaps it was the room. "Stephen, I'm Do-Yeong Kim." The Asian man on the mat, also dressed in red, stepped into the observation room. He looked young, despite his salt-and-pepper hair. "I'm one of the combat instructors."

Stephen knew little about many of the Mighty at this point, but he knew a red uniform meant Kim was a priest. Reading his mind wouldn't likely be possible. Stephen shook his hand. "Nice to meet you."

Kim pointed at a doorway connected to the observation room. "That's the men's locker room. Just inside, you'll find a change of clothes and sparring gear. Get changed, and I'll see you back here in a few."

"Sounds good." Stephen sped to the locker room where he found a bag with his name on it. A bag with Vincent's name laid open and empty next to his. Stephen pulled out a set of black training clothes from his own bag and changed. All Mighty knew the three colors associated with the classes: blue for prophets, yellow for warriors, and red for priests. *Why black?*

Stephen walked over to the sink and looked in the mirror. *Why am I nervous? This isn't a real fight.* He wanted to impress people. More than that, he didn't want to let anyone down. He knew how the anger felt when he fought, how his flesh wanted to take control, and it felt good to give in.

When he walked back into the observation room, Vincent sat alone. His sparring gear lay on the floor next to him.

"Good luck," Vincent grunted through what appeared to be a forced smile.

"Thanks. Are you gonna stay and watch?"

"If you don't mind, I thought I might for a few minutes."

Stephen laughed. "You're still recovering, aren't you?"

Vincent nodded and took a sip of water from his jug.

"Mr. Cross."

Stephen turned back to the floor.

"Please take a few minutes to warm up and stretch." Kim stood in the middle of the mat with Shannon. "I recommend a few laps around the room, some squats, push-ups, and jumping jacks to get your blood flowing. Then, take a minute to do some stretches, legs, arms, back—stretch it all out."

Stephen nodded and began jogging around the room as Mr. Kim and Shannon chatted in the center. Stephen tried to listen to her thoughts, hoping to hear something about strategy. It didn't work. Kim must be guarding Shannon's mind too.

He continued his exercises until he felt sufficiently loose. He couldn't help feeling something was wrong. It didn't make sense to have him do combat training with a priest. Stephen's warrior abilities alone would be too much for Kim.

Stephen approached the two still standing in the middle.

Shannon smiled mischievously. "Good luck, Stephen." She turned and walked toward the outer edge of the mat, near the observation area.

"Are you ready?" Kim asked.

Stephen nodded.

"No questions?"

Stephen thought for a moment and looked toward Vincent before turning back to his instructor. “Yeah. Why am I wearing black?”

“No one is certain which class to put you in just yet. So, I pulled you a black uniform. Honestly, I’m jealous. I’m not partial to red.” Mr. Kim smiled and paused before continuing. “Anything else?”

Stephen shook his head.

He had barely gotten the word out before Kim’s fist smacked the side of his helmet. Stephen jumped back. He had tried to evade it but was too slow. *How?* The strike wasn’t hard, but it got his attention. He heard snickers coming from the observation area. He maneuvered so that he could see both Vincent and Shannon without losing sight of Kim. He shrugged and they laughed more.

“Very good, Stephen. You didn’t turn your head to look at them. You changed your line of sight instead.”

Stephen swung. He felt slow and weak. What was happening? Kim parried his punch and the battle began. They went back and forth with punches and kicks. Both landed and missed their fair share of strikes. Stephen, however, felt as though he improved as the match went on. Still, it did little to help his now bruised ego. The argument could be made that Kim was beginning to tire, having already sparred Vincent.

Kim lunged at Stephen, throwing a punch at his head. Stephen, in anticipation, jumped into the air and connected with a spinning side kick, which launched Kim several feet backward, landing him on his side. For the first time in the match, Stephen smiled. He tried not to enjoy it, but it was hard. He watched as Kim struggled to his feet. As Stephen stepped forward, Kim held up his hand.

"I'm done," Kim said. "You're as good as they said, and tough too."

"Thanks," Stephen said half-heartedly.

"Seriously, I stopped pulling punches almost immediately."

Stephen reached up and wiped a trickle of blood from his nose, then smiled. "I noticed."

Kim walked over to him. "Then why do I get the impression you aren't happy with your performance?"

"I'm usually much faster and stronger than this. Something's off. I think I'm sick."

Laughter came from the observation area. The two men turned their attention toward Shannon and Vincent.

"Why are they laughing?"

Kim sighed. "I'm guessing it's because they didn't tell you about the combat room."

Stephen looked at his instructor, confused. "What about it?"

"It neutralizes abilities to allow better focus on combat training and techniques."

"What?" Stephen asked, dumbstruck.

He turned back toward the observation area to see Shannon walking toward him on the mat. She unzipped her hoodie. She wore black training clothes underneath.

"Sorry, Stephen," Shannon offered. "I couldn't resist. Today is when we evaluate your skill level. I wanted to see your true skill level, no powers."

"Well, then," Stephen said with slight agitation. "How'd I do?"

"Well, you passed the intermediate level."

Stephen looked at Kim. "You're intermediate?"

Kim bowed modestly and smiled at Stephen. Then he nodded toward Shannon. "You'll enjoy this one."

Stephen wasn't sure if Kim made that remark to him or Shannon. He looked back at Shannon in time to see her foot, just before it smacked into the side of his head. He heard ringing as he struggled to stay on his feet, staggering around. He shook his head, an effort to compose himself.

Kim walked over to Vincent and called back to Shannon and Stephen. "We'll leave you two to train. Good luck!"

"Thanks!" Stephen called out. He looked back at Shannon. "I have to fight you?"

"You don't have to. It'll be more fun if you do though." Shannon smiled. Stephen felt nervous once more, as the ringing faded away. He cautiously approached her, and the fight resumed.

The fog on the mirror made it hard for Stephen to see. No matter how many times he wiped it away with his towel, it fogged right back up. Still, the shiner around his left eye appeared obvious enough, even through the fogged-up glass. His shaggy brown hair wasn't quite long enough to cover it up. His swollen bottom lip made the cut on it more obvious. He had an abrasion on his right cheekbone. He dared not count the bruises on his body.

"Eh." He pulled away after dabbing his blackened eye with a towel. The physical discomfort felt bad enough. His pride, however, had suffered a harder blow. How could he ever live it down? He had been beaten by a girl.

Stephen slammed his fist on the counter, leaving a deep and crackled impression next to the sink. *Calm down.* Although he had been controlling his abilities well enough, he still feared that the madness that drove him back to Waltz—the memories and voices of all those whose minds he had forced his way into—might return. He splashed some water on his face before drying off and putting on clean clothes. Aches and pains settled over his body, causing his movements to be tentative.

Just as he eased down on the bed to relax and unwind, someone knocked on the door. *Really?* He slowly got up and made his way to the door, hoping for some good news on the other side. Stephen opened the door to his temporary compartment. Patty stood grinning, as though she already knew about his defeat. Still, it was Patty, which was good news.

"Hey, babe," she said as she brushed his wet hair away from his left eye. "You okay?"

She didn't sound concerned as much as patronizing.

Stephen pulled away and grabbed her hand to hold it. "Yeah, I'm fine." He paused while Patty kissed his injured eye. "So, news travels fast."

"Yes, it does."

"Well, she's good. I guess I never knew just how much my powers helped me."

"Stephen, don't be hard on yourself. Shannon, Mr. Kim, the other Mighty, they've all had training. This was a combat training assessment. Only a few of us who know how big your ego can be, found it funny. Everyone else seems to be impressed with how well you did."

"I guess," Stephen replied. "I just don't understand. She said that she occasionally trained people in combat. I really didn't expect her to be *that* good...and brutal."

Patty smirked. "Because she's a girl?"

"Hold up, Patty." Stephen responded with haste, knowing hesitation could send the conversation sideways in a hurry. "You know I'm not like that. She just doesn't look the part is all."

"I know." Patty winked. "I just like to see you squirm."

"As do I." Vincent walked in the door. He looked better than Stephen, but not much. His nose was bruised with some darkening around his left eye.

"Just be glad you didn't have to fight Shannon," Stephen said.

Patty giggled, glancing quickly at Vincent and then away.

"What was that?" Stephen asked, looking at both of them.

"What?" the two replied in near unison.

"Something's up."

The two remained silent.

"Come on! I can't even read you two..." Stephen debated in his head for only a moment. He *could* read Patty but had promised not to. "Really?"

"Well, I am hungry. I worked up an appetite earlier. I figured you had too." Vincent looked at Stephen. "Would you two like to get a bite in the mess hall?"

"We'd love to," Patty said in a chipper voice, taking Stephen by the arm.

Stephen knew when to give in. Patty was probably the most stubborn person he had ever come across, other than himself. "Yeah," he half-heartedly said. "I'm hungry. Let's go."

The trio navigated the halls a little easier each day. They had yet to venture through all the underground tunnels and hidden places, but they knew their way around well enough. Meals were about the only time the three could get together. Patty studied what she was allowed to learn of the Mighty and continued to manage the operations for the warehousing division of Stephen's company—Stockton Family Holdings, LLC, back in St. Louis. Stephen spent what spare moments he had checking in with the head of the various subsidiaries to make sure the business continued to thrive. Some days, the three didn't see each other at all. Still, he hoped that once this impending battle was over, they could return to their somewhat normal lives.

As they walked down the hall, they passed more kids. Some seemed so small. The older teens blended in with the adults much easier, though Stephen could feel the difference just being around them. Their thoughts and emotions were much more sporadic, less controlled.

Stephen heard footsteps rushing up from behind. He turned to see a darker-skinned, lean young man running toward them.

"Hey, guys!" the boy called out as he slowed his pace, drawing near.

Stephen gave the teen a fist bump. "What's up, Jax?"

Vincent stepped forward to give the young man a fist bump. "Hello, Jax." No matter what Vincent did, he always looked awkward and rigid.

Stephen turned to Patty. "You've heard me talk about Jax. We've had some classes together."

Jax shook her hand, a bright smile on his face. "Hello, Mrs. Patty..."

"Just Patty, please. I'm not that much older than you," Patty replied.

"Okay, *Patty*." Jax nodded toward Stephen. "You know, this guy here is *crazy* about you. He's concerned you might be feeling out of place."

Stephen rolled his eyes, covering his face with his hand. Why did he think telling a teenager something like that was a good idea? He nudged Jax. "Not cool."

Vincent looked at Stephen. "I have told you more than once that you do talk too much."

"I guess I do."

"Patty," Jax said. "Did you know Waltz well too?"

Stephen felt Patty's emotions swell. He dipped inside her mind, sharing what he felt when he remembered his time with Waltz, the feeling of being loved.

Patty glanced at Stephen and mouthed, "Thank you," before turning back to Jax. "Yes, I knew him well. He was a good man who seemed to only know how to love."

"That's how I remember him too," Jax replied. "I was young the last time I saw him."

"But you are young now," Vincent said.

"Vincent," Patty snapped. "You know what he meant."

"I do," Vincent replied. "I was merely pointing out—
"

"Stop!" Patty said.

Vincent grimaced, but Stephen and Jax laughed.

"I see who the boss is in this group," Jax said. "It was nice meeting you, Patty." He turned to Stephen. "I'll see you in class tomorrow." He nodded down the hall, an infectious smile adorning his face. "I gotta get to session. It's warrior training. I get to try turning it up a notch today! Between prophets, priests, and warriors, I'm sure glad I'm a warrior. There's nothing better."

"Well, have fun!" Stephen tapped Jax's chest. "Do some damage for me."

Jax took off back the way he had come. “You know I will!”

“That’s a good kid,” Stephen said. “He’s my favorite so far.”

“Really? Why is that?” Vincent asked.

“There’s something familiar about him. Plus, he doesn’t have a hateful bone in his body. I just hope he doesn’t let life break him down.”

“Well, maybe you can help him with that.” Patty wrapped her arm around Stephen’s.

“Maybe...” Stephen turned the corner. Before he managed to get fully turned around, he felt someone bump into him. “Whoa...” He reached to grab the man, catching him just before he hit the ground, but not before sunglasses fell from the man’s face. His solid white eyes made his skin seem all the darker. Vincent grabbed the glasses from the floor and placed them in the man’s hand.

“Thank you, Vincent,” the older man said, raising the glasses back on his face.

Vincent nodded and attempted a smile.

“I-I’m sorry. I didn’t notice...” Stephen paused, looking at the man, who continued to look straight ahead. He listened briefly to the man’s thoughts. “You’re—”

“Blind,” the man interrupted. “I sensed you poking around in there. You must be Stephen.”

“Excuse me,” Patty said. “But if you’re blind—”

“How do I know that you’re Patty, he’s Stephen, and the awkward gentleman that nodded at me as though I can see is Vincent?”

Stephen and Patty looked at Vincent who blushed a little.

"I'm Joe, Jackson's dad. I thought I heard him."

"He just took off," Stephen said.

"Oh." Joe reached for Stephen's arm. "I was just wanting to chat. Would you mind if I accompanied you three to the mess hall?"

"You're a prophet?" Patty asked.

Joe smiled. "I prefer seer. I've never parted water or anything like that. I just see things."

"That is ironic." Vincent had barely gotten the words out when Stephen and Patty both glared at him.

Joe chuckled. "Yes, I suppose it is ironic for a seer to be blind."

Joe turned in the direction of the mess hall, still holding onto Stephen's arm. As the group walked, Joe assured them that they'd settle in sooner than later.

Upon nearing the cafeteria, Joe asked for a moment alone with Stephen. Vincent and Patty obliged and continued onward. Stephen suspected Joe wanted to talk about his son. Jax looked up to Stephen and seemed to have a strong, almost brotherly affection for him, though Stephen wasn't sure why.

"Stephen, you don't remember Jackson, do you?"

Stephen had never seen Jax before they started classes in Enclave. "I'm not sure I understand."

"You used to call him *little* Jack."

Stephen felt his legs go weak. The impact was strong and immediate. Looking at Joe, he could barely see it, the resemblance. Joe was much smaller. Still, something about his smile looked familiar, jogging his memory. "You're Joe Thompson, Bernie's cousin."

Joe nodded. "I am."

"And Jax is little Jack!" He paused while running his hand through his hair, as though this would help the news settle in easier. "He came to visit us one summer. Bernard and I were in high school. Jack was like nine or ten. That boy followed me everywhere."

"He came home and talked about you for a while after that." Joe smiled. "He wanted to go back the next summer. I almost let him."

"Why didn't you?"

"His ability started to show that year. It wasn't enough that anyone would've noticed at the time. But, once it starts, you don't always know how quickly it will progress. I knew Waltz and Bernie would understand. I was concerned about you." He smiled again and paused to bite his lower lip for a moment. "It's kind of funny how things turn out. When Jackson learned about being Mighty, he was upset because he couldn't share it with you. You should've seen him when he heard you were coming here."

Stephen smiled. "How did I not know? Sure, he's a lot bigger now, but..." The realization that Joe was Bernie's family hit him. After all, he was the one responsible for having Bernie locked up. He had never even considered that Bernie would have family who were also gifted. He felt sadness fall on him as he struggled for words. "Joe, I-I, about Uncle Bernie..."

"Hey, Stephen. Don't you worry none about that. No, it ain't pleasant, but Bernie made his choices himself. You didn't make him do anything." Joe spoke with certainty. "And right now, Jackson needs someone to look up to more than ever. You and I are the closest family he has. Hey! Why don't y'all come visit us down south sometime? It'd be nice to have y'ins."

Stephen smiled. Since being at Enclave, he had found new friends and was excited at the prospect of having family. Knowing Jax had been family all along put him at ease.

"Joe, if either of you ever need me—"

"We know, Stephen." Joe wrapped his arms around him and gave a gentle squeeze.

Joe gasped, before snatching his hands back and stepping away. "Stephen." Joe's voice wavered as he now staggered backward. His eyes widened, and his lip quivered as he held his arms out, reaching for the wall to steady himself.

"What is it, Joe?" Stephen watched as Joe's body began to shake.

"I need to sit down."

Stephen grabbed him and helped him to a seat in the cafeteria. "Joe?" Stephen said more firmly.

"Let me help."

Stephen turned to see where the deep voice had come from. A tall, muscular man with white hair and wearing a stone insignia on his collar kneeled next to Joe. "Do you know what's wrong?" Stephen asked.

"Nothing's wrong. He's seeing something, but not like usual. He's having a vision. He'll be fine. We need to get him to his room."

Stephen saw Patty and Vincent rushing over. "Is everything okay?" Vincent's usual stoic expression was replaced with concern.

"I think so," Stephen replied.

"Yes," the tall man replied. "He'll be fine. We just need to get him to his bed."

"Can we do anything?" Patty asked.

"If you two want to bring some food to his living quarters, he'll be hungry when he comes to. His visions can be physically exhausting. He'll feel drained."

Patty and Vincent headed toward the kitchen.

"Water too," the man called out.

Vincent waved in acknowledgement as they hurried along.

The man turned to Stephen. "I'll carry him. Will you get the doors?"

"I may not look it, but I'm stronger than you. I should probably carry him." Stephen reached to lift Joe. He froze. His mind flooded with images of Joe. All at once, he knew everything about Joe's gift that the man next to him knew.

"Do you understand?" the man asked.

Stephen nodded and went for the door as the man carried Joe into the hallway. Stephen followed.

"You must be Stephen. I'm Colvin Middleton. I'm Chief Arbiter here."

"Arbiter, like a judge?" Stephen said.

"Yes, exactly. Arbiters handle disputes and preside over trials and discipline. All arbiters are prophets."

They hurried down the hallway toward to the personal compartments.

"So, Joe really is okay?"

"Yes, he's good. His gift is somewhat unique. Not many can see the things he sees. But you already know that much, don't you?"

"I guess I do."

When they arrived at Joe's quarters, Stephen opened the door. Clothing items lay on the bed. Stephen moved them to the desk so Colvin could lay Joe down. Together, they situated pillows and blankets to make Joe comfortable.

"He'll be fine here. I'm guessing it'll be a little while before he wakes."

Stephen glanced around the room. There was a picture of Jax on the wall, just as he remembered him when he stayed with them over the summer.

"What's it like, Stephen?"

He turned back to Colvin. "What's what like?"

Colvin nodded toward the bed Joe laid on. "That type of vision."

"Uh, I..." Stephen wasn't sure what to say. He wasn't comfortable with everyone knowing so much about him.

"Most of us, prophets that is, have some type of communication from God. Sometimes it's as simple as being able to notice things others don't see. God reveals himself to us in this way." Colvin sat in a chair on the other side of the room. The lamp next to him made his wrinkles more apparent. "Few of us actually talk to angels. Very few ever see God."

"Well—" Stephen looked around for a chair. Pulling out the one from underneath the desk, he sat down. "It's humbling. I knew in an instant just how insignificant I was. Yet, I felt so much love. We're nothing compared to Him, compared to God. But, because of Him, our worth can never be measured. My body knew to kneel before Him. The angel Areli told me to get up. I imagine that had God Himself spoken to me in his glory-filled form, I would have burst into flames."

One side of Colvin's lips turned upward. His eyes softened. "That sounds amazing."

"The truth is, I could spend the rest of my life trying to explain it and never get it right."

"Stephen!" Patty called from the hallway.

"I'm closer. I've got it," the Chief Arbiter offered.

Colvin stood outside the door. "Down here." He re-entered, Patty and Vincent in tow. They placed the food in the compact kitchen area where only a sink, mini-fridge, and microwave were available. The smell of the food made Stephen's stomach growl. He ignored it.

"What happened to Joe?" Vincent sounded concerned, which was something that didn't come naturally.

Colvin looked at Stephen. "I know you three are close, but I don't know just how close."

Stephen nodded. "It's okay. You can tell 'em." Stephen looked back at Joe, noticing his eyelids twitch as though dreaming.

Colvin took a deep breath and began explaining. "This is an extension of Joe's gifts. He also sees visions of things that haven't happened yet, but not just any vision. Joe is what we call a harbinger."

Patty and Vincent looked at each other. Patty's face scrunched up and her eyebrows wrinkled, a look of confusion Stephen was familiar with. Vincent, however, looked lost in thought—his gaze drifted away. His eyes continued moving back and forth as if searching for something.

After a moment of silence, Vincent turned to Colvin. "A harbinger generally announces some type of change. So, what kinds of things does Joe see?"

"Big changes. And not always good." Colvin looked to Joe and then to Stephen.

Stephen hadn't really been paying attention. He had been watching Joe, wondering what he was seeing. Still, he was suddenly aware that everyone's focus had shifted to him. In an instant, he soaked up their present thoughts and understood what was going on.

"Colvin doesn't want to tell you that Joe has an unfortunate nickname, "Harbinger of Death." He heard Patty gasp but continued. "Often, the change that Joe sees is preceded or succeeded by death, but not always.

"There is more to it?" Vincent asked.

"His visions are set off by contact. In other words, whatever he's seeing or saw has to do with me." Stephen continued looking at Joe, tempted to try and see inside his mind.

"How long before we know?" Patty asked.

Stephen looked at her. He could tell from the tone in her voice she was working hard to hold herself together.

"Joe," Colvin started, "will come to in an hour or two. But it may be awhile before he can fully process what he saw. It's taken as long as a week. Even then, there is always room for interpretation."

"But we need to know!" Patty didn't contain her panic any longer. "We just went through so much. How long do we have? The guys are still in training." The more she spoke, the faster and louder she got. "We need answers."

Stephen sprang from his seat and headed for the door but kissed Patty on the cheek before leaving the room. He heard Patty call out behind him.

"Where are you going?"

"To get some answers."

Find more Exciting Titles from

JUMPMASTER PRESS™

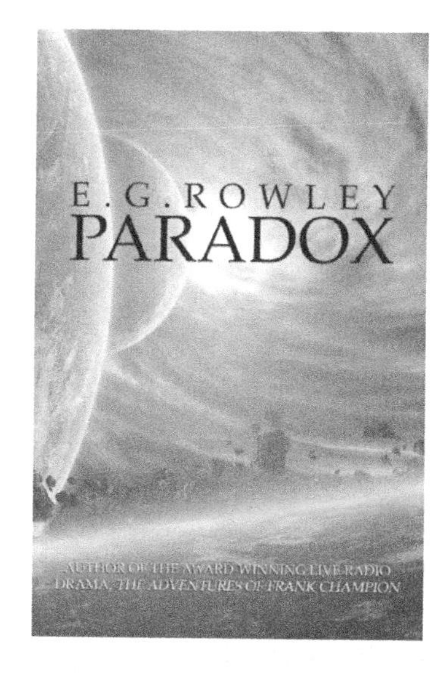

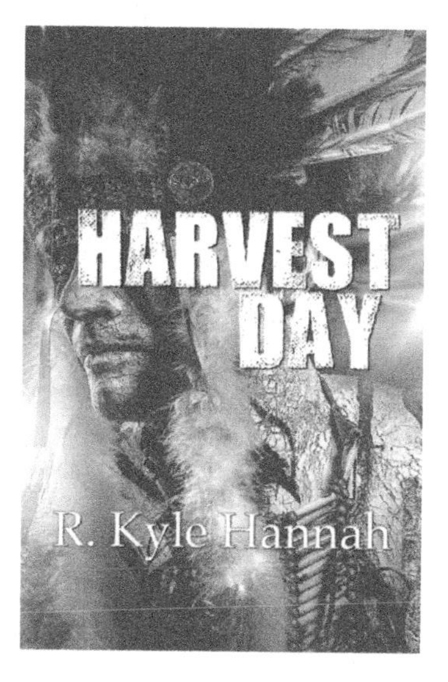

About The Author

Kenyon grew up in the south and has lived most of his life in Northwest Georgia. The youngest of his six siblings, he always felt the need to prove himself, especially compared to his three older brothers. Kenyon is a black belt in Tae Kwon Do competing in Edinburgh, Scotland in the WKA World Championship.

He enjoys writing poems, short stories, novels, songs, and maintains an inspirational blog. In addition, he holds onto the hope of one becoming a producer of inspirational films with a dark side. Aside from that, being Superman would be a fun job too!

Being involved in his church and community is a must for Kenyon. His goal in life is to leave a positive impact on the world around him. He and his wife formed a blended family and have six kids between them. Kenyon is also the founder of Next Chapter Convention & Xpo, a book expo held annually in Ringgold, GA. Aside from writing, he enjoys spending time with his family and traveling to new places.

Made in the USA
Columbia, SC
01 August 2021